INFINITE DARK

VOLUME 1

Published by
TOP COW PRODUCTIONS, INC.
Los Angeles

For Top Cow Productions, Inc.

For Top Cow Productions, Inc.

Marc Silvestri - CEO

Matt Hawkins - President & COO

Elena Salcedo - Vice President of Operations

Henry Barajas - Director of Operations

Vincent Valentine - Production Manager

Dylan Gray - Marketing Director

To find the comic
shop nearest you, call:
1-888-COMICBOOK

Want more? Check out:
www.topcow.com
for news & exclusive Top Cow merchandise!

INFINITE DARK, VOL. 1. First printing. March 2019. Published by Image Comics, Inc. Office of publication: 2701 NW Vaughn St., Suite 780, Portland, OR 97210. Copyright © 2019 Ryan Cady and Top Cow Productions, Inc. All rights reserved. Contains material originally published in single magazine form as INFINITE DARK #1–4. "Infinite Dark," its logos, and the likenesses of all characters herein are trademarks of Ryan Cady and Top Cow Productions, Inc., unless otherwise noted. "Image" and the Image Comics logos are registered trademarks of Image Comics, Inc. No part of this publication may be reproduced or transmitted, in any form or by any means (except for short excerpts for journalistic or review purposes), without the express written permission of Ryan Cady and Top Cow Productions, Inc., or Image Comics, Inc. All names, characters, events, and locales in this publication are entirely fictional. Any resemblance to actual persons (living or dead), events, or places, without satirical intent, is coincidental. Printed in the USA. For information regarding the CPSIA on this printed material call: 203-595-3636. For international rights, contact: foreignlicensing@imagecomics.com. ISBN: 978-1-5343-1056-8.

INFINITE DARK

VOLUME 1

WRITER **RYAN CADY**
@RYCADY

ARTIST **ANDREA MUTTI**
@ANDREAMUTTI9

COLORIST **K. MICHAEL RUSSELL**
@KMICHAELRUSSELL

LETTERER **TROY PETERI OF A LARGER WORLD**
@A_LARGER_WORLD

STORY EDITOR **ALEX LU**
@WAXENWINGS

EDITOR IN CHIEF **MATT HAWKINS**
@TOPCOWMATT

EDITOR **ELENA SALCEDO**

PRODUCTION **VINCENT VALENTINE**

CHAPTER
ONE

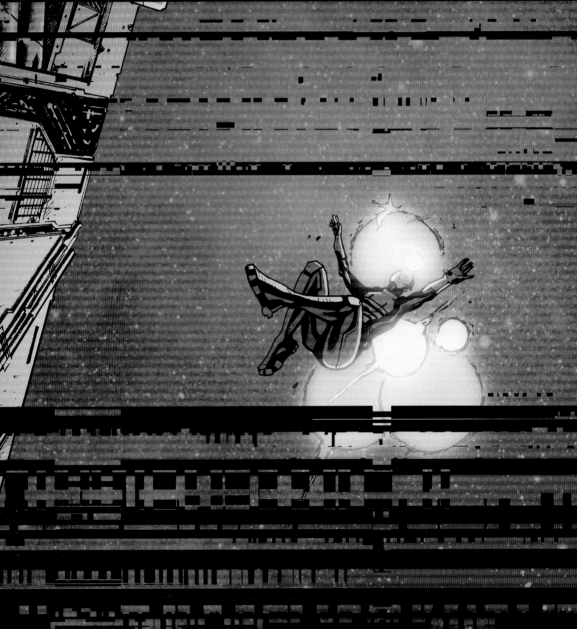

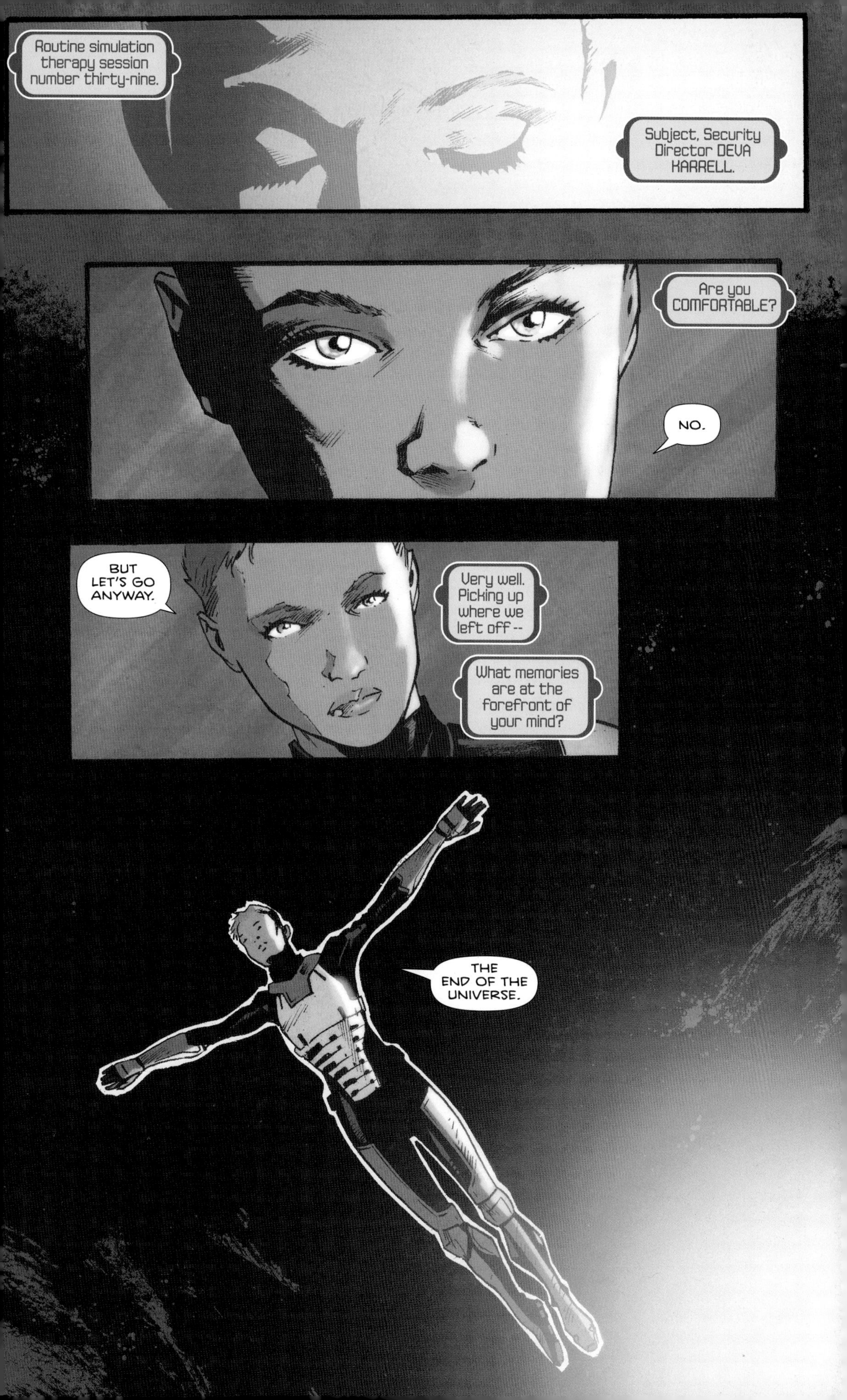
Routine simulation therapy session number thirty-nine.
Subject, Security Director DEVA KARRELL.
Are you COMFORTABLE?
NO.
BUT LET'S GO ANYWAY.
Very well. Picking up where we left off --
What memories are at the forefront of your mind?
THE END OF THE UNIVERSE.

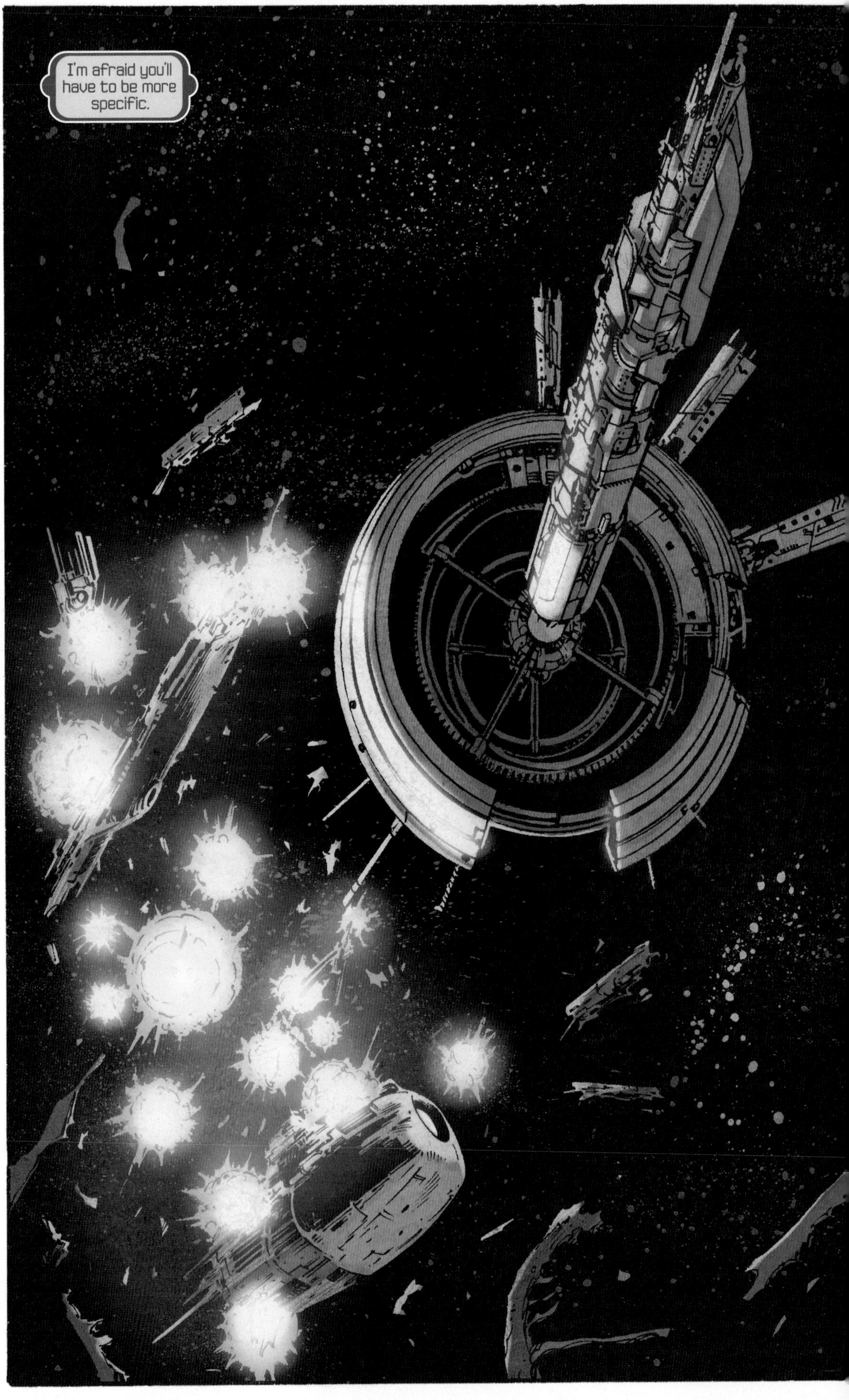
I'm afraid you'll have to be more specific.

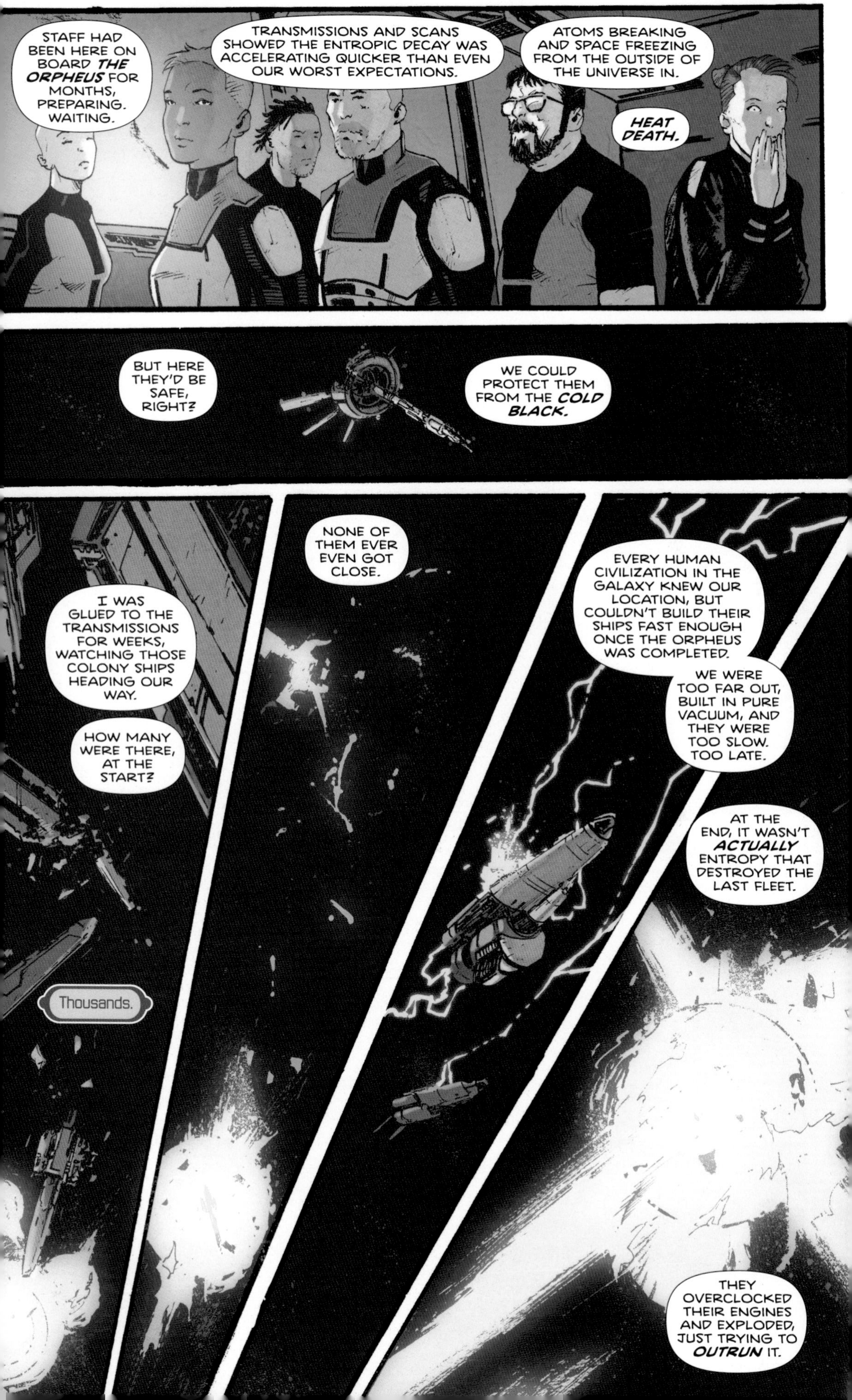
STAFF HAD BEEN HERE ON BOARD THE ORPHEUS FOR MONTHS, PREPARING. WAITING.
TRANSMISSIONS AND SCANS SHOWED THE ENTROPIC DECAY WAS ACCELERATING QUICKER THAN EVEN OUR WORST EXPECTATIONS.
ATOMS BREAKING AND SPACE FREEZING FROM THE OUTSIDE OF THE UNIVERSE IN.
HEAT DEATH.
BUT HERE THEY'D BE SAFE, RIGHT?
WE COULD PROTECT THEM FROM THE COLD BLACK.
I WAS GLUED TO THE TRANSMISSIONS FOR WEEKS, WATCHING THOSE COLONY SHIPS HEADING OUR WAY.
HOW MANY WERE THERE, AT THE START?
Thousands.
NONE OF THEM EVER EVEN GOT CLOSE.
EVERY HUMAN CIVILIZATION IN THE GALAXY KNEW OUR LOCATION, BUT COULDN'T BUILD THEIR SHIPS FAST ENOUGH ONCE THE ORPHEUS WAS COMPLETED.
WE WERE TOO FAR OUT, BUILT IN PURE VACUUM, AND THEY WERE TOO SLOW. TOO LATE.
AT THE END, IT WASN'T ACTUALLY ENTROPY THAT DESTROYED THE LAST FLEET.
THEY OVERCLOCKED THEIR ENGINES AND EXPLODED, JUST TRYING TO OUTRUN IT.

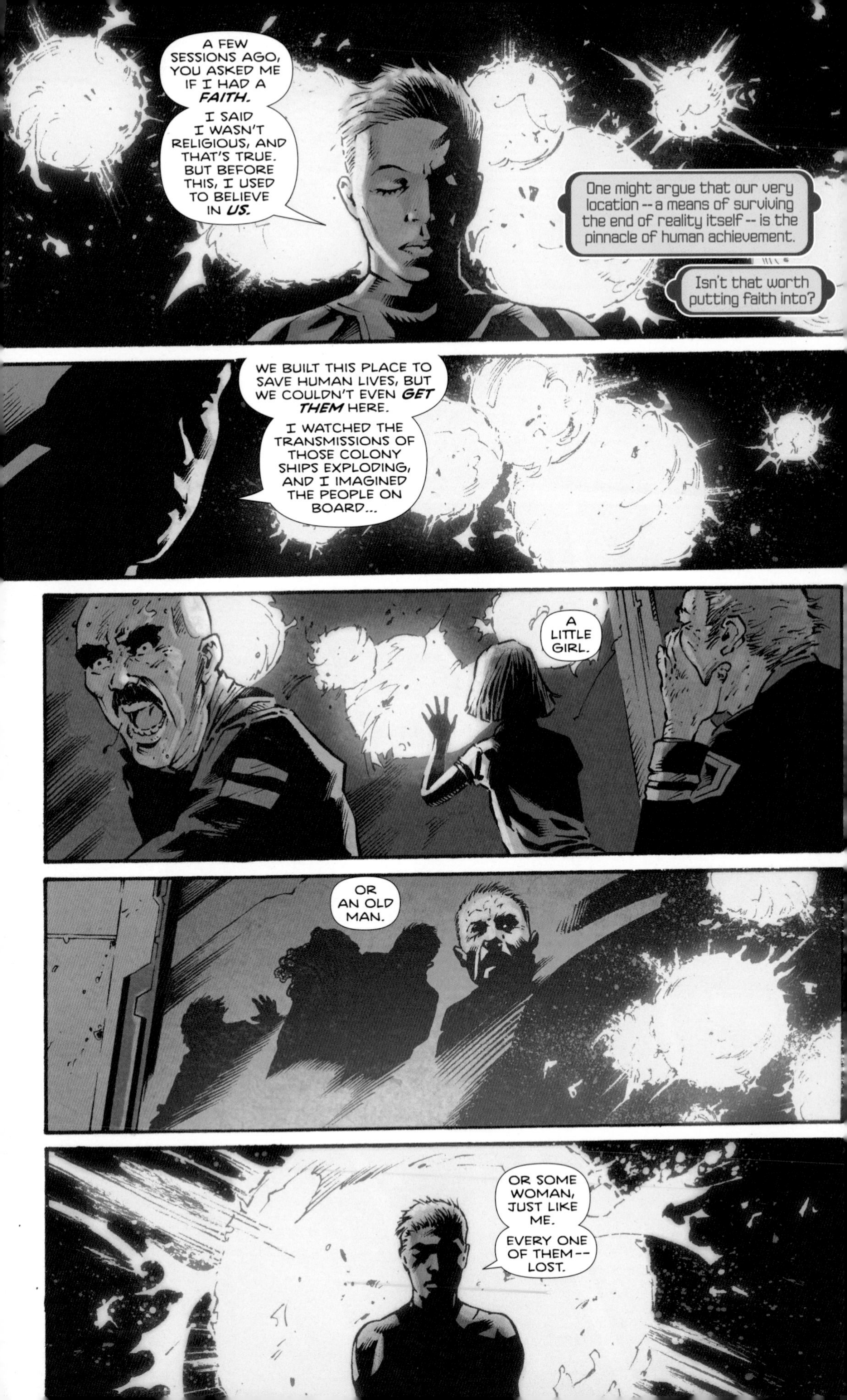
A FEW SESSIONS AGO, YOU ASKED ME IF I HAD A *FAITH.*
I SAID I WASN'T RELIGIOUS, AND THAT'S TRUE. BUT BEFORE THIS, I USED TO BELIEVE IN *US.*
One might argue that our very location -- a means of surviving the end of reality itself -- is the pinnacle of human achievement.
Isn't that worth putting faith into?
WE BUILT THIS PLACE TO SAVE HUMAN LIVES, BUT WE COULDN'T EVEN *GET THEM* HERE.
I WATCHED THE TRANSMISSIONS OF THOSE COLONY SHIPS EXPLODING, AND I IMAGINED THE PEOPLE ON BOARD...
A LITTLE GIRL.
OR AN OLD MAN.
OR SOME WOMAN, JUST LIKE ME.
EVERY ONE OF THEM-- LOST.

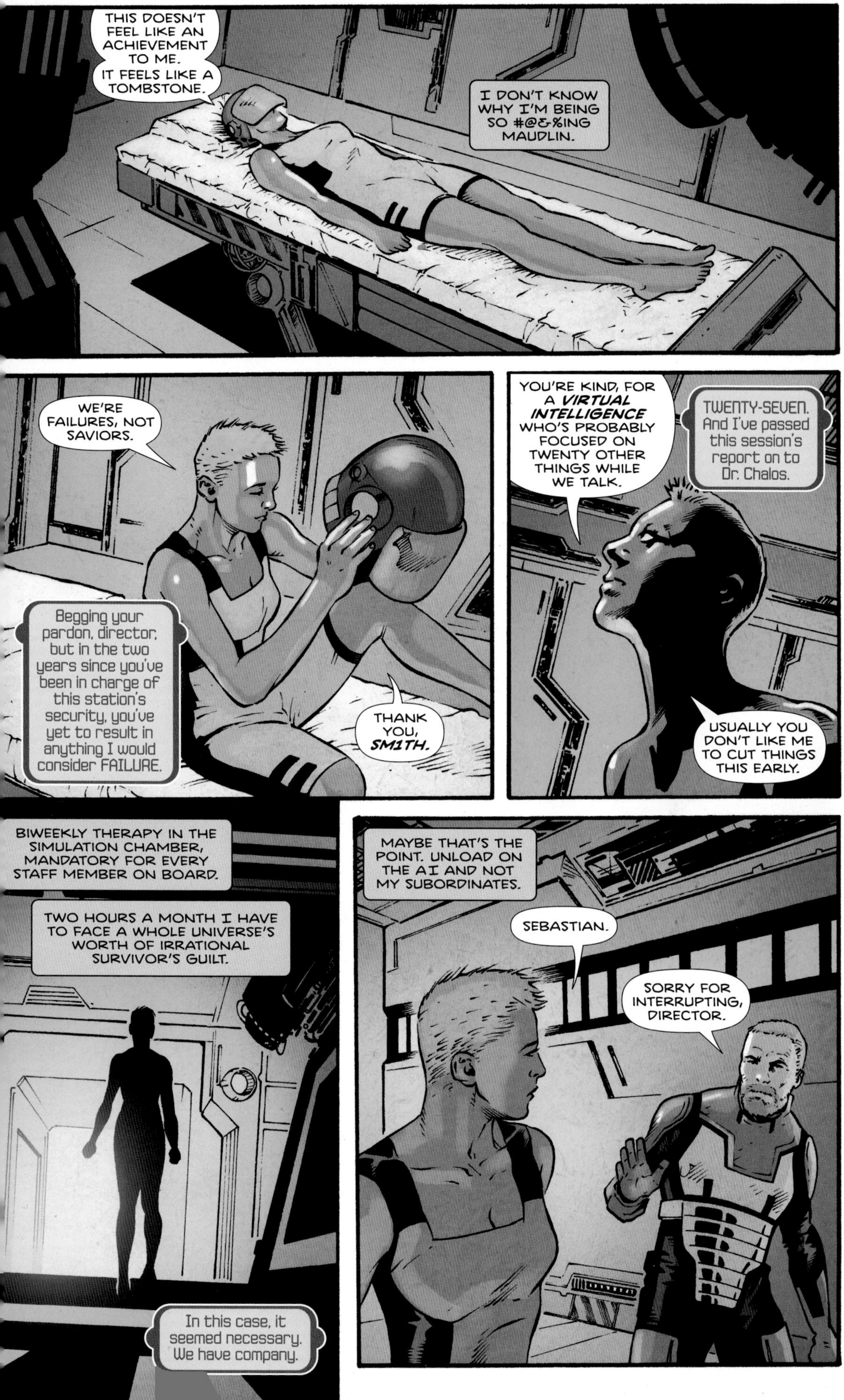
THIS DOESN'T FEEL LIKE AN ACHIEVEMENT TO ME. IT FEELS LIKE A TOMBSTONE.
I DON'T KNOW WHY I'M BEING SO #@&%ING MAUDLIN.
WE'RE FAILURES, NOT SAVIORS.
Begging your pardon, director, but in the two years since you've been in charge of this station's security, you've yet to result in anything I would consider FAILURE.
THANK YOU, SM1TH.
YOU'RE KIND, FOR A VIRTUAL INTELLIGENCE WHO'S PROBABLY FOCUSED ON TWENTY OTHER THINGS WHILE WE TALK.
TWENTY-SEVEN. And I've passed this session's report on to Dr. Chalos.
USUALLY YOU DON'T LIKE ME TO CUT THINGS THIS EARLY.
BIWEEKLY THERAPY IN THE SIMULATION CHAMBER, MANDATORY FOR EVERY STAFF MEMBER ON BOARD.
TWO HOURS A MONTH I HAVE TO FACE A WHOLE UNIVERSE'S WORTH OF IRRATIONAL SURVIVOR'S GUILT.
In this case, it seemed necessary. We have company.
MAYBE THAT'S THE POINT. UNLOAD ON THE AI AND NOT MY SUBORDINATES.
SEBASTIAN.
SORRY FOR INTERRUPTING, DIRECTOR.

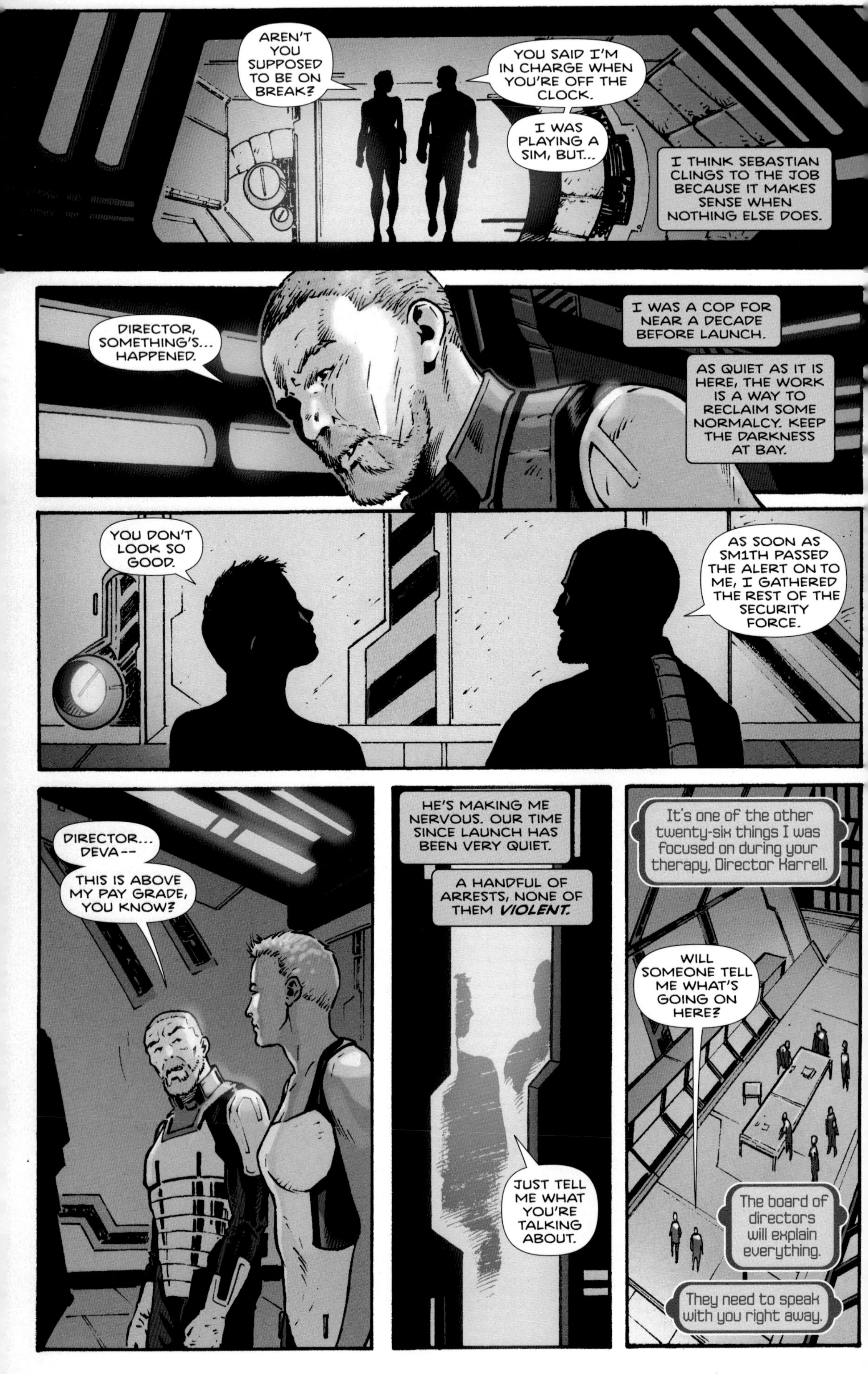
AREN'T YOU SUPPOSED TO BE ON BREAK?
YOU SAID I'M IN CHARGE WHEN YOU'RE OFF THE CLOCK.
I WAS PLAYING A SIM, BUT...
I THINK SEBASTIAN CLINGS TO THE JOB BECAUSE IT MAKES SENSE WHEN NOTHING ELSE DOES.
DIRECTOR, SOMETHING'S... HAPPENED.
I WAS A COP FOR NEAR A DECADE BEFORE LAUNCH.
AS QUIET AS IT IS HERE, THE WORK IS A WAY TO RECLAIM SOME NORMALCY. KEEP THE DARKNESS AT BAY.
YOU DON'T LOOK SO GOOD.
AS SOON AS SM1TH PASSED THE ALERT ON TO ME, I GATHERED THE REST OF THE SECURITY FORCE.
DIRECTOR... DEVA--
THIS IS ABOVE MY PAY GRADE, YOU KNOW?
HE'S MAKING ME NERVOUS. OUR TIME SINCE LAUNCH HAS BEEN VERY QUIET.
A HANDFUL OF ARRESTS, NONE OF THEM *VIOLENT.*
JUST TELL ME WHAT YOU'RE TALKING ABOUT.
It's one of the other twenty-six things I was focused on during your therapy, Director Karrell.
WILL SOMEONE TELL ME WHAT'S GOING ON HERE?
The board of directors will explain everything.
They need to speak with you right away.

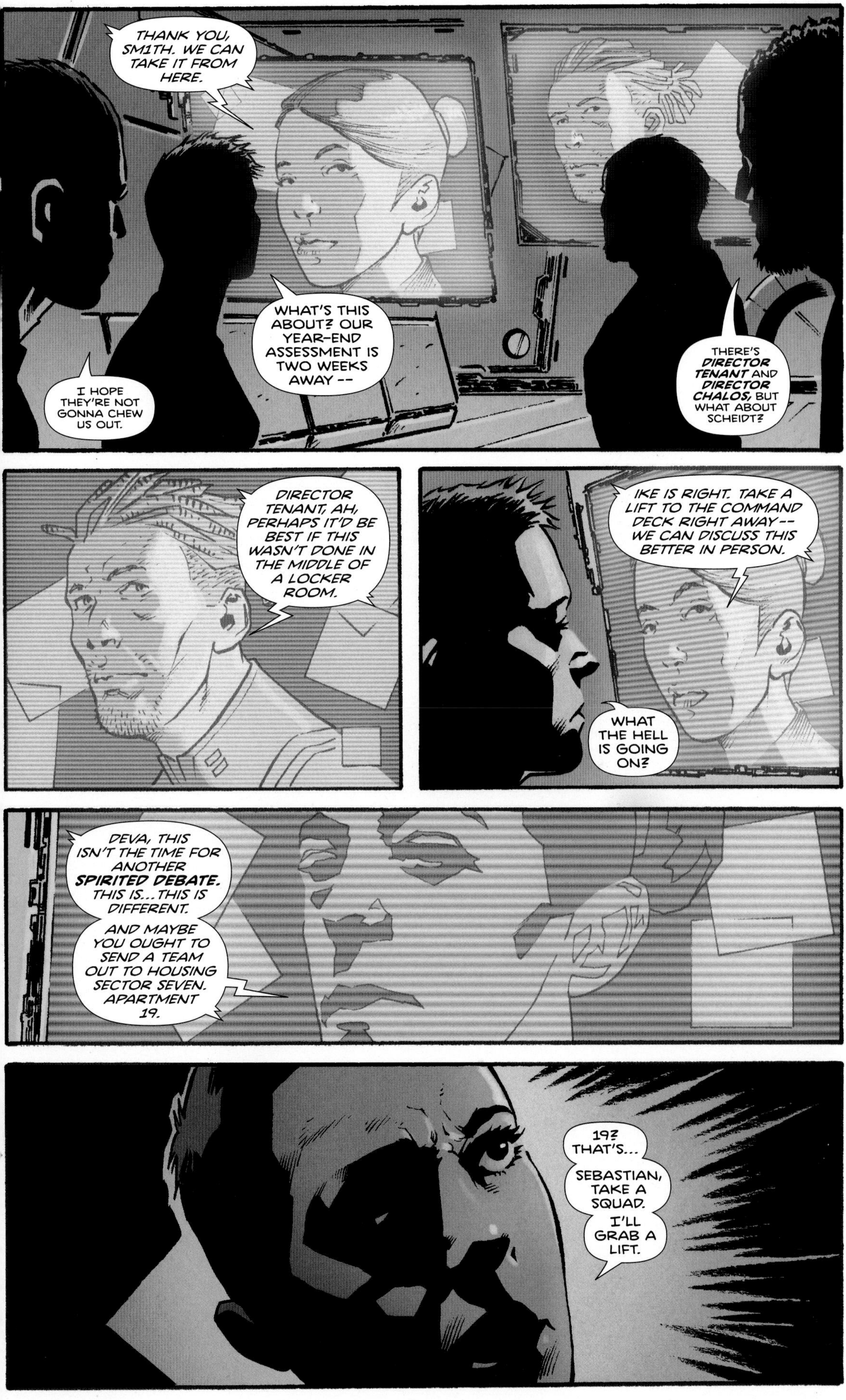
THANK YOU, SM1TH. WE CAN TAKE IT FROM HERE.
I HOPE THEY'RE NOT GONNA CHEW US OUT.
WHAT'S THIS ABOUT? OUR YEAR-END ASSESSMENT IS TWO WEEKS AWAY --
THERE'S DIRECTOR TENANT AND DIRECTOR CHALOS, BUT WHAT ABOUT SCHEIDT?
DIRECTOR TENANT, AH, PERHAPS IT'D BE BEST IF THIS WASN'T DONE IN THE MIDDLE OF A LOCKER ROOM.
IKE IS RIGHT. TAKE A LIFT TO THE COMMAND DECK RIGHT AWAY -- WE CAN DISCUSS THIS BETTER IN PERSON.
WHAT THE HELL IS GOING ON?
DEVA, THIS ISN'T THE TIME FOR ANOTHER SPIRITED DEBATE. THIS IS... THIS IS DIFFERENT.
AND MAYBE YOU OUGHT TO SEND A TEAM OUT TO HOUSING SECTOR SEVEN. APARTMENT 19.
19? THAT'S...
SEBASTIAN, TAKE A SQUAD.
I'LL GRAB A LIFT.

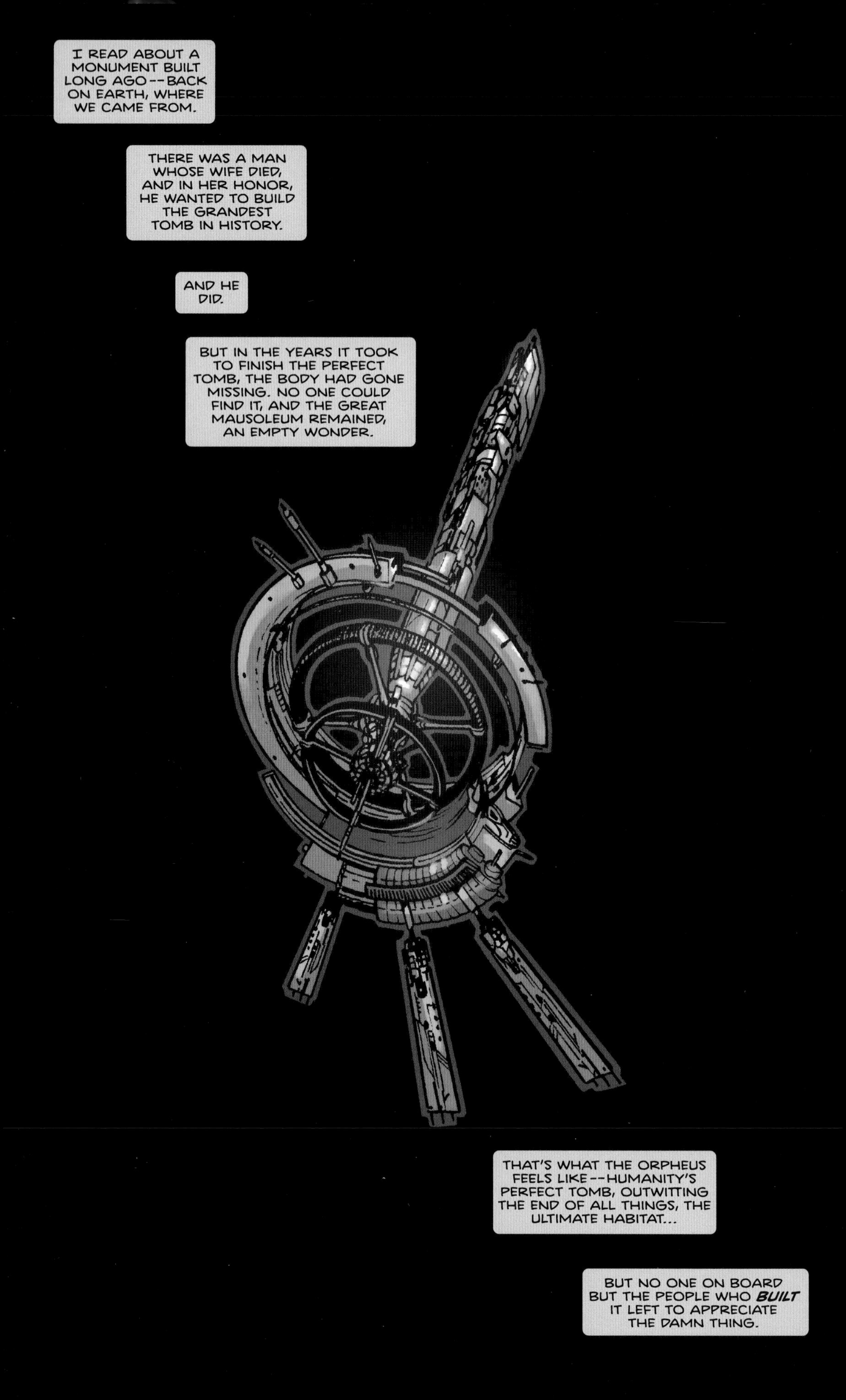
I READ ABOUT A MONUMENT BUILT LONG AGO--BACK ON EARTH, WHERE WE CAME FROM.
THERE WAS A MAN WHOSE WIFE DIED, AND IN HER HONOR, HE WANTED TO BUILD THE GRANDEST TOMB IN HISTORY.
AND HE DID.
BUT IN THE YEARS IT TOOK TO FINISH THE PERFECT TOMB, THE BODY HAD GONE MISSING. NO ONE COULD FIND IT, AND THE GREAT MAUSOLEUM REMAINED, AN EMPTY WONDER.
THAT'S WHAT THE ORPHEUS FEELS LIKE--HUMANITY'S PERFECT TOMB, OUTWITTING THE END OF ALL THINGS, THE ULTIMATE HABITAT...
BUT NO ONE ON BOARD BUT THE PEOPLE WHO *BUILT* IT LEFT TO APPRECIATE THE DAMN THING.

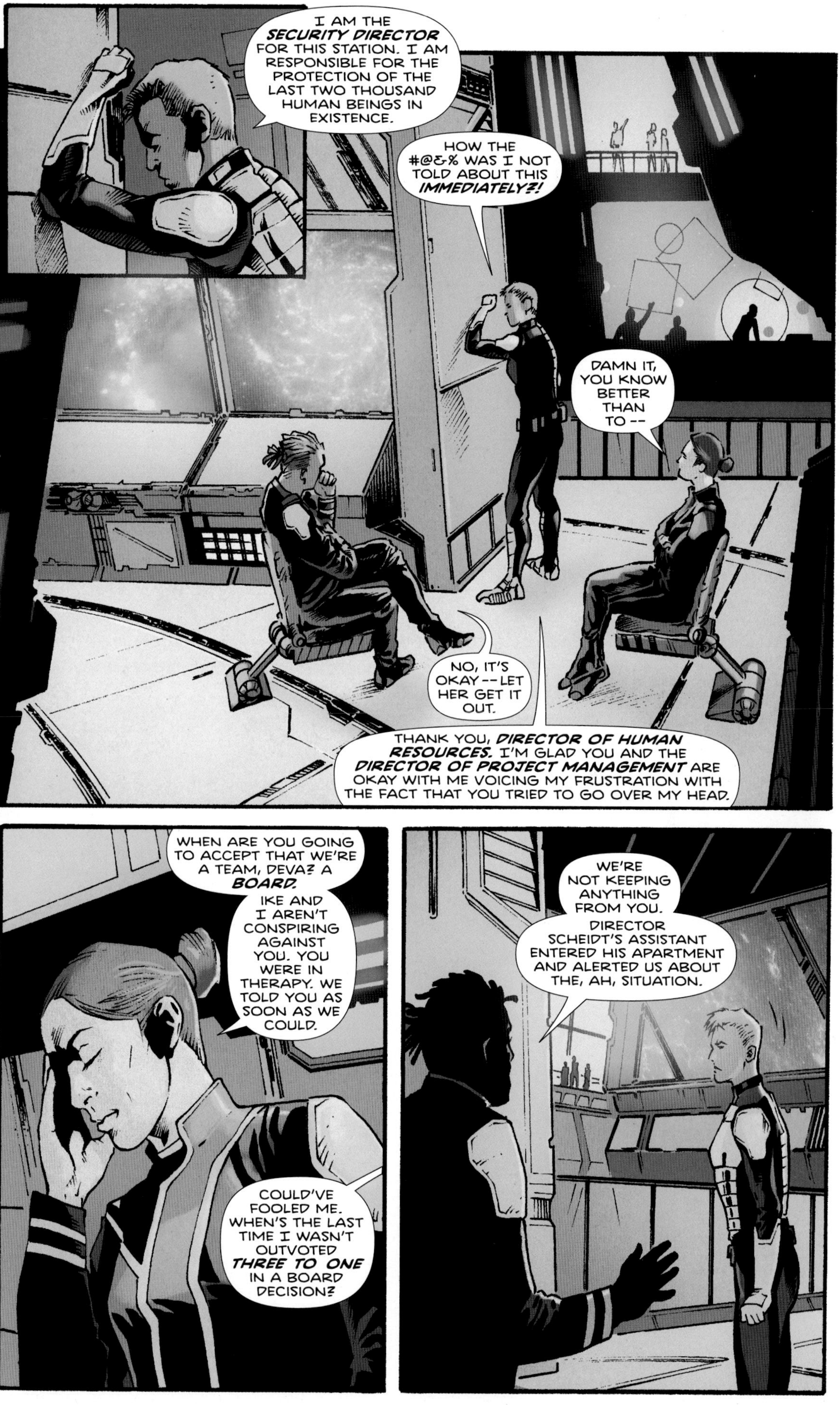
I AM THE SECURITY DIRECTOR FOR THIS STATION. I AM RESPONSIBLE FOR THE PROTECTION OF THE LAST TWO THOUSAND HUMAN BEINGS IN EXISTENCE.
HOW THE #@&% WAS I NOT TOLD ABOUT THIS IMMEDIATELY?!
DAMN IT, YOU KNOW BETTER THAN TO --
NO, IT'S OKAY -- LET HER GET IT OUT.
THANK YOU, DIRECTOR OF HUMAN RESOURCES. I'M GLAD YOU AND THE DIRECTOR OF PROJECT MANAGEMENT ARE OKAY WITH ME VOICING MY FRUSTRATION WITH THE FACT THAT YOU TRIED TO GO OVER MY HEAD.
WHEN ARE YOU GOING TO ACCEPT THAT WE'RE A TEAM, DEVA? A BOARD.
IKE AND I AREN'T CONSPIRING AGAINST YOU. YOU WERE IN THERAPY. WE TOLD YOU AS SOON AS WE COULD.
COULD'VE FOOLED ME. WHEN'S THE LAST TIME I WASN'T OUTVOTED THREE TO ONE IN A BOARD DECISION?
WE'RE NOT KEEPING ANYTHING FROM YOU.
DIRECTOR SCHEIDT'S ASSISTANT ENTERED HIS APARTMENT AND ALERTED US ABOUT THE, AH, SITUATION.

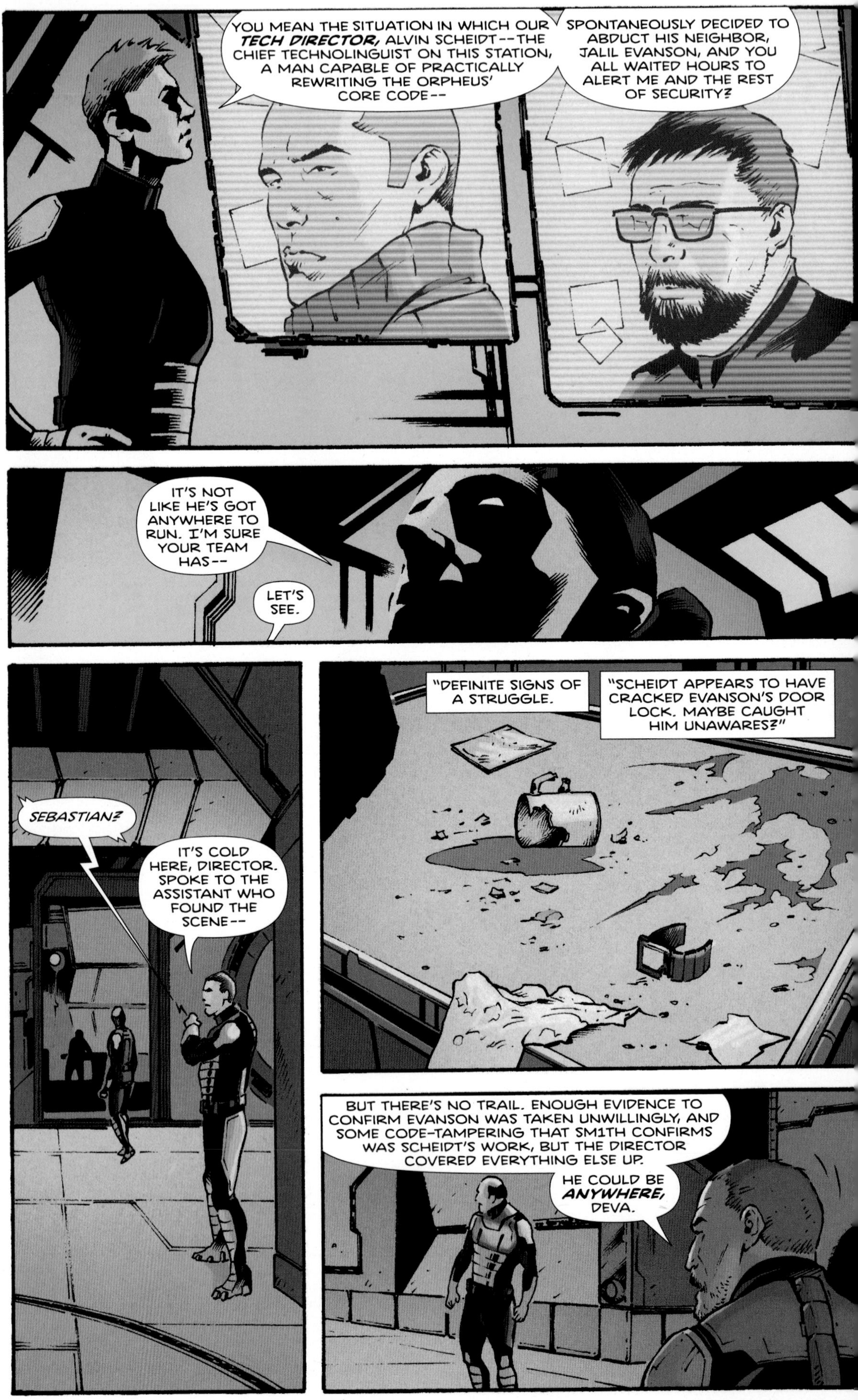
YOU MEAN THE SITUATION IN WHICH OUR *TECH DIRECTOR,* ALVIN SCHEIDT--THE CHIEF TECHNOLINGUIST ON THIS STATION, A MAN CAPABLE OF PRACTICALLY REWRITING THE ORPHEUS' CORE CODE--
SPONTANEOUSLY DECIDED TO ABDUCT HIS NEIGHBOR, JALIL EVANSON, AND YOU ALL WAITED HOURS TO ALERT ME AND THE REST OF SECURITY?
IT'S NOT LIKE HE'S GOT ANYWHERE TO RUN. I'M SURE YOUR TEAM HAS--
LET'S SEE.
SEBASTIAN?
IT'S COLD HERE, DIRECTOR. SPOKE TO THE ASSISTANT WHO FOUND THE SCENE--
"DEFINITE SIGNS OF A STRUGGLE.
"SCHEIDT APPEARS TO HAVE CRACKED EVANSON'S DOOR LOCK. MAYBE CAUGHT HIM UNAWARES?"
BUT THERE'S NO TRAIL. ENOUGH EVIDENCE TO CONFIRM EVANSON WAS TAKEN UNWILLINGLY, AND SOME CODE-TAMPERING THAT SM1TH CONFIRMS WAS SCHEIDT'S WORK, BUT THE DIRECTOR COVERED EVERYTHING ELSE UP.
HE COULD BE *ANYWHERE,* DEVA.

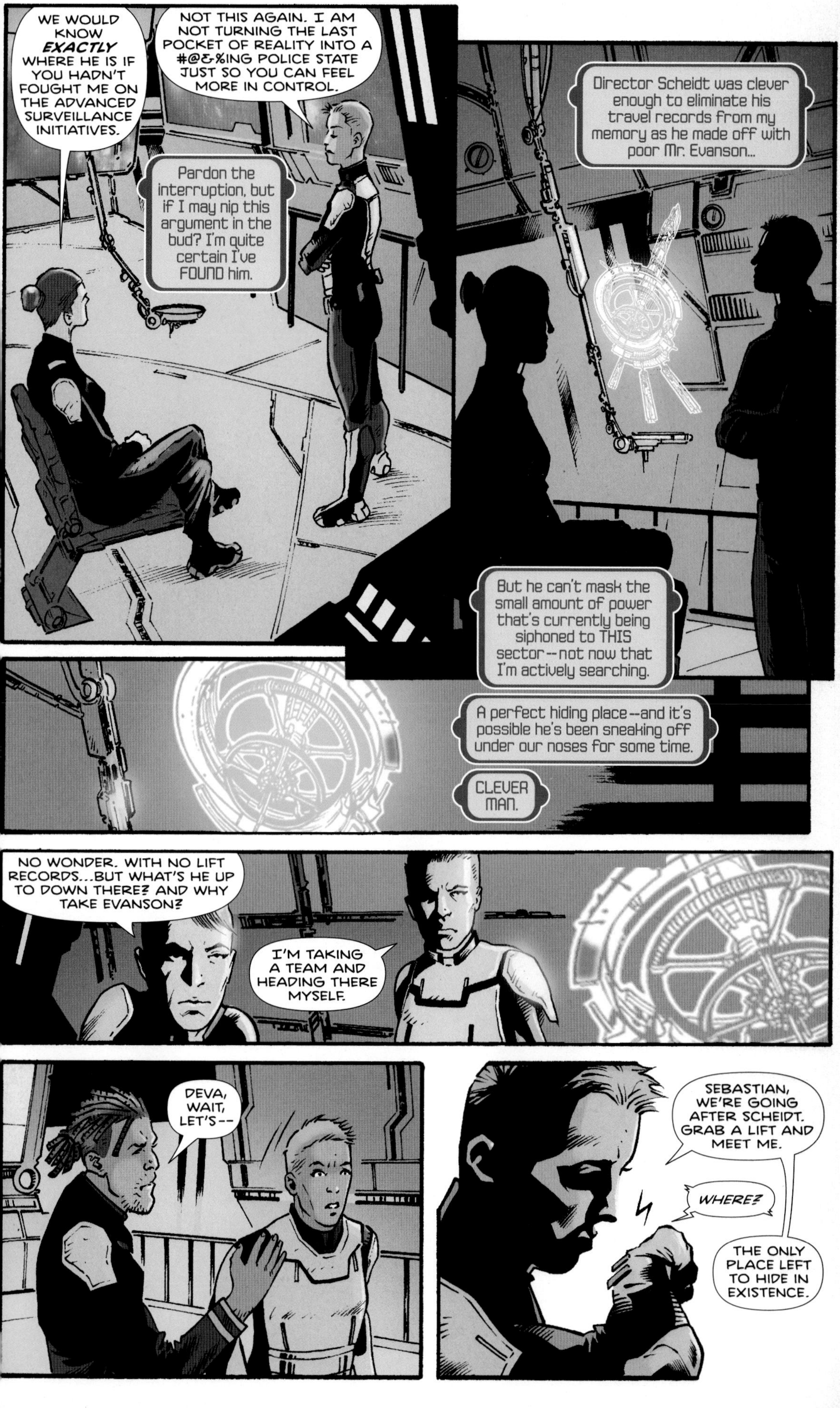
WE WOULD KNOW *EXACTLY* WHERE HE IS IF YOU HADN'T FOUGHT ME ON THE ADVANCED SURVEILLANCE INITIATIVES.
NOT THIS AGAIN. I AM NOT TURNING THE LAST POCKET OF REALITY INTO A #@&%ING POLICE STATE JUST SO YOU CAN FEEL MORE IN CONTROL.
Pardon the interruption, but if I may nip this argument in the bud? I'm quite certain I've FOUND him.
Director Scheidt was clever enough to eliminate his travel records from my memory as he made off with poor Mr. Evanson...
But he can't mask the small amount of power that's currently being siphoned to THIS sector--not now that I'm actively searching.
A perfect hiding place--and it's possible he's been sneaking off under our noses for some time.
CLEVER MAN.
NO WONDER. WITH NO LIFT RECORDS...BUT WHAT'S HE UP TO DOWN THERE? AND WHY TAKE EVANSON?
I'M TAKING A TEAM AND HEADING THERE MYSELF.
DEVA, WAIT, LET'S--
SEBASTIAN, WE'RE GOING AFTER SCHEIDT. GRAB A LIFT AND MEET ME.
WHERE?
THE ONLY PLACE LEFT TO HIDE IN EXISTENCE.

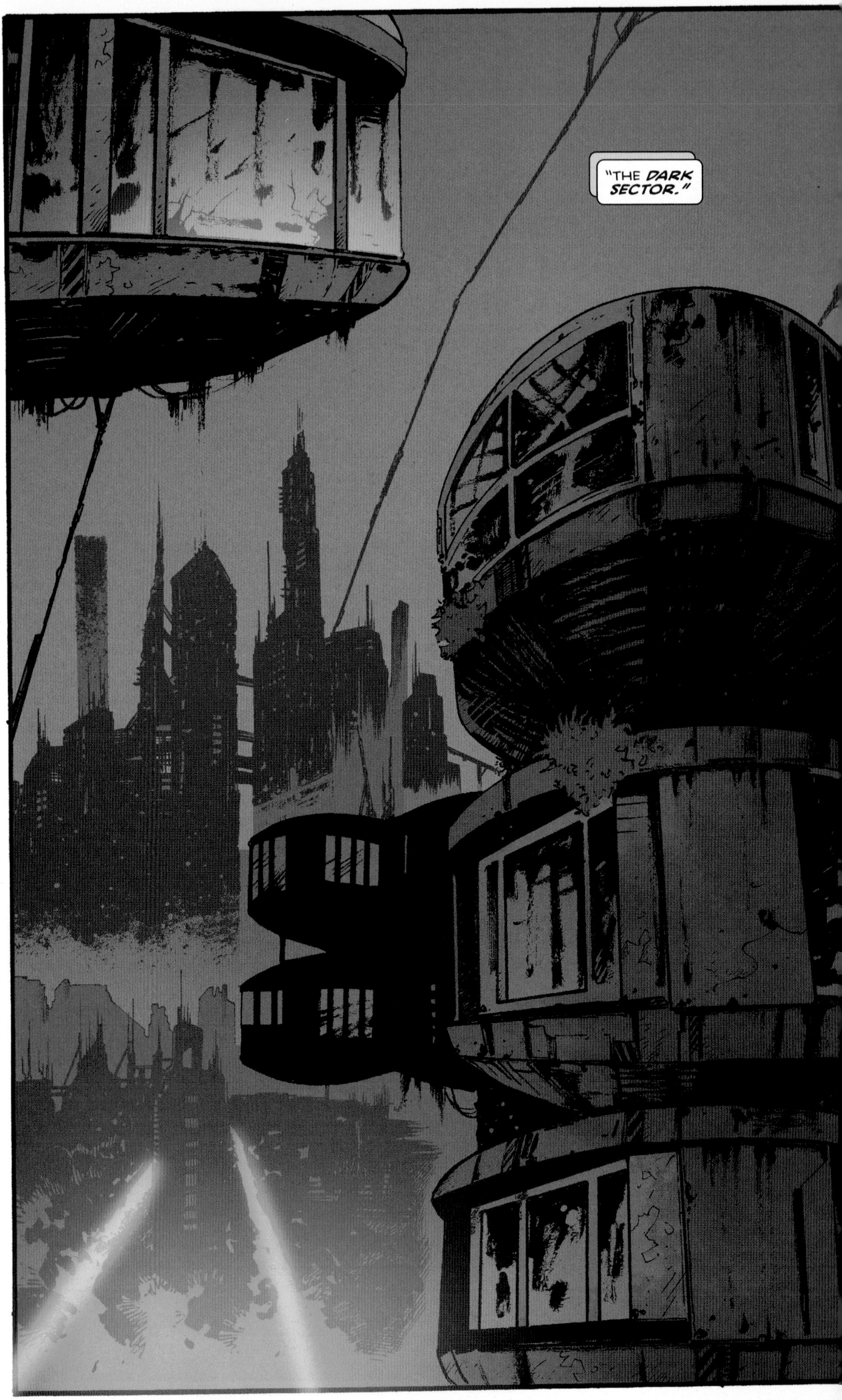
"THE DARK SECTOR."

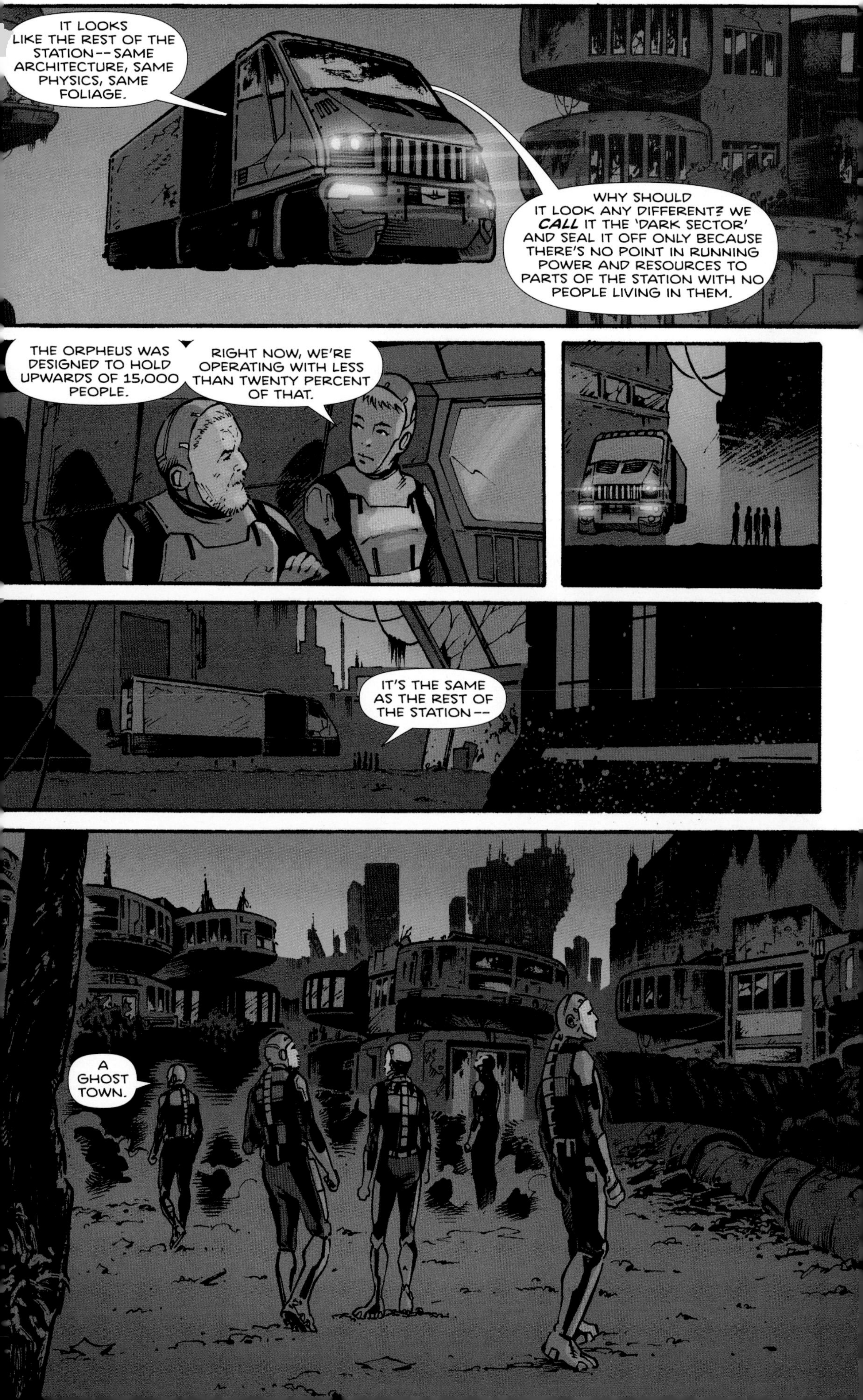
IT LOOKS LIKE THE REST OF THE STATION--SAME ARCHITECTURE, SAME PHYSICS, SAME FOLIAGE.
WHY SHOULD IT LOOK ANY DIFFERENT? WE *CALL* IT THE 'DARK SECTOR' AND SEAL IT OFF ONLY BECAUSE THERE'S NO POINT IN RUNNING POWER AND RESOURCES TO PARTS OF THE STATION WITH NO PEOPLE LIVING IN THEM.
THE ORPHEUS WAS DESIGNED TO HOLD UPWARDS OF 15,000 PEOPLE.
RIGHT NOW, WE'RE OPERATING WITH LESS THAN TWENTY PERCENT OF THAT.
IT'S THE SAME AS THE REST OF THE STATION--
A GHOST TOWN.

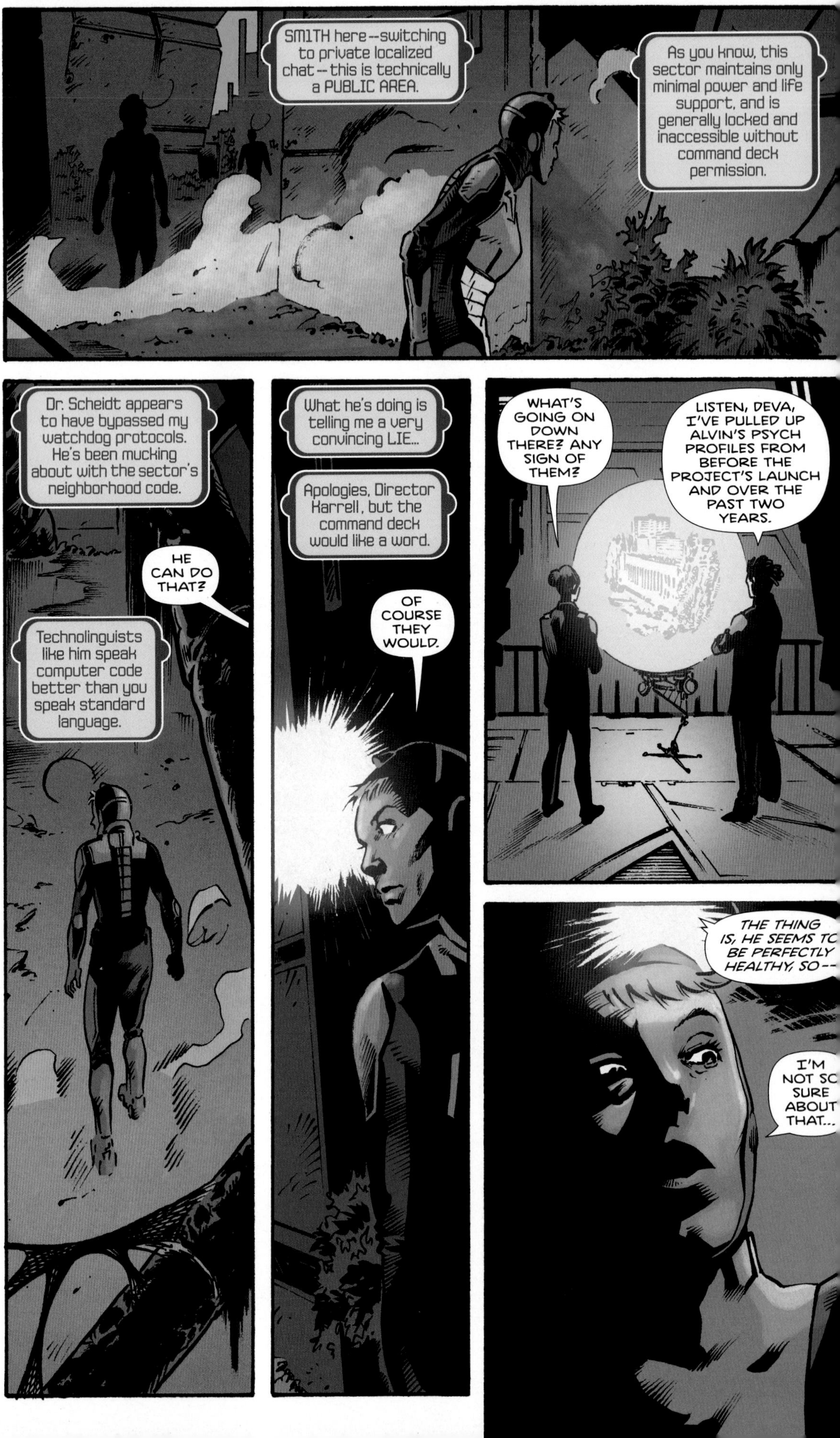
SM1TH here--switching to private localized chat--this is technically a PUBLIC AREA.
As you know, this sector maintains only minimal power and life support, and is generally locked and inaccessible without command deck permission.
Dr. Scheidt appears to have bypassed my watchdog protocols. He's been mucking about with the sector's neighborhood code.
HE CAN DO THAT?
Technolinguists like him speak computer code better than you speak standard language.
What he's doing is telling me a very convincing LIE...
Apologies, Director Karrell, but the command deck would like a word.
OF COURSE THEY WOULD.
WHAT'S GOING ON DOWN THERE? ANY SIGN OF THEM?
LISTEN, DEVA, I'VE PULLED UP ALVIN'S PSYCH PROFILES FROM BEFORE THE PROJECT'S LAUNCH AND OVER THE PAST TWO YEARS.
THE THING IS, HE SEEMS TO BE PERFECTLY HEALTHY, SO--
I'M NOT SO SURE ABOUT THAT...

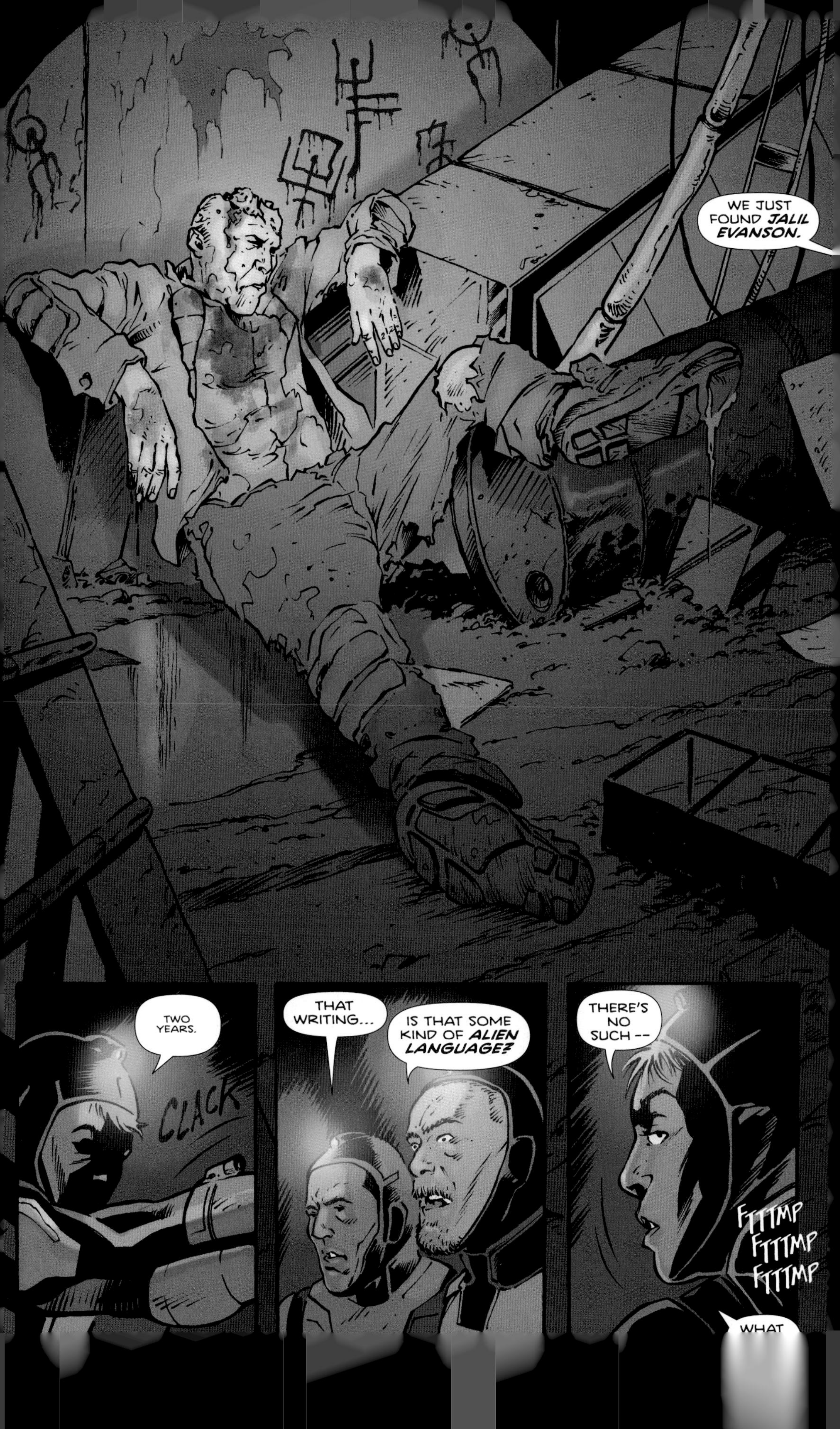
WE JUST FOUND JALIL EVANSON.
TWO YEARS.
CLACK
THAT WRITING...
IS THAT SOME KIND OF ALIEN LANGUAGE?
THERE'S NO SUCH --
FTTTMP
FTTTMP
FTTTMP
WHAT

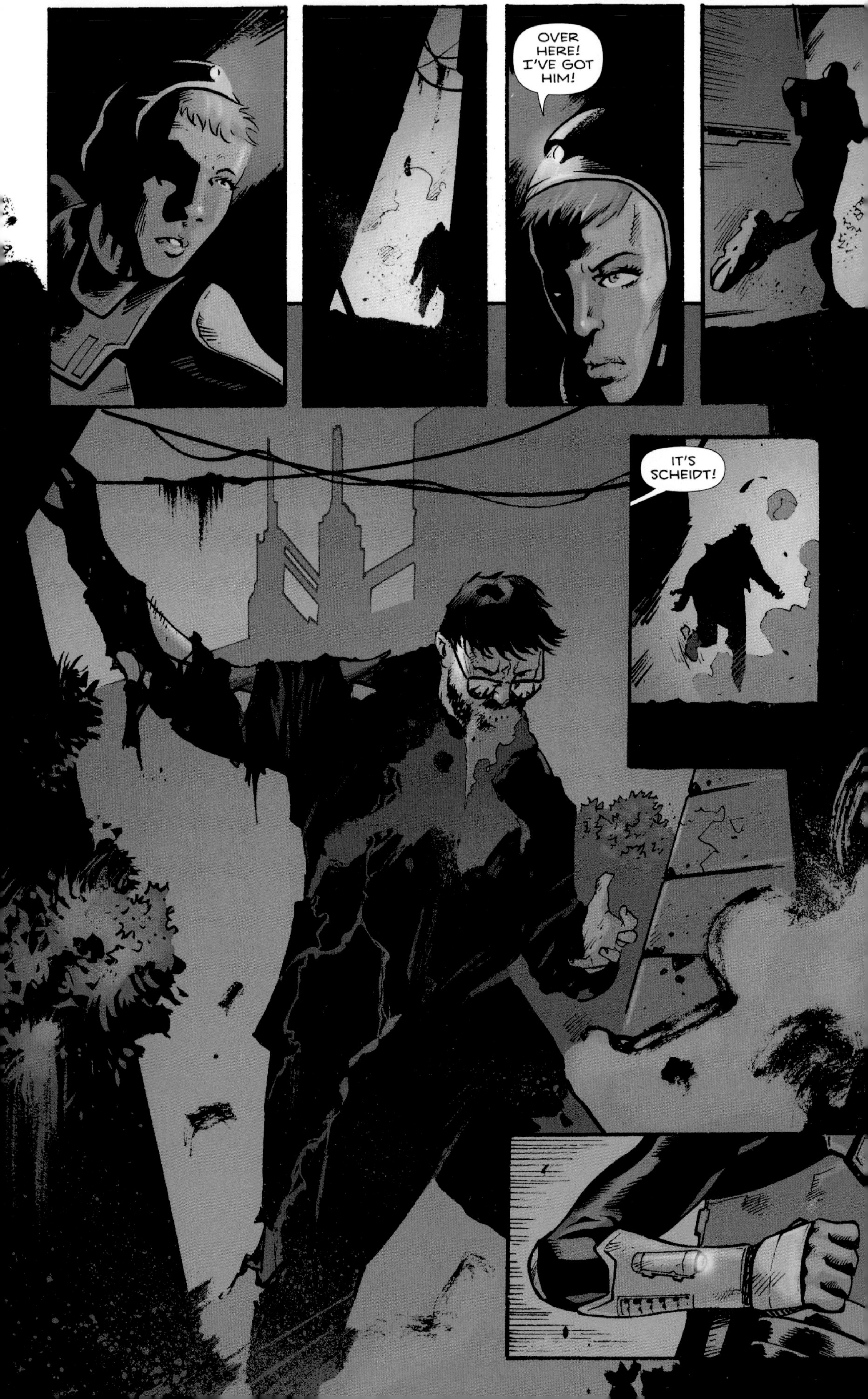
OVER HERE! I'VE GOT HIM!
IT'S SCHEIDT!

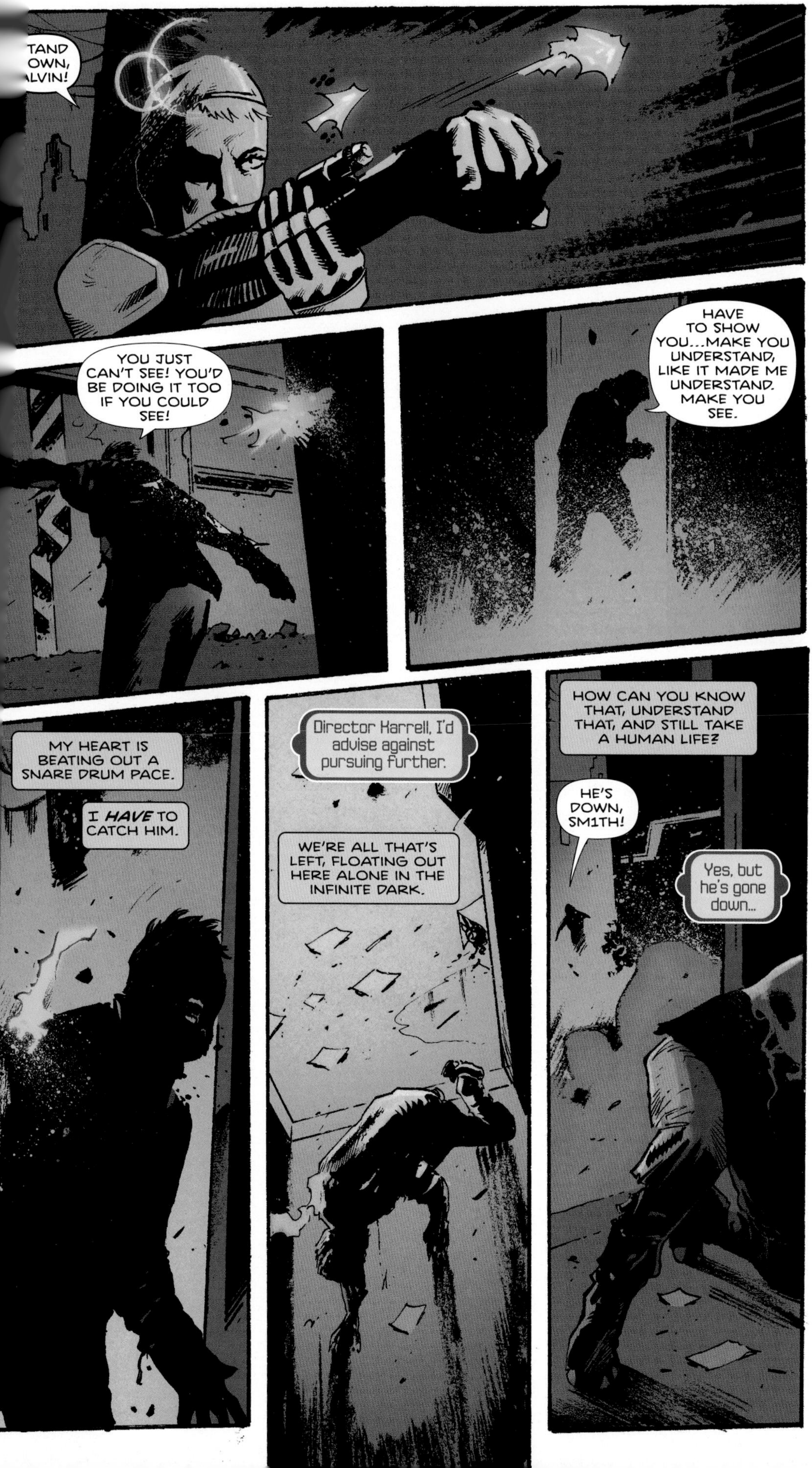
TAND OWN, ALVIN!
YOU JUST CAN'T SEE! YOU'D BE DOING IT TOO IF YOU COULD SEE!
HAVE TO SHOW YOU...MAKE YOU UNDERSTAND, LIKE IT MADE ME UNDERSTAND. MAKE YOU SEE.
MY HEART IS BEATING OUT A SNARE DRUM PACE.
I *HAVE* TO CATCH HIM.
Director Karrell, I'd advise against pursuing further.
WE'RE ALL THAT'S LEFT, FLOATING OUT HERE ALONE IN THE INFINITE DARK.
HOW CAN YOU KNOW THAT, UNDERSTAND THAT, AND STILL TAKE A HUMAN LIFE?
HE'S DOWN, SM1TH!
Yes, but he's gone down...

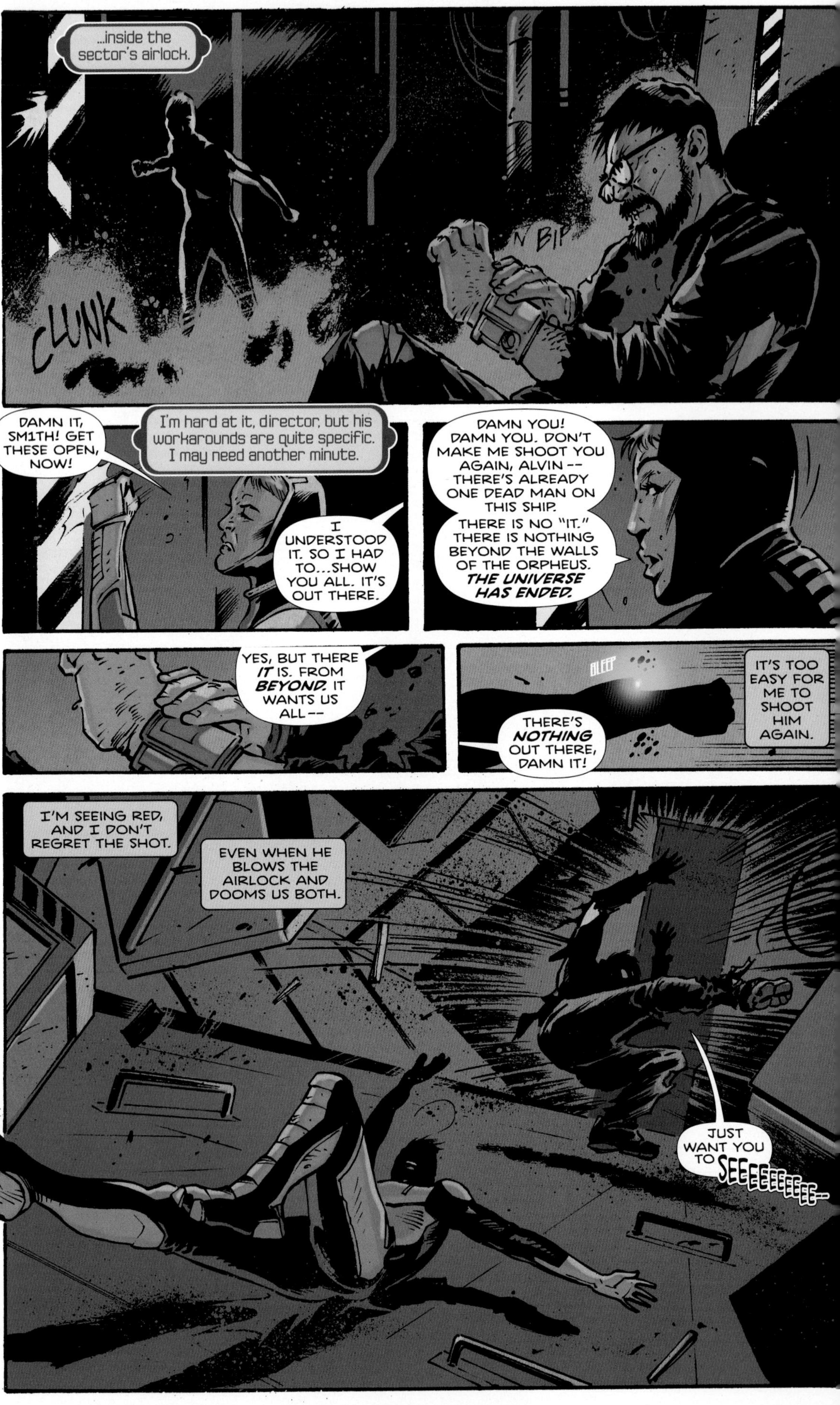
...inside the sector's airlock.
N BIP
CLUNK
DAMN IT, SM1TH! GET THESE OPEN, NOW!
I'm hard at it, director, but his workarounds are quite specific. I may need another minute.
I UNDERSTOOD IT. SO I HAD TO...SHOW YOU ALL. IT'S OUT THERE.
DAMN YOU! DAMN YOU. DON'T MAKE ME SHOOT YOU AGAIN, ALVIN -- THERE'S ALREADY ONE DEAD MAN ON THIS SHIP.
THERE IS NO "IT." THERE IS NOTHING BEYOND THE WALLS OF THE ORPHEUS. THE UNIVERSE HAS ENDED.
YES, BUT THERE IT IS. FROM BEYOND. IT WANTS US ALL--
BLEEP
THERE'S NOTHING OUT THERE, DAMN IT!
IT'S TOO EASY FOR ME TO SHOOT HIM AGAIN.
I'M SEEING RED, AND I DON'T REGRET THE SHOT.
EVEN WHEN HE BLOWS THE AIRLOCK AND DOOMS US BOTH.
JUST WANT YOU TO SEEEEEEEEEE--

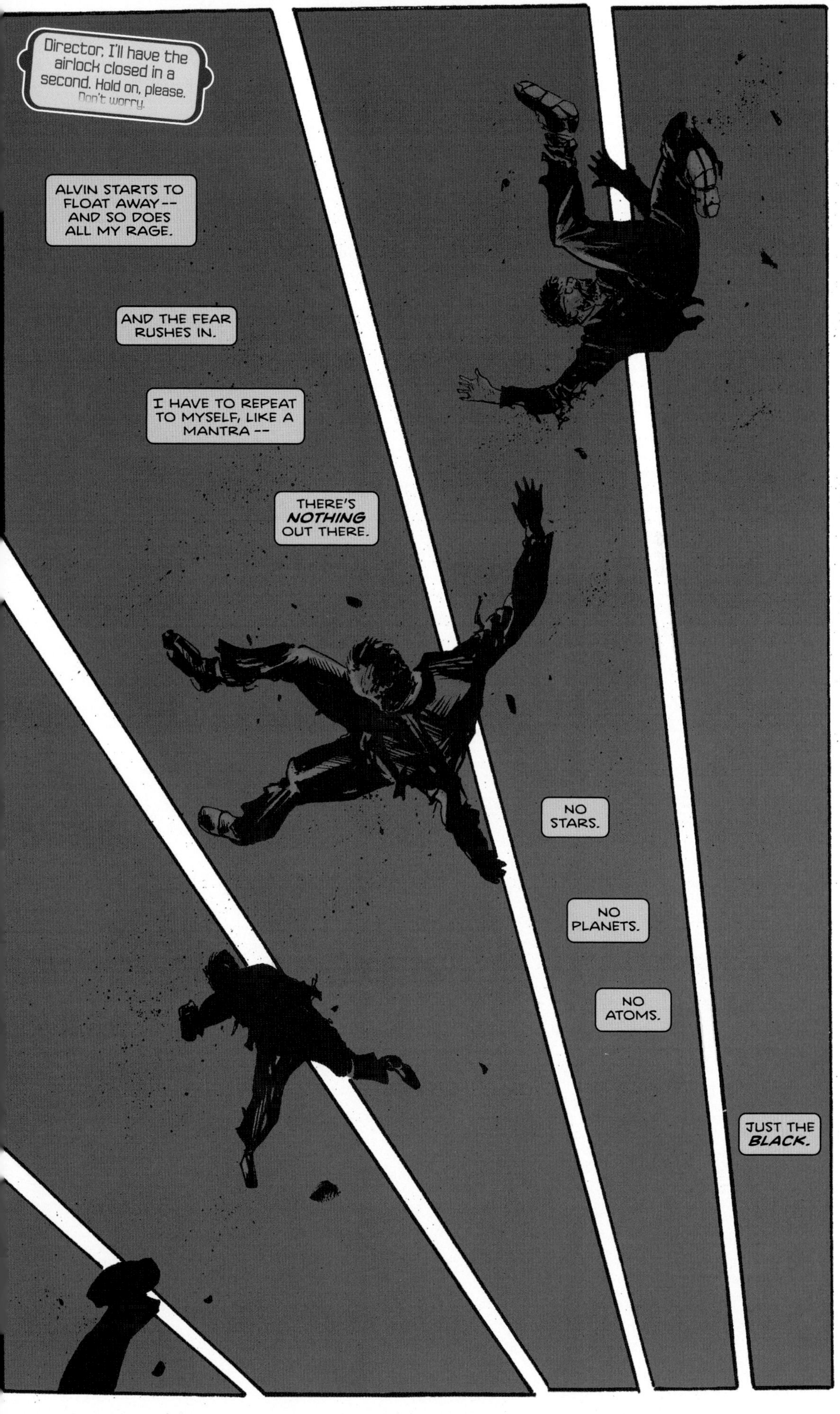
Director, I'll have the airlock closed in a second. Hold on, please. Don't worry.
ALVIN STARTS TO FLOAT AWAY-- AND SO DOES ALL MY RAGE.
AND THE FEAR RUSHES IN.
I HAVE TO REPEAT TO MYSELF, LIKE A MANTRA --
THERE'S *NOTHING* OUT THERE.
NO STARS.
NO PLANETS.
NO ATOMS.
JUST THE *BLACK.*

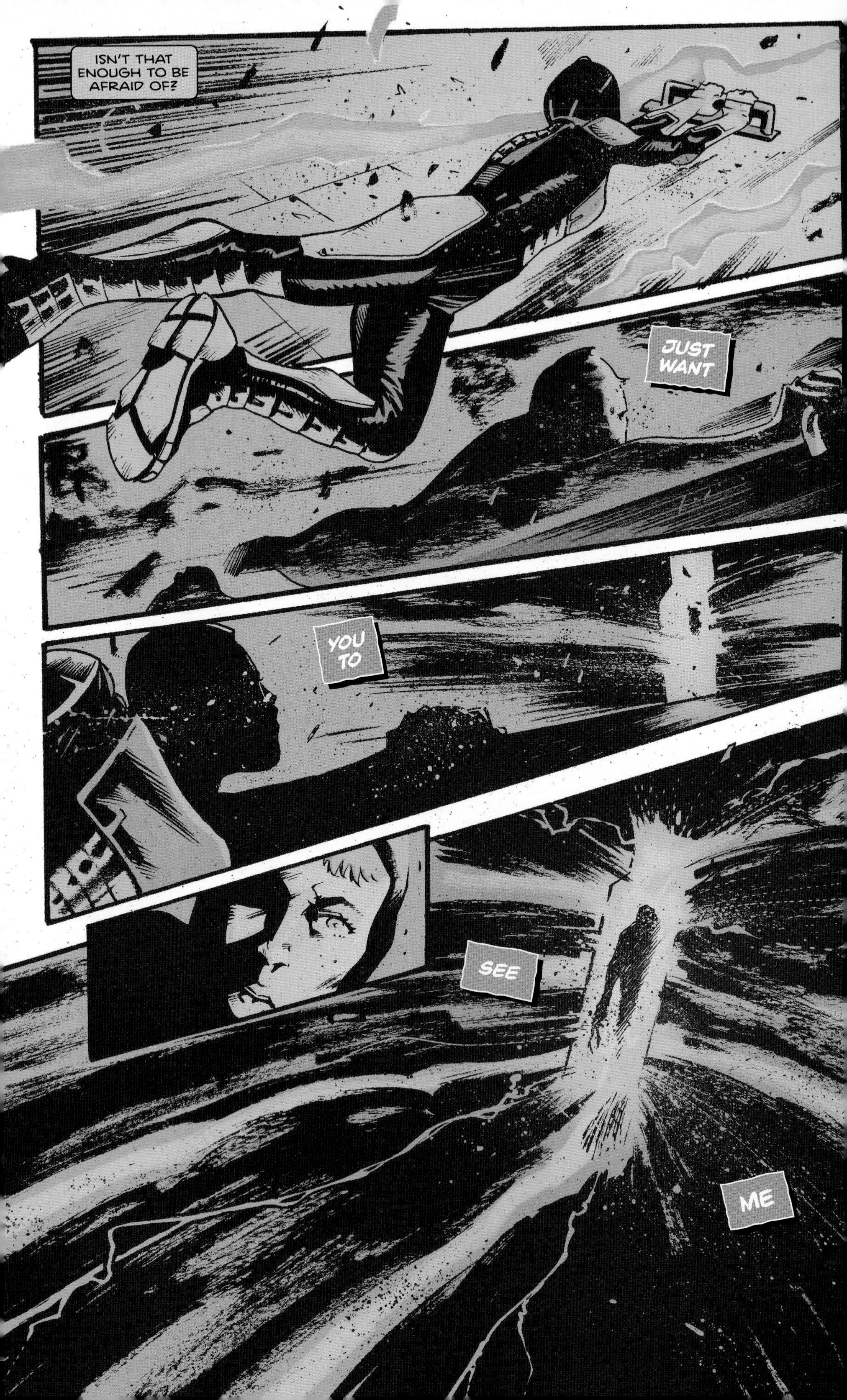
ISN'T THAT ENOUGH TO BE AFRAID OF?
JUST WANT
YOU TO
SEE
ME

CHAPTER TWO

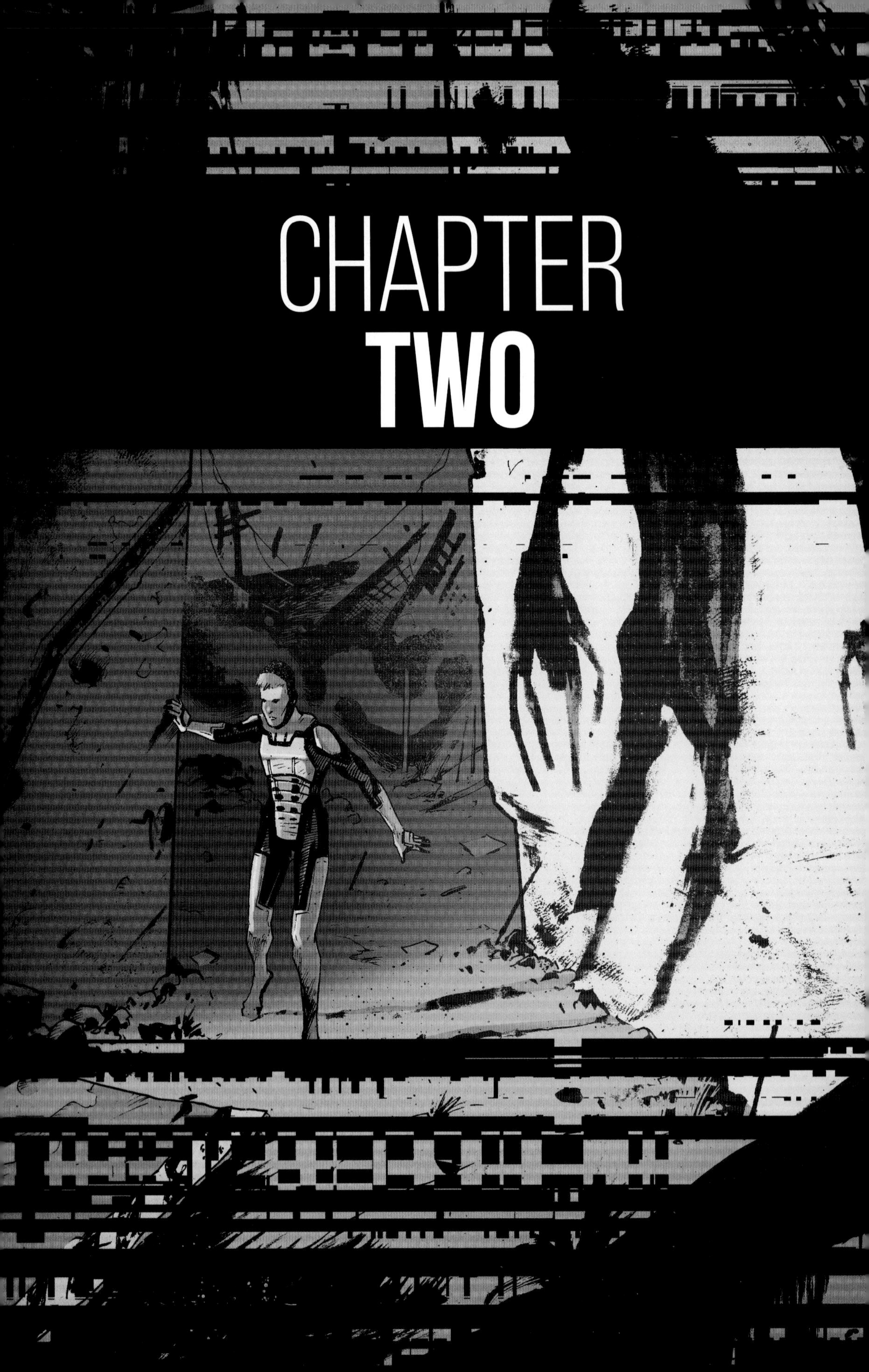

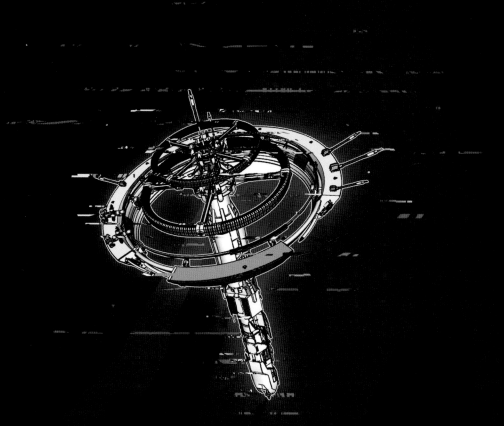

" STARING INTO PURE OBLIVION...
IT CAN REALLY DAMAGE A PERSON. "

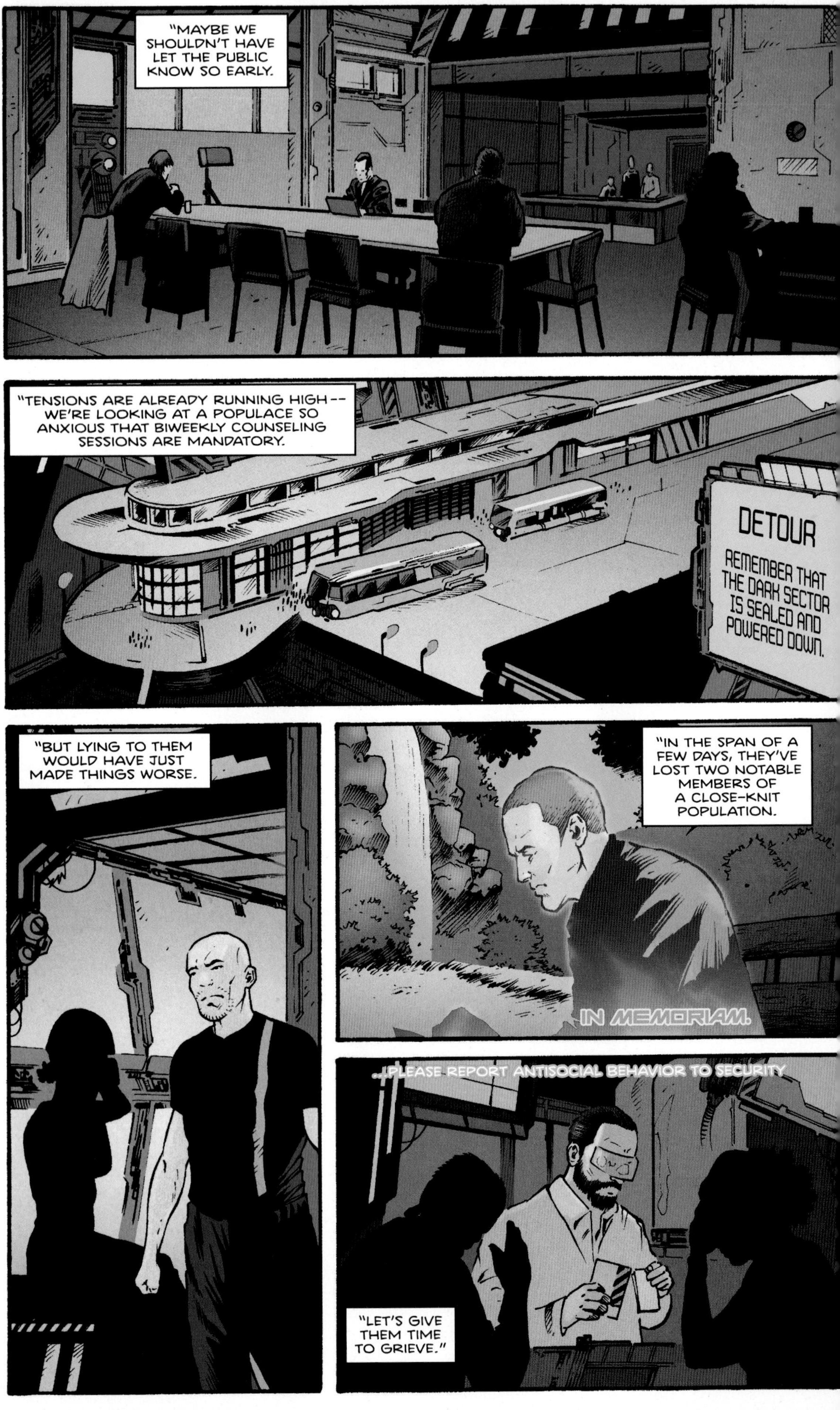
"MAYBE WE SHOULDN'T HAVE LET THE PUBLIC KNOW SO EARLY.
"TENSIONS ARE ALREADY RUNNING HIGH-- WE'RE LOOKING AT A POPULACE SO ANXIOUS THAT BIWEEKLY COUNSELING SESSIONS ARE MANDATORY.
DETOUR
REMEMBER THAT THE DARK SECTOR IS SEALED AND POWERED DOWN.
"BUT LYING TO THEM WOULD HAVE JUST MADE THINGS WORSE.
"IN THE SPAN OF A FEW DAYS, THEY'VE LOST TWO NOTABLE MEMBERS OF A CLOSE-KNIT POPULATION.
IN MEMORIAM.
...PLEASE REPORT ANTISOCIAL BEHAVIOR TO SECURITY
"LET'S GIVE THEM TIME TO GRIEVE."

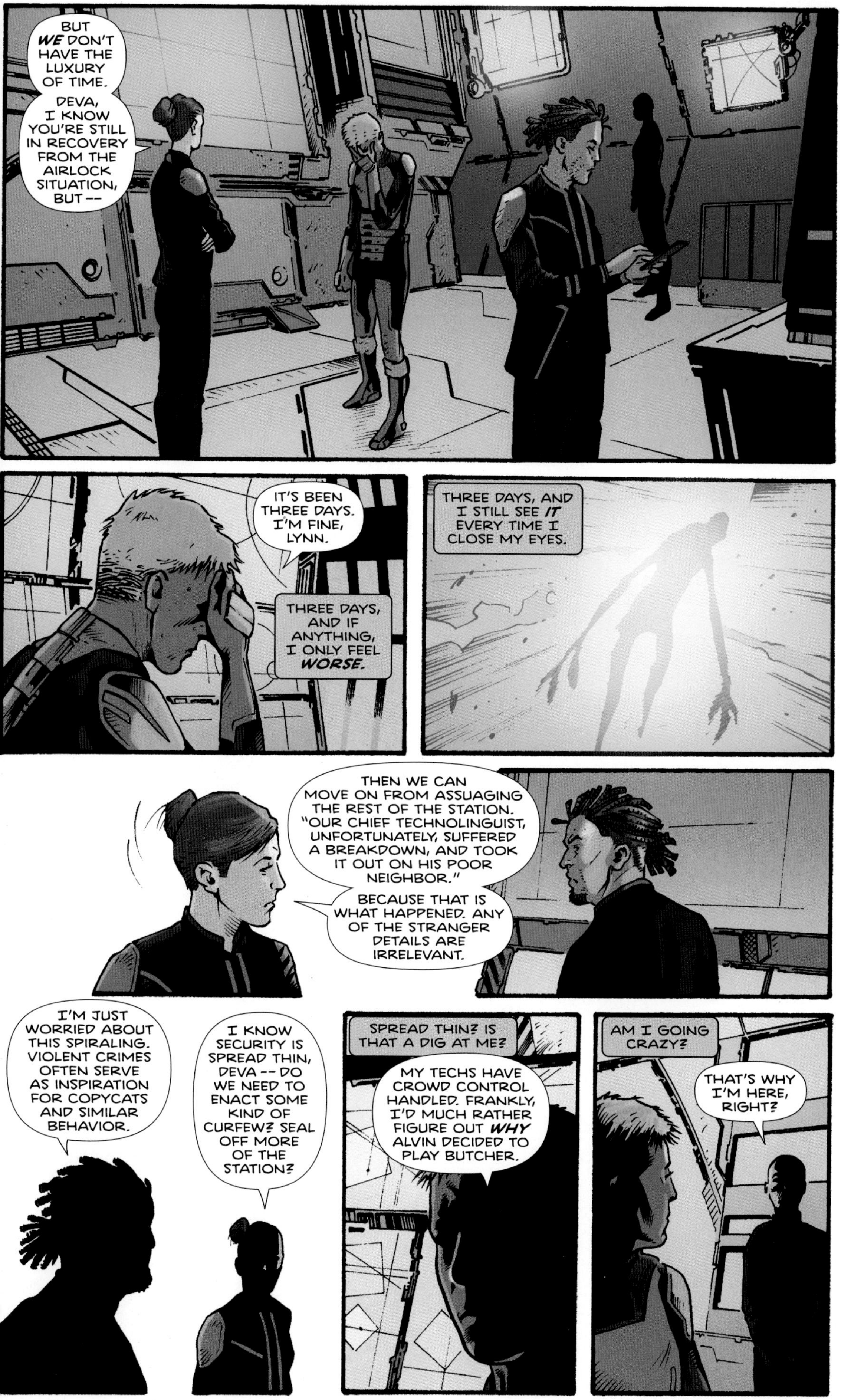
BUT *WE* DON'T HAVE THE LUXURY OF TIME.
DEVA, I KNOW YOU'RE STILL IN RECOVERY FROM THE AIRLOCK SITUATION, BUT --
IT'S BEEN THREE DAYS. I'M FINE, LYNN.
THREE DAYS, AND IF ANYTHING, I ONLY FEEL *WORSE.*
THREE DAYS, AND I STILL SEE *IT* EVERY TIME I CLOSE MY EYES.
THEN WE CAN MOVE ON FROM ASSUAGING THE REST OF THE STATION. "OUR CHIEF TECHNOLINGUIST, UNFORTUNATELY, SUFFERED A BREAKDOWN, AND TOOK IT OUT ON HIS POOR NEIGHBOR."
BECAUSE THAT IS WHAT HAPPENED. ANY OF THE STRANGER DETAILS ARE IRRELEVANT.
I'M JUST WORRIED ABOUT THIS SPIRALING. VIOLENT CRIMES OFTEN SERVE AS INSPIRATION FOR COPYCATS AND SIMILAR BEHAVIOR.
I KNOW SECURITY IS SPREAD THIN, DEVA -- DO WE NEED TO ENACT SOME KIND OF CURFEW? SEAL OFF MORE OF THE STATION?
SPREAD THIN? IS THAT A DIG AT ME?
MY TECHS HAVE CROWD CONTROL HANDLED. FRANKLY, I'D MUCH RATHER FIGURE OUT *WHY* ALVIN DECIDED TO PLAY BUTCHER.
AM I GOING CRAZY?
THAT'S WHY I'M HERE, RIGHT?

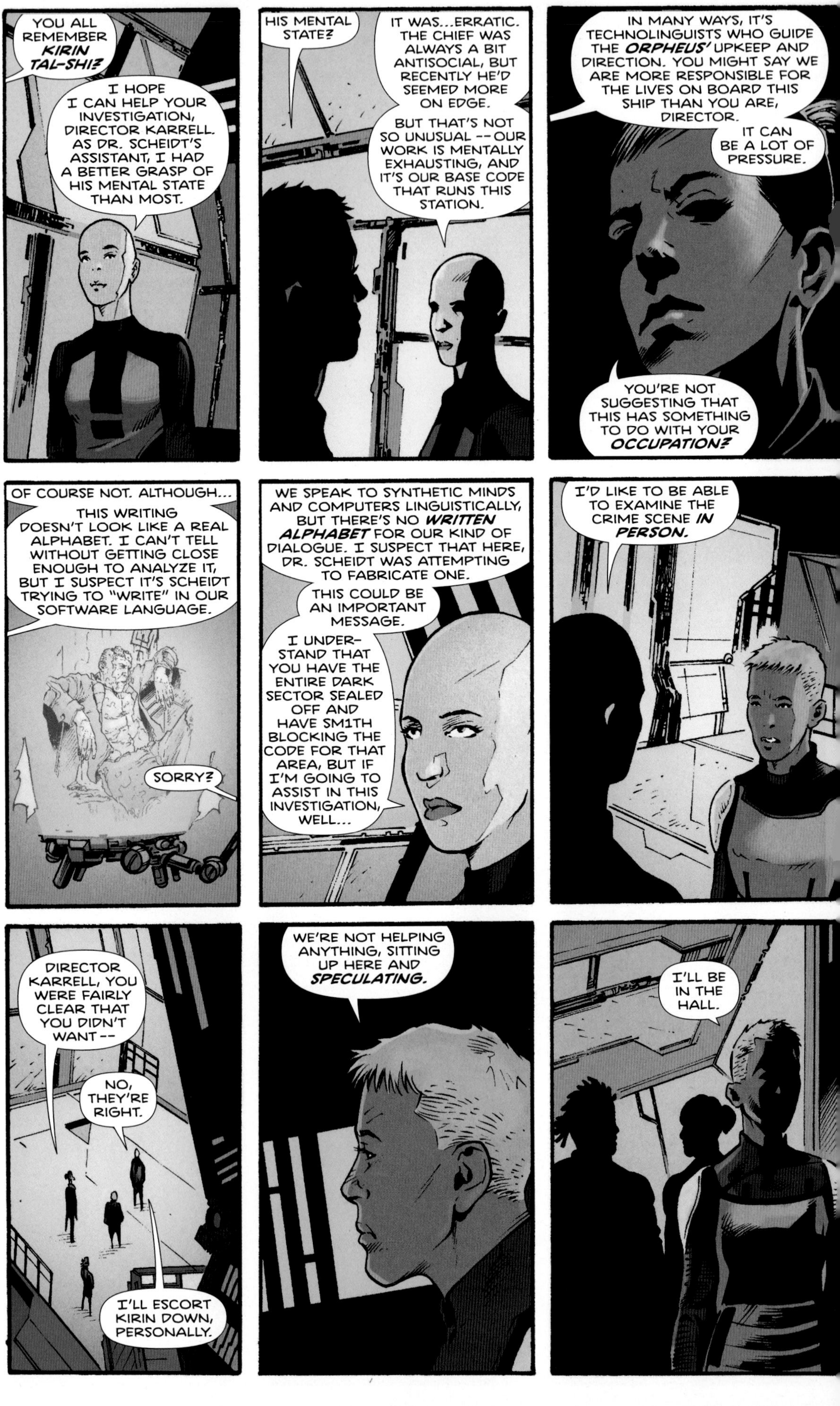
YOU ALL REMEMBER *KIRIN TAL-SHI?*
I HOPE I CAN HELP YOUR INVESTIGATION, DIRECTOR KARRELL. AS DR. SCHEIDT'S ASSISTANT, I HAD A BETTER GRASP OF HIS MENTAL STATE THAN MOST.
HIS MENTAL STATE?
IT WAS...ERRATIC. THE CHIEF WAS ALWAYS A BIT ANTISOCIAL, BUT RECENTLY HE'D SEEMED MORE ON EDGE.
BUT THAT'S NOT SO UNUSUAL -- OUR WORK IS MENTALLY EXHAUSTING, AND IT'S OUR BASE CODE THAT RUNS THIS STATION.
IN MANY WAYS, IT'S TECHNOLINGUISTS WHO GUIDE THE *ORPHEUS'* UPKEEP AND DIRECTION. YOU MIGHT SAY WE ARE MORE RESPONSIBLE FOR THE LIVES ON BOARD THIS SHIP THAN YOU ARE, DIRECTOR.
IT CAN BE A LOT OF PRESSURE.
YOU'RE NOT SUGGESTING THAT THIS HAS SOMETHING TO DO WITH YOUR *OCCUPATION?*
OF COURSE NOT. ALTHOUGH...
THIS WRITING DOESN'T LOOK LIKE A REAL ALPHABET. I CAN'T TELL WITHOUT GETTING CLOSE ENOUGH TO ANALYZE IT, BUT I SUSPECT IT'S SCHEIDT TRYING TO "WRITE" IN OUR SOFTWARE LANGUAGE.
SORRY?
WE SPEAK TO SYNTHETIC MINDS AND COMPUTERS LINGUISTICALLY, BUT THERE'S NO *WRITTEN ALPHABET* FOR OUR KIND OF DIALOGUE. I SUSPECT THAT HERE, DR. SCHEIDT WAS ATTEMPTING TO FABRICATE ONE.
THIS COULD BE AN IMPORTANT MESSAGE.
I UNDERSTAND THAT YOU HAVE THE ENTIRE DARK SECTOR SEALED OFF AND HAVE SM1TH BLOCKING THE CODE FOR THAT AREA, BUT IF I'M GOING TO ASSIST IN THIS INVESTIGATION, WELL...
I'D LIKE TO BE ABLE TO EXAMINE THE CRIME SCENE *IN PERSON.*
DIRECTOR KARRELL, YOU WERE FAIRLY CLEAR THAT YOU DIDN'T WANT --
NO, THEY'RE RIGHT.
I'LL ESCORT KIRIN DOWN, PERSONALLY.
WE'RE NOT HELPING ANYTHING, SITTING UP HERE AND *SPECULATING.*
I'LL BE IN THE HALL.

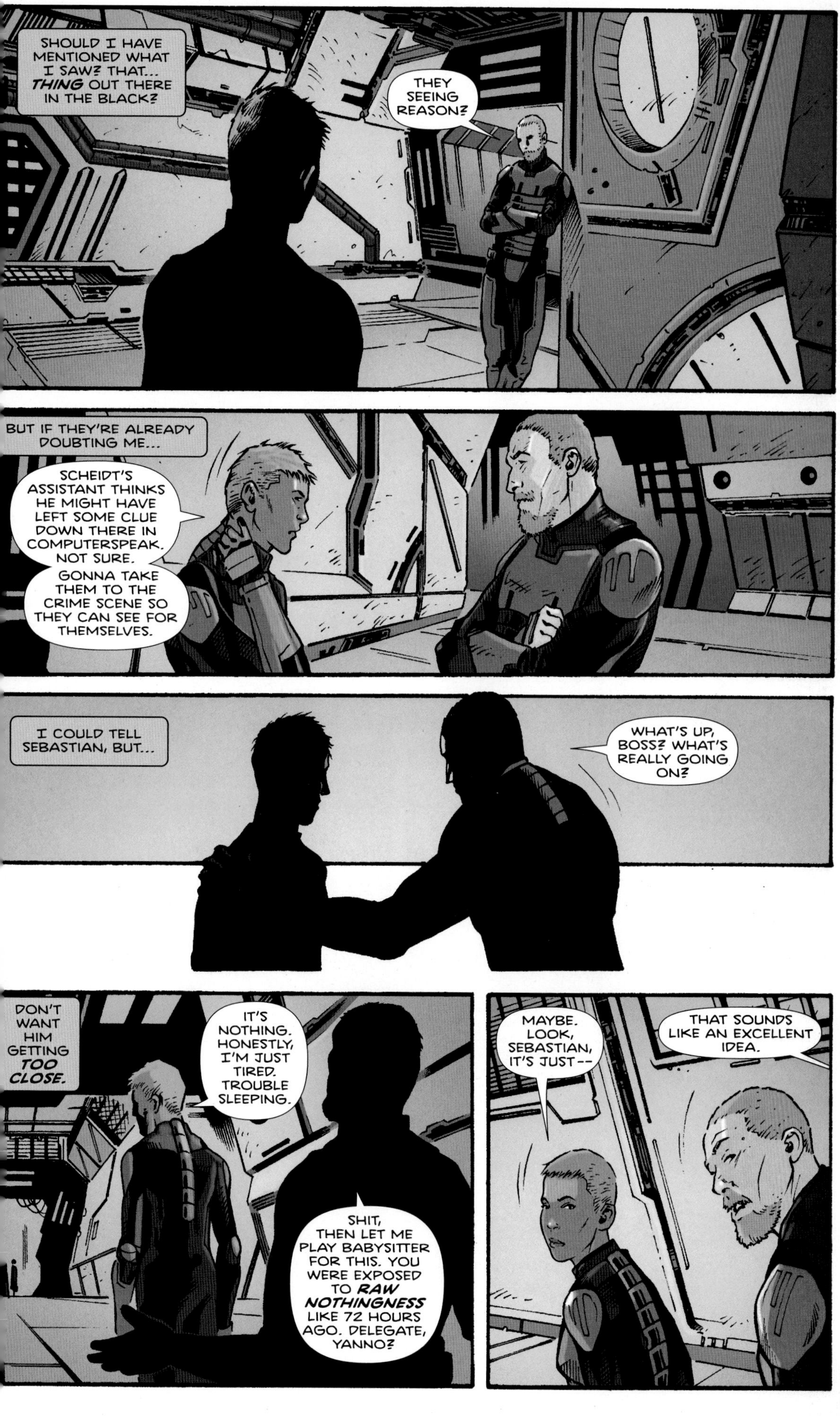
SHOULD I HAVE MENTIONED WHAT I SAW? THAT... *THING* OUT THERE IN THE BLACK?
THEY SEEING REASON?
BUT IF THEY'RE ALREADY DOUBTING ME...
SCHEIDT'S ASSISTANT THINKS HE MIGHT HAVE LEFT SOME CLUE DOWN THERE IN COMPUTERSPEAK. NOT SURE.
GONNA TAKE THEM TO THE CRIME SCENE SO THEY CAN SEE FOR THEMSELVES.
I COULD TELL SEBASTIAN, BUT...
WHAT'S UP, BOSS? WHAT'S REALLY GOING ON?
DON'T WANT HIM GETTING *TOO CLOSE.*
IT'S NOTHING. HONESTLY, I'M JUST TIRED. TROUBLE SLEEPING.
SHIT, THEN LET ME PLAY BABYSITTER FOR THIS. YOU WERE EXPOSED TO *RAW NOTHINGNESS* LIKE 72 HOURS AGO. DELEGATE, YANNO?
MAYBE. LOOK, SEBASTIAN, IT'S JUST--
THAT SOUNDS LIKE AN EXCELLENT IDEA.

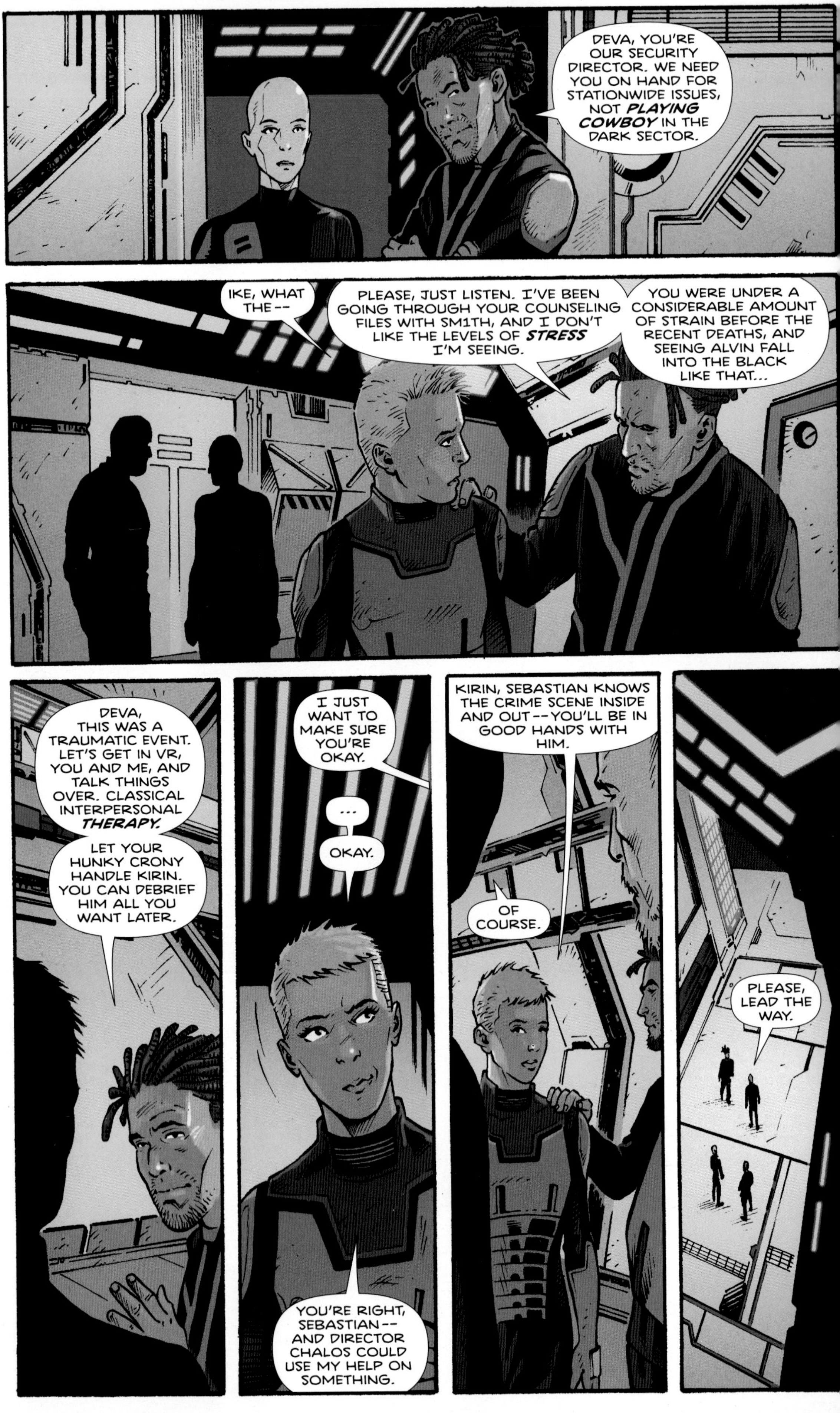
DEVA, YOU'RE OUR SECURITY DIRECTOR. WE NEED YOU ON HAND FOR STATIONWIDE ISSUES, NOT PLAYING COWBOY IN THE DARK SECTOR.
IKE, WHAT THE--
PLEASE, JUST LISTEN. I'VE BEEN GOING THROUGH YOUR COUNSELING FILES WITH SM1TH, AND I DON'T LIKE THE LEVELS OF STRESS I'M SEEING.
YOU WERE UNDER A CONSIDERABLE AMOUNT OF STRAIN BEFORE THE RECENT DEATHS, AND SEEING ALVIN FALL INTO THE BLACK LIKE THAT...
DEVA, THIS WAS A TRAUMATIC EVENT. LET'S GET IN VR, YOU AND ME, AND TALK THINGS OVER. CLASSICAL INTERPERSONAL THERAPY.
LET YOUR HUNKY CRONY HANDLE KIRIN. YOU CAN DEBRIEF HIM ALL YOU WANT LATER.
I JUST WANT TO MAKE SURE YOU'RE OKAY.
...
OKAY.
YOU'RE RIGHT, SEBASTIAN-- AND DIRECTOR CHALOS COULD USE MY HELP ON SOMETHING.
KIRIN, SEBASTIAN KNOWS THE CRIME SCENE INSIDE AND OUT--YOU'LL BE IN GOOD HANDS WITH HIM.
OF COURSE.
PLEASE, LEAD THE WAY.

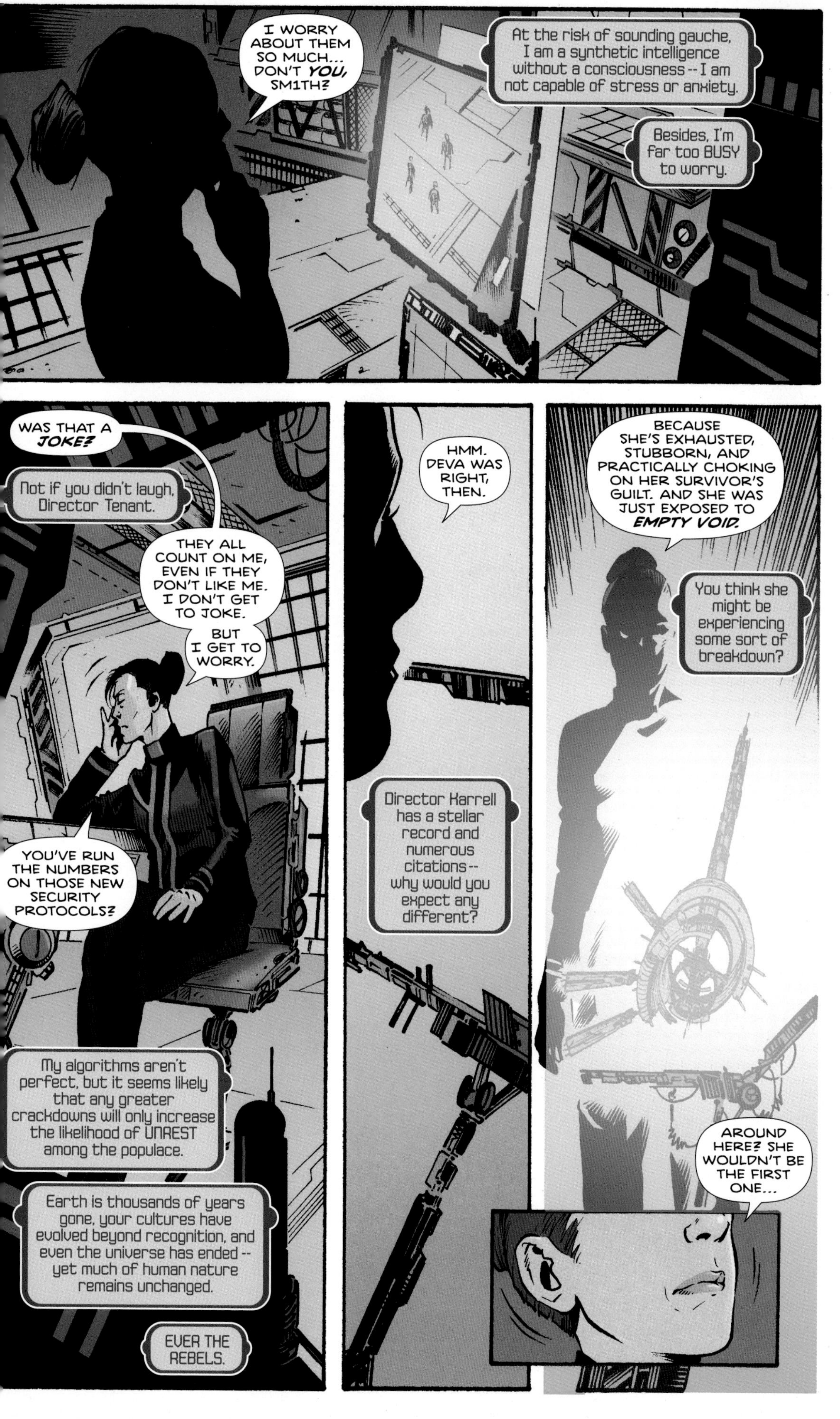

I WORRY ABOUT THEM SO MUCH... DON'T *YOU,* SM1TH?
At the risk of sounding gauche, I am a synthetic intelligence without a consciousness -- I am not capable of stress or anxiety.
Besides, I'm far too BUSY to worry.
WAS THAT A *JOKE?*
Not if you didn't laugh, Director Tenant.
THEY ALL COUNT ON ME, EVEN IF THEY DON'T LIKE ME. I DON'T GET TO JOKE.
BUT I GET TO WORRY.
YOU'VE RUN THE NUMBERS ON THOSE NEW SECURITY PROTOCOLS?
My algorithms aren't perfect, but it seems likely that any greater crackdowns will only increase the likelihood of UNREST among the populace.
Earth is thousands of years gone, your cultures have evolved beyond recognition, and even the universe has ended -- yet much of human nature remains unchanged.
EVER THE REBELS.
HMM. DEVA WAS RIGHT, THEN.
Director Harrell has a stellar record and numerous citations -- why would you expect any different?
BECAUSE SHE'S EXHAUSTED, STUBBORN, AND PRACTICALLY CHOKING ON HER SURVIVOR'S GUILT. AND SHE WAS JUST EXPOSED TO *EMPTY VOID.*
You think she might be experiencing some sort of breakdown?
AROUND HERE? SHE WOULDN'T BE THE FIRST ONE...

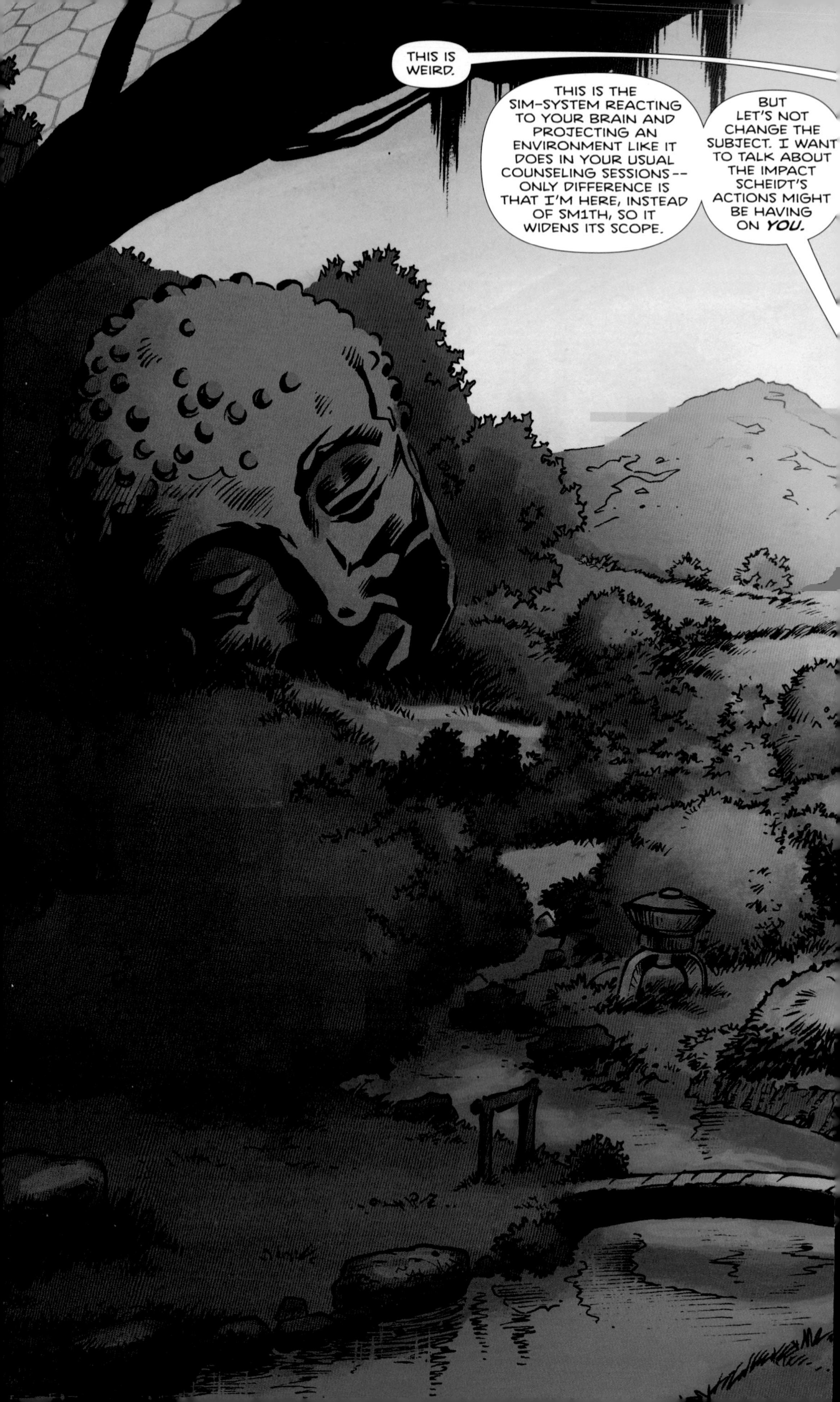
THIS IS WEIRD.
THIS IS THE SIM-SYSTEM REACTING TO YOUR BRAIN AND PROJECTING AN ENVIRONMENT LIKE IT DOES IN YOUR USUAL COUNSELING SESSIONS-- ONLY DIFFERENCE IS THAT I'M HERE, INSTEAD OF SM1TH, SO IT WIDENS ITS SCOPE.
BUT LET'S NOT CHANGE THE SUBJECT. I WANT TO TALK ABOUT THE IMPACT SCHEIDT'S ACTIONS MIGHT BE HAVING ON *YOU.*

I DID EVERYTHING I COULD TO SAVE HIM. *EVERYTHING.*
YOU EXPOSED YOURSELF TO THE BLACK. WATCHED ALVIN SLIP OUT PAST OUR *PSEUDOREALITY FIELD* AND DISSOLVE INTO PURE ENTROPY.
THAT'S NOT AN EASY THING TO SHAKE, DEVA.
WHEN THEY DRAGGED YOU OUT OF THE AIRLOCK, YOU WERE FROZEN HALF TO DEATH, BABBLING ABOUT ALVIN TRYING TO MAKE YOU SEE SOMETHING -- SOMETHING OUT THERE IN THE DARK.

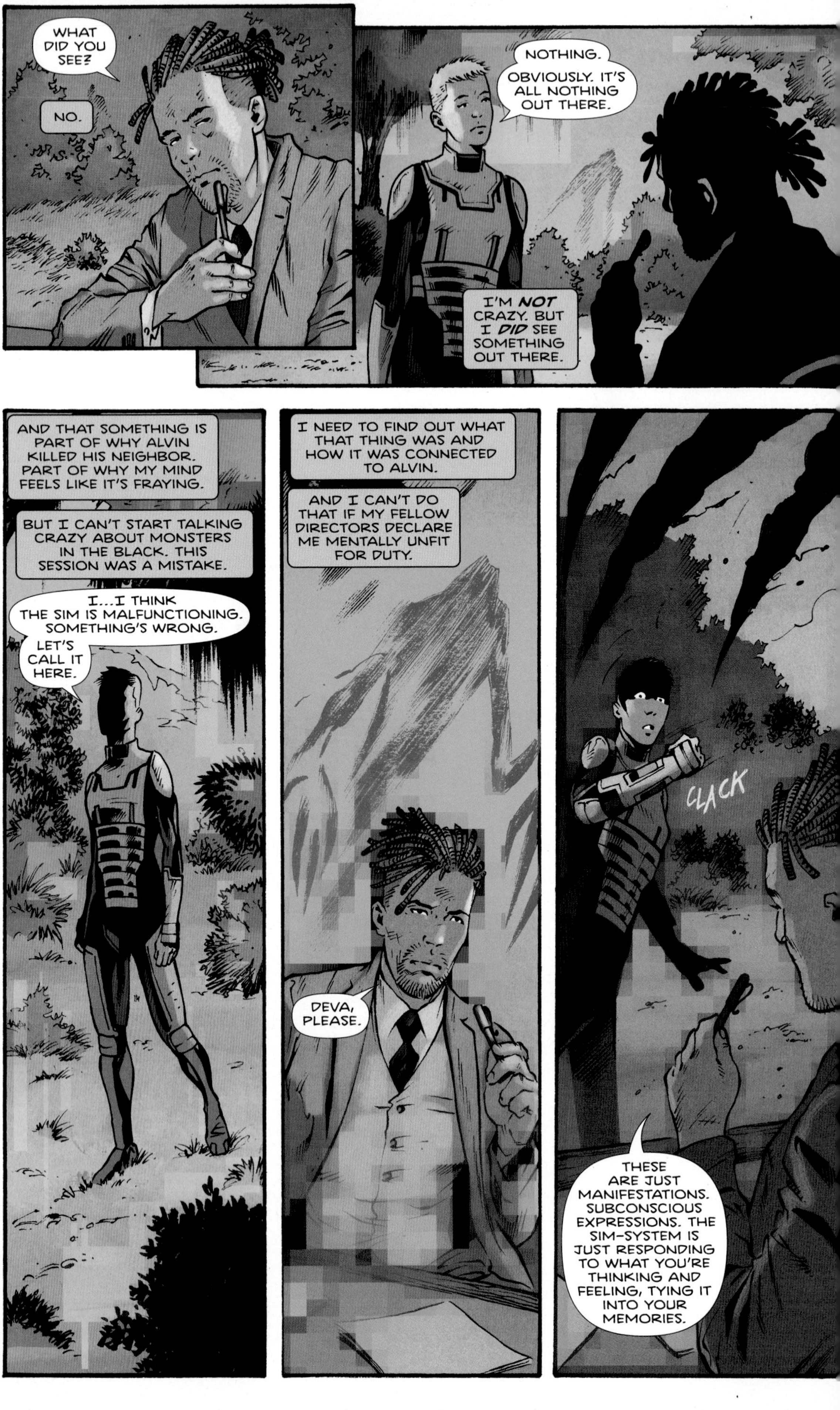
WHAT DID YOU SEE?
NO.
NOTHING.
OBVIOUSLY. IT'S ALL NOTHING OUT THERE.
I'M **NOT** CRAZY. BUT I ***DID*** SEE SOMETHING OUT THERE.
AND THAT SOMETHING IS PART OF WHY ALVIN KILLED HIS NEIGHBOR. PART OF WHY MY MIND FEELS LIKE IT'S FRAYING.
BUT I CAN'T START TALKING CRAZY ABOUT MONSTERS IN THE BLACK. THIS SESSION WAS A MISTAKE.
I...I THINK THE SIM IS MALFUNCTIONING. SOMETHING'S WRONG.
LET'S CALL IT HERE.
I NEED TO FIND OUT WHAT THAT THING WAS AND HOW IT WAS CONNECTED TO ALVIN.
AND I CAN'T DO THAT IF MY FELLOW DIRECTORS DECLARE ME MENTALLY UNFIT FOR DUTY.
DEVA, PLEASE.
CLACK
THESE ARE JUST MANIFESTATIONS. SUBCONSCIOUS EXPRESSIONS. THE SIM-SYSTEM IS JUST RESPONDING TO WHAT YOU'RE THINKING AND FEELING, TYING IT INTO YOUR MEMORIES.

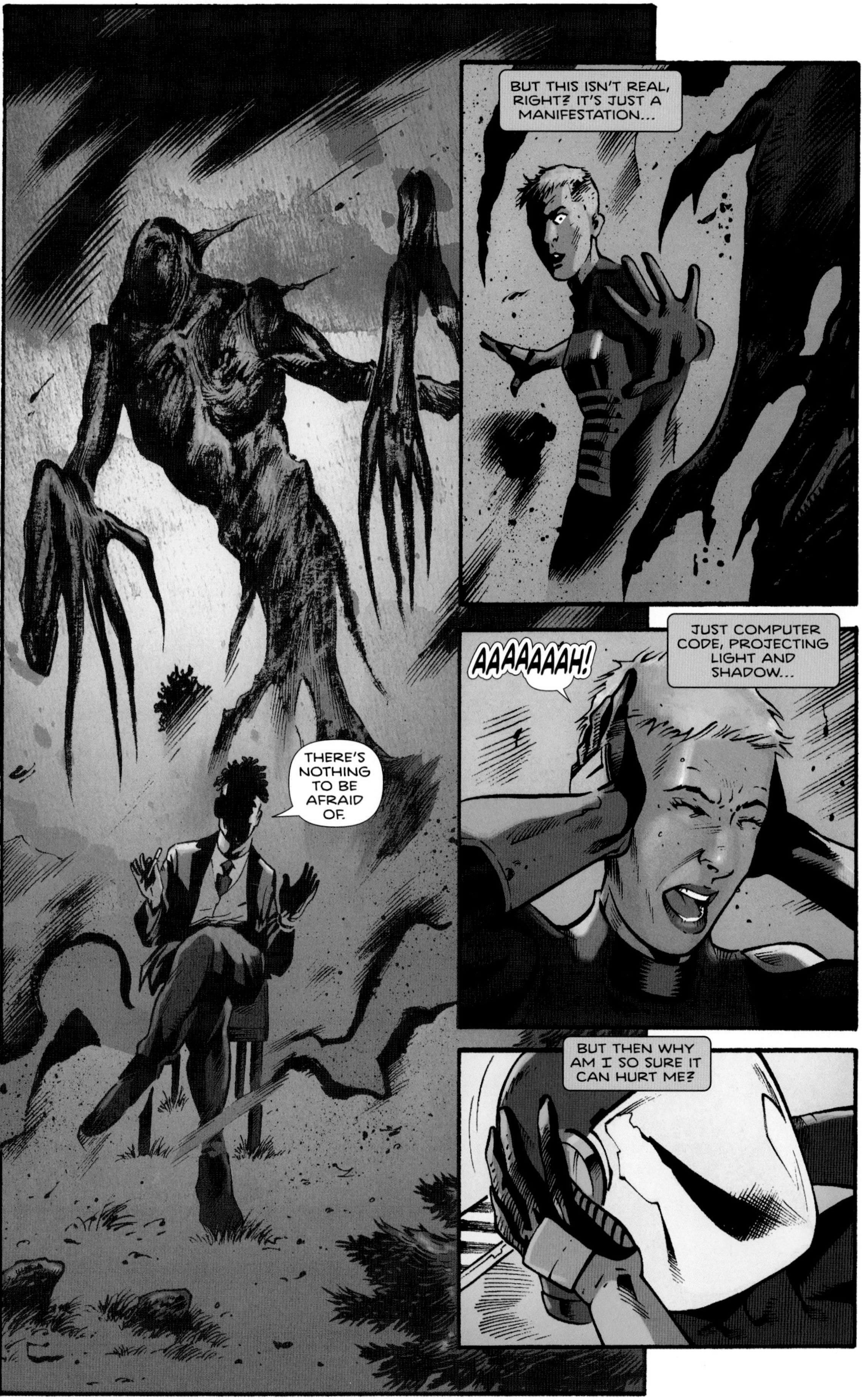
THERE'S NOTHING TO BE AFRAID OF.
BUT THIS ISN'T REAL, RIGHT? IT'S JUST A MANIFESTATION...
JUST COMPUTER CODE, PROJECTING LIGHT AND SHADOW...
AAAAAAAH!
BUT THEN WHY AM I SO SURE IT CAN HURT ME?

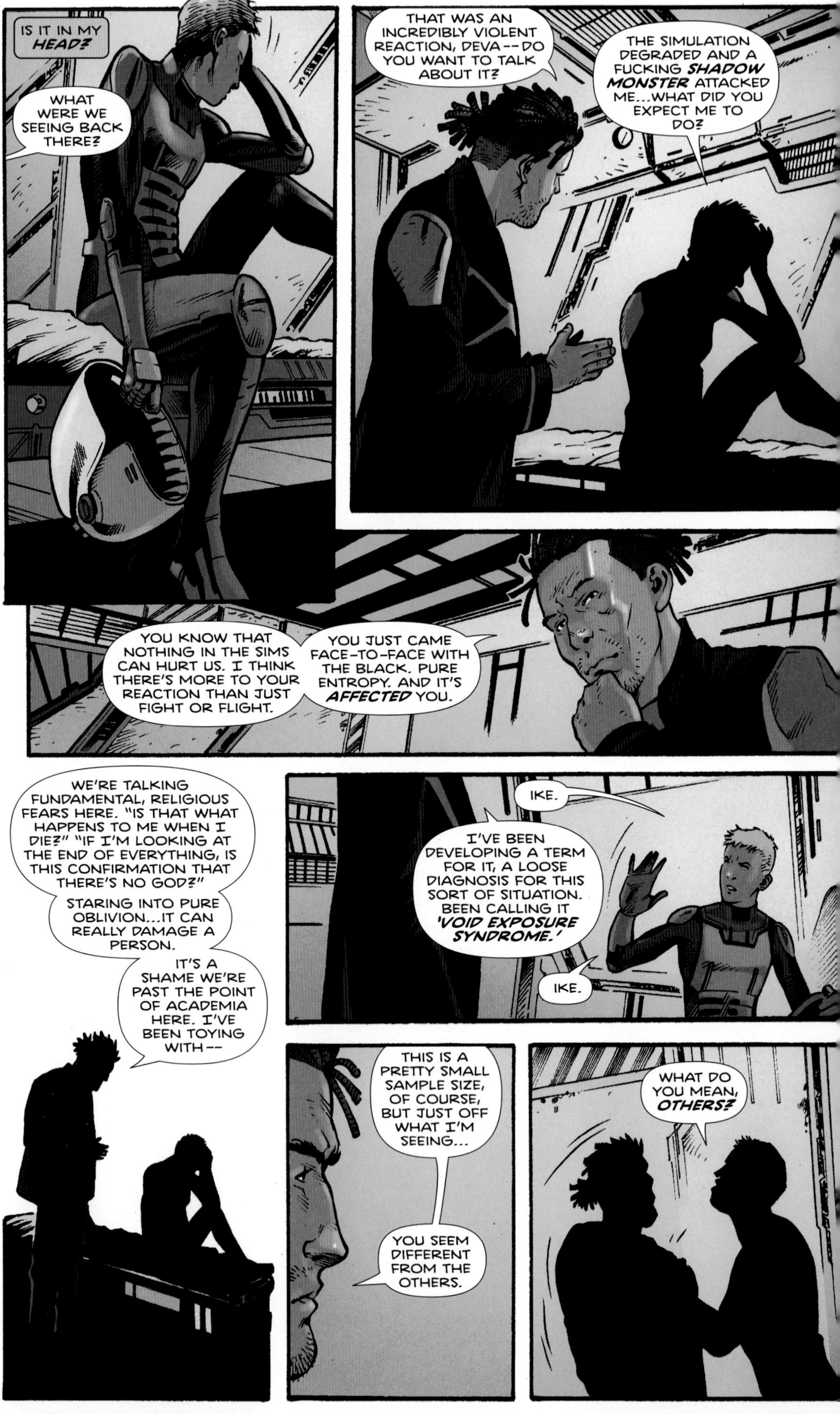

IS IT IN MY HEAD?
WHAT WERE WE SEEING BACK THERE?
THAT WAS AN INCREDIBLY VIOLENT REACTION, DEVA--DO YOU WANT TO TALK ABOUT IT?
THE SIMULATION DEGRADED AND A FUCKING SHADOW MONSTER ATTACKED ME...WHAT DID YOU EXPECT ME TO DO?
YOU KNOW THAT NOTHING IN THE SIMS CAN HURT US. I THINK THERE'S MORE TO YOUR REACTION THAN JUST FIGHT OR FLIGHT.
YOU JUST CAME FACE-TO-FACE WITH THE BLACK. PURE ENTROPY. AND IT'S AFFECTED YOU.
WE'RE TALKING FUNDAMENTAL, RELIGIOUS FEARS HERE. "IS THAT WHAT HAPPENS TO ME WHEN I DIE?" "IF I'M LOOKING AT THE END OF EVERYTHING, IS THIS CONFIRMATION THAT THERE'S NO GOD?"
STARING INTO PURE OBLIVION...IT CAN REALLY DAMAGE A PERSON.
IT'S A SHAME WE'RE PAST THE POINT OF ACADEMIA HERE. I'VE BEEN TOYING WITH--
IKE.
I'VE BEEN DEVELOPING A TERM FOR IT, A LOOSE DIAGNOSIS FOR THIS SORT OF SITUATION. BEEN CALLING IT 'VOID EXPOSURE SYNDROME.'
IKE.
THIS IS A PRETTY SMALL SAMPLE SIZE, OF COURSE, BUT JUST OFF WHAT I'M SEEING...
YOU SEEM DIFFERENT FROM THE OTHERS.
WHAT DO YOU MEAN, OTHERS?

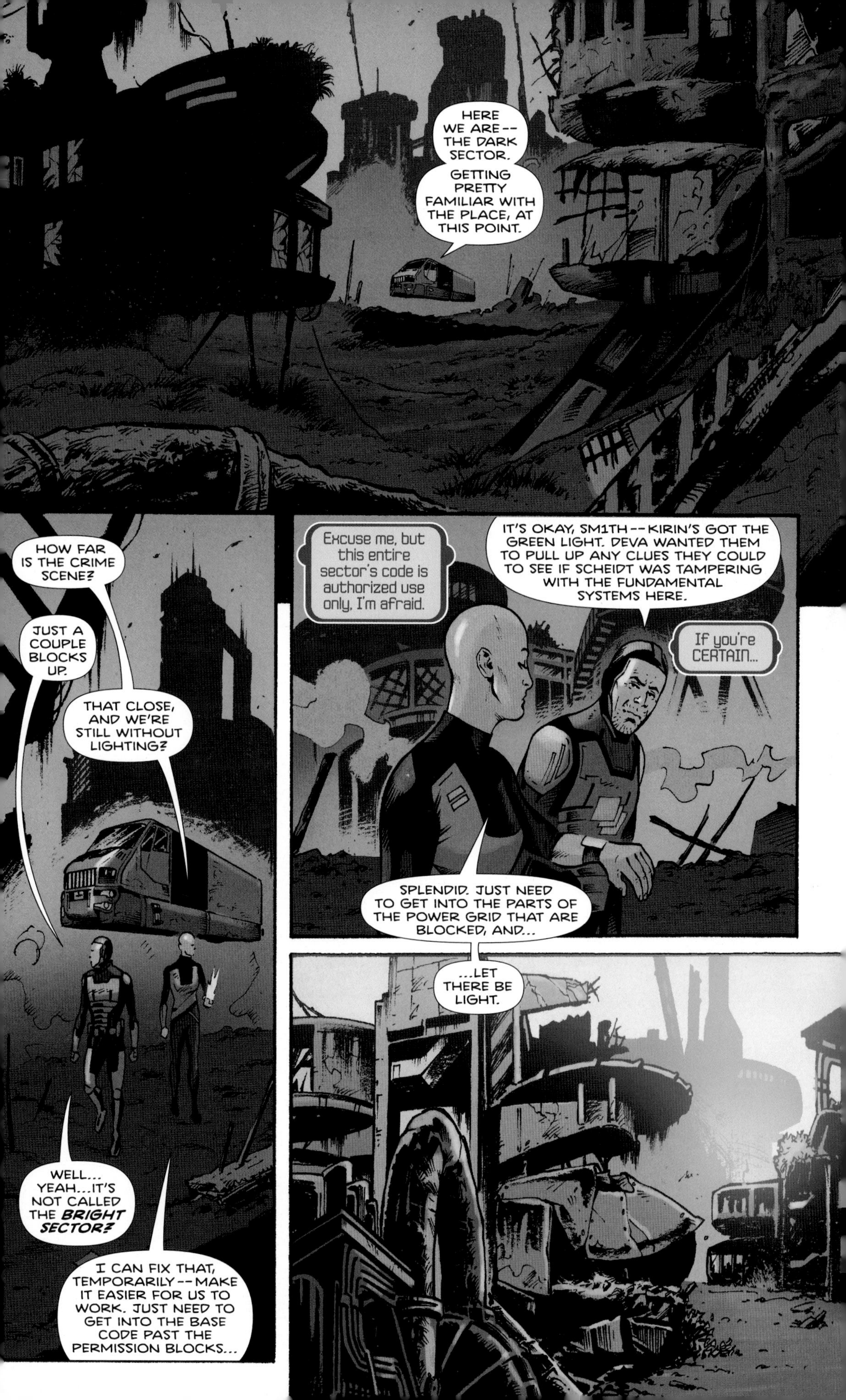
HERE WE ARE-- THE DARK SECTOR.
GETTING PRETTY FAMILIAR WITH THE PLACE, AT THIS POINT.
HOW FAR IS THE CRIME SCENE?
JUST A COUPLE BLOCKS UP.
THAT CLOSE, AND WE'RE STILL WITHOUT LIGHTING?
WELL... YEAH...IT'S NOT CALLED THE BRIGHT SECTOR?
I CAN FIX THAT, TEMPORARILY--MAKE IT EASIER FOR US TO WORK. JUST NEED TO GET INTO THE BASE CODE PAST THE PERMISSION BLOCKS...
Excuse me, but this entire sector's code is authorized use only, I'm afraid.
IT'S OKAY, SM1TH--KIRIN'S GOT THE GREEN LIGHT. DEVA WANTED THEM TO PULL UP ANY CLUES THEY COULD TO SEE IF SCHEIDT WAS TAMPERING WITH THE FUNDAMENTAL SYSTEMS HERE.
If you're CERTAIN...
SPLENDID. JUST NEED TO GET INTO THE PARTS OF THE POWER GRID THAT ARE BLOCKED, AND...
...LET THERE BE LIGHT.

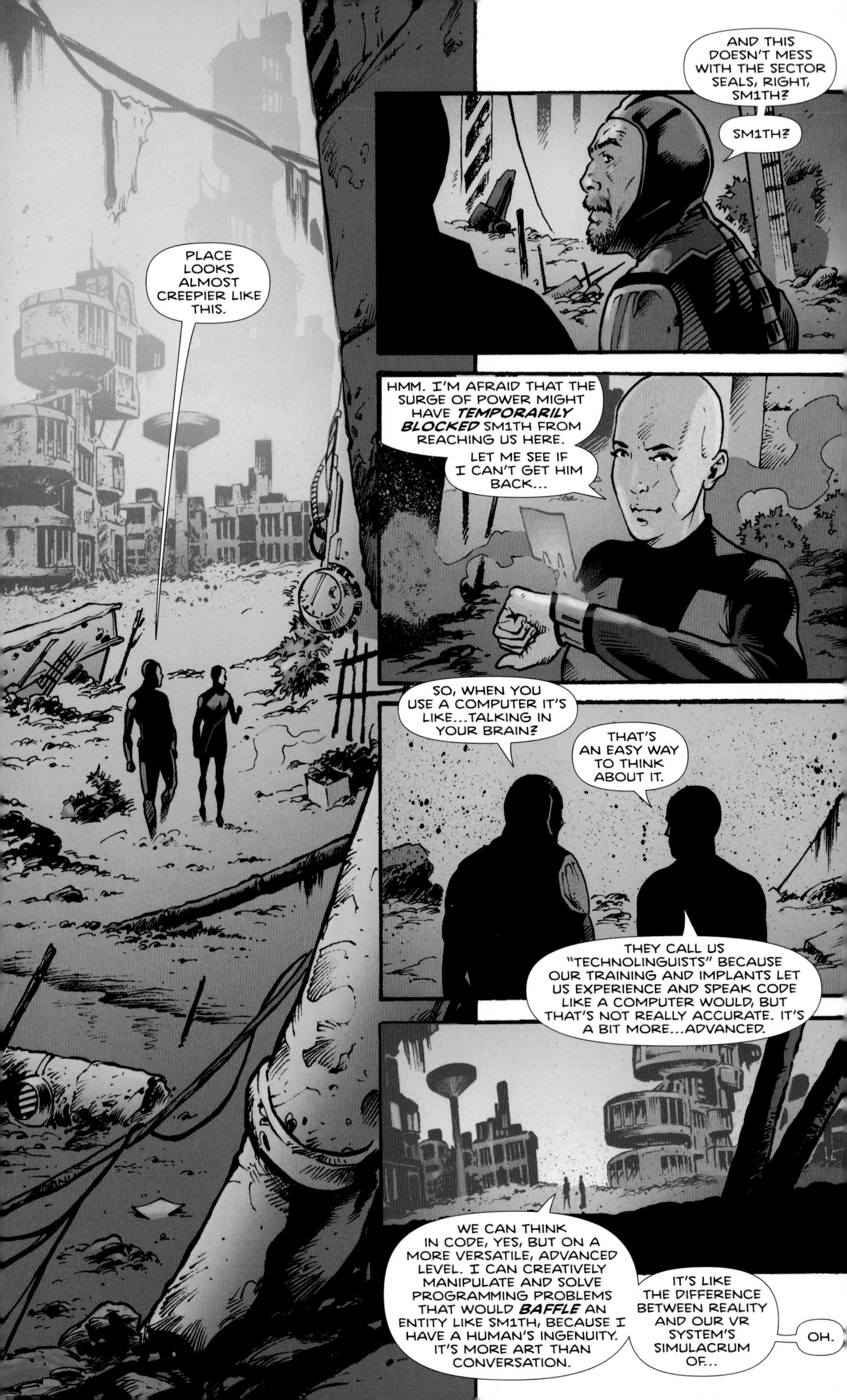
PLACE LOOKS ALMOST CREEPIER LIKE THIS.
AND THIS DOESN'T MESS WITH THE SECTOR SEALS, RIGHT, SM1TH?
SM1TH?
HMM. I'M AFRAID THAT THE SURGE OF POWER MIGHT HAVE TEMPORARILY BLOCKED SM1TH FROM REACHING US HERE.
LET ME SEE IF I CAN'T GET HIM BACK...
SO, WHEN YOU USE A COMPUTER IT'S LIKE...TALKING IN YOUR BRAIN?
THAT'S AN EASY WAY TO THINK ABOUT IT.
THEY CALL US "TECHNOLINGUISTS" BECAUSE OUR TRAINING AND IMPLANTS LET US EXPERIENCE AND SPEAK CODE LIKE A COMPUTER WOULD, BUT THAT'S NOT REALLY ACCURATE. IT'S A BIT MORE...ADVANCED.
WE CAN THINK IN CODE, YES, BUT ON A MORE VERSATILE, ADVANCED LEVEL. I CAN CREATIVELY MANIPULATE AND SOLVE PROGRAMMING PROBLEMS THAT WOULD BAFFLE AN ENTITY LIKE SM1TH, BECAUSE I HAVE A HUMAN'S INGENUITY. IT'S MORE ART THAN CONVERSATION.
IT'S LIKE THE DIFFERENCE BETWEEN REALITY AND OUR VR SYSTEM'S SIMULACRUM OF...
OH.

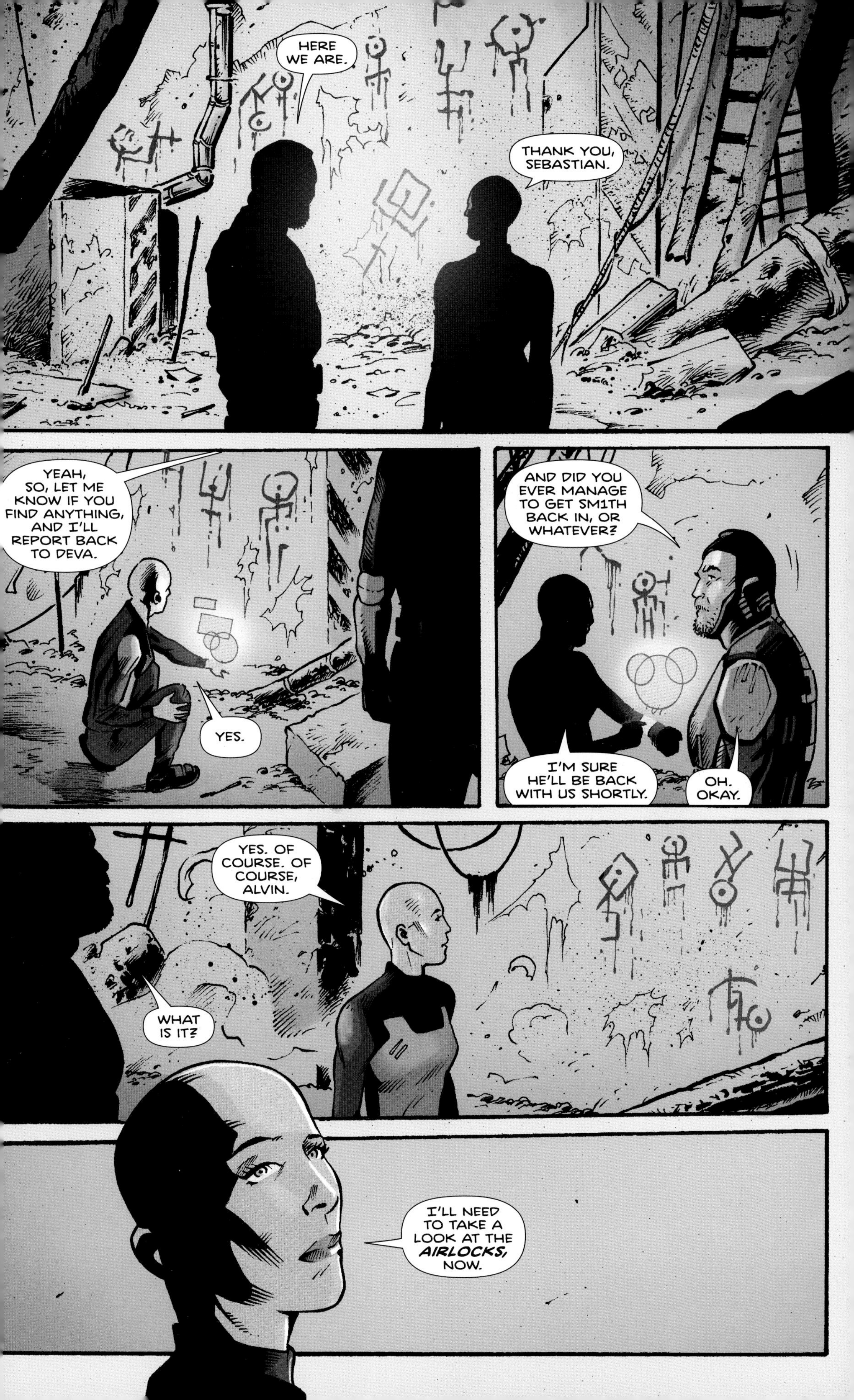
HERE WE ARE.
THANK YOU, SEBASTIAN.
YEAH, SO, LET ME KNOW IF YOU FIND ANYTHING, AND I'LL REPORT BACK TO DEVA.
YES.
AND DID YOU EVER MANAGE TO GET SM1TH BACK IN, OR WHATEVER?
I'M SURE HE'LL BE BACK WITH US SHORTLY.
OH. OKAY.
YES. OF COURSE. OF COURSE, ALVIN.
WHAT IS IT?
I'LL NEED TO TAKE A LOOK AT THE *AIRLOCKS,* NOW.

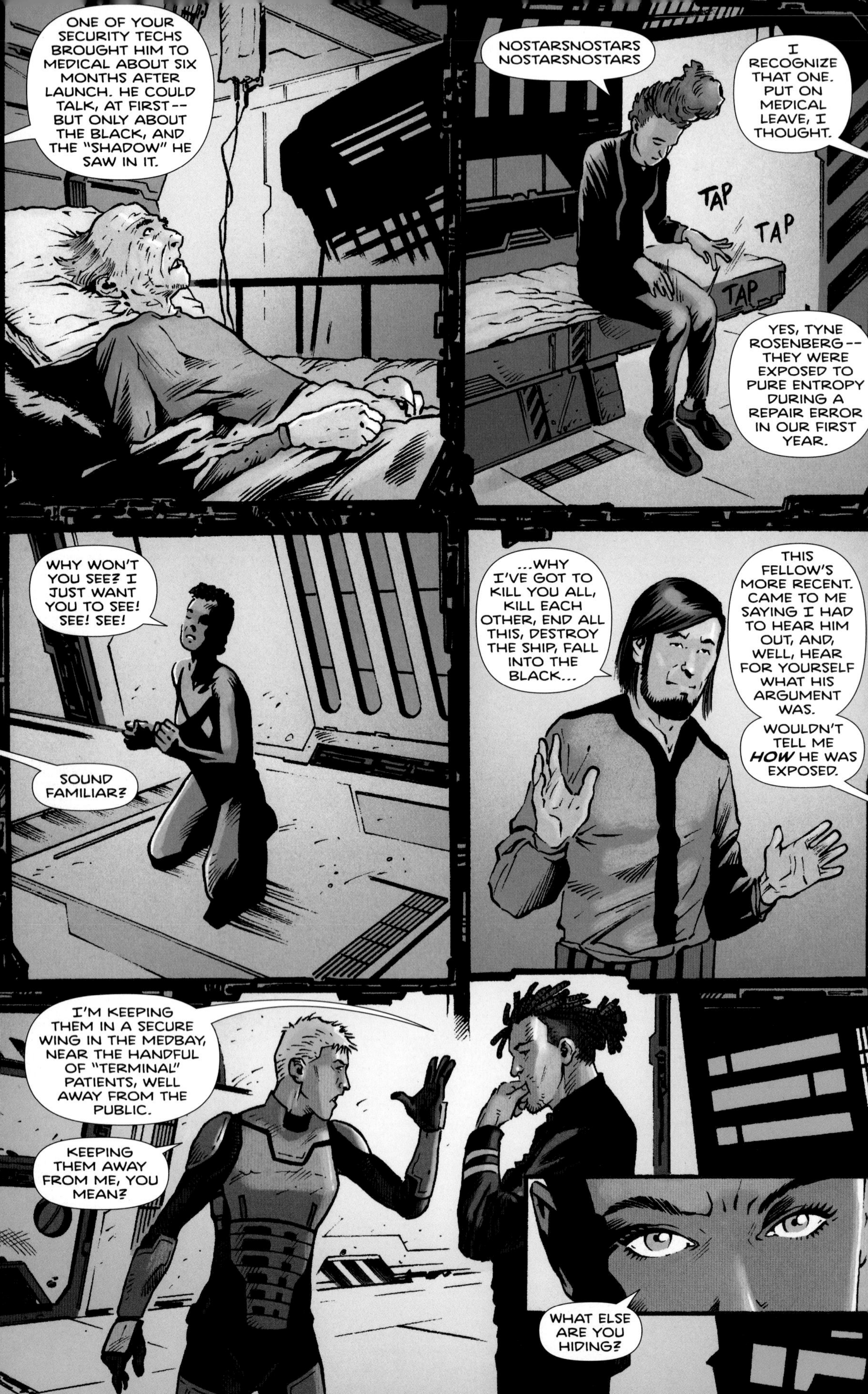
ONE OF YOUR SECURITY TECHS BROUGHT HIM TO MEDICAL ABOUT SIX MONTHS AFTER LAUNCH. HE COULD TALK, AT FIRST-- BUT ONLY ABOUT THE BLACK, AND THE "SHADOW" HE SAW IN IT.
NOSTARSNOSTARS NOSTARSNOSTARS
I RECOGNIZE THAT ONE. PUT ON MEDICAL LEAVE, I THOUGHT.
TAP
TAP
TAP
YES, TYNE ROSENBERG-- THEY WERE EXPOSED TO PURE ENTROPY DURING A REPAIR ERROR IN OUR FIRST YEAR.
WHY WON'T YOU SEE? I JUST WANT YOU TO SEE! SEE! SEE!
SOUND FAMILIAR?
...WHY I'VE GOT TO KILL YOU ALL, KILL EACH OTHER, END ALL THIS, DESTROY THE SHIP, FALL INTO THE BLACK...
THIS FELLOW'S MORE RECENT. CAME TO ME SAYING I HAD TO HEAR HIM OUT, AND, WELL, HEAR FOR YOURSELF WHAT HIS ARGUMENT WAS.
WOULDN'T TELL ME *HOW* HE WAS EXPOSED.
I'M KEEPING THEM IN A SECURE WING IN THE MEDBAY, NEAR THE HANDFUL OF "TERMINAL" PATIENTS, WELL AWAY FROM THE PUBLIC.
KEEPING THEM AWAY FROM ME, YOU MEAN?
WHAT ELSE ARE YOU HIDING?

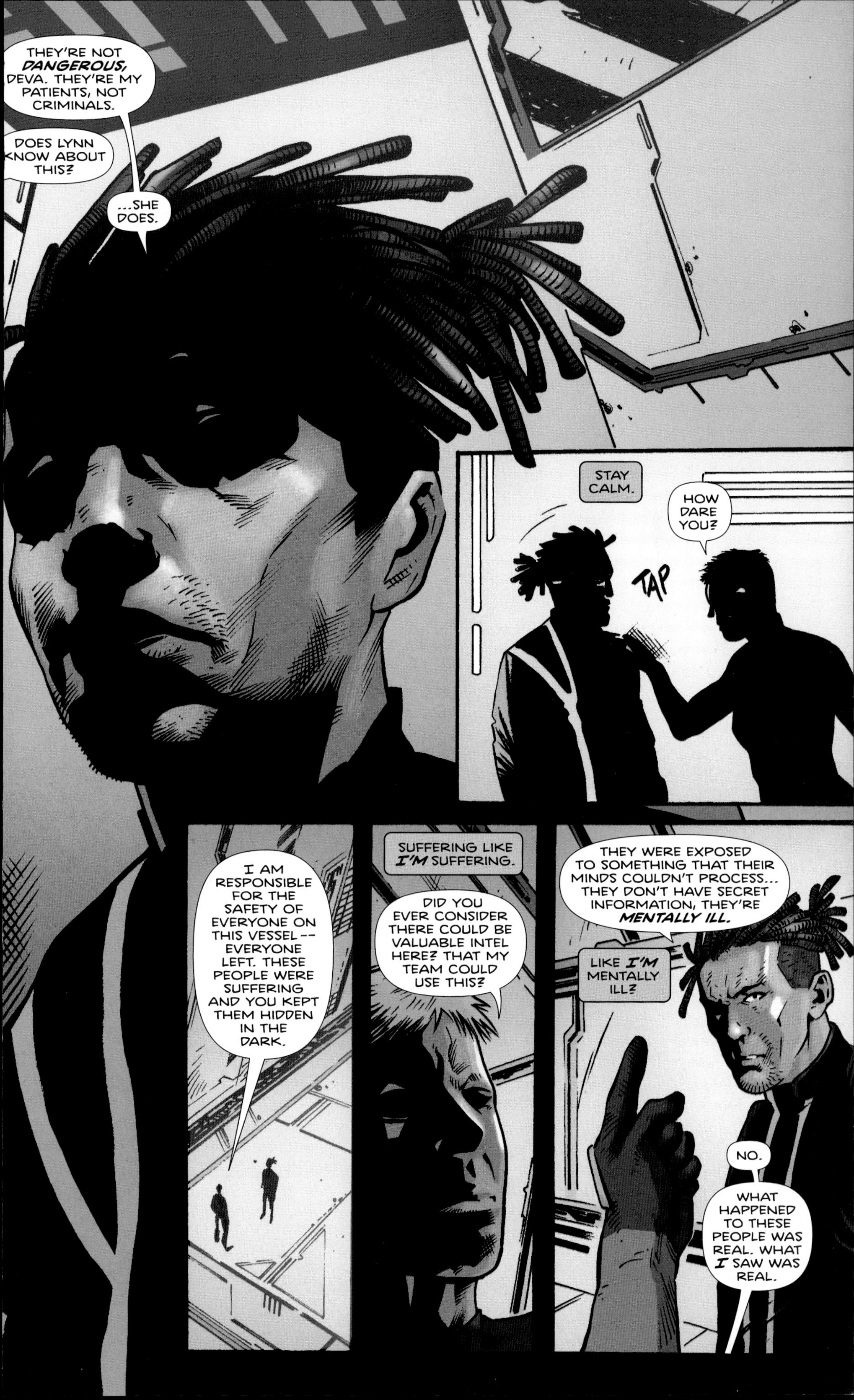
THEY'RE NOT *DANGEROUS,* DEVA. THEY'RE MY PATIENTS, NOT CRIMINALS.
DOES LYNN KNOW ABOUT THIS?
...SHE DOES.
STAY CALM.
HOW DARE YOU?
TAP
I AM RESPONSIBLE FOR THE SAFETY OF EVERYONE ON THIS VESSEL-- EVERYONE LEFT. THESE PEOPLE WERE SUFFERING AND YOU KEPT THEM HIDDEN IN THE DARK.
SUFFERING LIKE *I'M* SUFFERING.
DID YOU EVER CONSIDER THERE COULD BE VALUABLE INTEL HERE? THAT MY TEAM COULD USE THIS?
THEY WERE EXPOSED TO SOMETHING THAT THEIR MINDS COULDN'T PROCESS... THEY DON'T HAVE SECRET INFORMATION, THEY'RE *MENTALLY ILL.*
LIKE *I'M* MENTALLY ILL?
NO.
WHAT HAPPENED TO THESE PEOPLE WAS REAL. WHAT *I* SAW WAS REAL.

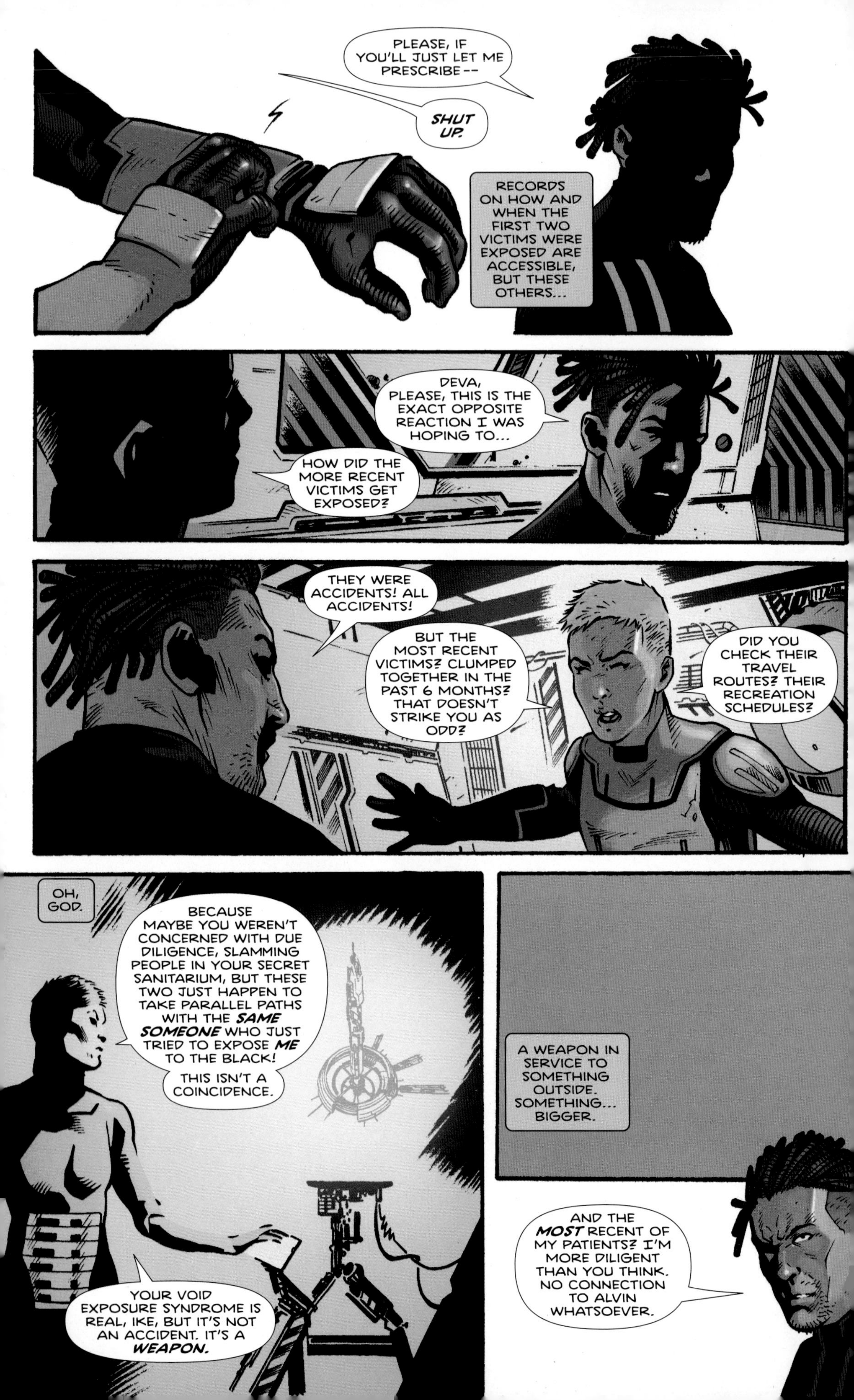
PLEASE, IF YOU'LL JUST LET ME PRESCRIBE--
SHUT UP.
RECORDS ON HOW AND WHEN THE FIRST TWO VICTIMS WERE EXPOSED ARE ACCESSIBLE, BUT THESE OTHERS...
DEVA, PLEASE, THIS IS THE EXACT OPPOSITE REACTION I WAS HOPING TO...
HOW DID THE MORE RECENT VICTIMS GET EXPOSED?
THEY WERE ACCIDENTS! ALL ACCIDENTS!
BUT THE MOST RECENT VICTIMS? CLUMPED TOGETHER IN THE PAST 6 MONTHS? THAT DOESN'T STRIKE YOU AS ODD?
DID YOU CHECK THEIR TRAVEL ROUTES? THEIR RECREATION SCHEDULES?
OH, GOD.
BECAUSE MAYBE YOU WEREN'T CONCERNED WITH DUE DILIGENCE, SLAMMING PEOPLE IN YOUR SECRET SANITARIUM, BUT THESE TWO JUST HAPPEN TO TAKE PARALLEL PATHS WITH THE SAME SOMEONE WHO JUST TRIED TO EXPOSE ME TO THE BLACK!
THIS ISN'T A COINCIDENCE.
YOUR VOID EXPOSURE SYNDROME IS REAL, IKE, BUT IT'S NOT AN ACCIDENT. IT'S A WEAPON.
A WEAPON IN SERVICE TO SOMETHING OUTSIDE. SOMETHING... BIGGER.
AND THE MOST RECENT OF MY PATIENTS? I'M MORE DILIGENT THAN YOU THINK. NO CONNECTION TO ALVIN WHATSOEVER.

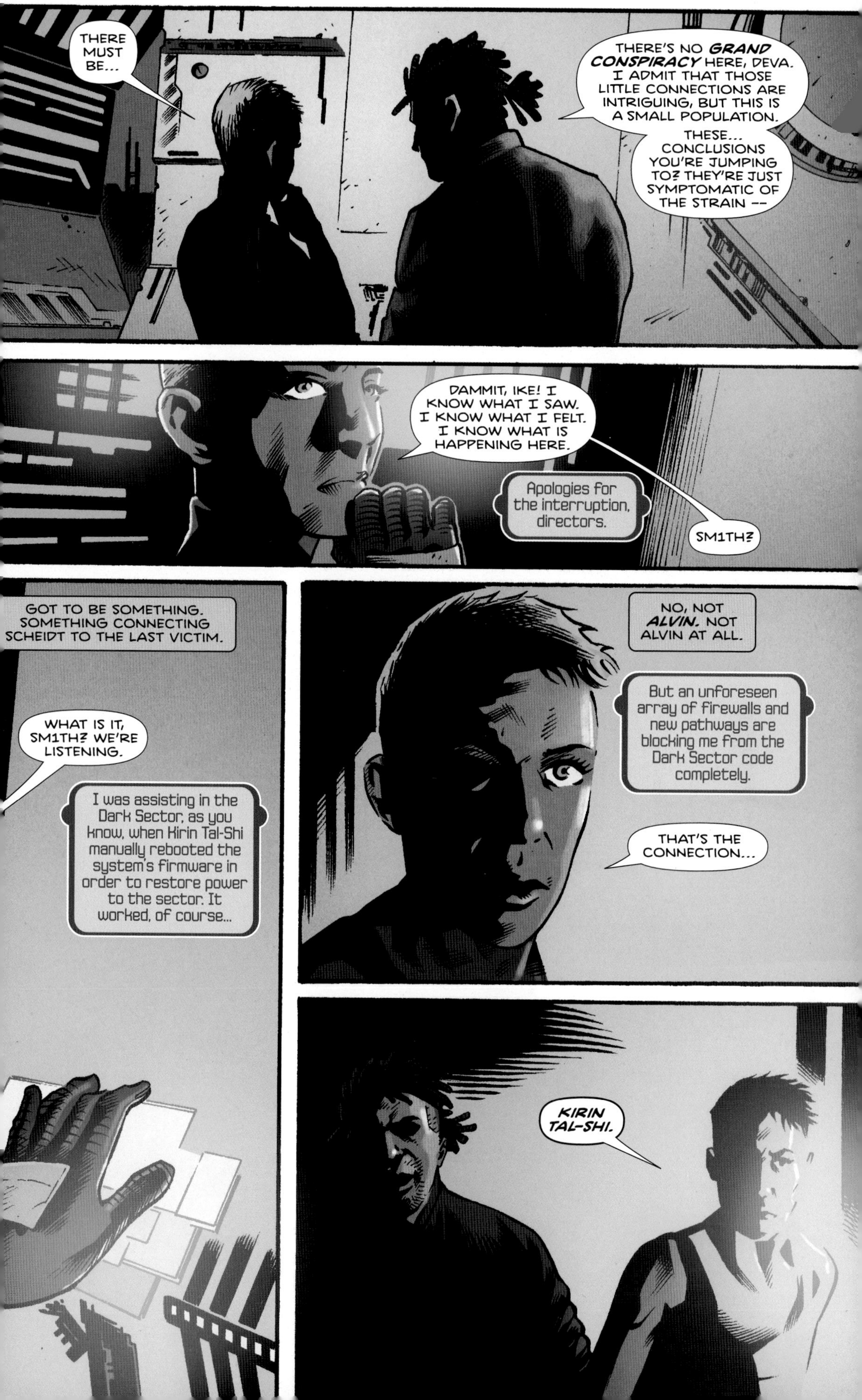
THERE MUST BE...
THERE'S NO GRAND CONSPIRACY HERE, DEVA. I ADMIT THAT THOSE LITTLE CONNECTIONS ARE INTRIGUING, BUT THIS IS A SMALL POPULATION.
THESE... CONCLUSIONS YOU'RE JUMPING TO? THEY'RE JUST SYMPTOMATIC OF THE STRAIN --
DAMMIT, IKE! I KNOW WHAT I SAW. I KNOW WHAT I FELT. I KNOW WHAT IS HAPPENING HERE.
Apologies for the interruption, directors.
SM1TH?
GOT TO BE SOMETHING. SOMETHING CONNECTING SCHEIDT TO THE LAST VICTIM.
WHAT IS IT, SM1TH? WE'RE LISTENING.
I was assisting in the Dark Sector, as you know, when Kirin Tal-Shi manually rebooted the system's firmware in order to restore power to the sector. It worked, of course...
NO, NOT ALVIN. NOT ALVIN AT ALL.
But an unforeseen array of firewalls and new pathways are blocking me from the Dark Sector code completely.
THAT'S THE CONNECTION...
KIRIN TAL-SHI.

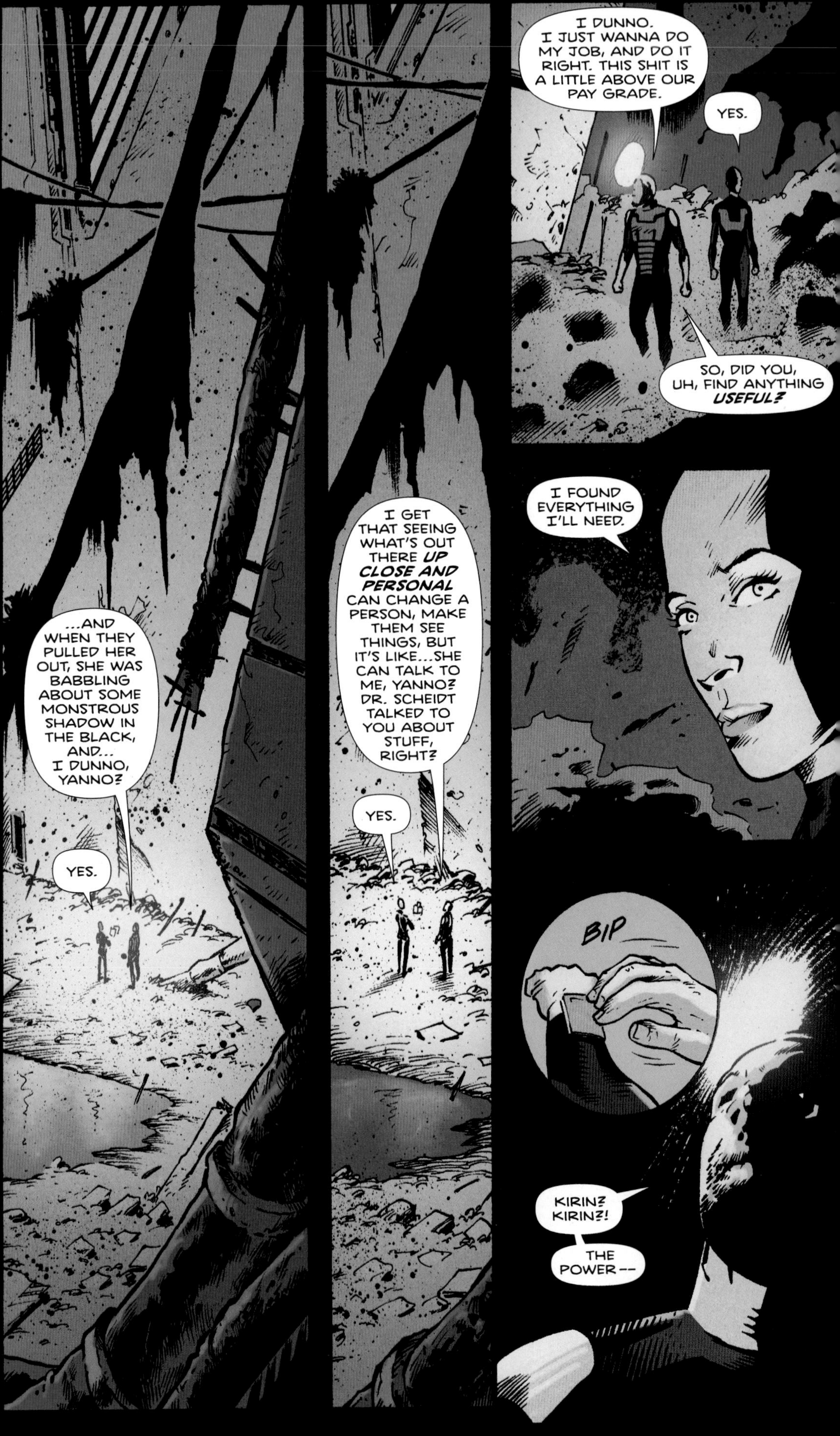

...AND WHEN THEY PULLED HER OUT, SHE WAS BABBLING ABOUT SOME MONSTROUS SHADOW IN THE BLACK, AND... I DUNNO, YANNO?
YES.
I GET THAT SEEING WHAT'S OUT THERE UP CLOSE AND PERSONAL CAN CHANGE A PERSON, MAKE THEM SEE THINGS, BUT IT'S LIKE...SHE CAN TALK TO ME, YANNO? DR. SCHEIDT TALKED TO YOU ABOUT STUFF, RIGHT?
YES.
I DUNNO. I JUST WANNA DO MY JOB, AND DO IT RIGHT. THIS SHIT IS A LITTLE ABOVE OUR PAY GRADE.
YES.
SO, DID YOU, UH, FIND ANYTHING USEFUL?
I FOUND EVERYTHING I'LL NEED.
BIP
KIRIN? KIRIN?!
THE POWER--

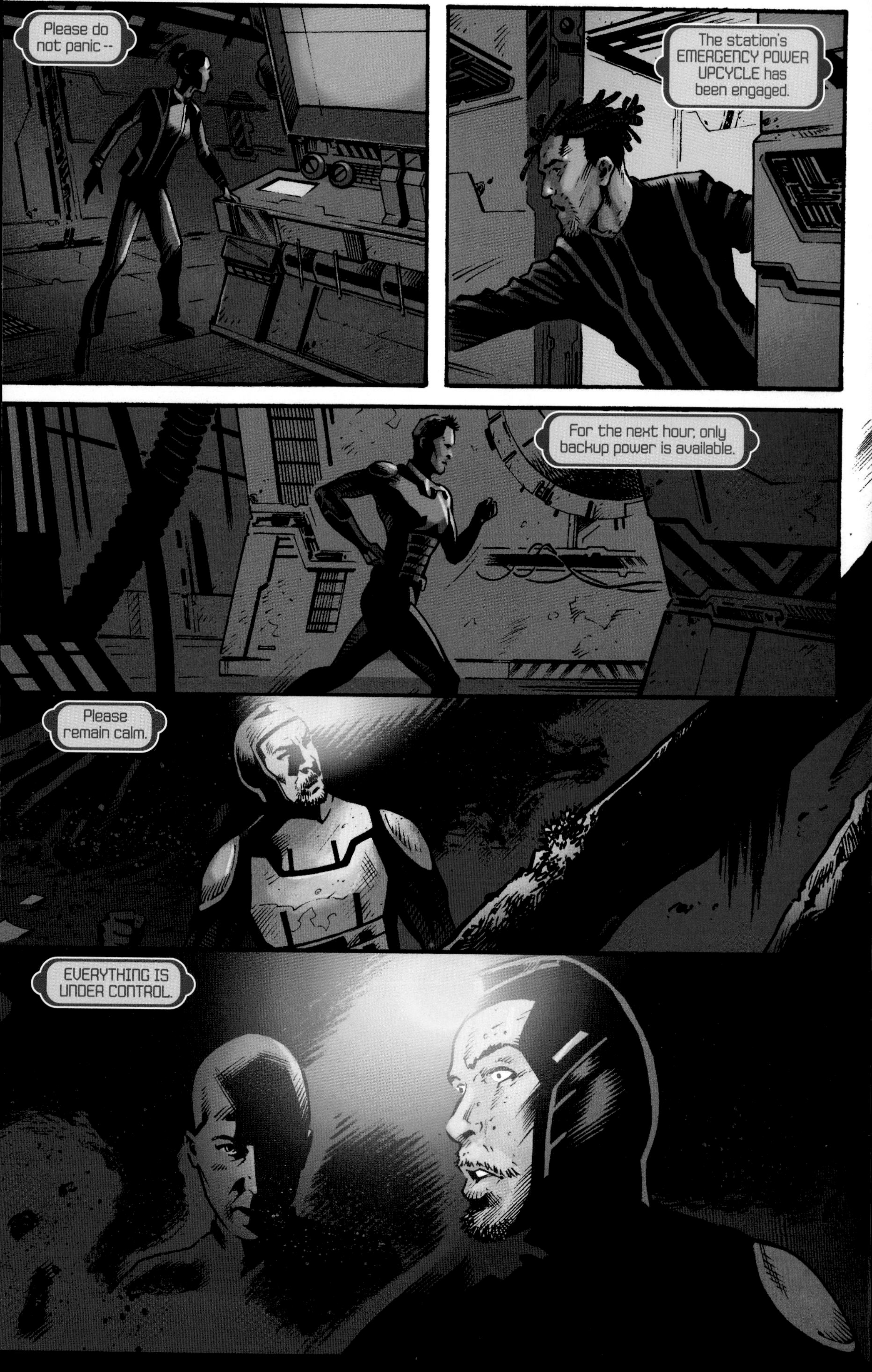
Please do not panic --
The station's EMERGENCY POWER UPCYCLE has been engaged.
For the next hour, only backup power is available.
Please remain calm.
EVERYTHING IS UNDER CONTROL.

CHAPTER **THREE**

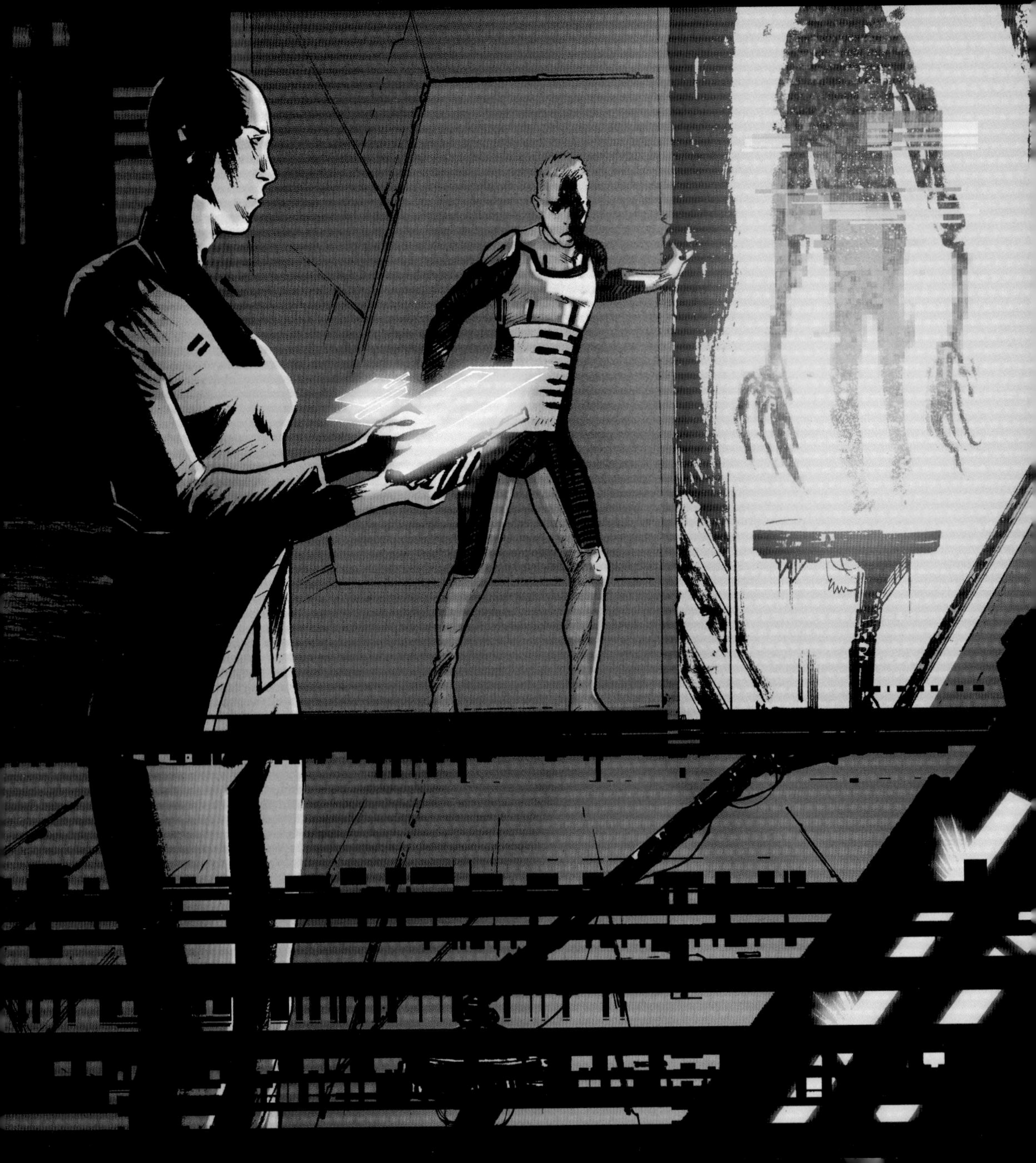

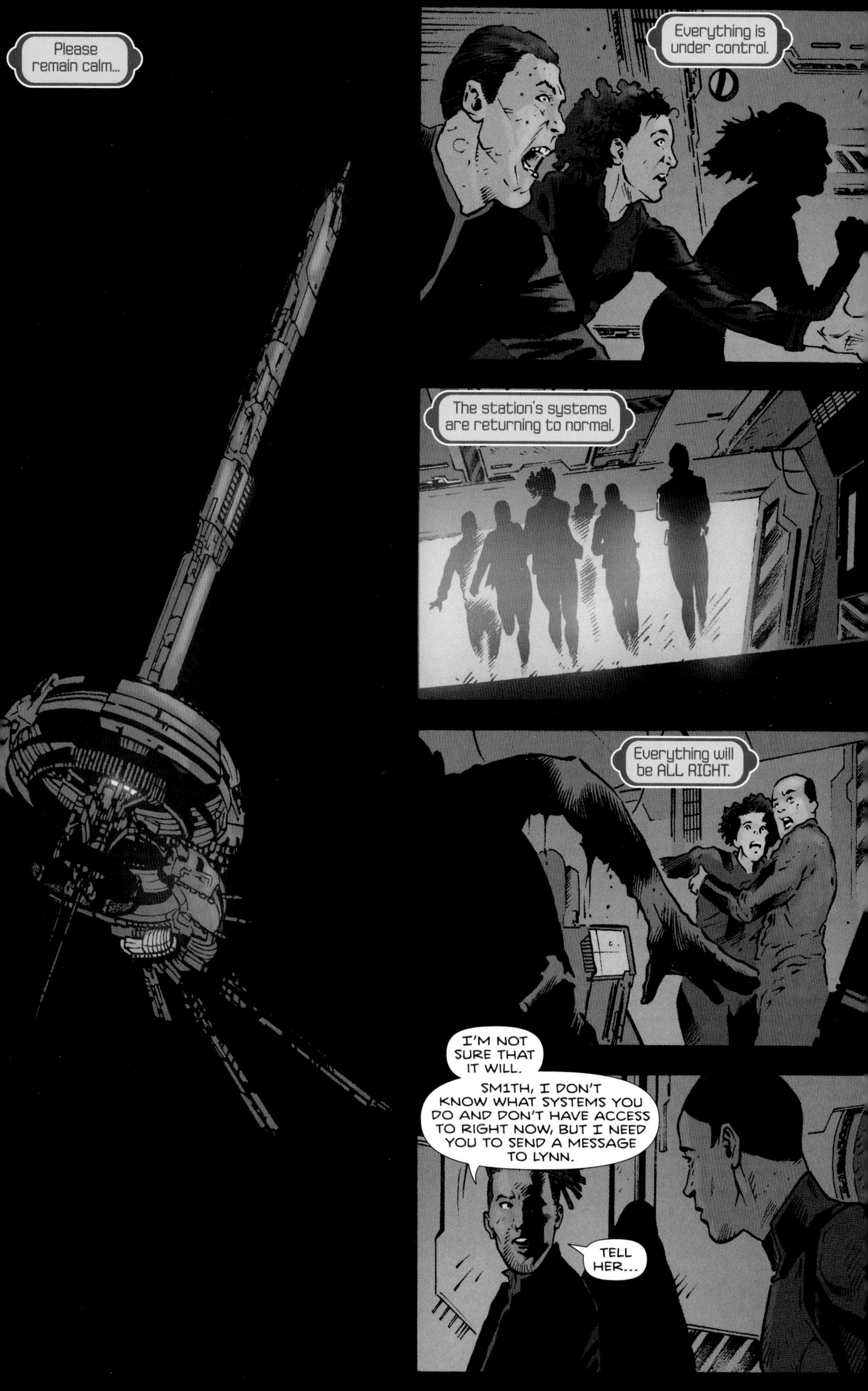
Please remain calm...
Everything is under control.
The station's systems are returning to normal.
Everything will be ALL RIGHT.
I'M NOT SURE THAT IT WILL.
SM1TH, I DON'T KNOW WHAT SYSTEMS YOU DO AND DON'T HAVE ACCESS TO RIGHT NOW, BUT I NEED YOU TO SEND A MESSAGE TO LYNN.
TELL HER...

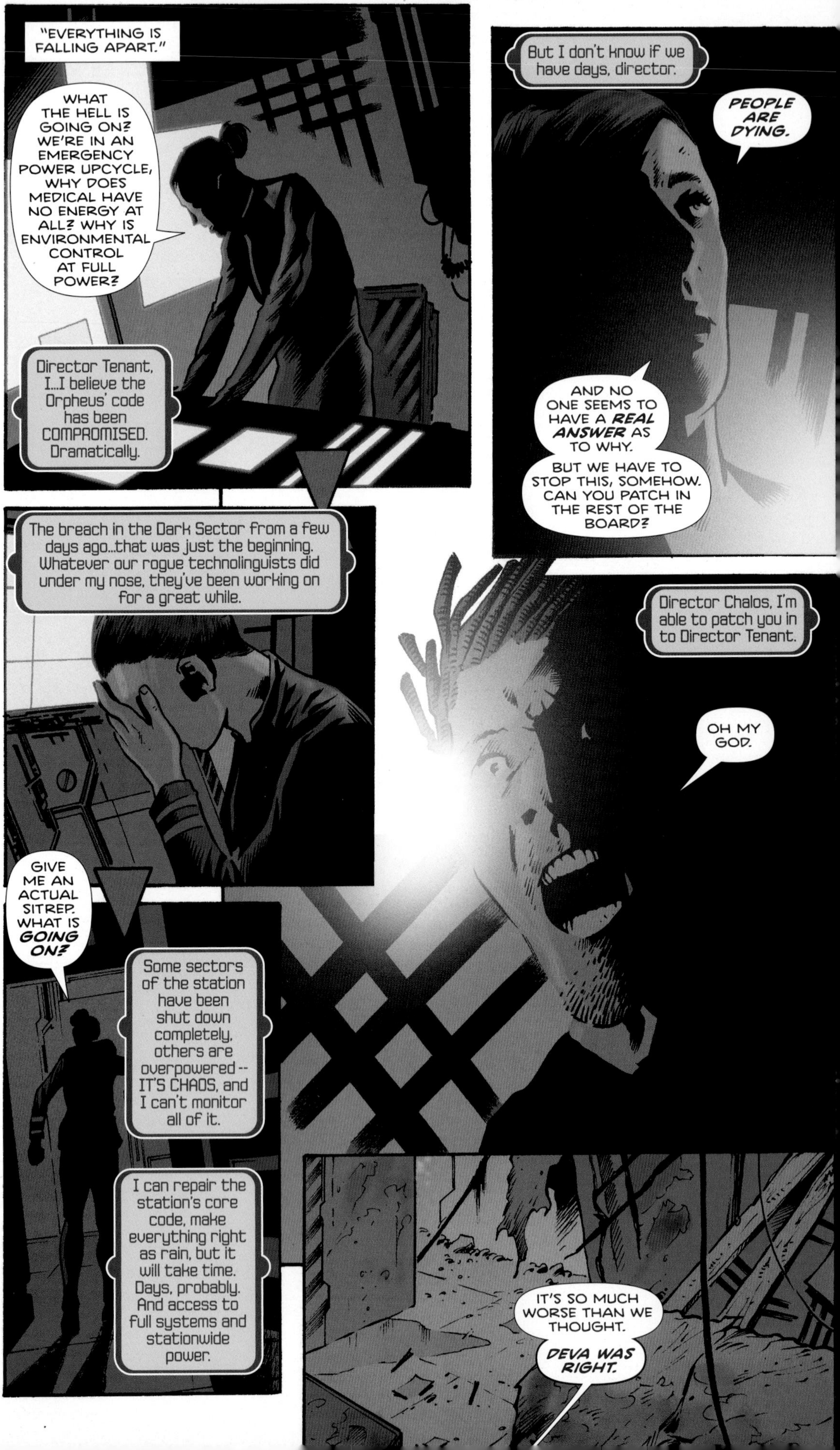
"EVERYTHING IS FALLING APART."
WHAT THE HELL IS GOING ON? WE'RE IN AN EMERGENCY POWER UPCYCLE, WHY DOES MEDICAL HAVE NO ENERGY AT ALL? WHY IS ENVIRONMENTAL CONTROL AT FULL POWER?
Director Tenant, I...I believe the Orpheus' code has been COMPROMISED. Dramatically.
The breach in the Dark Sector from a few days ago...that was just the beginning. Whatever our rogue technolinguists did under my nose, they've been working on for a great while.
GIVE ME AN ACTUAL SITREP. WHAT IS GOING ON?
Some sectors of the station have been shut down completely, others are overpowered -- IT'S CHAOS, and I can't monitor all of it.
I can repair the station's core code, make everything right as rain, but it will take time. Days, probably. And access to full systems and stationwide power.
But I don't know if we have days, director.
PEOPLE ARE DYING.
AND NO ONE SEEMS TO HAVE A REAL ANSWER AS TO WHY.
BUT WE HAVE TO STOP THIS, SOMEHOW. CAN YOU PATCH IN THE REST OF THE BOARD?
Director Chalos, I'm able to patch you in to Director Tenant.
OH MY GOD.
IT'S SO MUCH WORSE THAN WE THOUGHT.
DEVA WAS RIGHT.

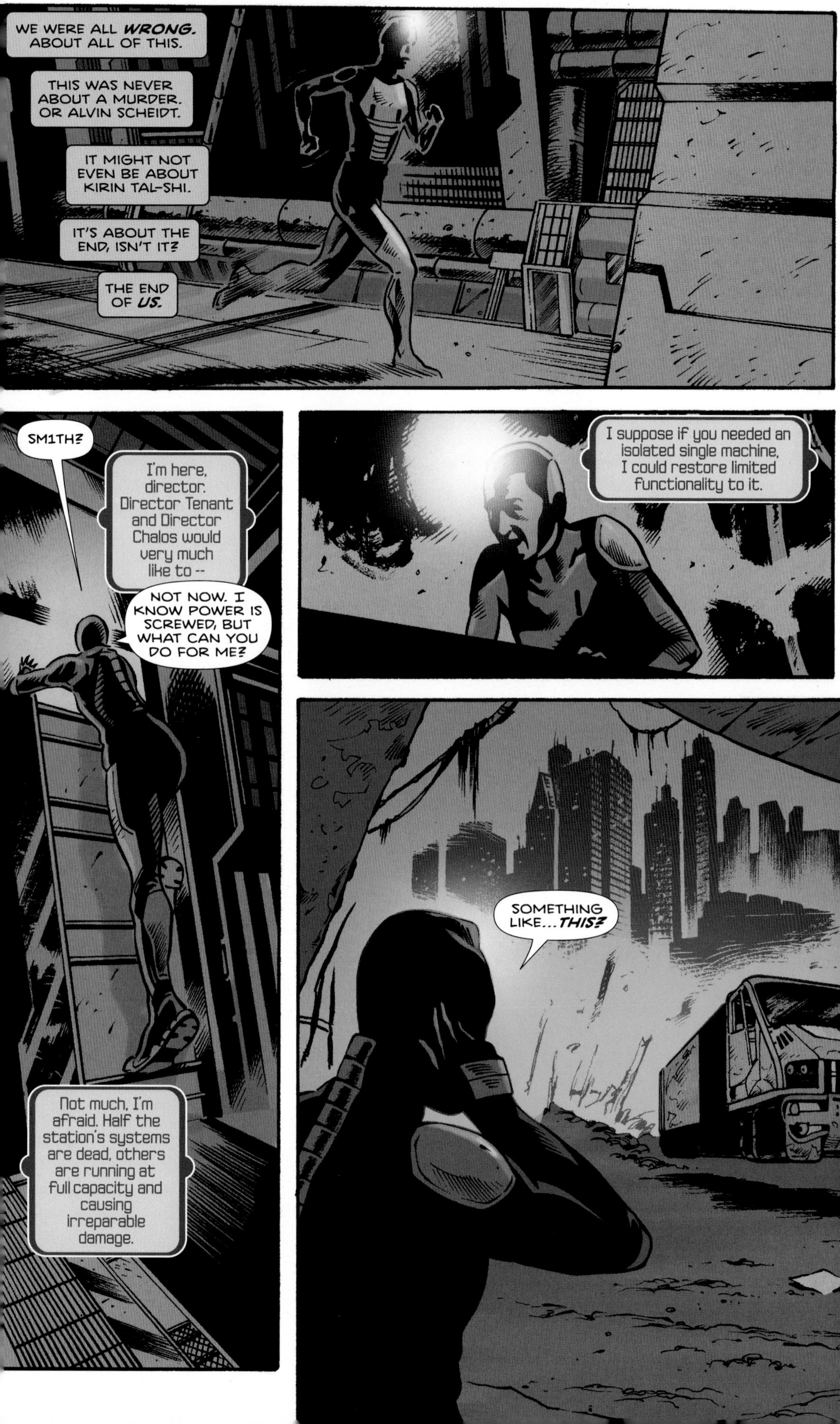
WE WERE ALL WRONG. ABOUT ALL OF THIS.
THIS WAS NEVER ABOUT A MURDER. OR ALVIN SCHEIDT.
IT MIGHT NOT EVEN BE ABOUT KIRIN TAL-SHI.
IT'S ABOUT THE END, ISN'T IT?
THE END OF US.
SM1TH?
I'm here, director. Director Tenant and Director Chalos would very much like to --
NOT NOW. I KNOW POWER IS SCREWED, BUT WHAT CAN YOU DO FOR ME?
Not much, I'm afraid. Half the station's systems are dead, others are running at full capacity and causing irreparable damage.
I suppose if you needed an isolated single machine, I could restore limited functionality to it.
SOMETHING LIKE...THIS?

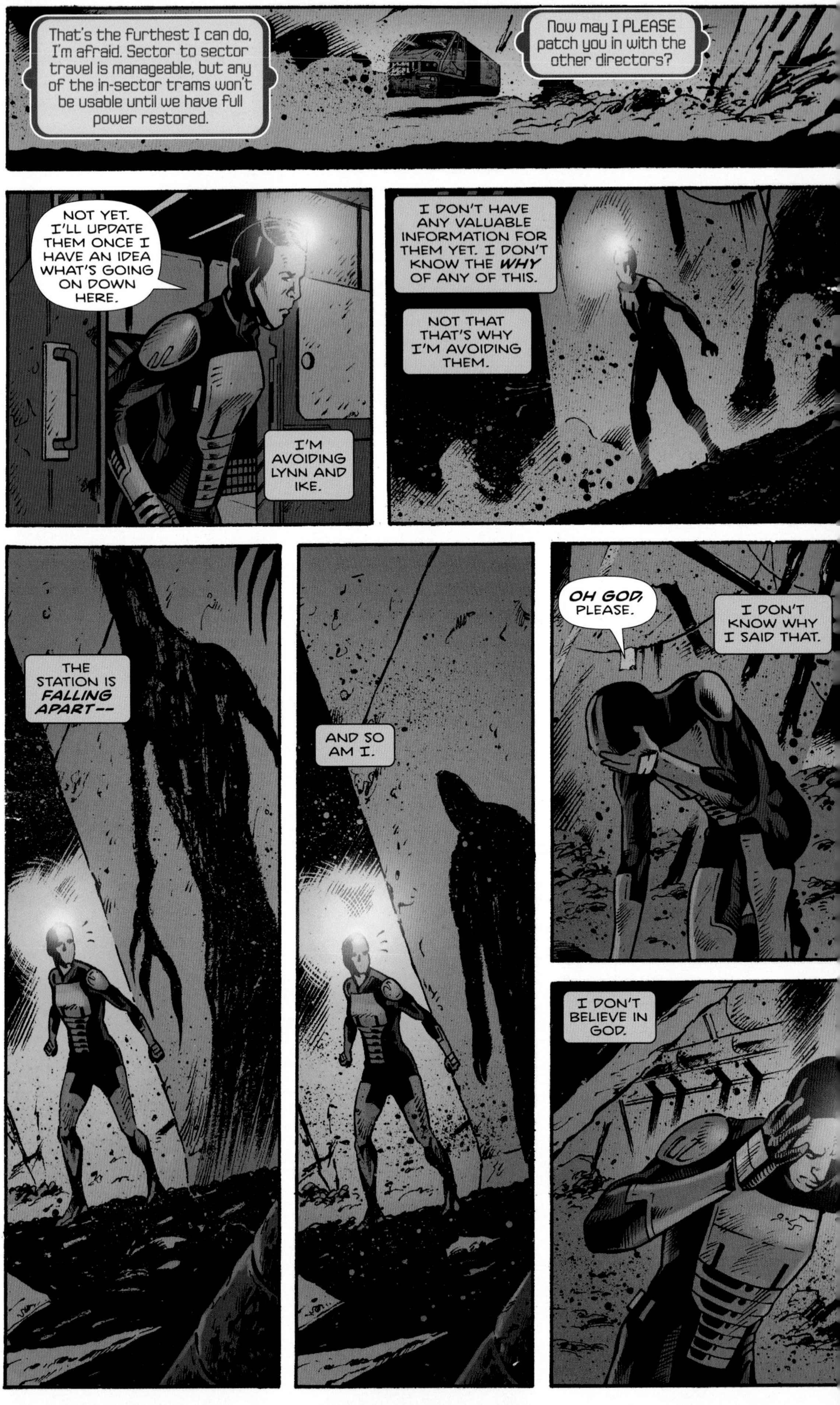

That's the furthest I can do, I'm afraid. Sector to sector travel is manageable, but any of the in-sector trams won't be usable until we have full power restored.
Now may I PLEASE patch you in with the other directors?
NOT YET. I'LL UPDATE THEM ONCE I HAVE AN IDEA WHAT'S GOING ON DOWN HERE.
I'M AVOIDING LYNN AND IKE.
I DON'T HAVE ANY VALUABLE INFORMATION FOR THEM YET. I DON'T KNOW THE *WHY* OF ANY OF THIS.
NOT THAT THAT'S WHY I'M AVOIDING THEM.
THE STATION IS *FALLING APART--*
AND SO AM I.
OH GOD, PLEASE.
I DON'T KNOW WHY I SAID THAT.
I DON'T BELIEVE IN GOD.

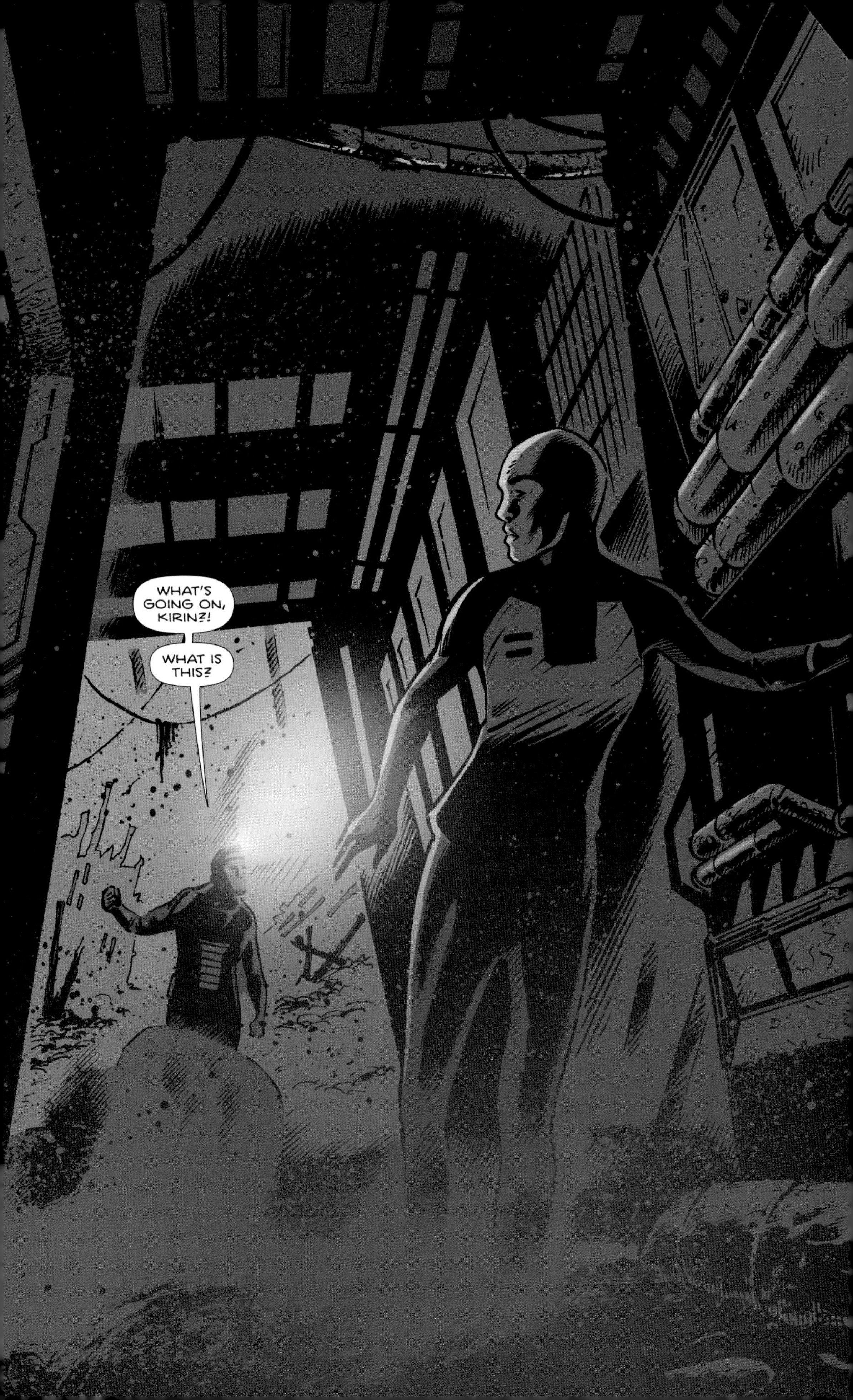
WHAT'S GOING ON, KIRIN?!
WHAT IS THIS?

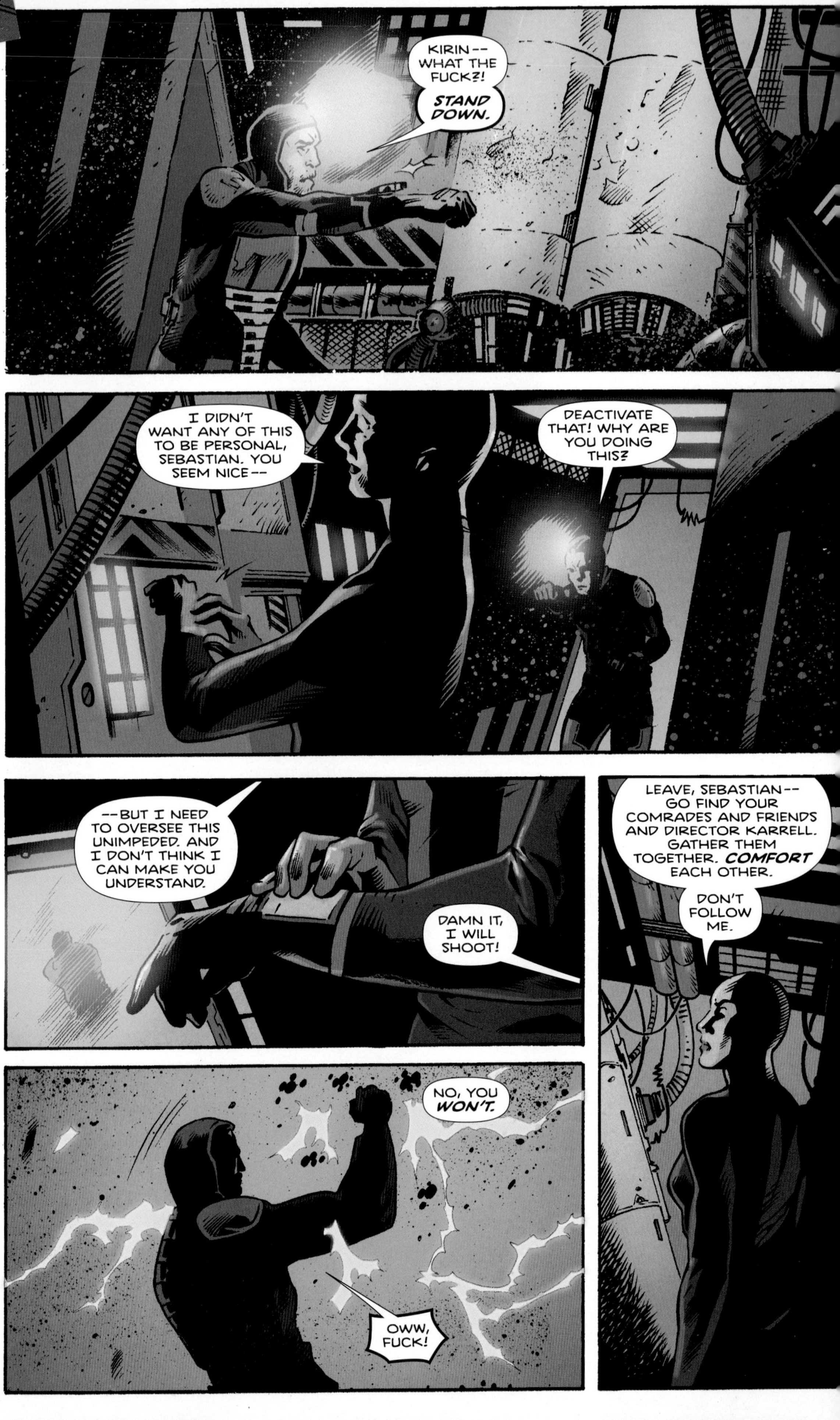
KIRIN-- WHAT THE FUCK?!
STAND DOWN.
I DIDN'T WANT ANY OF THIS TO BE PERSONAL, SEBASTIAN. YOU SEEM NICE--
DEACTIVATE THAT! WHY ARE YOU DOING THIS?
--BUT I NEED TO OVERSEE THIS UNIMPEDED. AND I DON'T THINK I CAN MAKE YOU UNDERSTAND.
DAMN IT, I WILL SHOOT!
LEAVE, SEBASTIAN-- GO FIND YOUR COMRADES AND FRIENDS AND DIRECTOR KARRELL. GATHER THEM TOGETHER. COMFORT EACH OTHER.
DON'T FOLLOW ME.
NO, YOU WON'T.
OWW, FUCK!

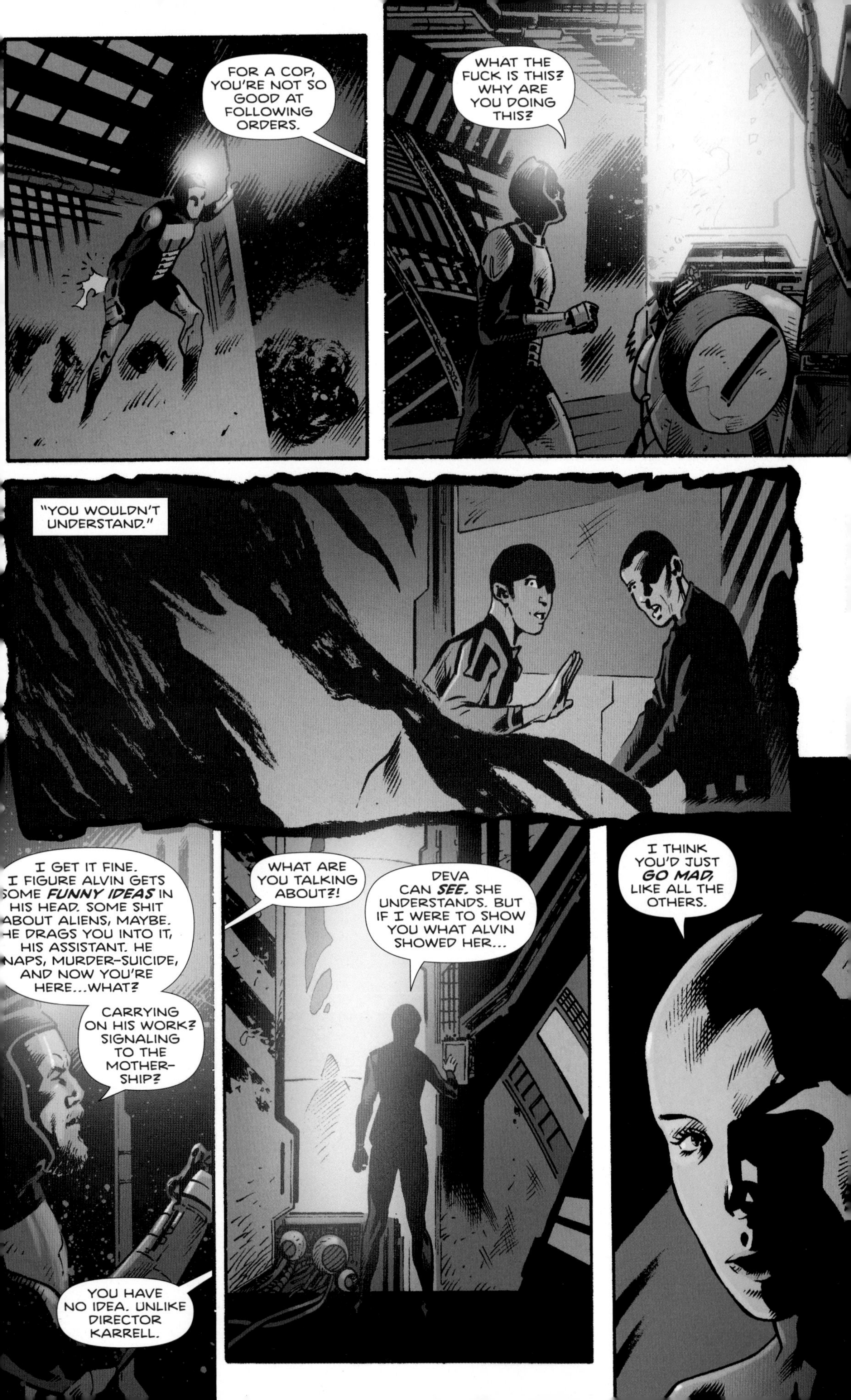
FOR A COP, YOU'RE NOT SO GOOD AT FOLLOWING ORDERS.
WHAT THE FUCK IS THIS? WHY ARE YOU DOING THIS?
"YOU WOULDN'T UNDERSTAND."
I GET IT FINE. I FIGURE ALVIN GETS SOME FUNNY IDEAS IN HIS HEAD. SOME SHIT ABOUT ALIENS, MAYBE. HE DRAGS YOU INTO IT, HIS ASSISTANT. HE NAPS, MURDER-SUICIDE, AND NOW YOU'RE HERE...WHAT?
CARRYING ON HIS WORK? SIGNALING TO THE MOTHER-SHIP?
YOU HAVE NO IDEA. UNLIKE DIRECTOR KARRELL.
WHAT ARE YOU TALKING ABOUT?!
DEVA CAN SEE. SHE UNDERSTANDS. BUT IF I WERE TO SHOW YOU WHAT ALVIN SHOWED HER...
I THINK YOU'D JUST GO MAD, LIKE ALL THE OTHERS.

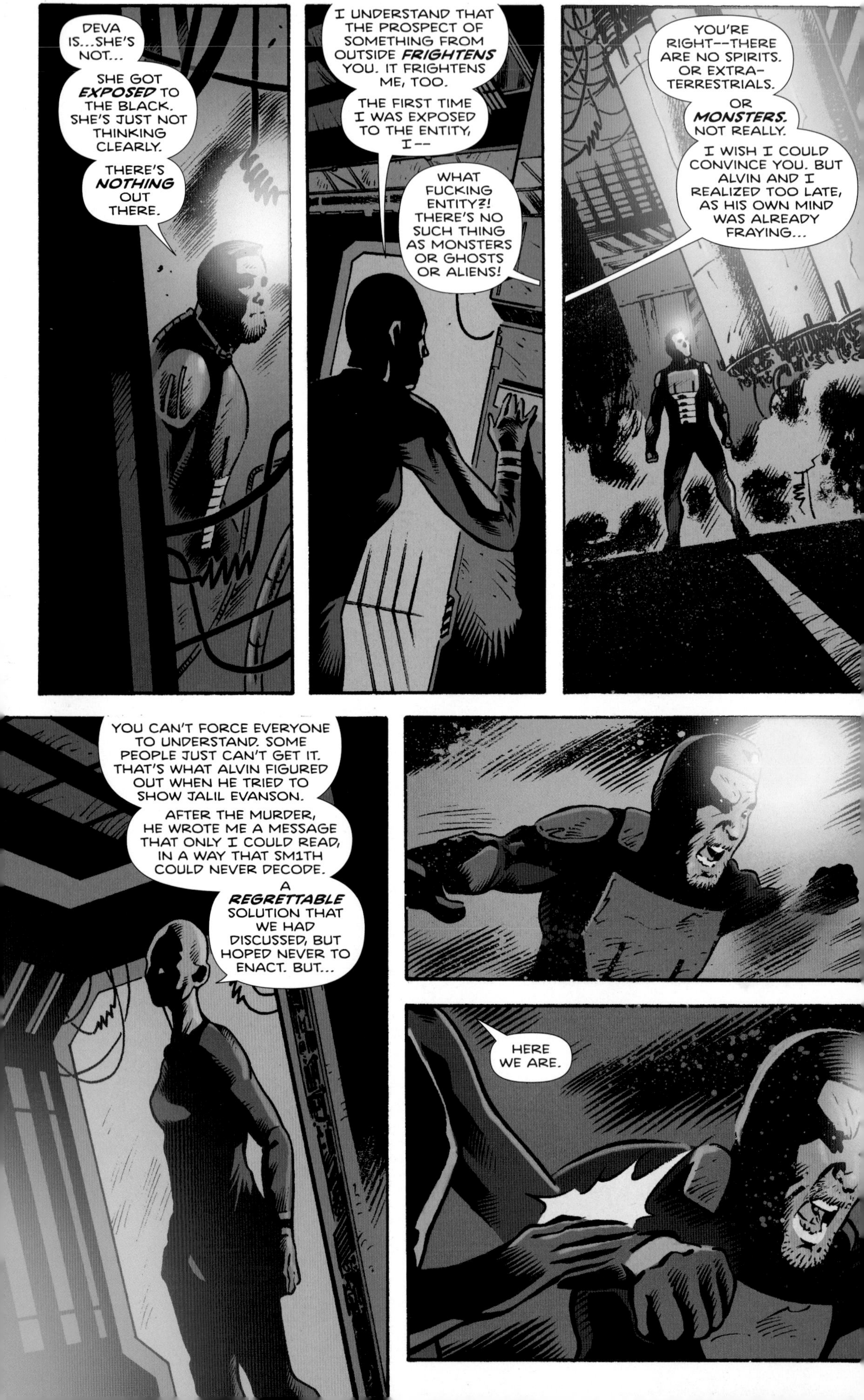
DEVA IS...SHE'S NOT...
SHE GOT EXPOSED TO THE BLACK. SHE'S JUST NOT THINKING CLEARLY.
THERE'S NOTHING OUT THERE.
I UNDERSTAND THAT THE PROSPECT OF SOMETHING FROM OUTSIDE FRIGHTENS YOU. IT FRIGHTENS ME, TOO.
THE FIRST TIME I WAS EXPOSED TO THE ENTITY, I--
WHAT FUCKING ENTITY?! THERE'S NO SUCH THING AS MONSTERS OR GHOSTS OR ALIENS!
YOU'RE RIGHT--THERE ARE NO SPIRITS. OR EXTRA-TERRESTRIALS.
OR MONSTERS. NOT REALLY.
I WISH I COULD CONVINCE YOU. BUT ALVIN AND I REALIZED TOO LATE, AS HIS OWN MIND WAS ALREADY FRAYING...
YOU CAN'T FORCE EVERYONE TO UNDERSTAND. SOME PEOPLE JUST CAN'T GET IT. THAT'S WHAT ALVIN FIGURED OUT WHEN HE TRIED TO SHOW JALIL EVANSON.
AFTER THE MURDER, HE WROTE ME A MESSAGE THAT ONLY I COULD READ, IN A WAY THAT SM1TH COULD NEVER DECODE.
A REGRETTABLE SOLUTION THAT WE HAD DISCUSSED, BUT HOPED NEVER TO ENACT. BUT...
HERE WE ARE.

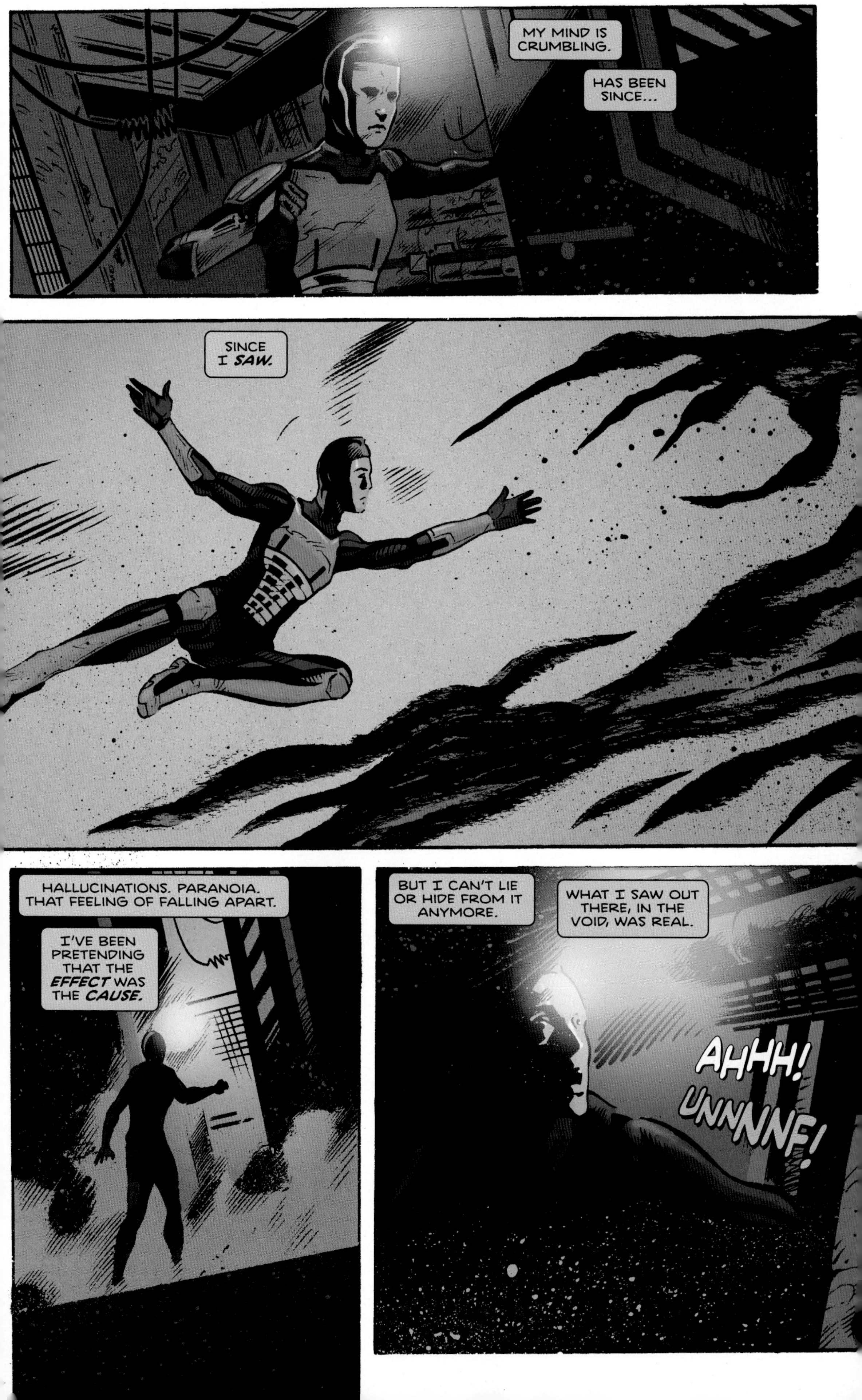

MY MIND IS CRUMBLING.
HAS BEEN SINCE...
SINCE I *SAW.*
HALLUCINATIONS. PARANOIA. THAT FEELING OF FALLING APART.
I'VE BEEN PRETENDING THAT THE *EFFECT* WAS THE *CAUSE.*
BUT I CAN'T LIE OR HIDE FROM IT ANYMORE.
WHAT I SAW OUT THERE, IN THE VOID, WAS REAL.
AHHH!
UNNNNF!

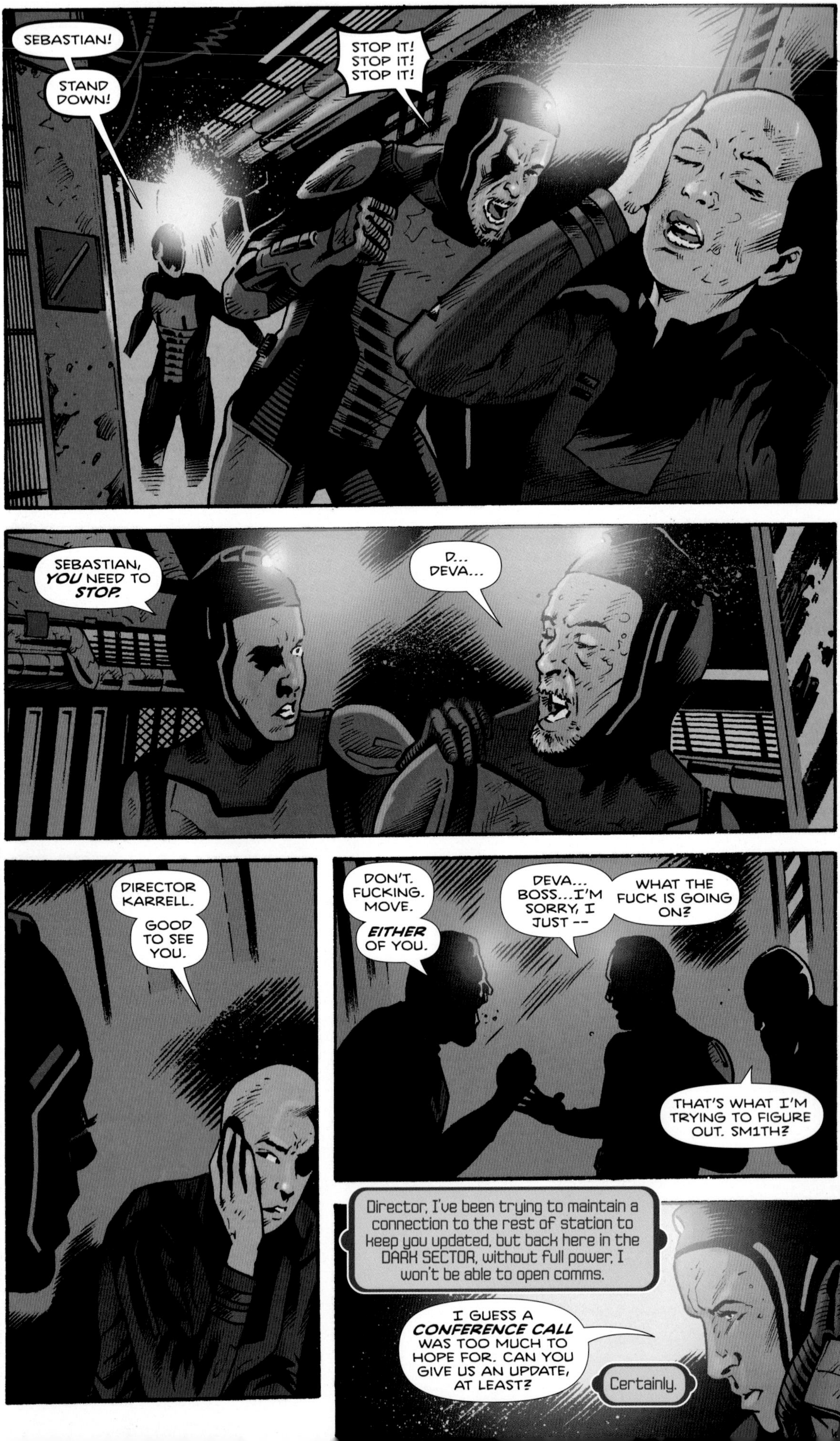
SEBASTIAN!
STAND DOWN!
STOP IT! STOP IT! STOP IT!
SEBASTIAN, YOU NEED TO STOP.
D... DEVA...
DIRECTOR KARRELL.
GOOD TO SEE YOU.
DON'T. FUCKING. MOVE.
EITHER OF YOU.
DEVA... BOSS...I'M SORRY, I JUST --
WHAT THE FUCK IS GOING ON?
THAT'S WHAT I'M TRYING TO FIGURE OUT. SM1TH?
Director, I've been trying to maintain a connection to the rest of station to keep you updated, but back here in the DARK SECTOR, without full power, I won't be able to open comms.
I GUESS A CONFERENCE CALL WAS TOO MUCH TO HOPE FOR. CAN YOU GIVE US AN UPDATE, AT LEAST?
Certainly.

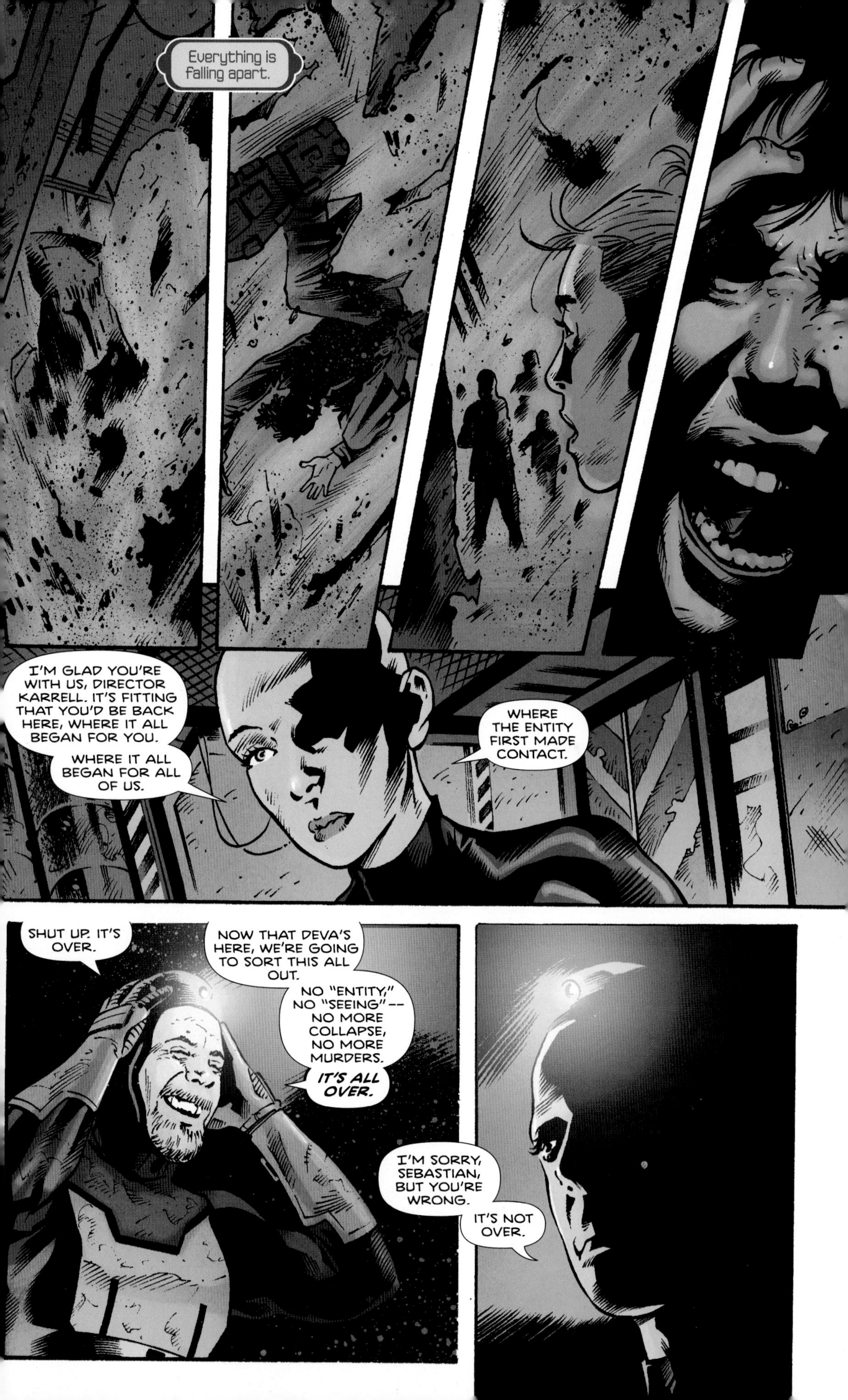
Everything is falling apart.
I'M GLAD YOU'RE WITH US, DIRECTOR KARRELL. IT'S FITTING THAT YOU'D BE BACK HERE, WHERE IT ALL BEGAN FOR YOU.
WHERE IT ALL BEGAN FOR ALL OF US.
WHERE THE ENTITY FIRST MADE CONTACT.
SHUT UP. IT'S OVER.
NOW THAT DEVA'S HERE, WE'RE GOING TO SORT THIS ALL OUT.
NO "ENTITY," NO "SEEING"-- NO MORE COLLAPSE, NO MORE MURDERS.
IT'S ALL OVER.
I'M SORRY, SEBASTIAN, BUT YOU'RE WRONG.
IT'S NOT OVER.

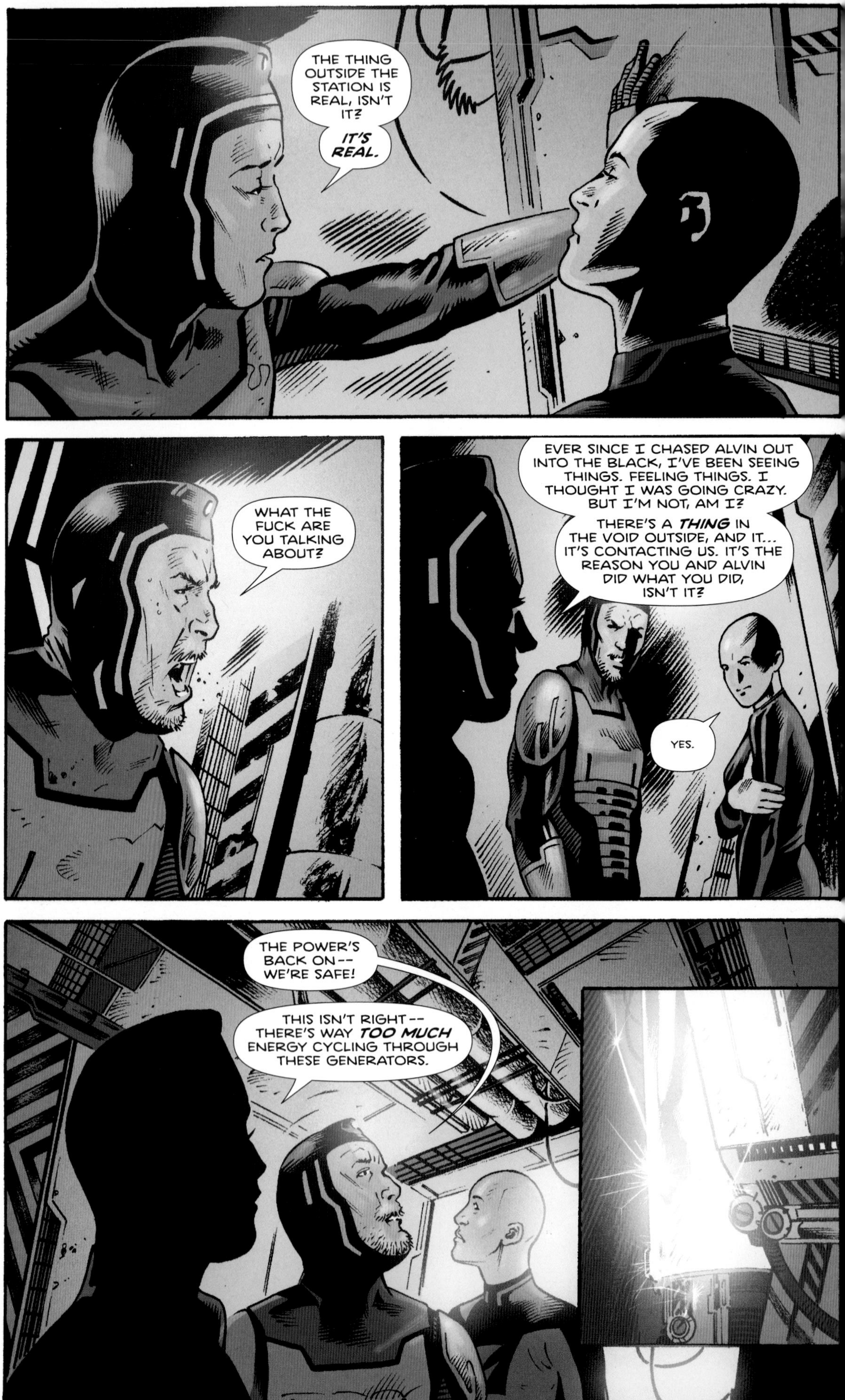
THE THING OUTSIDE THE STATION IS REAL, ISN'T IT?
IT'S REAL.
WHAT THE FUCK ARE YOU TALKING ABOUT?
EVER SINCE I CHASED ALVIN OUT INTO THE BLACK, I'VE BEEN SEEING THINGS. FEELING THINGS. I THOUGHT I WAS GOING CRAZY. BUT I'M NOT, AM I?
THERE'S A THING IN THE VOID OUTSIDE, AND IT... IT'S CONTACTING US. IT'S THE REASON YOU AND ALVIN DID WHAT YOU DID, ISN'T IT?
YES.
THE POWER'S BACK ON-- WE'RE SAFE!
THIS ISN'T RIGHT-- THERE'S WAY TOO MUCH ENERGY CYCLING THROUGH THESE GENERATORS.

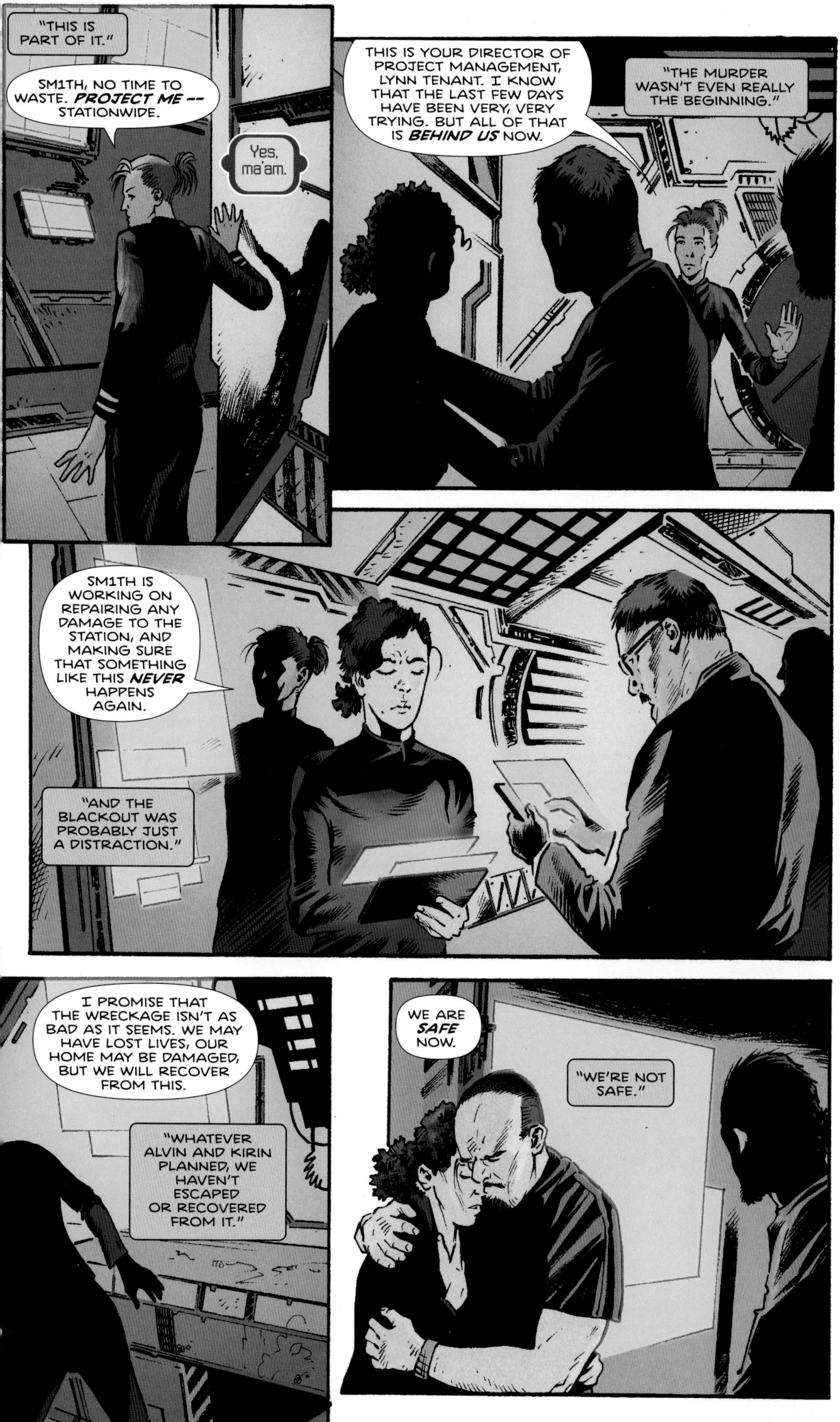
"THIS IS PART OF IT."
SM1TH, NO TIME TO WASTE. PROJECT ME -- STATIONWIDE.
Yes, ma'am.
THIS IS YOUR DIRECTOR OF PROJECT MANAGEMENT, LYNN TENANT. I KNOW THAT THE LAST FEW DAYS HAVE BEEN VERY, VERY TRYING. BUT ALL OF THAT IS BEHIND US NOW.
"THE MURDER WASN'T EVEN REALLY THE BEGINNING."
SM1TH IS WORKING ON REPAIRING ANY DAMAGE TO THE STATION, AND MAKING SURE THAT SOMETHING LIKE THIS NEVER HAPPENS AGAIN.
"AND THE BLACKOUT WAS PROBABLY JUST A DISTRACTION."
I PROMISE THAT THE WRECKAGE ISN'T AS BAD AS IT SEEMS. WE MAY HAVE LOST LIVES, OUR HOME MAY BE DAMAGED, BUT WE WILL RECOVER FROM THIS.
"WHATEVER ALVIN AND KIRIN PLANNED, WE HAVEN'T ESCAPED OR RECOVERED FROM IT."
WE ARE SAFE NOW.
"WE'RE NOT SAFE."

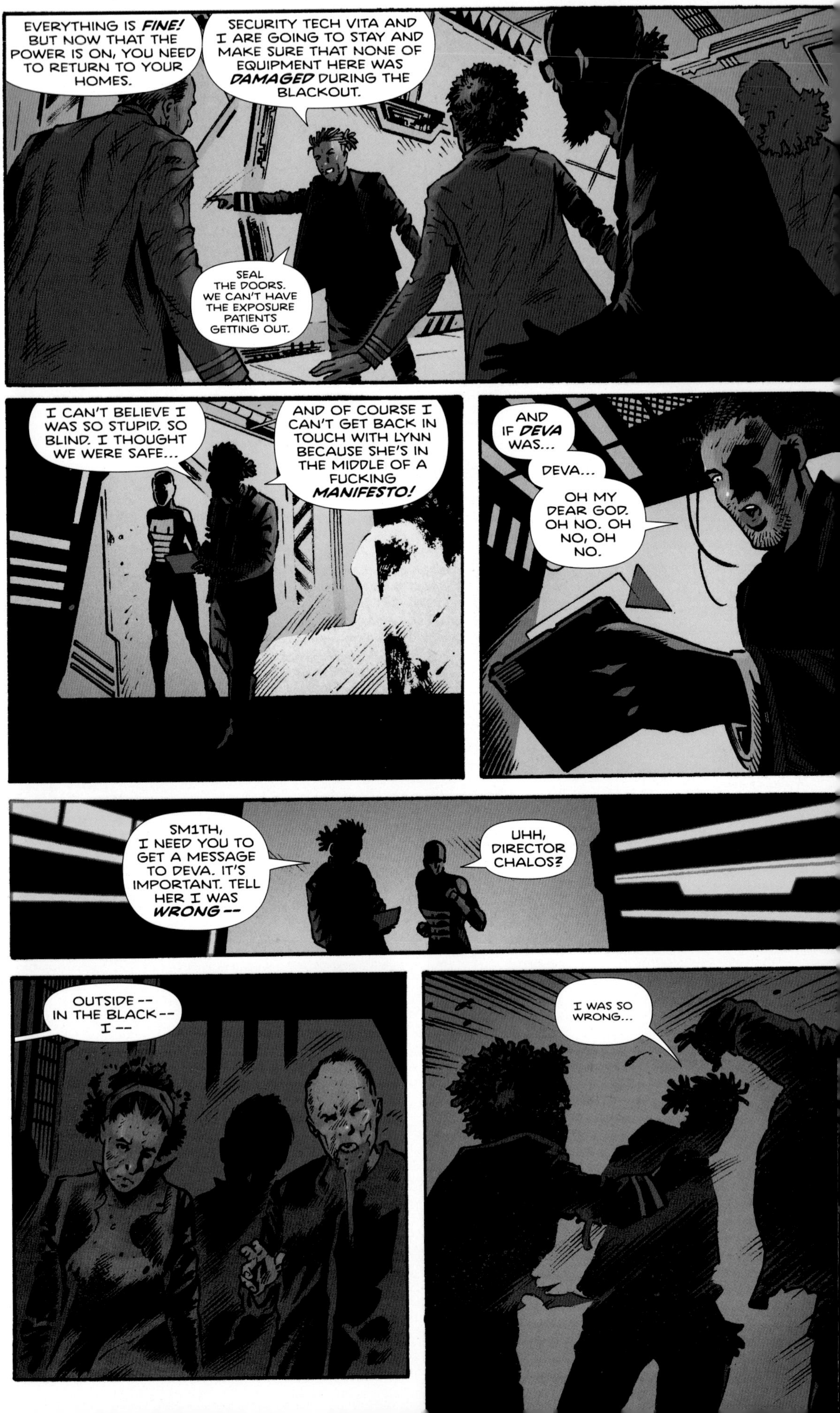
EVERYTHING IS *FINE!* BUT NOW THAT THE POWER IS ON, YOU NEED TO RETURN TO YOUR HOMES.
SECURITY TECH VITA AND I ARE GOING TO STAY AND MAKE SURE THAT NONE OF EQUIPMENT HERE WAS *DAMAGED* DURING THE BLACKOUT.
SEAL THE DOORS. WE CAN'T HAVE THE EXPOSURE PATIENTS GETTING OUT.
I CAN'T BELIEVE I WAS SO STUPID. SO BLIND. I THOUGHT WE WERE SAFE...
AND OF COURSE I CAN'T GET BACK IN TOUCH WITH LYNN BECAUSE SHE'S IN THE MIDDLE OF A FUCKING *MANIFESTO!*
AND IF *DEVA* WAS...
DEVA...
OH MY DEAR GOD. OH NO. OH NO, OH NO.
SM1TH, I NEED YOU TO GET A MESSAGE TO DEVA. IT'S IMPORTANT. TELL HER I WAS *WRONG --*
UHH, DIRECTOR CHALOS?
OUTSIDE -- IN THE BLACK -- I --
I WAS SO WRONG...

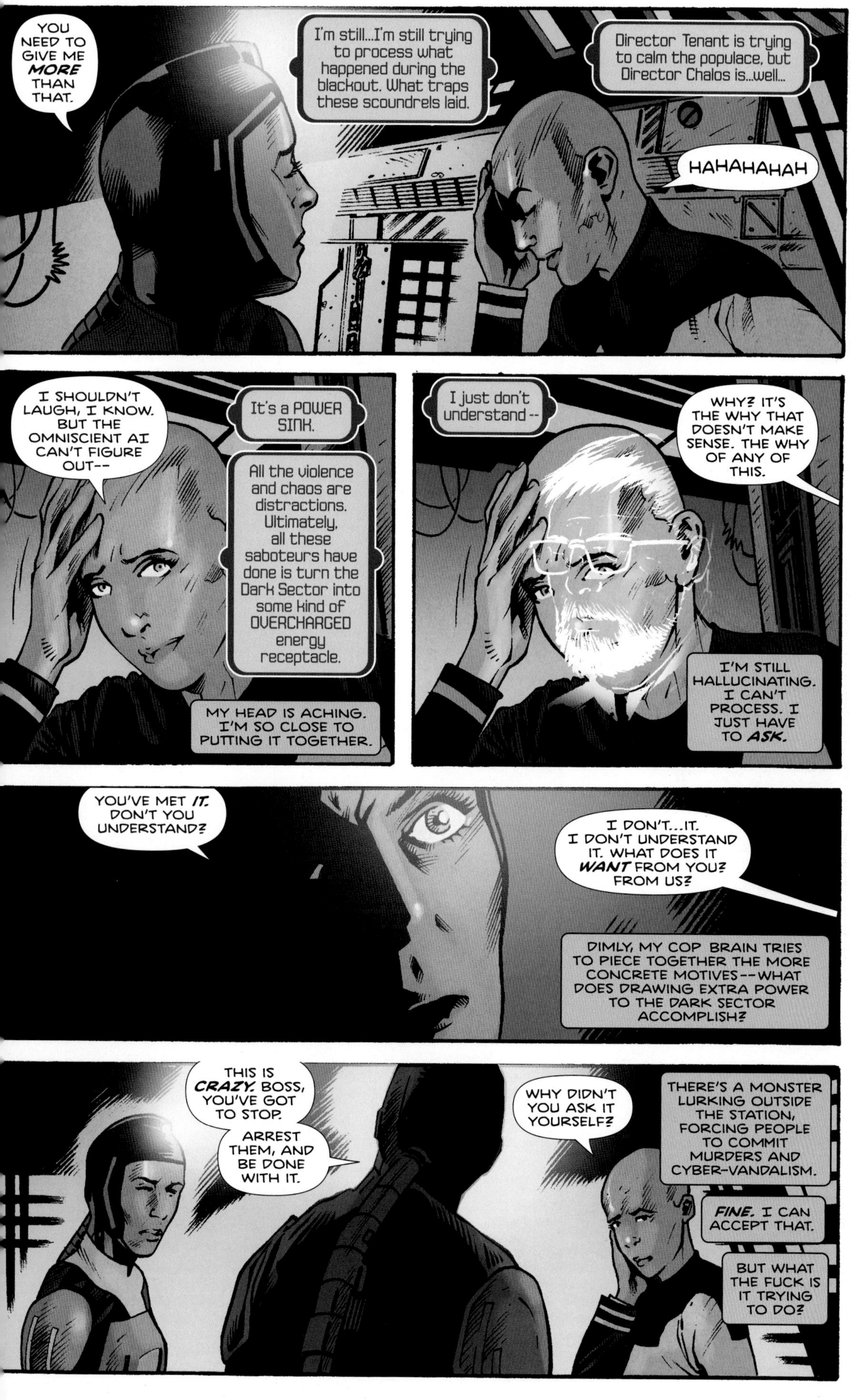
YOU NEED TO GIVE ME MORE THAN THAT.
I'm still...I'm still trying to process what happened during the blackout. What traps these scoundrels laid.
Director Tenant is trying to calm the populace, but Director Chalos is...well...
HAHAHAHAH
I SHOULDN'T LAUGH, I KNOW. BUT THE OMNISCIENT AI CAN'T FIGURE OUT--
It's a POWER SINK.
All the violence and chaos are distractions. Ultimately, all these saboteurs have done is turn the Dark Sector into some kind of OVERCHARGED energy receptacle.
MY HEAD IS ACHING. I'M SO CLOSE TO PUTTING IT TOGETHER.
I just don't understand --
WHY? IT'S THE WHY THAT DOESN'T MAKE SENSE. THE WHY OF ANY OF THIS.
I'M STILL HALLUCINATING. I CAN'T PROCESS. I JUST HAVE TO ASK.
YOU'VE MET IT. DON'T YOU UNDERSTAND?
I DON'T...IT. I DON'T UNDERSTAND IT. WHAT DOES IT WANT FROM YOU? FROM US?
DIMLY, MY COP BRAIN TRIES TO PIECE TOGETHER THE MORE CONCRETE MOTIVES--WHAT DOES DRAWING EXTRA POWER TO THE DARK SECTOR ACCOMPLISH?
THIS IS CRAZY. BOSS, YOU'VE GOT TO STOP.
ARREST THEM, AND BE DONE WITH IT.
WHY DIDN'T YOU ASK IT YOURSELF?
THERE'S A MONSTER LURKING OUTSIDE THE STATION, FORCING PEOPLE TO COMMIT MURDERS AND CYBER-VANDALISM.
FINE. I CAN ACCEPT THAT.
BUT WHAT THE FUCK IS IT TRYING TO DO?

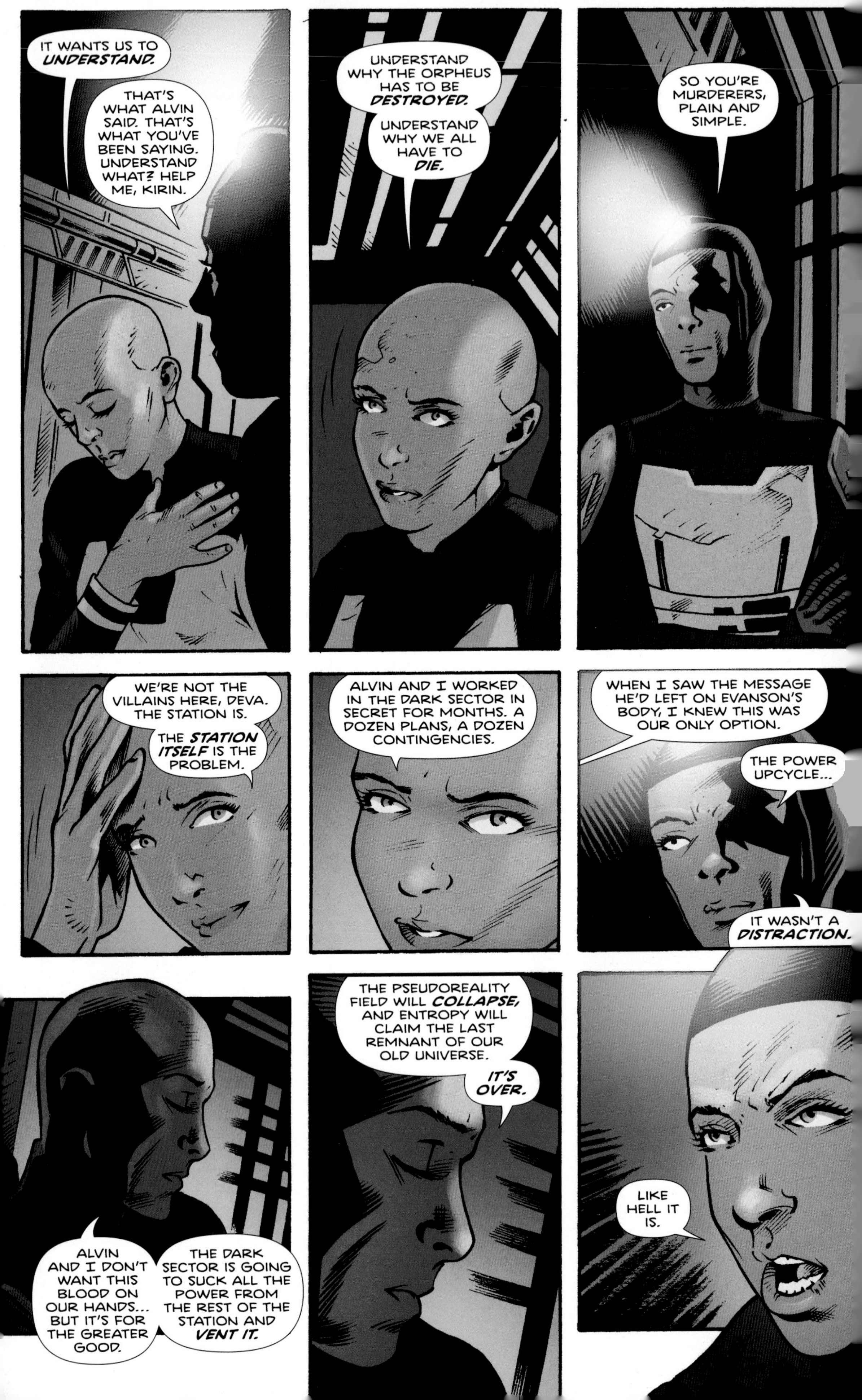

IT WANTS US TO UNDERSTAND.
THAT'S WHAT ALVIN SAID. THAT'S WHAT YOU'VE BEEN SAYING. UNDERSTAND WHAT? HELP ME, KIRIN.
UNDERSTAND WHY THE ORPHEUS HAS TO BE DESTROYED.
UNDERSTAND WHY WE ALL HAVE TO DIE.
SO YOU'RE MURDERERS, PLAIN AND SIMPLE.
WE'RE NOT THE VILLAINS HERE, DEVA. THE STATION IS.
THE STATION ITSELF IS THE PROBLEM.
ALVIN AND I WORKED IN THE DARK SECTOR IN SECRET FOR MONTHS. A DOZEN PLANS, A DOZEN CONTINGENCIES.
WHEN I SAW THE MESSAGE HE'D LEFT ON EVANSON'S BODY, I KNEW THIS WAS OUR ONLY OPTION.
THE POWER UPCYCLE...
IT WASN'T A DISTRACTION.
ALVIN AND I DON'T WANT THIS BLOOD ON OUR HANDS... BUT IT'S FOR THE GREATER GOOD.
THE DARK SECTOR IS GOING TO SUCK ALL THE POWER FROM THE REST OF THE STATION AND VENT IT.
THE PSEUDOREALITY FIELD WILL COLLAPSE, AND ENTROPY WILL CLAIM THE LAST REMNANT OF OUR OLD UNIVERSE.
IT'S OVER.
LIKE HELL IT IS.

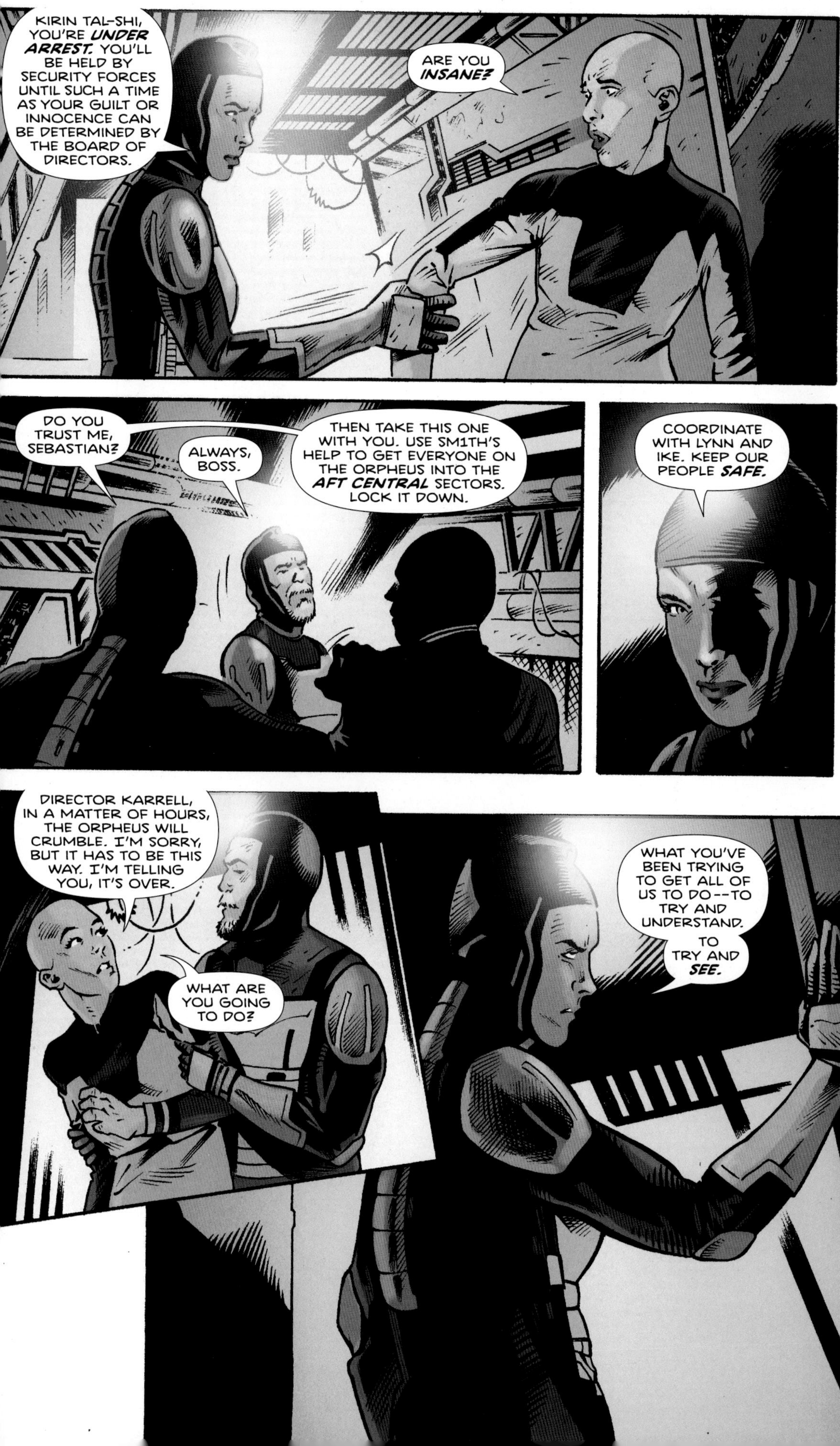
KIRIN TAL-SHI, YOU'RE *UNDER ARREST.* YOU'LL BE HELD BY SECURITY FORCES UNTIL SUCH A TIME AS YOUR GUILT OR INNOCENCE CAN BE DETERMINED BY THE BOARD OF DIRECTORS.
ARE YOU *INSANE?*
DO YOU TRUST ME, SEBASTIAN?
ALWAYS, BOSS.
THEN TAKE THIS ONE WITH YOU. USE SM1TH'S HELP TO GET EVERYONE ON THE ORPHEUS INTO THE *AFT CENTRAL* SECTORS. LOCK IT DOWN.
COORDINATE WITH LYNN AND IKE. KEEP OUR PEOPLE *SAFE.*
DIRECTOR KARRELL, IN A MATTER OF HOURS, THE ORPHEUS WILL CRUMBLE. I'M SORRY, BUT IT HAS TO BE THIS WAY. I'M TELLING YOU, IT'S OVER.
WHAT ARE YOU GOING TO DO?
WHAT YOU'VE BEEN TRYING TO GET ALL OF US TO DO--TO TRY AND UNDERSTAND.
TO TRY AND *SEE.*

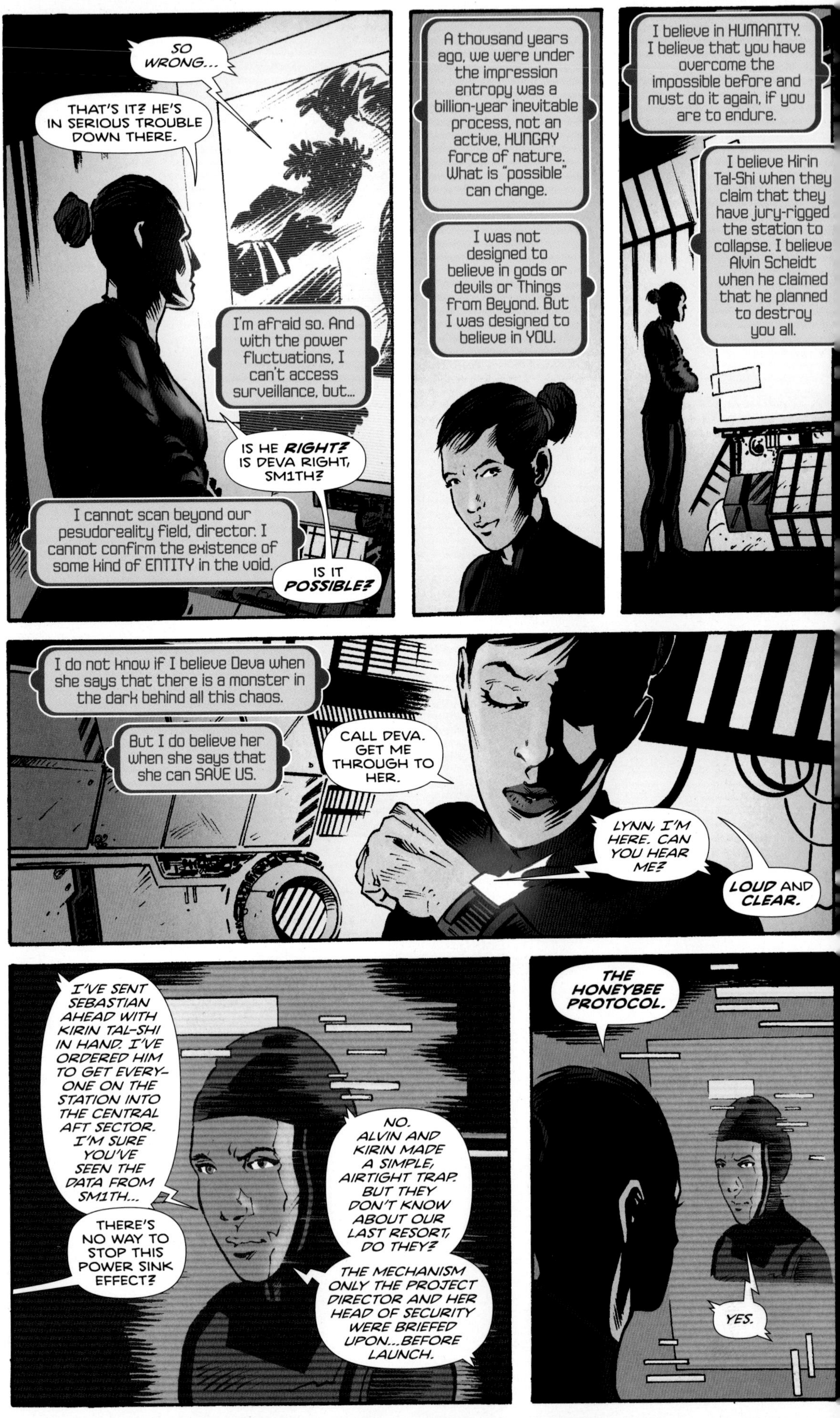
SO WRONG...
THAT'S IT? HE'S IN SERIOUS TROUBLE DOWN THERE.
I'm afraid so. And with the power fluctuations, I can't access surveillance, but...
IS HE RIGHT? IS DEVA RIGHT, SM1TH?
I cannot scan beyond our pesudoreality field, director. I cannot confirm the existence of some kind of ENTITY in the void.
IS IT POSSIBLE?
A thousand years ago, we were under the impression entropy was a billion-year inevitable process, not an active, HUNGRY force of nature. What is "possible" can change.
I was not designed to believe in gods or devils or Things from Beyond. But I was designed to believe in YOU.
I believe in HUMANITY. I believe that you have overcome the impossible before and must do it again, if you are to endure.
I believe Kirin Tal-Shi when they claim that they have jury-rigged the station to collapse. I believe Alvin Scheidt when he claimed that he planned to destroy you all.
I do not know if I believe Deva when she says that there is a monster in the dark behind all this chaos.
But I do believe her when she says that she can SAVE US.
CALL DEVA. GET ME THROUGH TO HER.
LYNN, I'M HERE. CAN YOU HEAR ME?
LOUD AND CLEAR.
I'VE SENT SEBASTIAN AHEAD WITH KIRIN TAL-SHI IN HAND. I'VE ORDERED HIM TO GET EVERY-ONE ON THE STATION INTO THE CENTRAL AFT SECTOR. I'M SURE YOU'VE SEEN THE DATA FROM SM1TH...
THERE'S NO WAY TO STOP THIS POWER SINK EFFECT?
NO. ALVIN AND KIRIN MADE A SIMPLE, AIRTIGHT TRAP. BUT THEY DON'T KNOW ABOUT OUR LAST RESORT, DO THEY?
THE MECHANISM ONLY THE PROJECT DIRECTOR AND HER HEAD OF SECURITY WERE BRIEFED UPON...BEFORE LAUNCH.
THE HONEYBEE PROTOCOL.
YES.

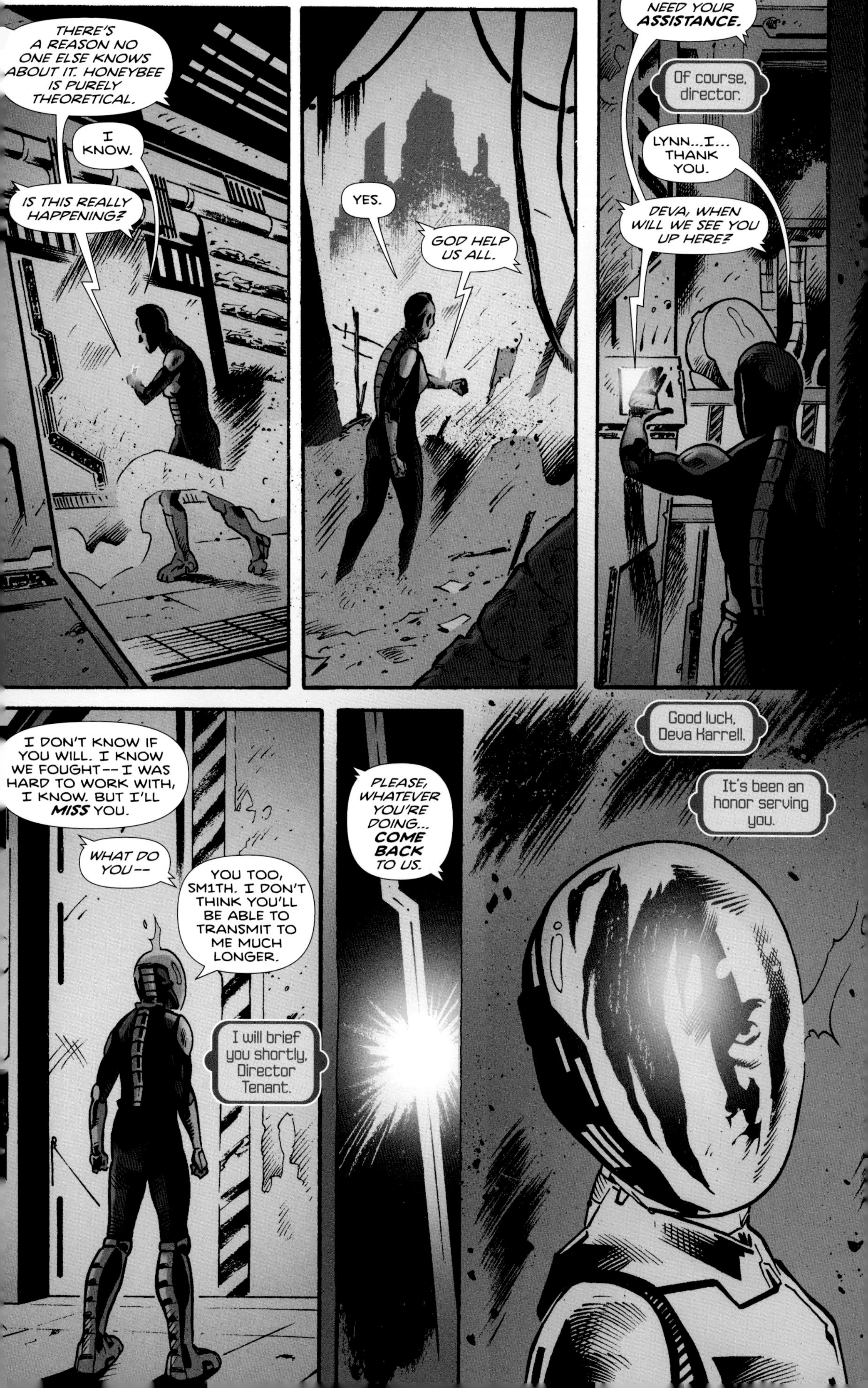
THERE'S A REASON NO ONE ELSE KNOWS ABOUT IT. HONEYBEE IS PURELY THEORETICAL.
I KNOW.
IS THIS REALLY HAPPENING?
YES.
GOD HELP US ALL.
SM1TH, I'LL NEED YOUR ASSISTANCE.
Of course, director.
LYNN...I... THANK YOU.
DEVA, WHEN WILL WE SEE YOU UP HERE?
I DON'T KNOW IF YOU WILL. I KNOW WE FOUGHT-- I WAS HARD TO WORK WITH, I KNOW. BUT I'LL MISS YOU.
WHAT DO YOU--
YOU TOO, SM1TH. I DON'T THINK YOU'LL BE ABLE TO TRANSMIT TO ME MUCH LONGER.
I will brief you shortly, Director Tenant.
PLEASE, WHATEVER YOU'RE DOING... COME BACK TO US.
Good luck, Deva Karrell.
It's been an honor serving you.

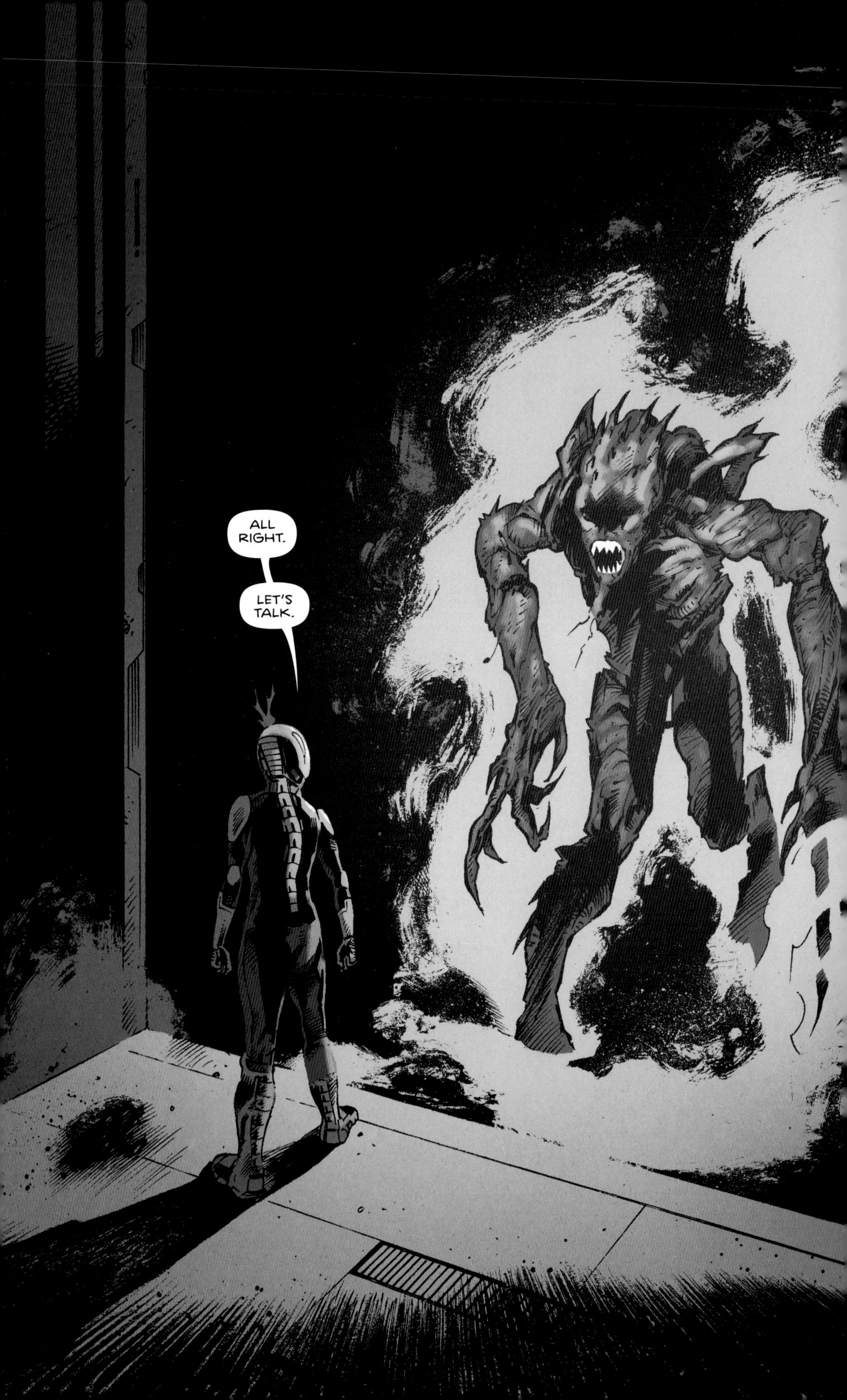
ALL RIGHT.
LET'S TALK.

CHAPTER
FOUR

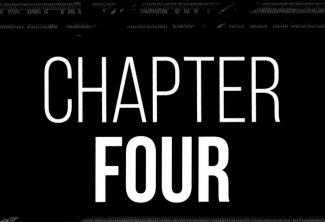

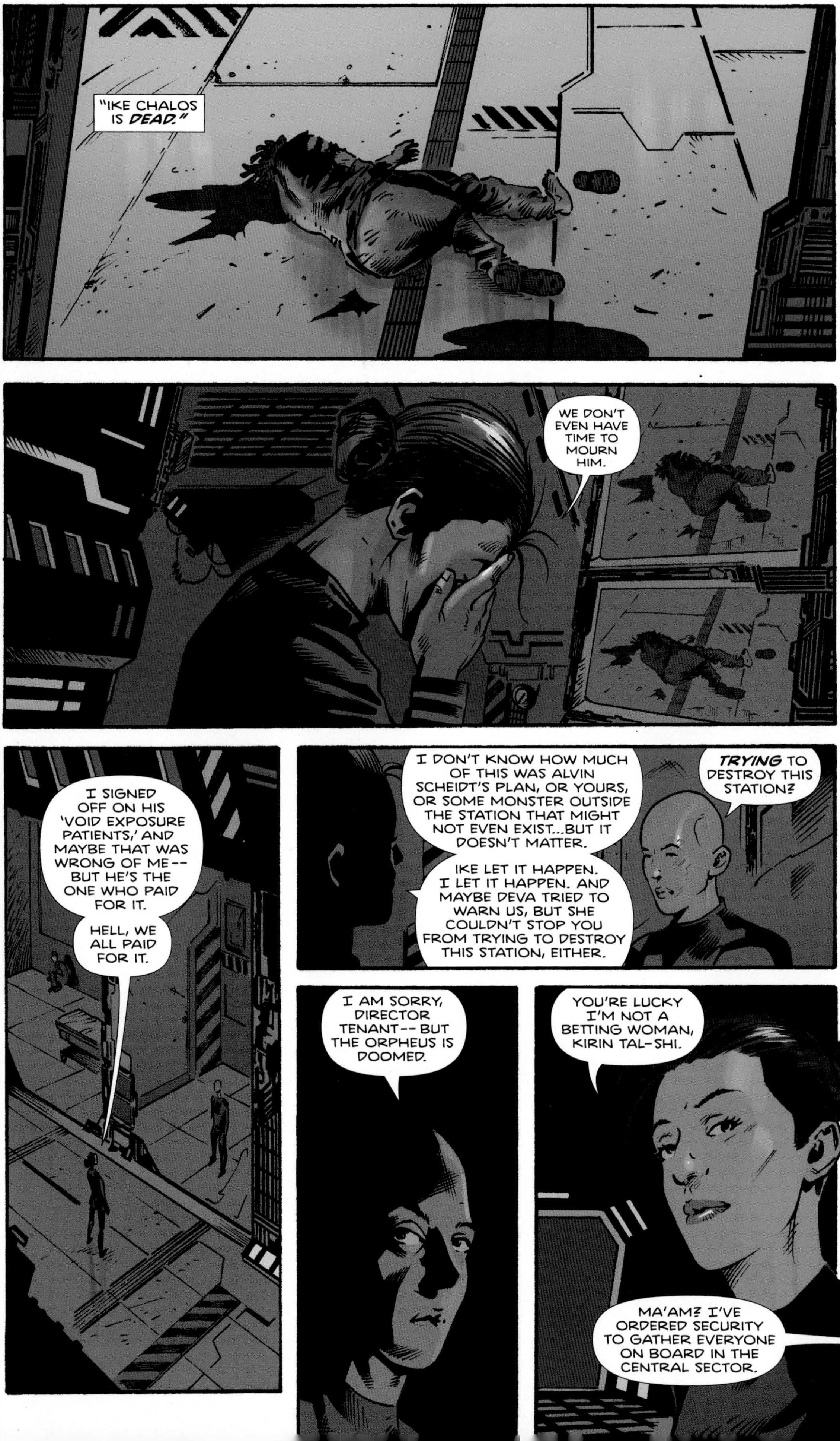
"IKE CHALOS IS DEAD."
WE DON'T EVEN HAVE TIME TO MOURN HIM.
I SIGNED OFF ON HIS 'VOID EXPOSURE PATIENTS,' AND MAYBE THAT WAS WRONG OF ME-- BUT HE'S THE ONE WHO PAID FOR IT.
HELL, WE ALL PAID FOR IT.
I DON'T KNOW HOW MUCH OF THIS WAS ALVIN SCHEIDT'S PLAN, OR YOURS, OR SOME MONSTER OUTSIDE THE STATION THAT MIGHT NOT EVEN EXIST...BUT IT DOESN'T MATTER.
IKE LET IT HAPPEN. I LET IT HAPPEN. AND MAYBE DEVA TRIED TO WARN US, BUT SHE COULDN'T STOP YOU FROM TRYING TO DESTROY THIS STATION, EITHER.
TRYING TO DESTROY THIS STATION?
I AM SORRY, DIRECTOR TENANT-- BUT THE ORPHEUS IS DOOMED.
YOU'RE LUCKY I'M NOT A BETTING WOMAN, KIRIN TAL-SHI.
MA'AM? I'VE ORDERED SECURITY TO GATHER EVERYONE ON BOARD IN THE CENTRAL SECTOR.

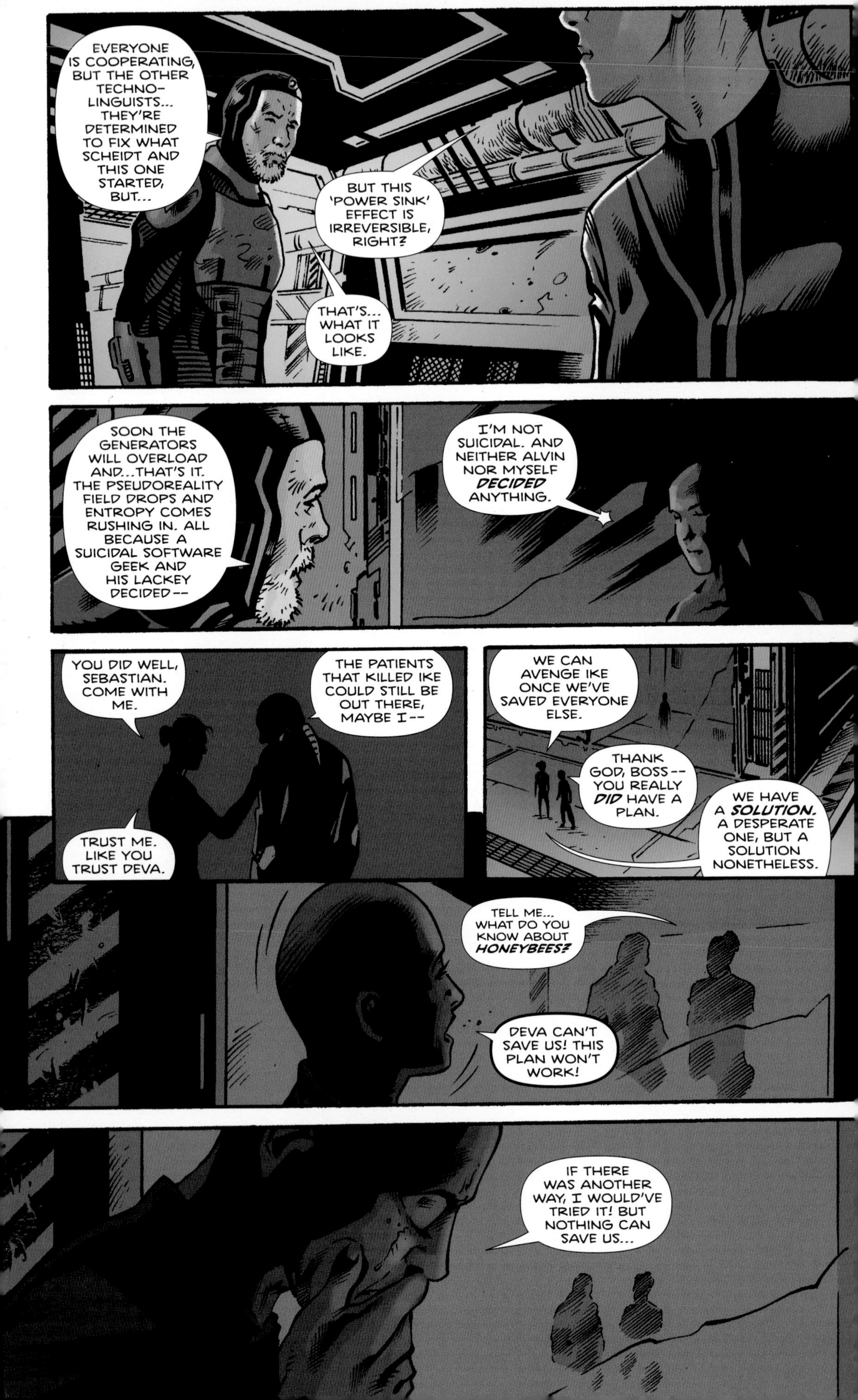
EVERYONE IS COOPERATING, BUT THE OTHER TECHNO-LINGUISTS... THEY'RE DETERMINED TO FIX WHAT SCHEIDT AND THIS ONE STARTED, BUT...
BUT THIS 'POWER SINK' EFFECT IS IRREVERSIBLE, RIGHT?
THAT'S... WHAT IT LOOKS LIKE.
SOON THE GENERATORS WILL OVERLOAD AND...THAT'S IT. THE PSEUDOREALITY FIELD DROPS AND ENTROPY COMES RUSHING IN. ALL BECAUSE A SUICIDAL SOFTWARE GEEK AND HIS LACKEY DECIDED--
I'M NOT SUICIDAL. AND NEITHER ALVIN NOR MYSELF DECIDED ANYTHING.
YOU DID WELL, SEBASTIAN. COME WITH ME.
THE PATIENTS THAT KILLED IKE COULD STILL BE OUT THERE, MAYBE I--
TRUST ME. LIKE YOU TRUST DEVA.
WE CAN AVENGE IKE ONCE WE'VE SAVED EVERYONE ELSE.
THANK GOD, BOSS-- YOU REALLY DID HAVE A PLAN.
WE HAVE A SOLUTION. A DESPERATE ONE, BUT A SOLUTION NONETHELESS.
TELL ME... WHAT DO YOU KNOW ABOUT HONEYBEES?
DEVA CAN'T SAVE US! THIS PLAN WON'T WORK!
IF THERE WAS ANOTHER WAY, I WOULD'VE TRIED IT! BUT NOTHING CAN SAVE US...

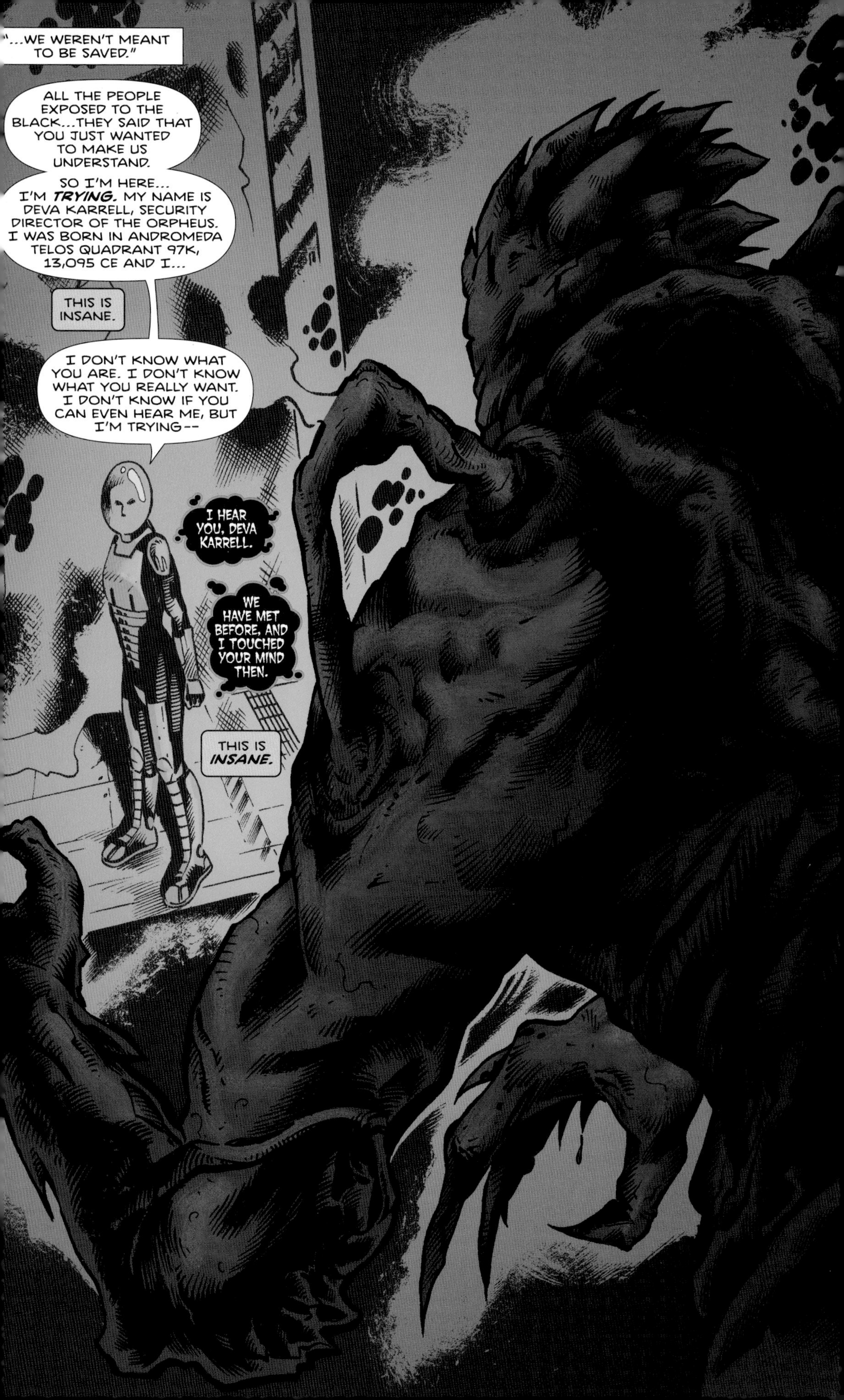
"...WE WEREN'T MEANT TO BE SAVED."
ALL THE PEOPLE EXPOSED TO THE BLACK...THEY SAID THAT YOU JUST WANTED TO MAKE US UNDERSTAND.
SO I'M HERE... I'M *TRYING.* MY NAME IS DEVA KARRELL, SECURITY DIRECTOR OF THE ORPHEUS. I WAS BORN IN ANDROMEDA TELOS QUADRANT 97K, 13,095 CE AND I...
THIS IS INSANE.
I DON'T KNOW WHAT YOU ARE. I DON'T KNOW WHAT YOU REALLY WANT. I DON'T KNOW IF YOU CAN EVEN HEAR ME, BUT I'M TRYING--
I HEAR YOU, DEVA KARRELL.
WE HAVE MET BEFORE, AND I TOUCHED YOUR MIND THEN.
THIS IS *INSANE.*

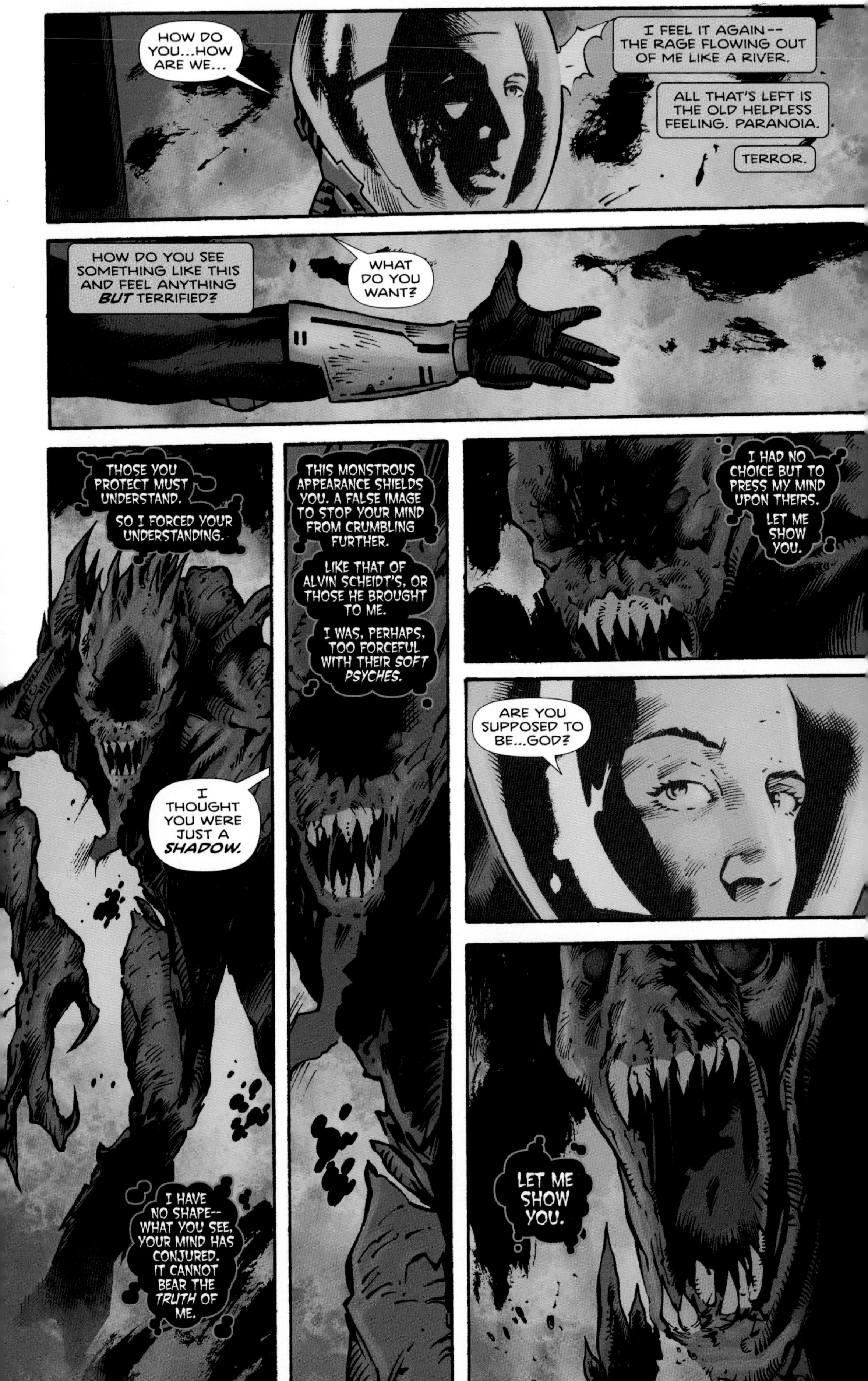
HOW DO YOU...HOW ARE WE...
I FEEL IT AGAIN-- THE RAGE FLOWING OUT OF ME LIKE A RIVER.
ALL THAT'S LEFT IS THE OLD HELPLESS FEELING. PARANOIA.
TERROR.
HOW DO YOU SEE SOMETHING LIKE THIS AND FEEL ANYTHING *BUT* TERRIFIED?
WHAT DO YOU WANT?
THOSE YOU PROTECT MUST UNDERSTAND.
SO I FORCED YOUR UNDERSTANDING.
I THOUGHT YOU WERE JUST A *SHADOW.*
I HAVE NO SHAPE-- WHAT YOU SEE, YOUR MIND HAS CONJURED. IT CANNOT BEAR THE *TRUTH* OF ME.
THIS MONSTROUS APPEARANCE SHIELDS YOU. A FALSE IMAGE TO STOP YOUR MIND FROM CRUMBLING FURTHER.
LIKE THAT OF ALVIN SCHEIDT'S, OR THOSE HE BROUGHT TO ME.
I WAS, PERHAPS, TOO FORCEFUL WITH THEIR *SOFT PSYCHES.*
I HAD NO CHOICE BUT TO PRESS MY MIND UPON THEIRS.
LET ME SHOW YOU.
ARE YOU SUPPOSED TO BE...GOD?
LET ME SHOW YOU.

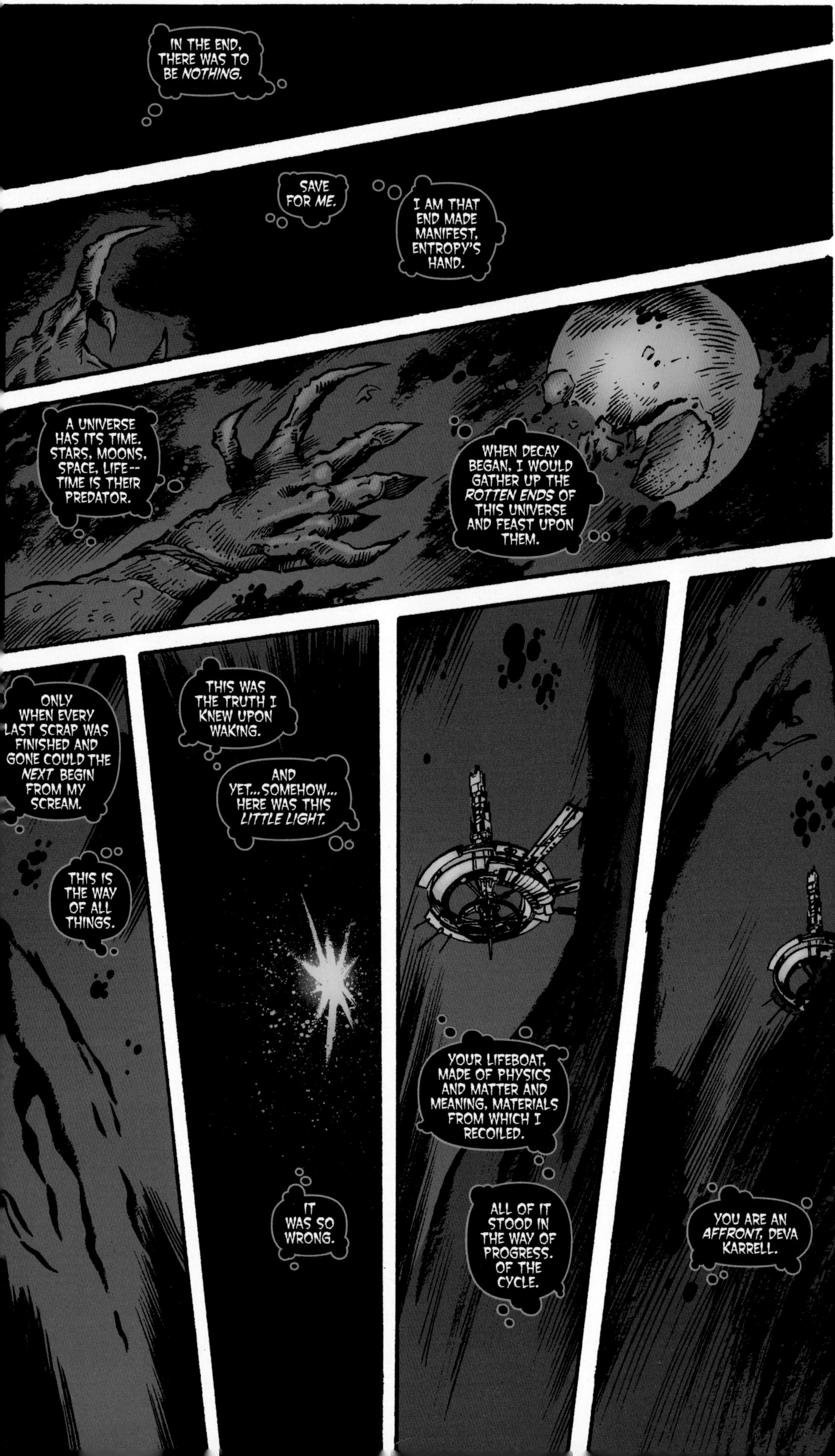

IN THE END, THERE WAS TO BE *NOTHING.*
SAVE FOR *ME.*
I AM THAT END MADE MANIFEST, ENTROPY'S HAND.
A UNIVERSE HAS ITS TIME. STARS, MOONS, SPACE, LIFE-- TIME IS THEIR PREDATOR.
WHEN DECAY BEGAN, I WOULD GATHER UP THE *ROTTEN ENDS* OF THIS UNIVERSE AND FEAST UPON THEM.
ONLY WHEN EVERY LAST SCRAP WAS FINISHED AND GONE COULD THE *NEXT* BEGIN FROM MY SCREAM.
THIS IS THE WAY OF ALL THINGS.
THIS WAS THE TRUTH I KNEW UPON WAKING.
AND YET...SOMEHOW... HERE WAS THIS *LITTLE LIGHT.*
IT WAS SO WRONG.
YOUR LIFEBOAT, MADE OF PHYSICS AND MATTER AND MEANING, MATERIALS FROM WHICH I RECOILED.
ALL OF IT STOOD IN THE WAY OF PROGRESS. OF THE CYCLE.
YOU ARE AN *AFFRONT,* DEVA KARRELL.

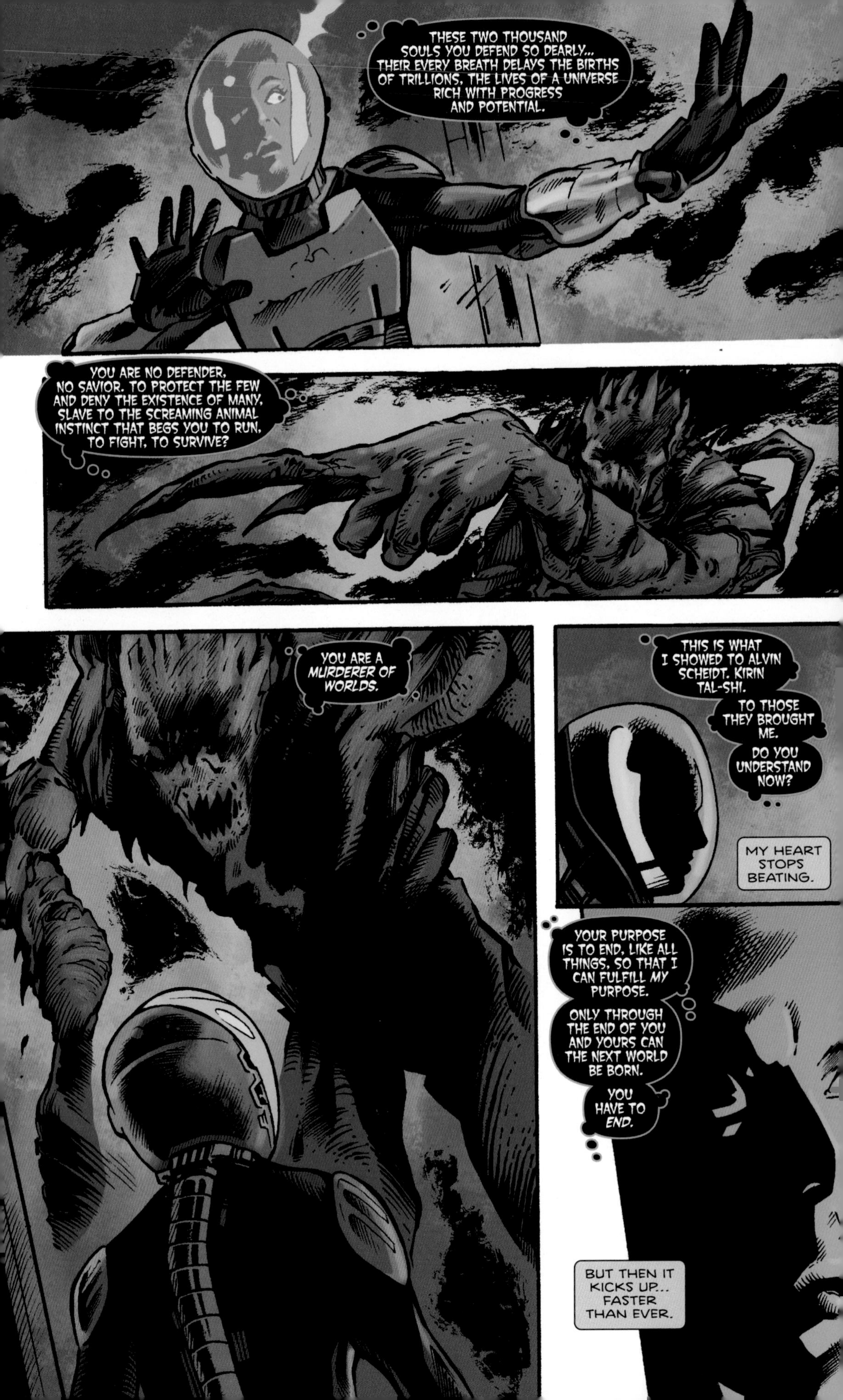

THESE TWO THOUSAND SOULS YOU DEFEND SO DEARLY... THEIR EVERY BREATH DELAYS THE BIRTHS OF TRILLIONS. THE LIVES OF A UNIVERSE RICH WITH PROGRESS AND POTENTIAL.
YOU ARE NO DEFENDER, NO SAVIOR. TO PROTECT THE FEW AND DENY THE EXISTENCE OF MANY, SLAVE TO THE SCREAMING ANIMAL INSTINCT THAT BEGS YOU TO RUN, TO FIGHT, TO SURVIVE?
YOU ARE A *MURDERER OF WORLDS.*
THIS IS WHAT I SHOWED TO ALVIN SCHEIDT. KIRIN TAL-SHI.
TO THOSE THEY BROUGHT ME.
DO YOU UNDERSTAND NOW?
MY HEART STOPS BEATING.
YOUR PURPOSE IS TO END, LIKE ALL THINGS, SO THAT I CAN FULFILL *MY* PURPOSE.
ONLY THROUGH THE END OF YOU AND YOURS CAN THE NEXT WORLD BE BORN.
YOU HAVE TO *END.*
BUT THEN IT KICKS UP... FASTER THAN EVER.

NO.

FOR A SECOND, IT ALMOST HAD ME.

JUST LIKE BEFORE, ALL THE GUILT AND SELF-DOUBT, THAT IMPULSE TO GIVE UP ON EVERYTHING...

BUT THAT'S A LIE.

EVERYTHING THIS MONSTER SAYS IS A LIE.

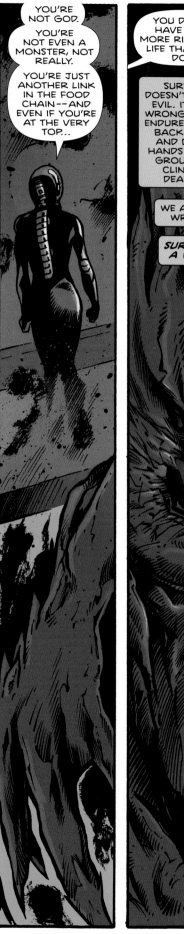

YOU'RE NOT GOD.

YOU'RE NOT EVEN A MONSTER, NOT REALLY.

YOU'RE JUST ANOTHER LINK IN THE FOOD CHAIN--AND EVEN IF YOU'RE AT THE VERY TOP...

YOU DON'T HAVE ANY MORE RIGHT TO LIFE THAN WE DO.

SURVIVING DOESN'T MAKE US EVIL. IT WASN'T WRONG OF US TO ENDURE, TO LOOK BACK AT HELL AND DIG OUR HANDS INTO THE GROUND AND CLING FOR DEAR LIFE.

WE ARE NOT WRONG.

SURVIVAL IS A VIRTUE.

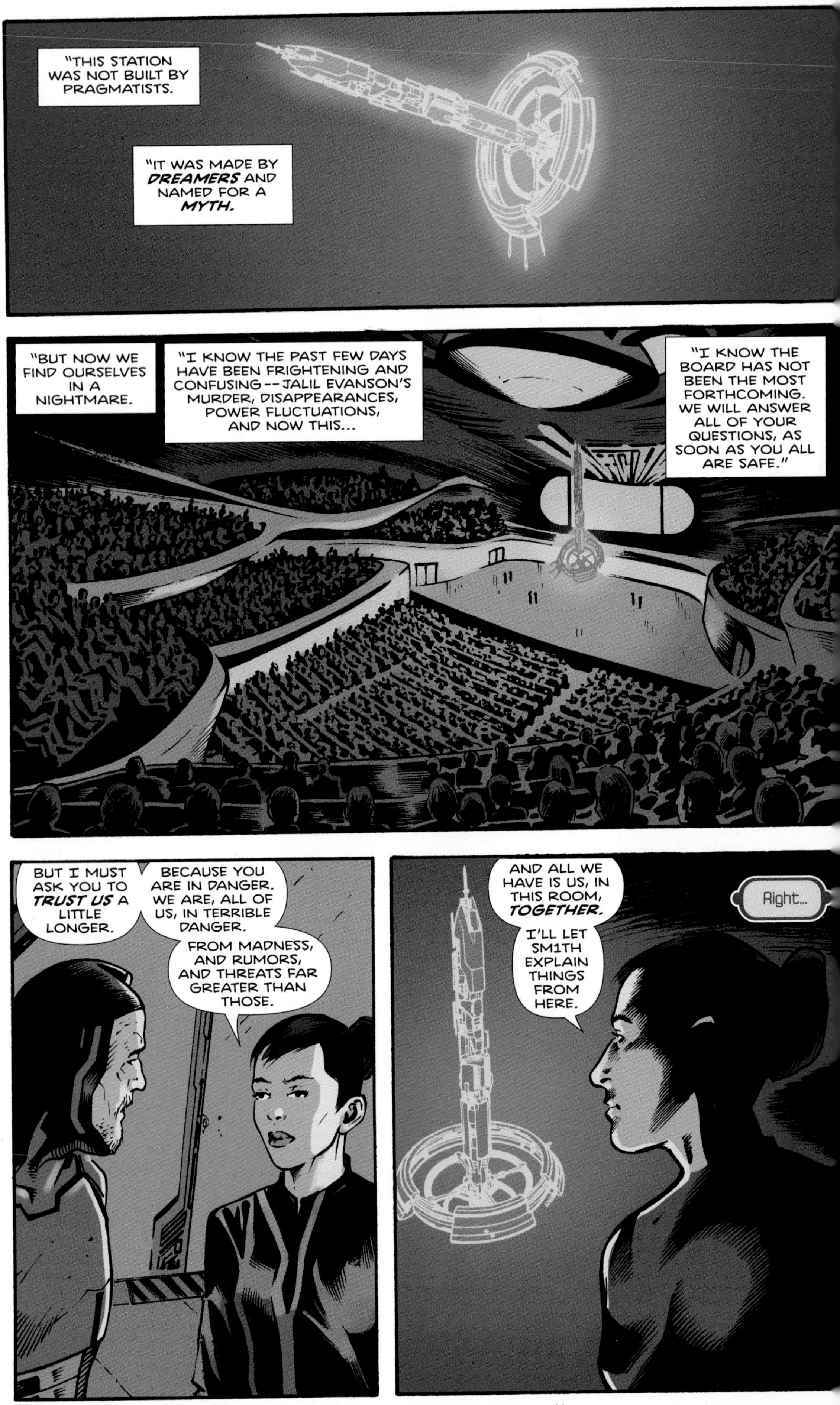
"THIS STATION WAS NOT BUILT BY PRAGMATISTS.
"IT WAS MADE BY *DREAMERS* AND NAMED FOR A *MYTH.*
"BUT NOW WE FIND OURSELVES IN A NIGHTMARE.
"I KNOW THE PAST FEW DAYS HAVE BEEN FRIGHTENING AND CONFUSING--JALIL EVANSON'S MURDER, DISAPPEARANCES, POWER FLUCTUATIONS, AND NOW THIS...
"I KNOW THE BOARD HAS NOT BEEN THE MOST FORTHCOMING. WE WILL ANSWER ALL OF YOUR QUESTIONS, AS SOON AS YOU ALL ARE SAFE."
BUT I MUST ASK YOU TO *TRUST US* A LITTLE LONGER.
BECAUSE YOU ARE IN DANGER. WE ARE, ALL OF US, IN TERRIBLE DANGER.
FROM MADNESS, AND RUMORS, AND THREATS FAR GREATER THAN THOSE.
AND ALL WE HAVE IS US, IN THIS ROOM, *TOGETHER.*
I'LL LET SM1TH EXPLAIN THINGS FROM HERE.
Right...

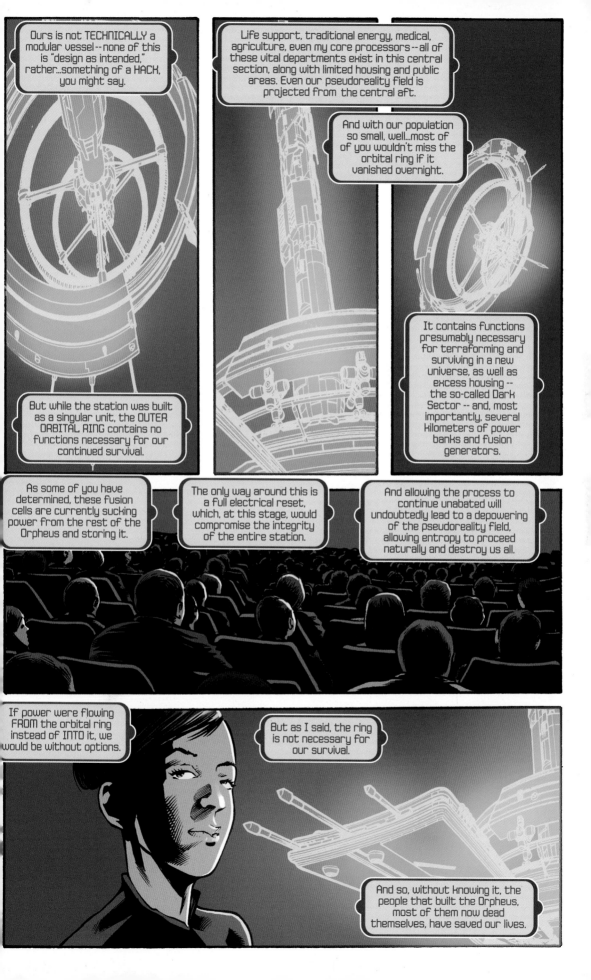

Ours is not TECHNICALLY a modular vessel -- none of this is "design as intended," rather...something of a HACK, you might say.

But while the station was built as a singular unit, the OUTER ORBITAL RING contains no functions necessary for our continued survival.

Life support, traditional energy, medical, agriculture, even my core processors -- all of these vital departments exist in this central section, along with limited housing and public areas. Even our pseudoreality field is projected from the central aft.

And with our population so small, well...most of of you wouldn't miss the orbital ring if it vanished overnight.

It contains functions presumably necessary for terraforming and surviving in a new universe, as well as excess housing -- the so-called Dark Sector -- and, most importantly, several kilometers of power banks and fusion generators.

As some of you have determined, these fusion cells are currently sucking power from the rest of the Orpheus and storing it.

The only way around this is a full electrical reset, which, at this stage, would compromise the integrity of the entire station.

And allowing the process to continue unabated will undoubtedly lead to a depowering of the pseudoreality field, allowing entropy to proceed naturally and destroy us all.

If power were flowing FROM the orbital ring instead of INTO it, we would be without options.

But as I said, the ring is not necessary for our survival.

And so, without knowing it, the people that built the Orpheus, most of them now dead themselves, have saved our lives.

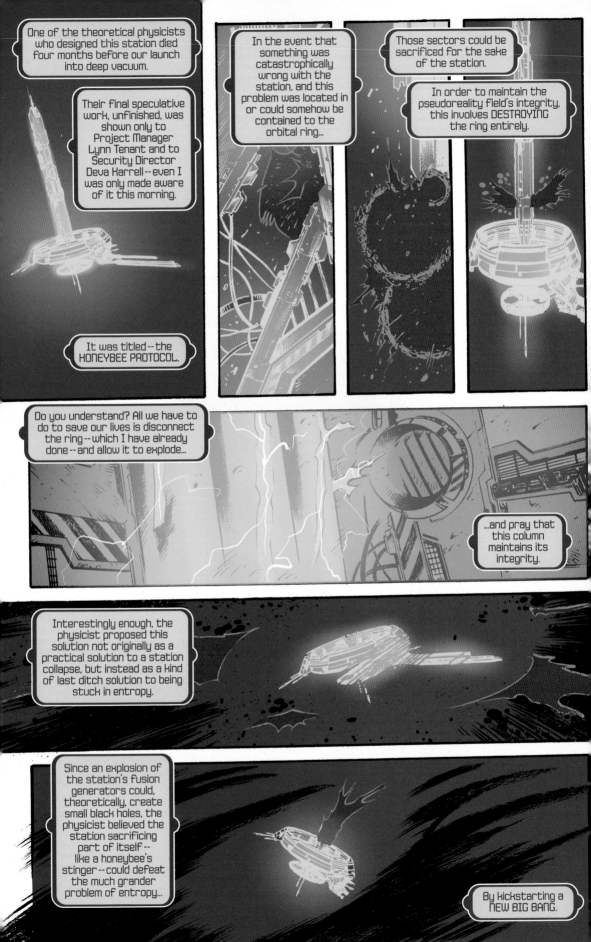

One of the theoretical physicists who designed this station died four months before our launch into deep vacuum.

Their final speculative work, unfinished, was shown only to Project Manager Lynn Tenant and to Security Director Deva Karrell -- even I was only made aware of it this morning.

It was titled -- the HONEYBEE PROTOCOL.

In the event that something was catastrophically wrong with the station, and this problem was located in or could somehow be contained to the orbital ring...

Those sectors could be sacrificed for the sake of the station.

In order to maintain the pseudoreality field's integrity, this involves DESTROYING the ring entirely.

Do you understand? All we have to do to save our lives is disconnect the ring -- which I have already done -- and allow it to explode...

...and pray that this column maintains its integrity.

Interestingly enough, the physicist proposed this solution not originally as a practical solution to a station collapse, but instead as a kind of last ditch solution to being stuck in entropy.

Since an explosion of the station's fusion generators could, theoretically, create small black holes, the physicist believed the station sacrificing part of itself -- like a honeybee's stinger -- could defeat the much grander problem of entropy...

By kickstarting a NEW BIG BANG.

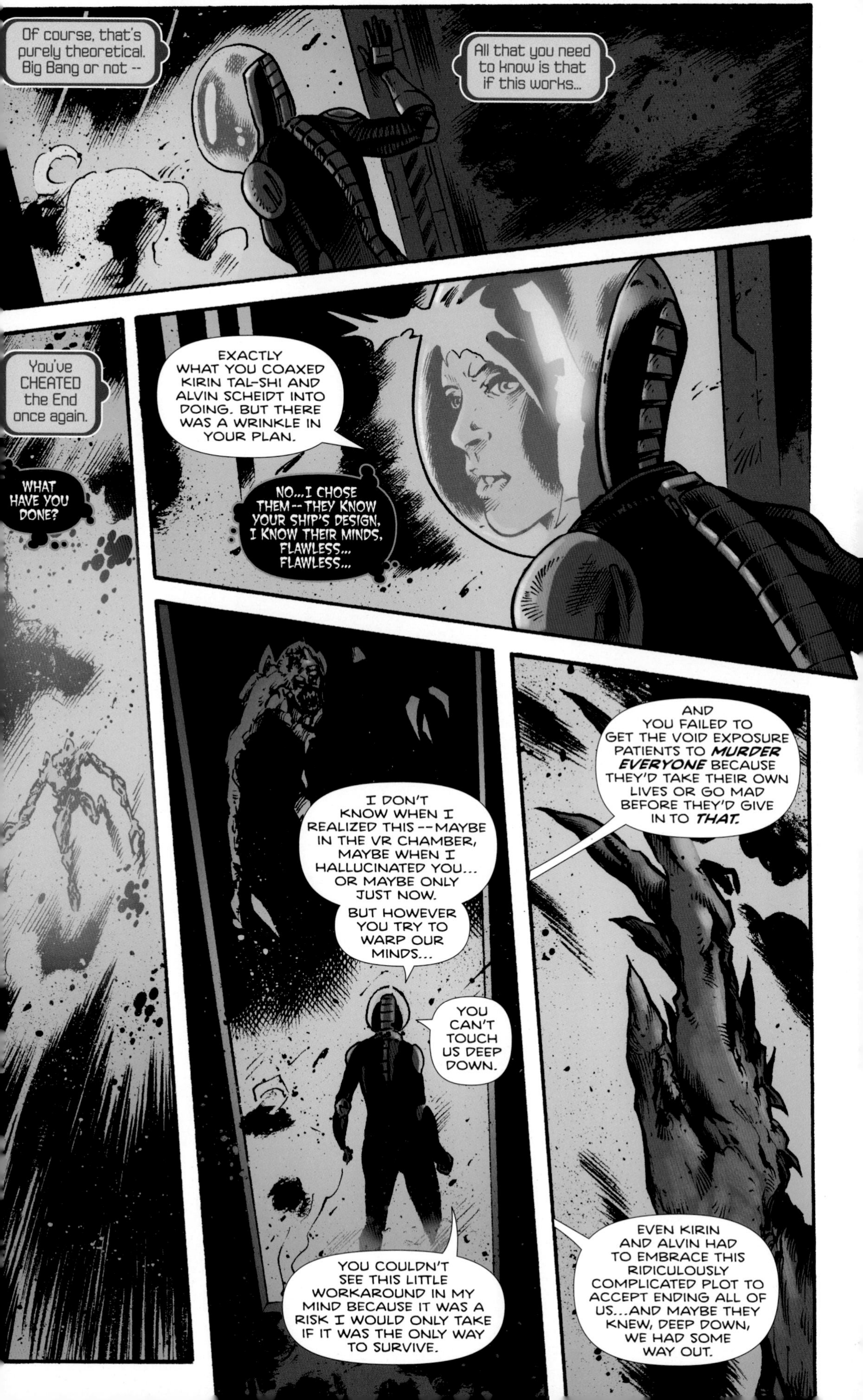
Of course, that's purely theoretical. Big Bang or not --
All that you need to know is that if this works...
You've CHEATED the End once again.
WHAT HAVE YOU DONE?
EXACTLY WHAT YOU COAXED KIRIN TAL-SHI AND ALVIN SCHEIDT INTO DOING. BUT THERE WAS A WRINKLE IN YOUR PLAN.
NO...I CHOSE THEM--THEY KNOW YOUR SHIP'S DESIGN, I KNOW THEIR MINDS, FLAWLESS... FLAWLESS...
I DON'T KNOW WHEN I REALIZED THIS--MAYBE IN THE VR CHAMBER, MAYBE WHEN I HALLUCINATED YOU... OR MAYBE ONLY JUST NOW.
BUT HOWEVER YOU TRY TO WARP OUR MINDS...
YOU CAN'T TOUCH US DEEP DOWN.
YOU COULDN'T SEE THIS LITTLE WORKAROUND IN MY MIND BECAUSE IT WAS A RISK I WOULD ONLY TAKE IF IT WAS THE ONLY WAY TO SURVIVE.
AND YOU FAILED TO GET THE VOID EXPOSURE PATIENTS TO MURDER EVERYONE BECAUSE THEY'D TAKE THEIR OWN LIVES OR GO MAD BEFORE THEY'D GIVE IN TO THAT.
EVEN KIRIN AND ALVIN HAD TO EMBRACE THIS RIDICULOUSLY COMPLICATED PLOT TO ACCEPT ENDING ALL OF US...AND MAYBE THEY KNEW, DEEP DOWN, WE HAD SOME WAY OUT.

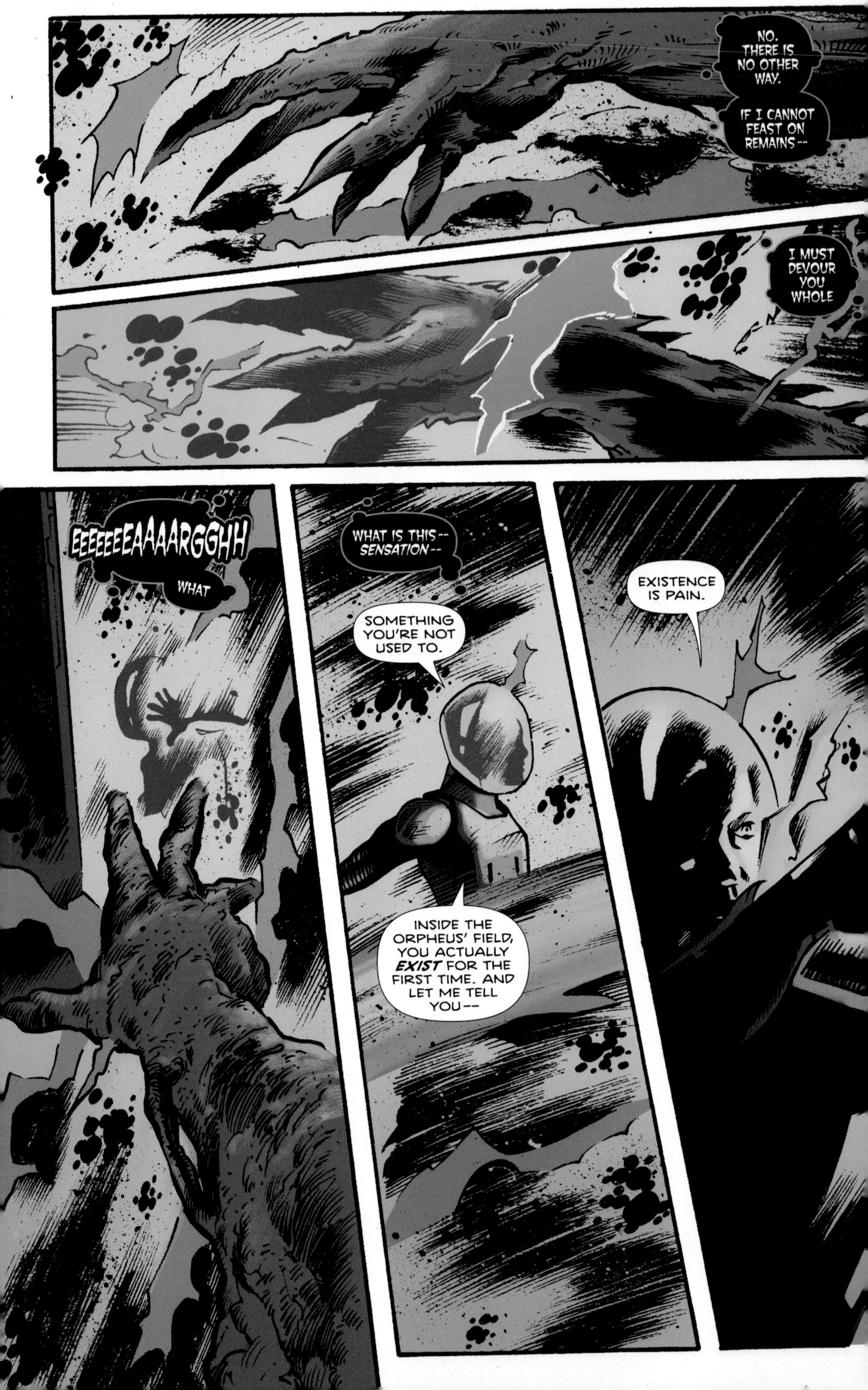
NO. THERE IS NO OTHER WAY.
IF I CANNOT FEAST ON REMAINS--
I MUST DEVOUR YOU WHOLE
EEEEEEEAAAARGGHH
WHAT
WHAT IS THIS-- SENSATION--
SOMETHING YOU'RE NOT USED TO.
INSIDE THE ORPHEUS' FIELD, YOU ACTUALLY EXIST FOR THE FIRST TIME. AND LET ME TELL YOU--
EXISTENCE IS PAIN.

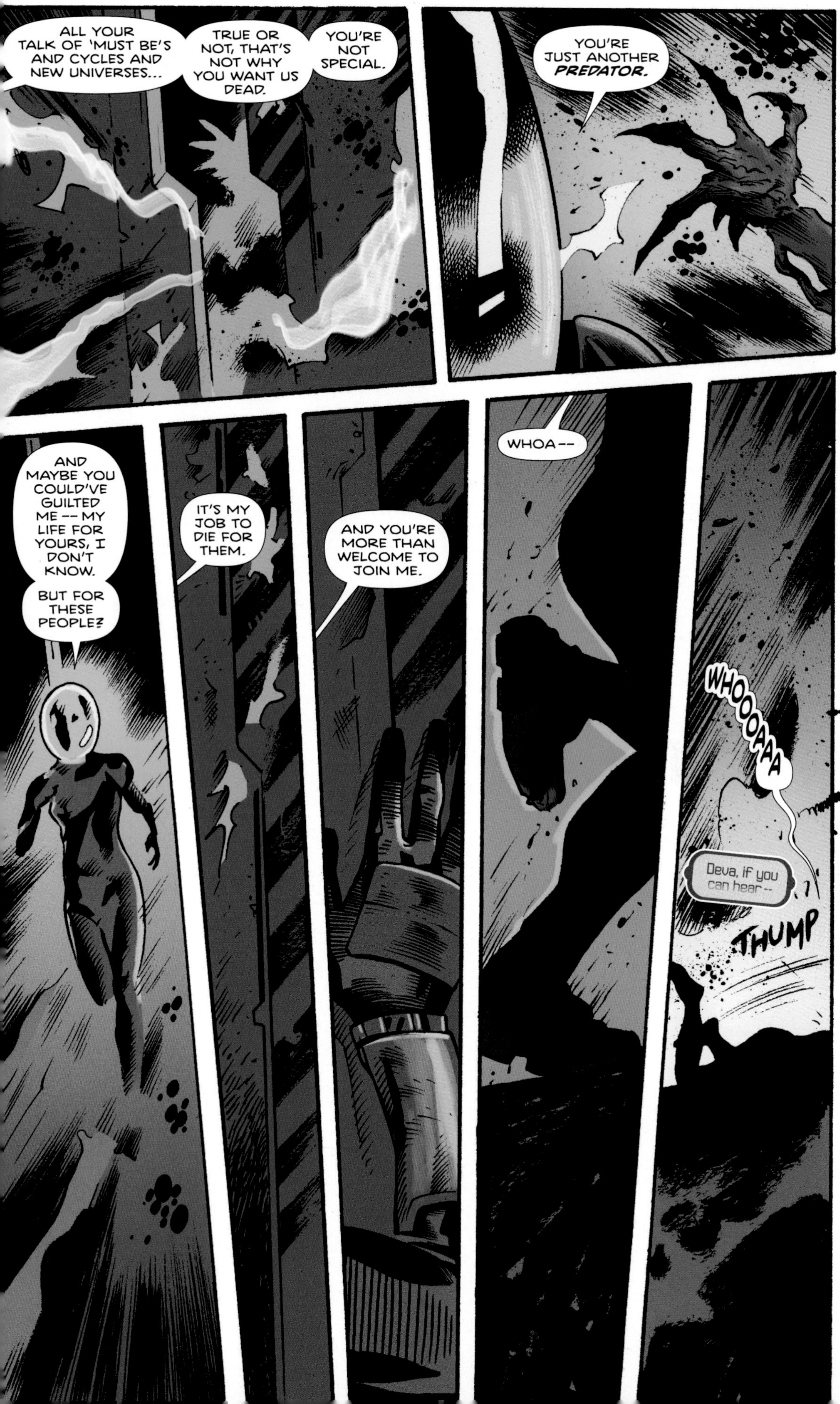
ALL YOUR TALK OF 'MUST BE'S AND CYCLES AND NEW UNIVERSES...
TRUE OR NOT, THAT'S NOT WHY YOU WANT US DEAD.
YOU'RE NOT SPECIAL.
YOU'RE JUST ANOTHER *PREDATOR.*
AND MAYBE YOU COULD'VE GUILTED ME -- MY LIFE FOR YOURS, I DON'T KNOW.
BUT FOR THESE PEOPLE?
IT'S MY JOB TO DIE FOR THEM.
AND YOU'RE MORE THAN WELCOME TO JOIN ME.
WHOA --
WHOOOAAA
Deva, if you can hear --
THUMP

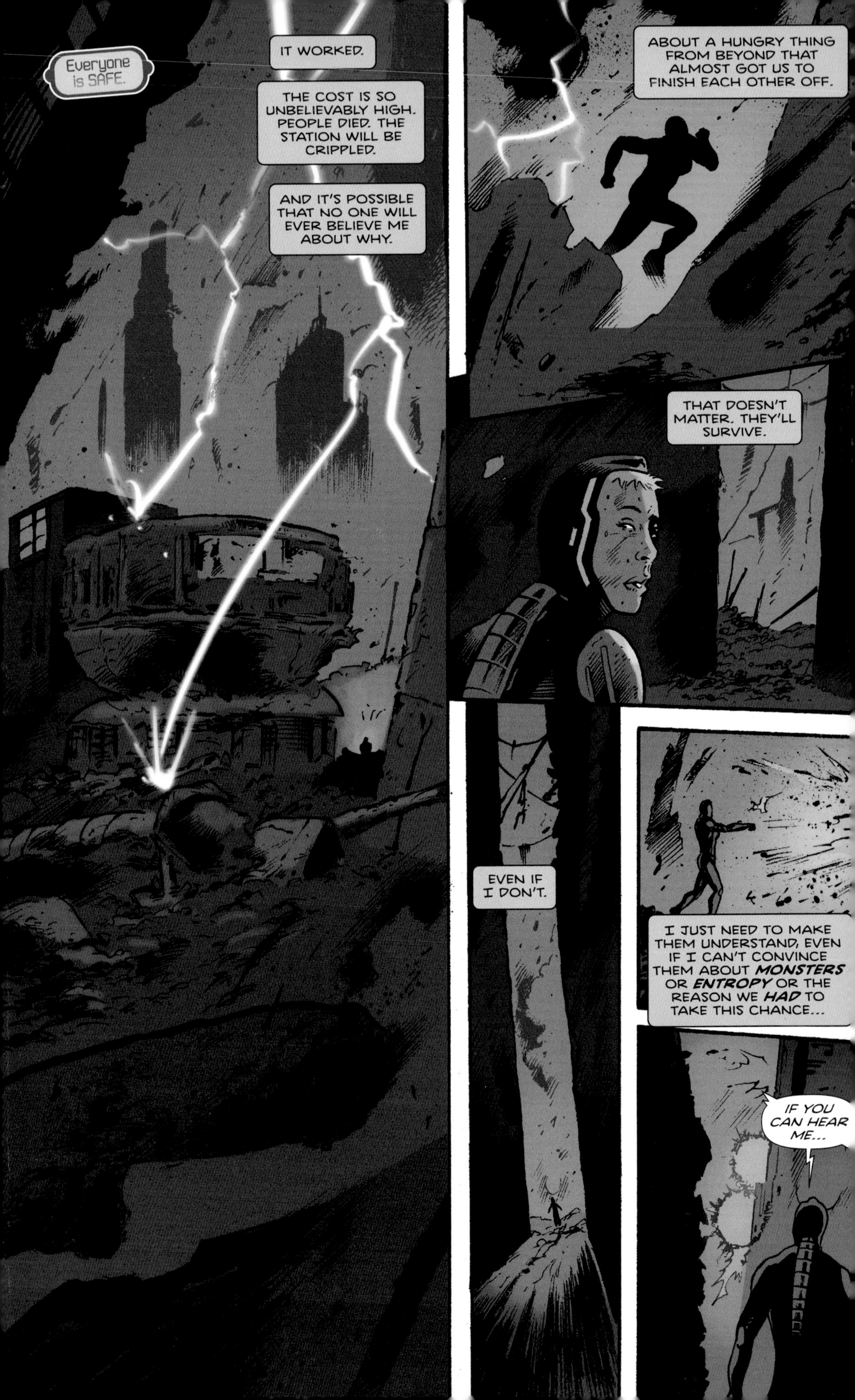
Everyone is SAFE.
IT WORKED.
THE COST IS SO UNBELIEVABLY HIGH. PEOPLE DIED. THE STATION WILL BE CRIPPLED.
AND IT'S POSSIBLE THAT NO ONE WILL EVER BELIEVE ME ABOUT WHY.
ABOUT A HUNGRY THING FROM BEYOND THAT ALMOST GOT US TO FINISH EACH OTHER OFF.
THAT DOESN'T MATTER. THEY'LL SURVIVE.
EVEN IF I DON'T.
I JUST NEED TO MAKE THEM UNDERSTAND, EVEN IF I CAN'T CONVINCE THEM ABOUT *MONSTERS* OR *ENTROPY* OR THE REASON WE *HAD* TO TAKE THIS CHANCE...
IF YOU CAN HEAR ME...

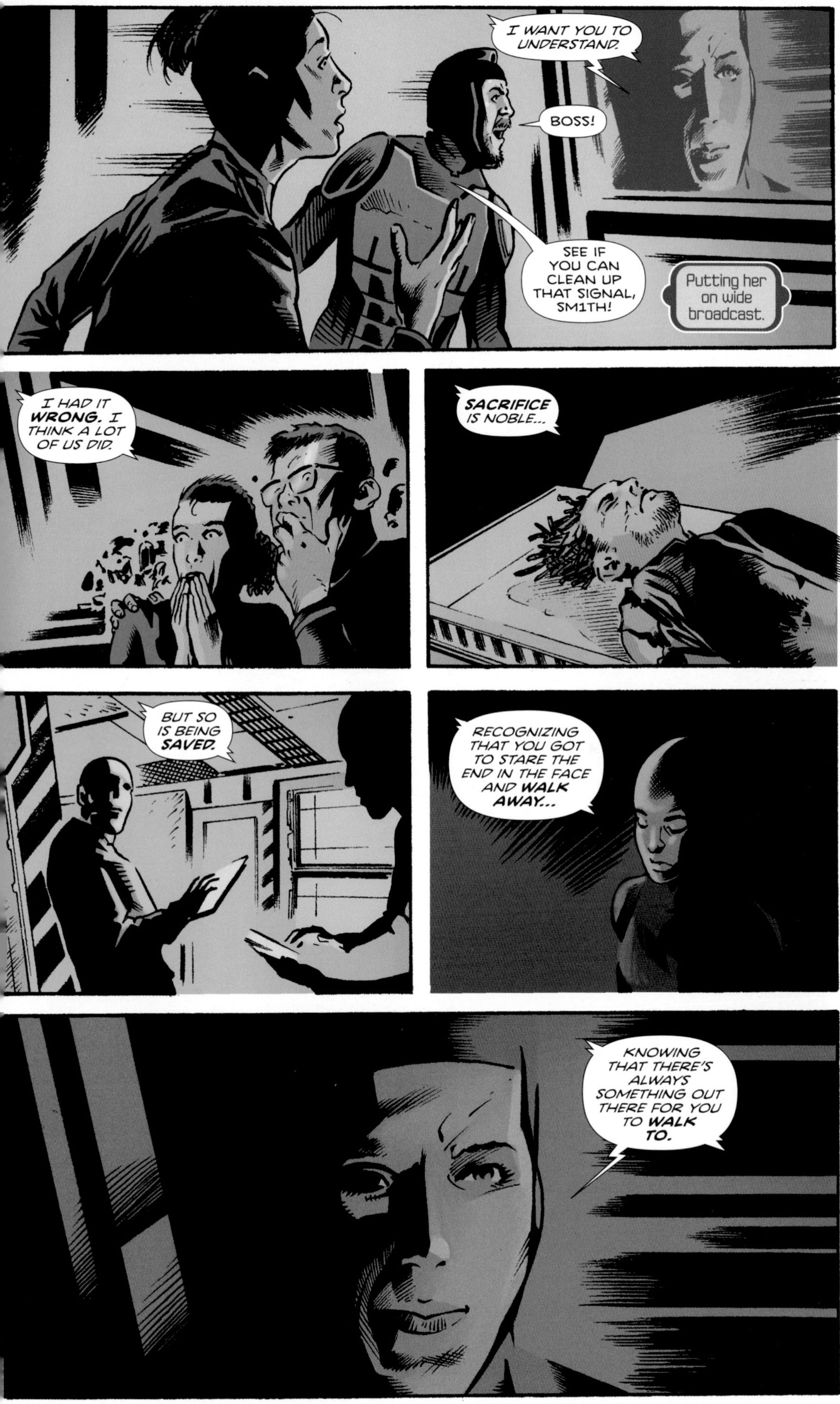
I WANT YOU TO UNDERSTAND.
BOSS!
SEE IF YOU CAN CLEAN UP THAT SIGNAL, SM1TH!
Putting her on wide broadcast.
I HAD IT WRONG. I THINK A LOT OF US DID.
SACRIFICE IS NOBLE...
BUT SO IS BEING SAVED.
RECOGNIZING THAT YOU GOT TO STARE THE END IN THE FACE AND WALK AWAY...
KNOWING THAT THERE'S ALWAYS SOMETHING OUT THERE FOR YOU TO WALK TO.

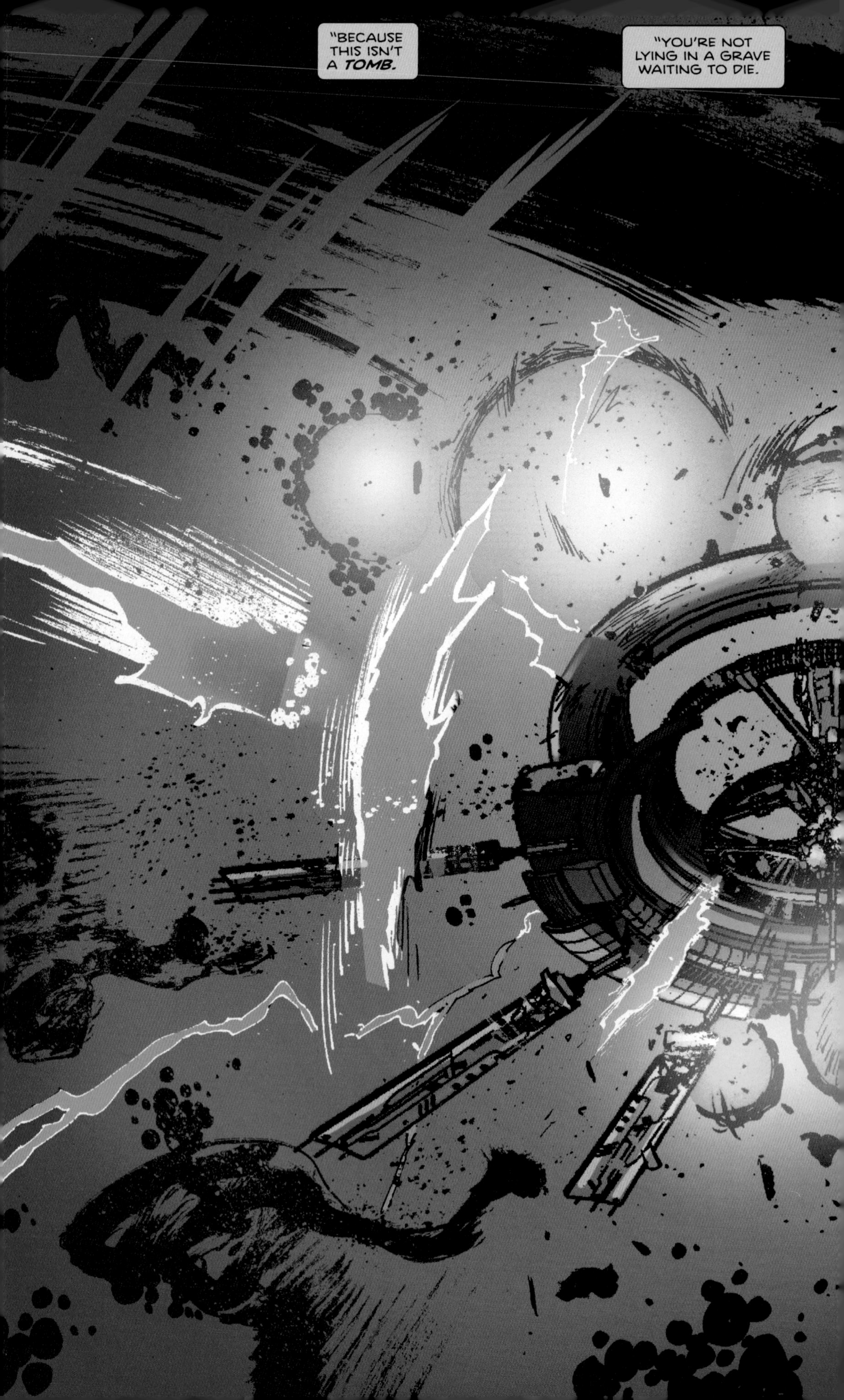
"BECAUSE THIS ISN'T A *TOMB.*
"YOU'RE NOT LYING IN A GRAVE WAITING TO DIE.

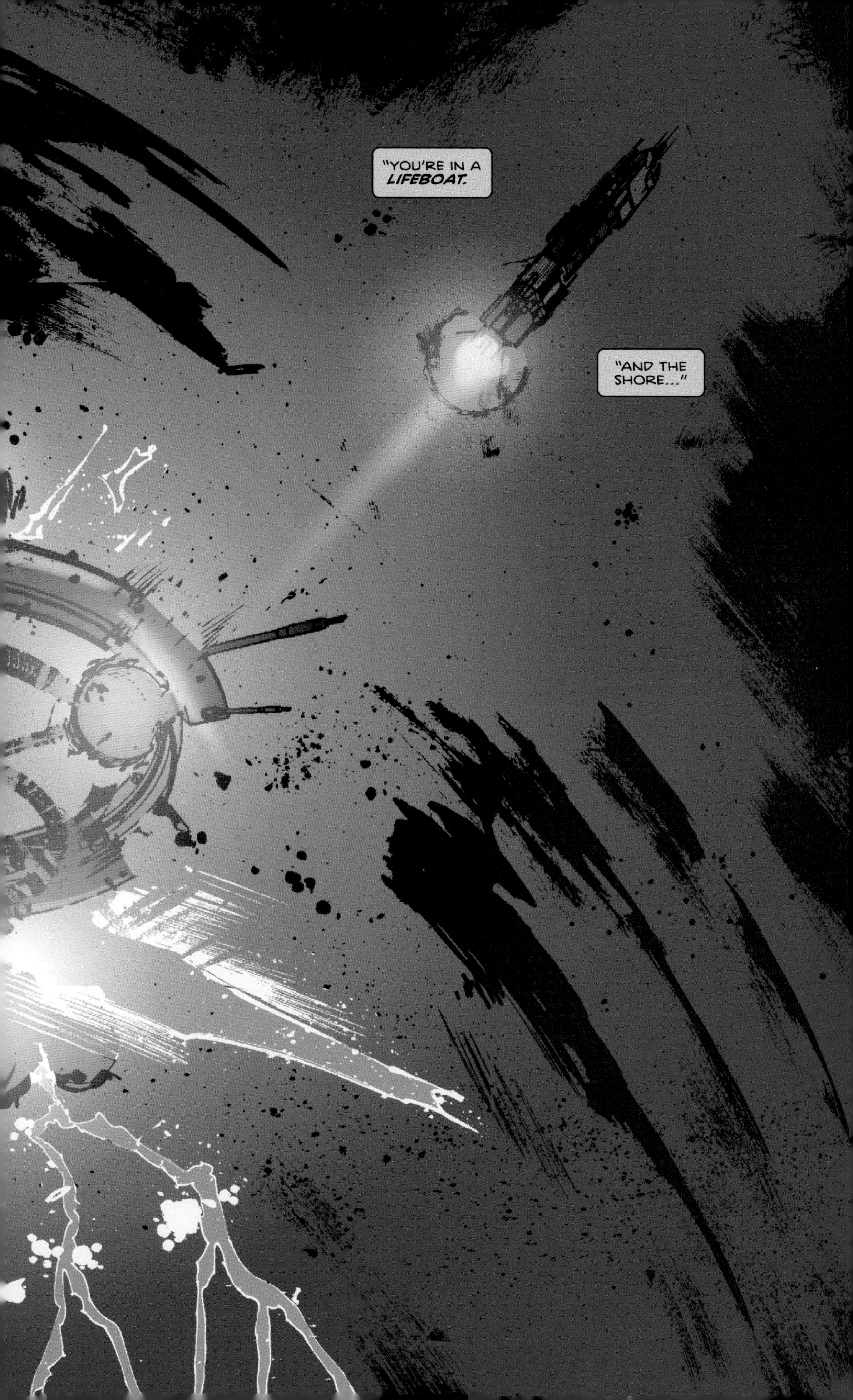
"YOU'RE IN A LIFEBOAT.
"AND THE SHORE..."

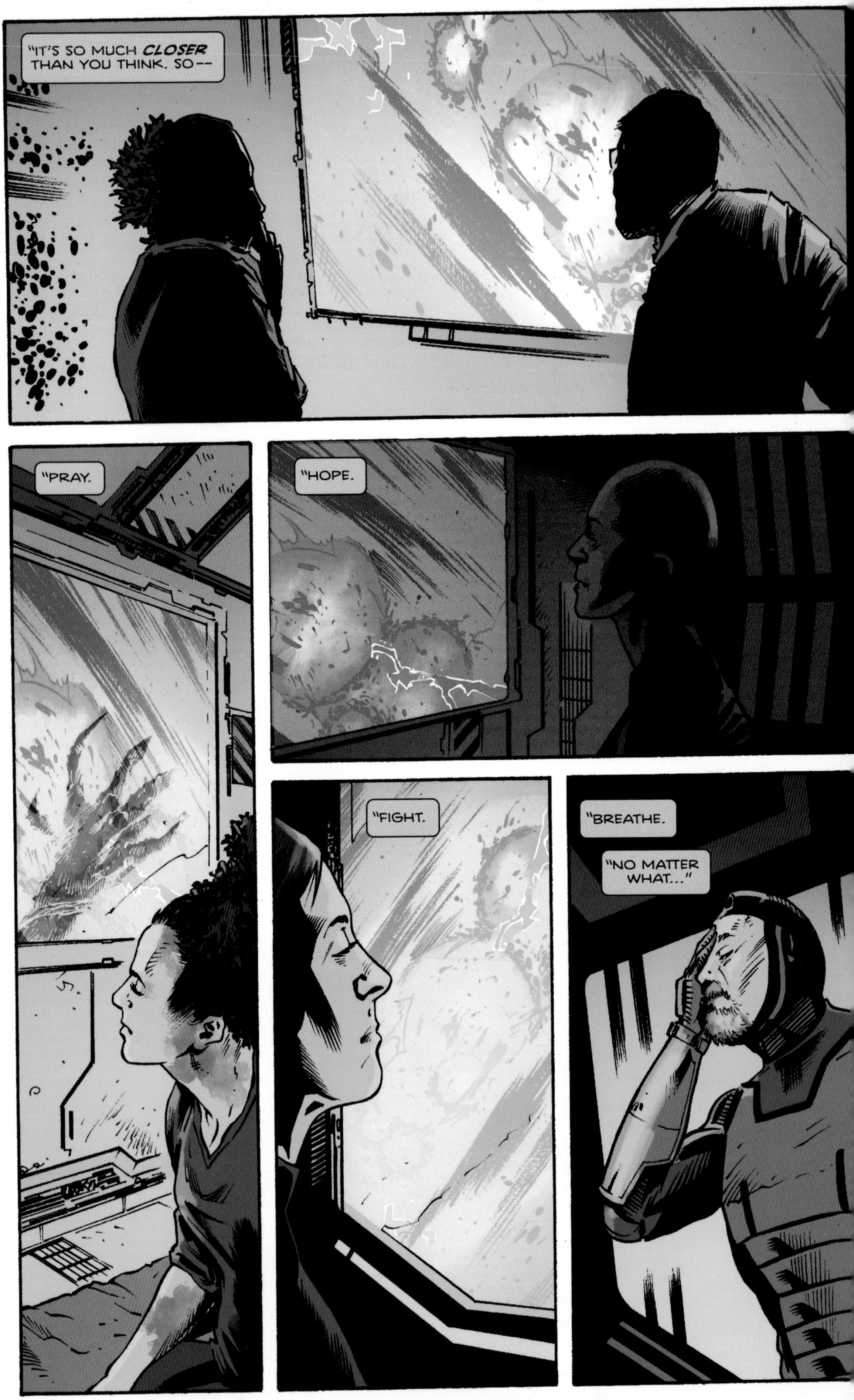
"IT'S SO MUCH *CLOSER* THAN YOU THINK. SO--
"PRAY.
"HOPE.
"FIGHT.
"BREATHE.
"NO MATTER WHAT..."

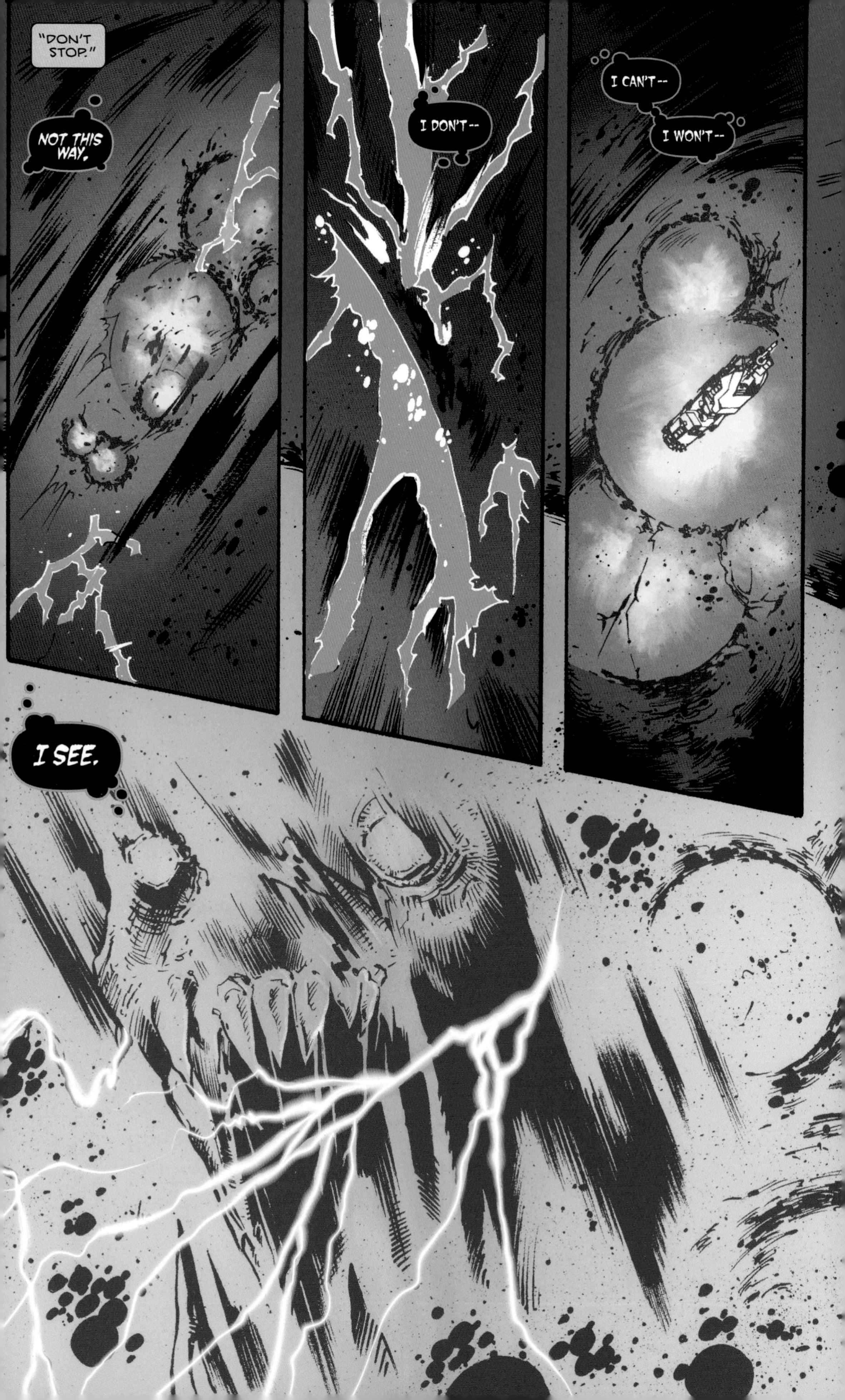
"DON'T STOP."
NOT THIS WAY.
I DON'T--
I CAN'T--
I WON'T--
I SEE.

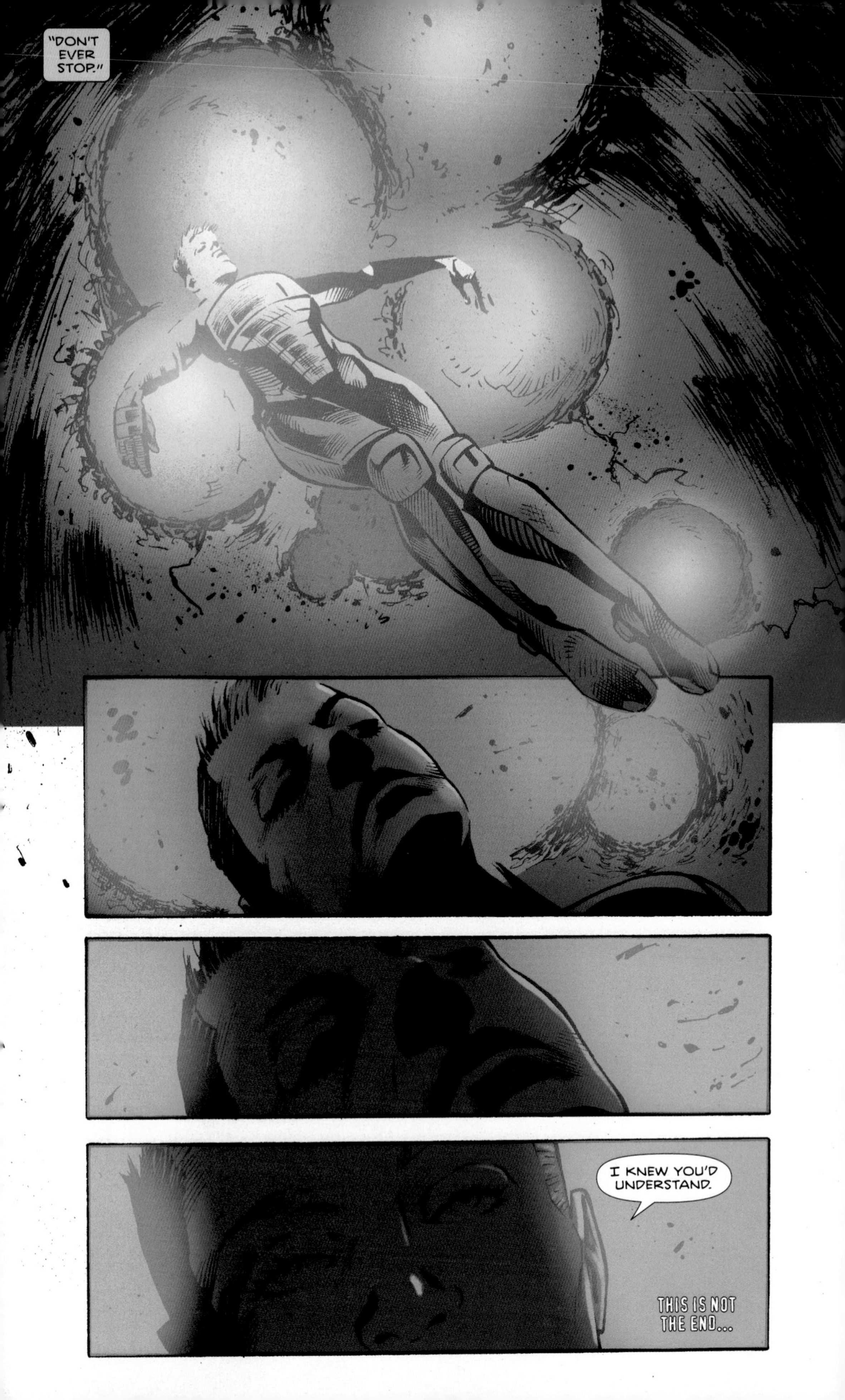
"DON'T EVER STOP."
I KNEW YOU'D UNDERSTAND.
THIS IS NOT THE END...

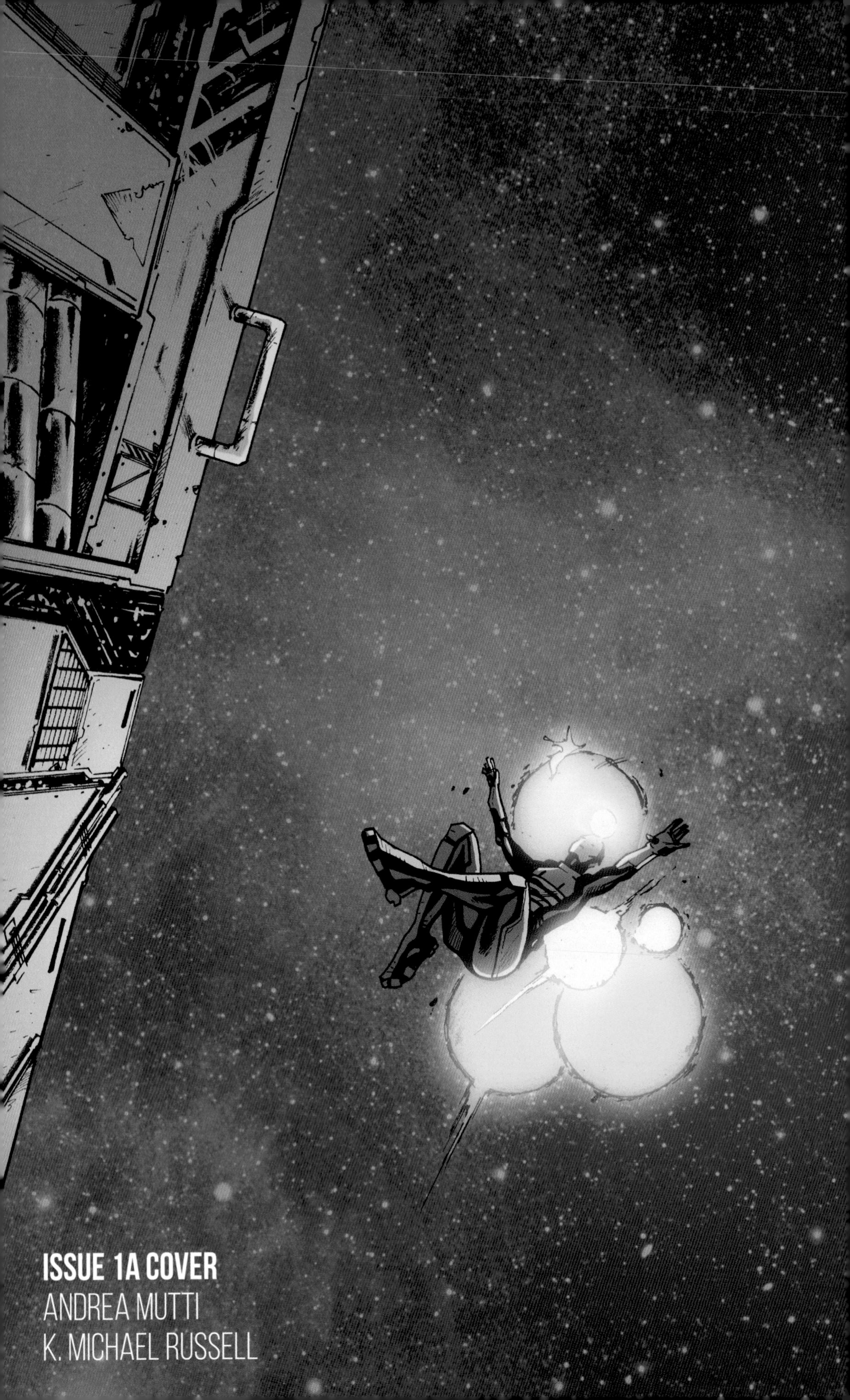

ISSUE 1A COVER
ANDREA MUTTI
K. MICHAEL RUSSELL

ISSUE 1B COVER
ANDREA MUTTI
K. MICHAEL RUSSELL

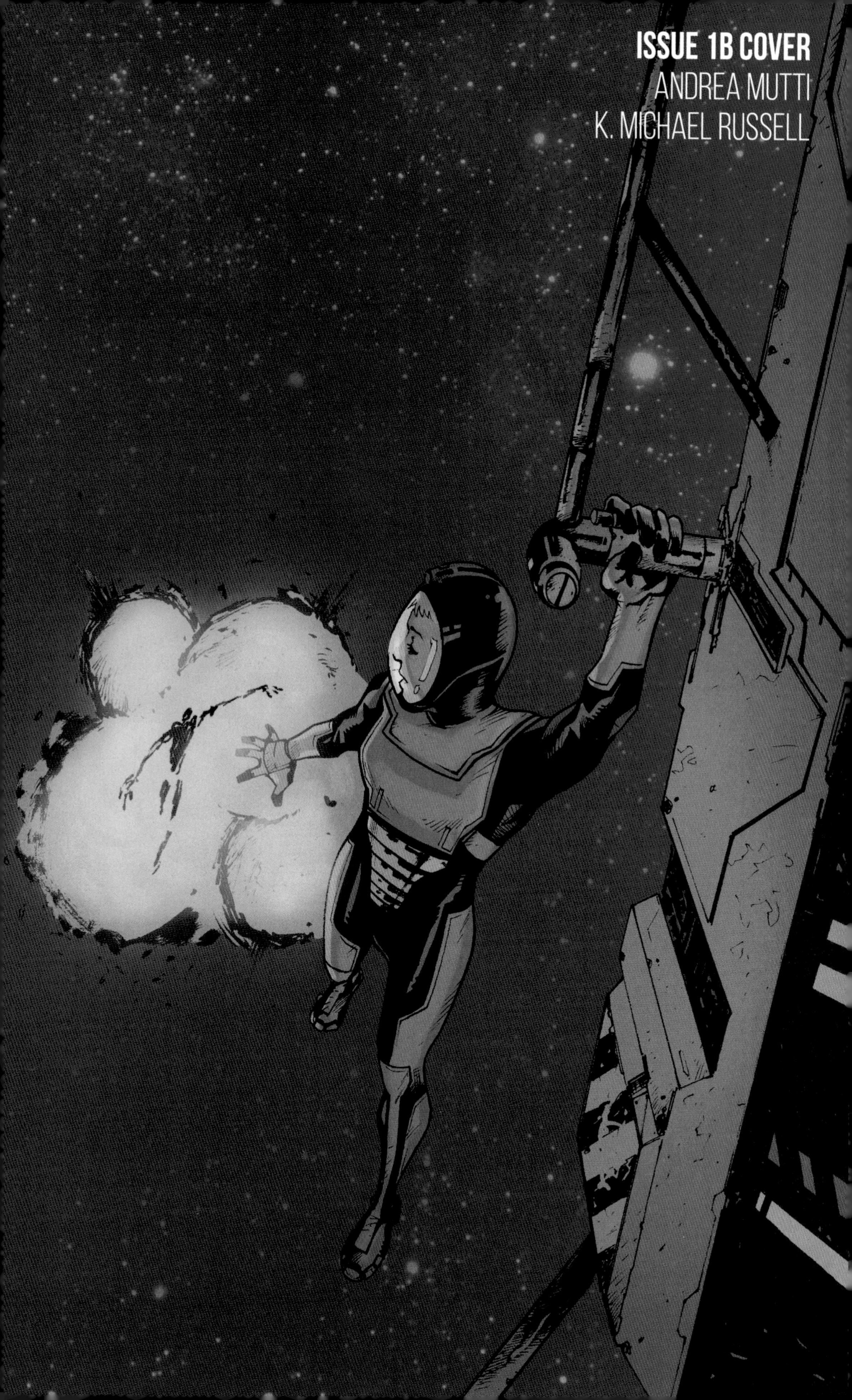

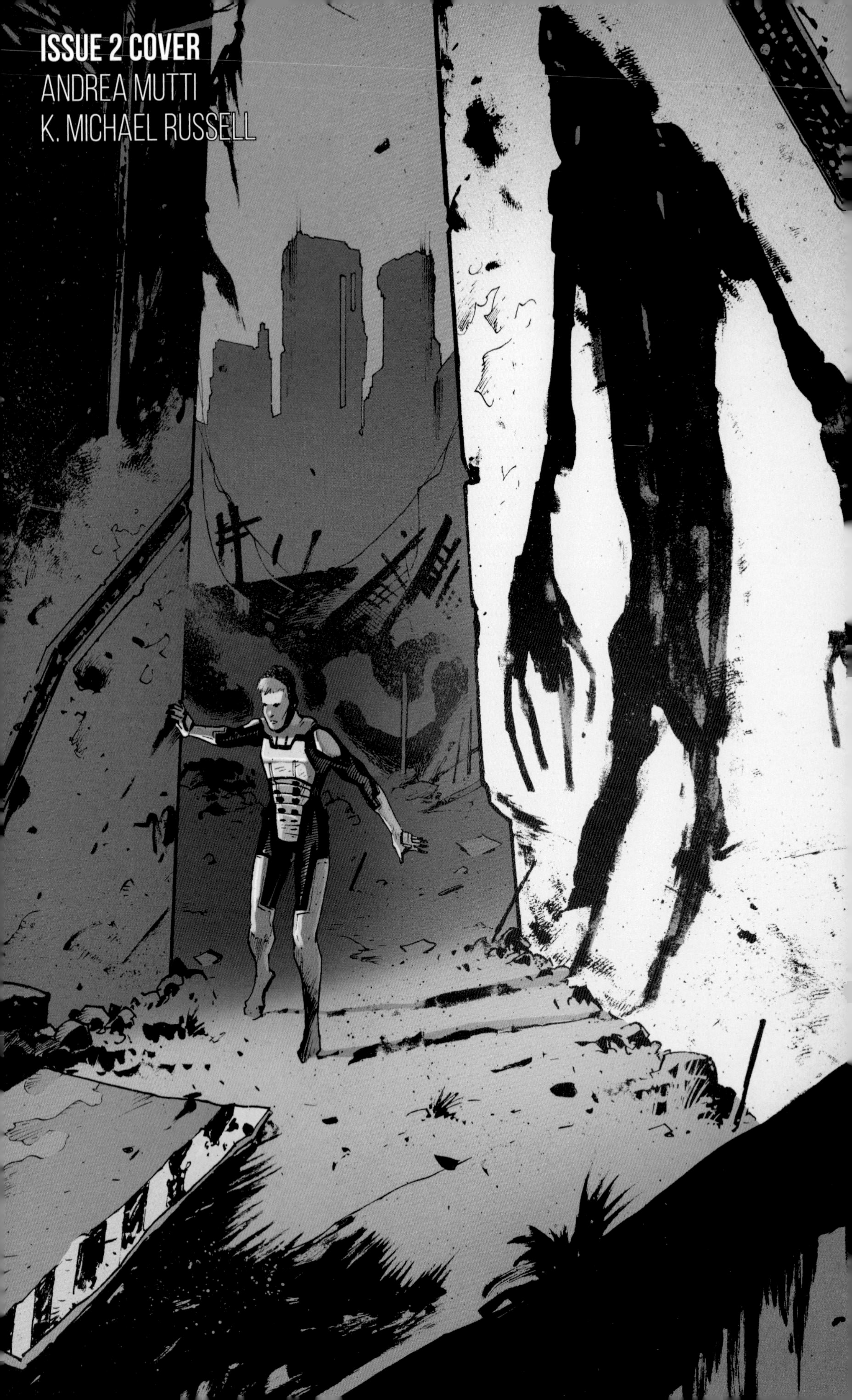

ISSUE 2 COVER
ANDREA MUTTI
K. MICHAEL RUSSELL

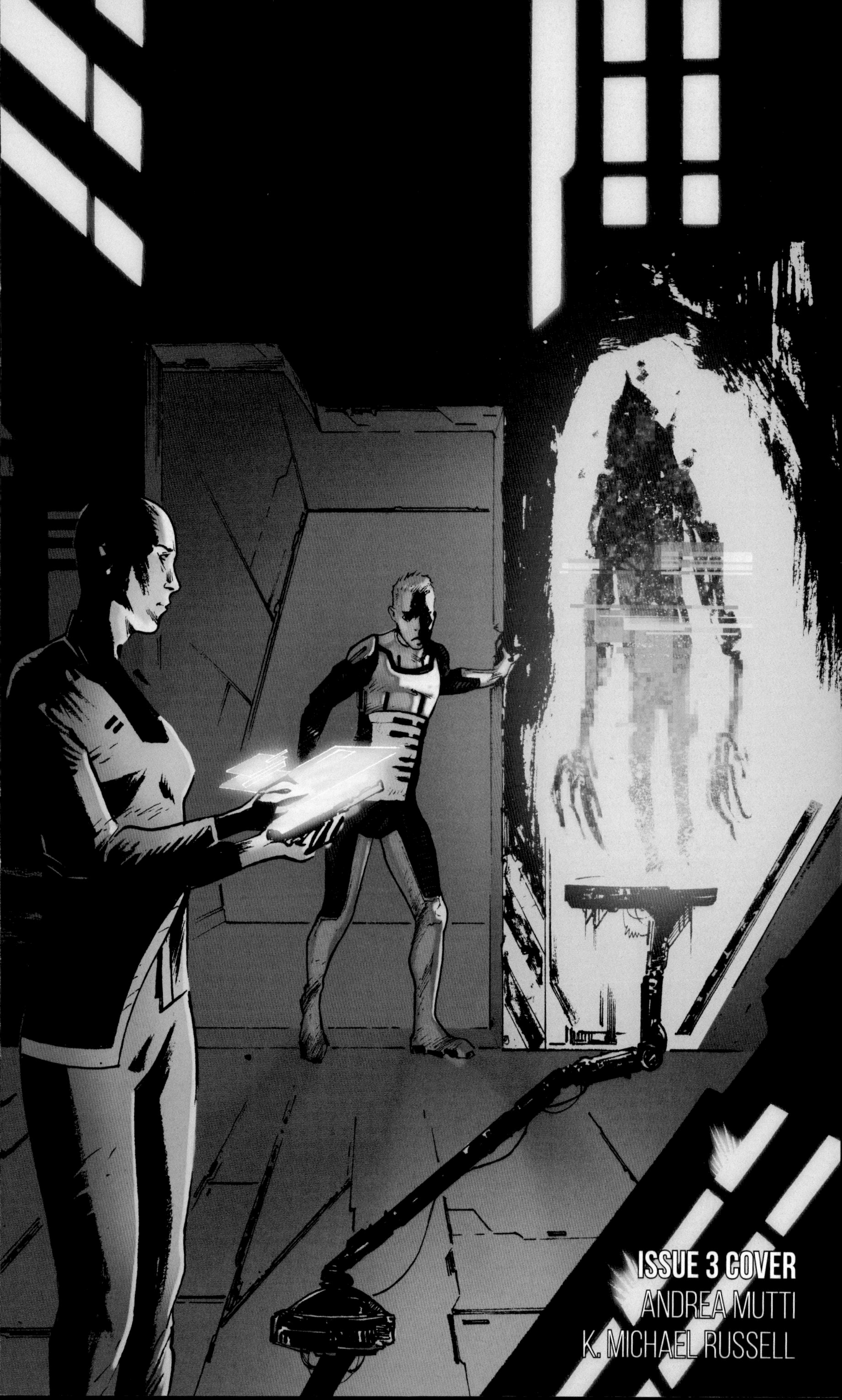
ISSUE 3 COVER
ANDREA MUTTI
K. MICHAEL RUSSELL

ISSUE 4 COVER
ANDREA MUTTI
K. MICHAEL RUSSELL

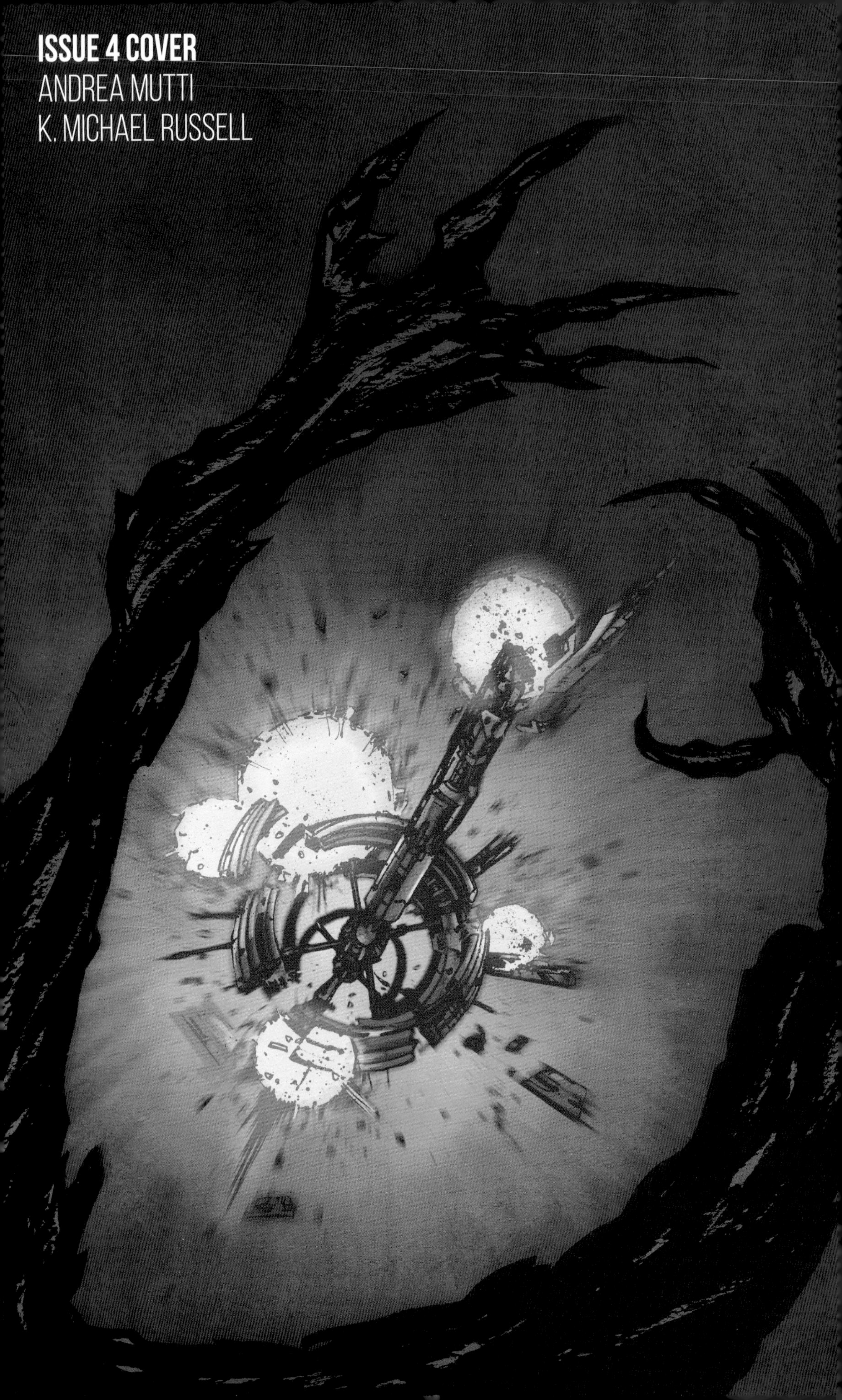

The original pitch for INFINITE DARK was called 'No Stars', and was intended to end at 5 issues, rather than multiple issue arcs.

On the following pages, you can see the original pitch document's 'cover', an inked version of the issue #1 cover, and the original colors for the issue #1 cover.

When we were still titling the book 'No Stars', we wanted to hammer home that emptiness, but it always looked weird on the page—especially colored. Eventually we went with a recolored image that had background.

Light and stars, justifying that it took place during Deva's first simulation and so there actually COULD be stellar bodies in the background. Plus, as Andrea pointed out, it just looked so much better that way.

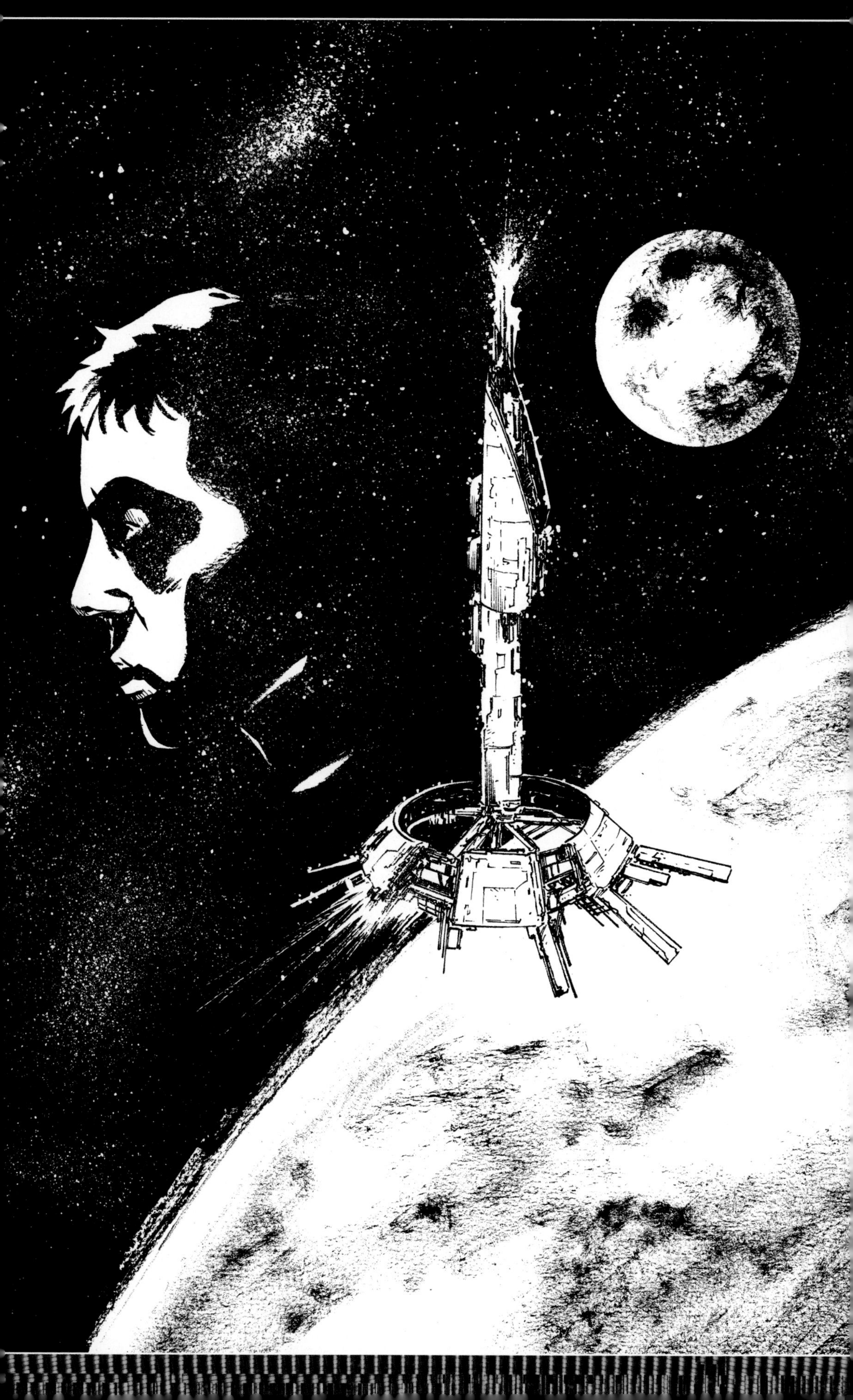

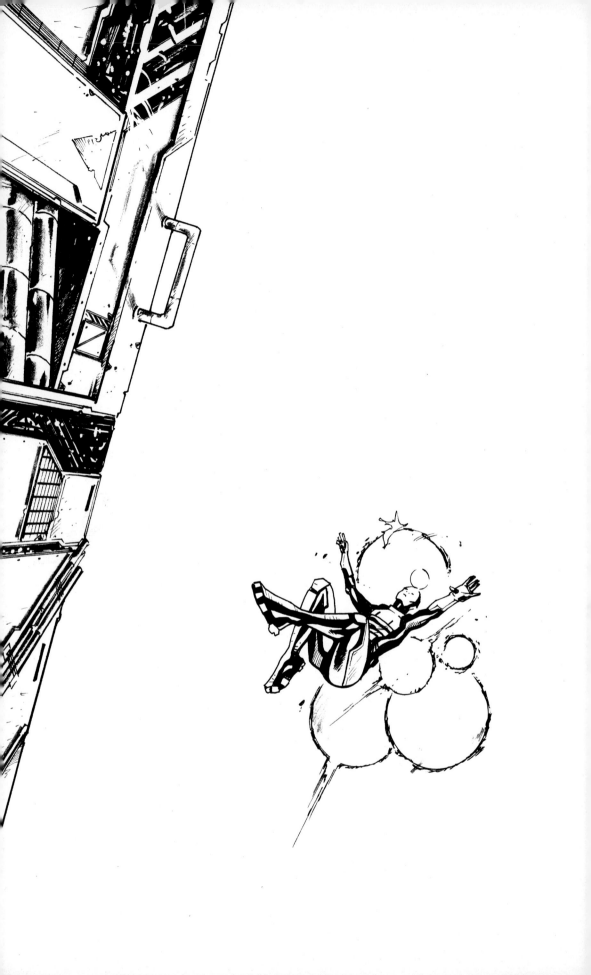

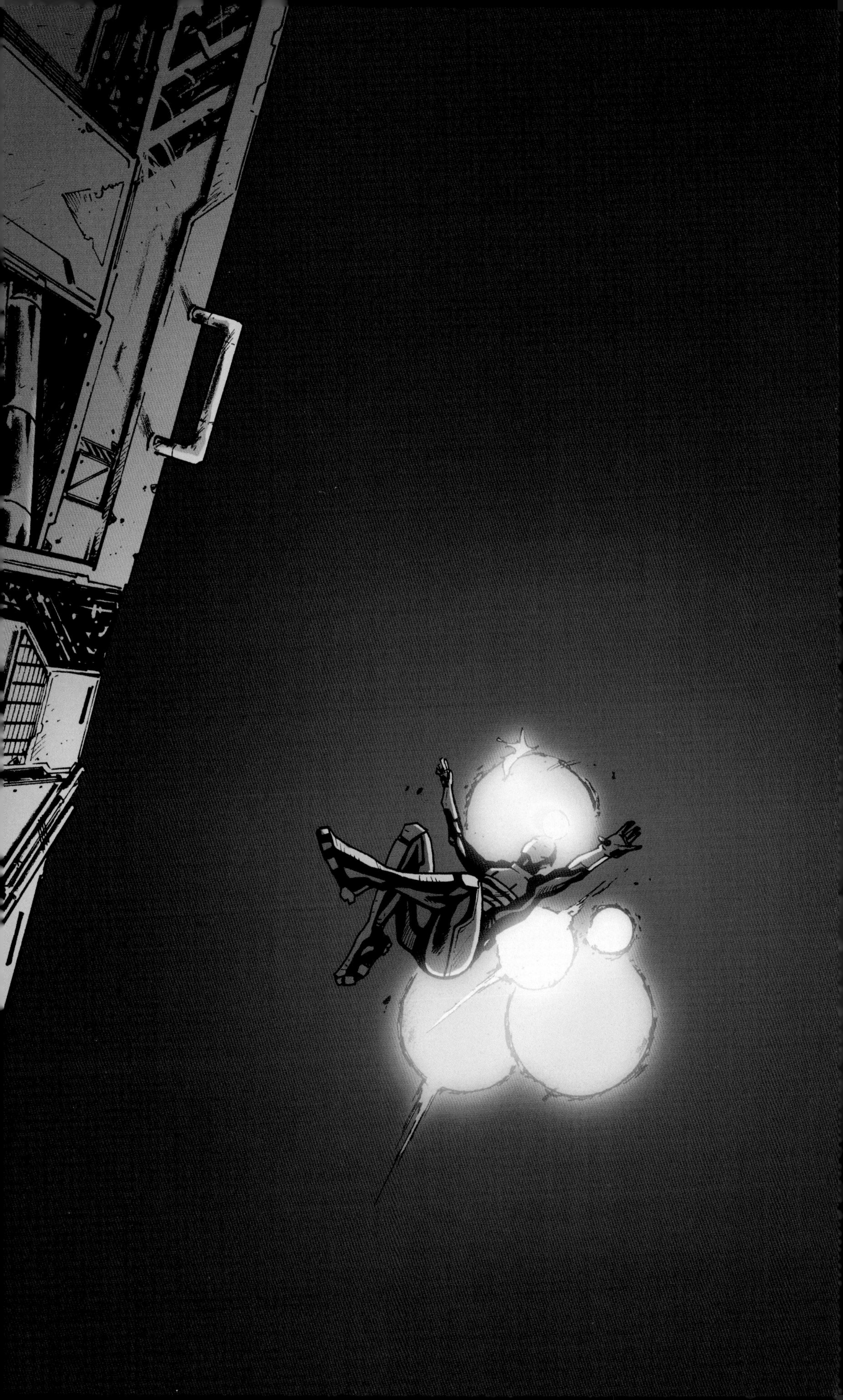

DISPATCHES FROM THE VOID

Horror can be a comfort.

It sounds strange, but even reading this final proof of this first issue, I find my anxieties about its launch – the maddening impostor syndrome that so many creators struggle with – taking a back seat. In the wake of a dead universe, in the face of a brutal murder in a shadowy space station, as a silhouette from the beyond the stars reaches out a hand to threaten the last human souls in existence… It's all too easy to lose myself in those big, primal terrors and let the day-to-day human problems fade away, for a little while.

DEVA KARREL

I started writing INFINITE DARK in June 2017, at that point in the midst of the worst depression of my life. I'd moved to New York City for reasons that felt all wrong, and I was feeling more and more like I'd made choices that were dooming me to feeling miserable and low and terrified of everything every day. I didn't know what to do or how to get out of it, but I knew that I needed to escape the cold, miserable feeling, and moreso that I needed to survive. So I worked on it, and I made some dramatic changes… and all the while, I was plugging away at this series.

I got better, of course. Not all the way, but better.

ALVIN SHEIDT

And helping me along the way wasn't just this project, but my old frightful friends – the *Alien* franchise, Stephen King novels, *Texas Chainsaw Massacre*, the *Outlast* games, and every spine-tingling, nightmare-inducing slice of spooky media I could get my hands on. I hope bits of them made it in here, too, even as they helped coax me out of my own rock bottom. Hopefully I've been able to show that strange comfort in INFINITE DARK – the knife edge between terror and wonder that something truly horrifying can bring. The fascination we have when facing down something that must not be merely endured or defeated but survived.

DR IKE CHALOS

When we first meet Deva in chapter one, she's in a bleak place – many of the residents on this void-ship are. She's carrying tons of irrational survivor's guilt. She lashes out at her friends and coworkers and berates herself later, lives with the day-to-day paranoia of maddening anxiety, and outside of every wall and window is the black, that void composed of pure entropy reminding her what's at stake, what she's outlived and enduring but is still there waiting for her should she fail.

And then along comes an Entity.

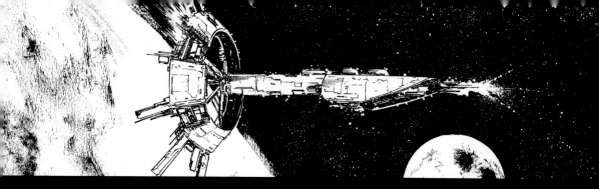

That was all a bit rambly, but what I'm trying to get across with this section is not just that working on this book was transformative for me when I was in a dark place – although it very much was – but moreso that for some of us, horror as a genre is a kind of balm for our wounded psyches.

For so many of my friends who live or die by the genre, we can readily think of times where some film or fiction with a monster or a murderer has helped us find new perspective on our depression, or give a strange face to our anxiety, or even just give us some blessedly big distraction when it seems like our own brains are more threatening than anything on the screen could be.

I've done my best to try and make that somewhat tangible for the characters in INFINITE DARK, and nothing would please me more than to hear that someone was helped or distracted by my spooky little book.

But this section – what I'm calling "Dispatches from the Void" – is for testimonials a little more in the abstract, a little rambly. Here some of the brightest and best horror writers and readers I know are going to talk about the two big themes at play in this book – Horror as a Genre, and Mental Health as a Monster – and how they've intersected in their own lives. And, in all likelihood, they'll do a much better job than I have.

So keep an eye on this space, and if you have your own thoughts on the matter, or just want to say something about the book in general, email submissions@topcow.com with "Dispatches from the Void" in the subject line, marked okay to print.

Thanks for reading, and I'll leave you with this comforting thought – one day, the universe will run out of time, and all reactions will stop as energy dwindles and all atoms freeze and crack. That is Heat Death, and it is inevitable and terrifying. But, lucky for you, you will be long, long dead before that happens.

-Ryan Cady

DISPATCHES FROM THE VOID

GUEST COLUMNISTS

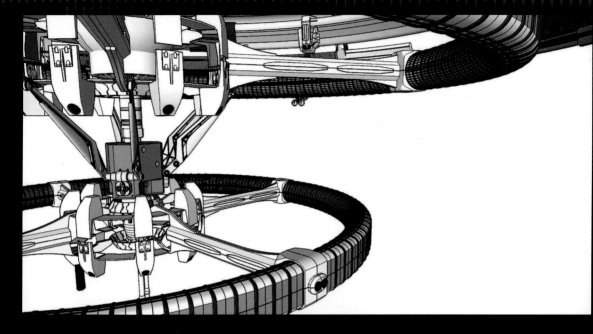

There's no point in starting this essay out by stating that horror has always reflected generational anxieties, even if that's what I want to talk about (to an extent). Every horror fan knows this. The idea of horror as a sort of societal coping mechanism to process the reintegration of Vietnam vets (the slasher boom) or the occupation of Iraq (torture porn) has been written about by people far smarter and more articulate than me. You already know the story. So instead let's talk about my parents' divorce.

About a year ago I found out they were separating. It's a weird thing to experience as an adult. I feel like we're conditioned to expect divorce to happen before we graduate high school and if we dodge that bullet before donning a cap and gown it'll never hit us. Unfortunately, divorce doesn't much care whether or not you see it coming. It was the conclusion of a drawn-out erosion that began with my sister's first attempt on her life and ended about four months after I moved out of state.

Watching your family implode from a distance allows you the luxury of putting the last couple of decades under a microscope and analyzing every moment when things went wrong. You notice cracks in the foundation that you didn't realize were there the whole time. And suddenly you realize that everything you understand about yourself is built on this foundation that you're only just now realizing, 26 years later, isn't as stable as you once realized. Your past can still kill you.

Does the idea of being left to deal with the consequences of the sins of a past generation sound familiar? If it does, congratulations, You Might Be A Millenial. We are a generation that has, over the last fifteen years or so, watched old men slowly fuck our world up irreparably. Climate change, healthcare, racial/gender/queer equality, you name it, they've fucked it up, beyond repair in some cases. And they'll be dead before they have to face the consequences. We are the ones inheriting their demons, the broken world they made. It will be up to us to fix it, if the fallout doesn't kill us first.

And yes, the idea of the past rearing its ugly head to ruin the lives of a bunch of innocent kids isn't exactly a recent convention in the genre. Still, it's hard to not notice it as a throughline in this modern golden age of horror. Films like *Insidious*, *It Follows*, and *Hereditary* follow characters who have evil thrust upon them, evil largely attached to a literal or figurative past generation. They're forced to grapple with these evils despite having done nothing to create them. It doesn't matter. Your past can still kill you.

I've found great comfort in these stories over the last year. From *The Guest* to *Oculus* and even the recent *The Haunting of Hill House* series, these stories have articulated my every anxiety about repeating the mistakes I didn't realize were shaping me. But as much as that potential terrifies me to my core, they've also provided a crucial assurance: even if you can't undo the sins of another, your future is yours to control.

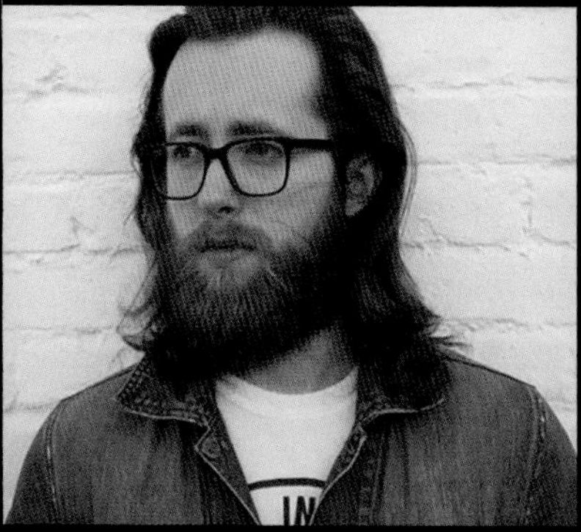

TRES DEAN (@tresdcomics) writes comics, including KILL THE DRUG WAR, DODGER, and JOEY RYAN: BIG IN JAPAN. He also writes words for the *Huffington Post*, *GQ*, *Men's Health*, and many others.

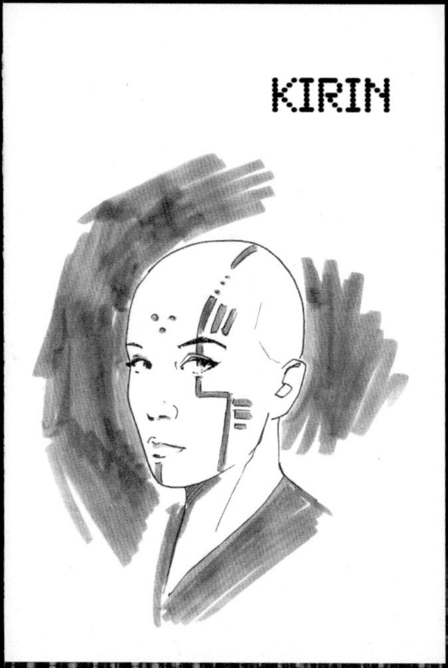
KIRIN

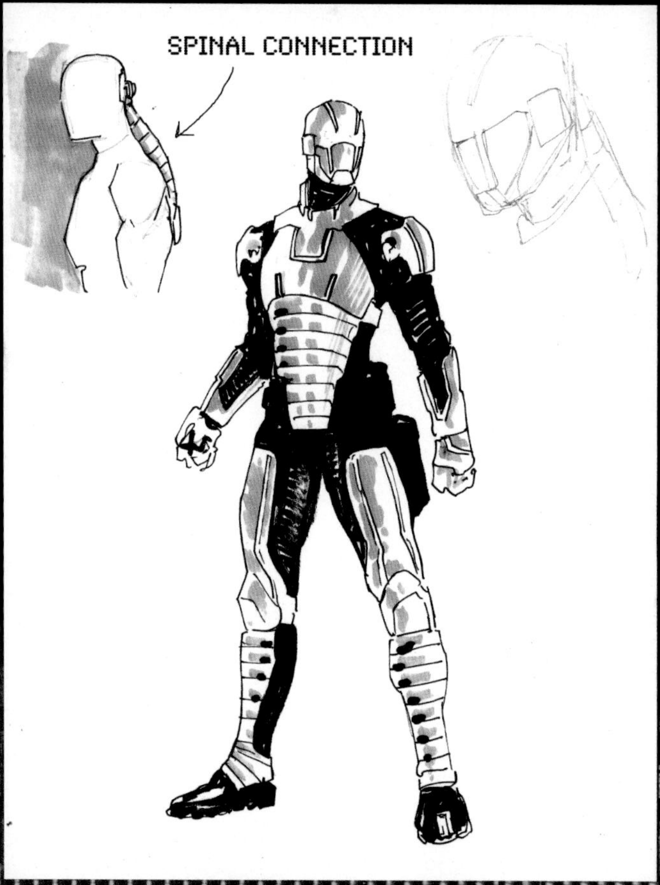
SPINAL CONNECTION

I've had a complicated relationship with horror. That is to say, when I was younger, I was so horror-sensitive that even looking at a movie poster for an incoming horror film would leave me lying awake in fear. As a child, my anxiety issues would manifest in the belief that I was in danger from whatever horrifying image I'd accidentally come across. I'd have constant nightmares and night terrors. I'd stay awake, believing that from the corner of my eye I could see something: Bloody Mary, that kid from *The Grudge*, a humanoid figment of my imagination with arms far, far too long. Hell, the very first *Pirates Of The Caribbean* film sent me screaming.

At some point, though, something shifted. I came across horror writing, which I loved, and which raised my curiosity for all the films I couldn't bring myself to watch. I started to test the edges of my fear, and my anxiety. I'd watch sections of horror movie clips, and when it was ultimately still too scary for me, I'd read the movie synopsis online. Trying out horror like this was a double-edged sword. When I was a teen, my anxiety was at its peak. Reading Lovecraft in those conditions only made me sure that my fears were real. There were demons under my couch. I would swear there was a whisper at my door. I would seek out a new horror figure to fear, and then be convinced it was coming for me, that I was not safe, I am in danger, I am in danger, I am in danger.

After I realized what a toll this behavior was taking on me, I stopped entirely. If anything remotely scary seemed like it was about to come on my screen, I would immediately mute the TV/video/whatever and turn away. My mental health improved, but I thought I was done with horror for good. That is, until I stumbled across a horror podcast. It had been years since I let myself interact with horror at all, and that old curiosity couldn't help but creep in me. Horror felt like it was no good for me, but I was drawn to it, I felt…well, comfortably uncomfortable in the space. Horror podcasts helped ease me in once more. I haven't turned back since.

I've realized now, more in control of my anxiety and more time to be introspective, why my complicated love for horror exists. Horror is a genre that validates the person saying, "Something is wrong." That person is always right, and usually survives in the end. That character, most times, uncovers a truth about the unknowable and dispels it forever with the newfound knowledge. I have anxiety. I know what it is to feel unreasonable terror, and to try to take it apart with logic. Even further, horror for me is to dive headfirst in the uneasiness of my mind. My fear might be real, but after the credits roll? I survived. Horror, for me, is surviving.

NADIA SHAMMAS (@Nadia_Shammas_) is a comic writer and editor best known for creating *CORPUS: A Comic Anthology of Bodily Ailments*. When not exploring the eldritch horrors of Brooklyn, she's working on her upcoming graphic novel or trying to win the love of her cat, Lilith.

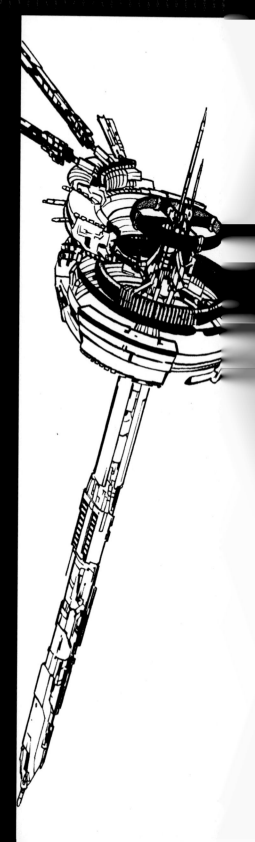

always tell folks that *Alien* is my favorite movie, but
that *The Texas Chain Saw Massacre* is my favorite
horror movie. It's not that I don't think *Alien* is a horror
movie (it is) or that I don't find it frightening on its own
terms (I do), but that *The Texas Chain Saw Massacre*
possesses one quality *Alien* never will: the It Could
Happen to You! factor. My chances of coming
face-to-Leatherface with a cannibal clan are low—
I live in Queens—but the odds of me ever qualifying
for space travel are infinitesimally smaller. I'm
claustrophobic, I have poor eyesight, and a flair for
vegan baking is not a skill that translates well to living
aboard the International Space Station.

Even supernatural horror movies possess more of
the It Could Happen to You! factor than the average
sci-fi terror tale. I've woken up in the middle of the
night, noticed an oddly shaped shadow in the corner,
and briefly convinced myself that I, of all the billions
of humans to have walked the Earth, was about to
experience the very first real ghost attack. It's an
utterly irrational thought, but unless NASA pays your
bills, it's much closer to the realm of reality than
worrying about getting stranded on an interstellar
cargo freighter with an acid-blooded extraterrestrial.

For the vast, vast majority of human beings, terra
firma is where we were born, and terra firma is where
we will die. And that's where the scary part comes in:

What if we had to leave?

In INFINITE DARK, the story opens after the heat
death of the universe, as a small band of humans
persist in the nothingness. In the months since
Ryan sent me the first issue, it's hit many of us that
making it to the end of the universe is an optimistic
fantasy. A highly publicized climate study posited that
we have just over a decade to come together and
address climate change on a scale the world has
never seen—during an era in which several of the
most crucial countries in the battle are led by far-right
hyper-capitalists who would chop down the last tree in
existence if they could use it to print another dollar.

One of my greatest anxieties isn't just death, but knowing that it's coming and that I can't stop it. Learning that certain ecological doom isn't just inevitable, but will make its presence known during my lifetime, is like receiving a terminal medical diagnosis on an almost incomprehensible scale. I'm depressed for my own future, sure, but now I look at my friends' new babies and wonder if they'll be *Mad Max* characters in 40 years—or if conditions will destabilize so massively that we suffocate or roast in one massive die-off.

When I watch *Alien* or *Event Horizon* or read something like INFINITE DARK, a quiet little part of me knows I'm witnessing a danger that I'll never experience in real life. But with each new sobering article I read about coral extinctions, collapsing ice shelves, and political decisions that further endanger our fragile ecosystem, being firmly planted here on Earth feels less like a safety blanket and more like a guillotine sliding closer to the nape of my neck. I shouldn't be envious of the crews of The Nostromo or The Orpheus, but outer space is starting to look like an escape hatch just out of reach. It's cold and dark and dangerous out there, sure, but—all things considered—I wouldn't mind the option.

STEVE FOXE is the author of many licensed children's books and a few really cool comics he can't talk about just yet. He is the editor for *Paste Magazine*'s comic section and lives in Queens, where he tweets about comics, horror movies, gay stuff, and his boyfriend's dog at @steve_foxe.

Werewolf in London. I watch it a few times a year, but this time I had to turn it off before the legendary transformation scene was complete. My skin was crawling, my arms were covered in goosebumps, and I was sweating...but not because I was afraid. Because I knew what it felt like. Every pop of David's vertebra, every grinding crunch of his distorting limbs, reminded me of my own shapeshifting experience.

You see, just over a year ago, I gave birth to my son. With all the changes of new parenthood, the most unexpected was how it altered my relationship to horror movies, particularly body horror. It no longer feels like exciting escapism but like a vivid documentary of some of the most bizarre moments of my life.

When I see a character contorting and writhing with the labors of their mutations, I think about the end of my first trimester when my body was flooded with the hormone, Relaxin. This hormone made my joints begin to spread, my pelvic ligaments stretch, upped my volume of blood by 50%, and increased elasticity in my connective tissue—basically, it expanded my body's capacity to hold a 14-week old parasite, reshaping my physical structure to accommodate its growth. And it hurt. My back ached as my spine shifted its curvature and I was often out of breath. Panting, bloated with blood, anatomy twisting into a new shape...sound familiar?

No good werewolf is complete without sprouting hair, and that phase of my transformation came with the second trimester. A bounty of estrogen made my curls grow in thicker, longer—and not just on my head. I was shaving my legs every single day, waxing my upper lip once a week, using some of my rapidly depleting energy to prevent myself from going full The Howling. And then the bleeding gums started. Sure, I had that stereotypical pregnancy glow, but no one noticed once they saw my red, oozing smile. Not that I was smiling much, since right around this time the hungers arrived.

The cravings were insatiable. I dreamt of devouring waterfalls of gravy...but thanks to my son's placement, his kicking limbs dislodged most of what I ate, causing me to throw up a few times a day. So, I had to stick to soft, low acid foods with tons of heartburn medication. To compensate for my primal longings, my body made me crave ice. And then I had an uncontrollable desire to chew on sponges. It sounds crazy in the abstract but when you think about it, it was as close to bones and flesh as I could get. Shredding sponges with my teeth and crunching shards of ice was pure ecstasy, and though it did nothing for my nutritional needs, it was a balm for my hormonal demands. Whenever I see a movie where a poor shifting creature runs to the fridge to make a meat-shake, I can't help but empathize, for I know what it means to have unnatural needs. Except mine were described as "magical" and "the beauty of nature" where theirs are more accurately labeled as horror.

The last phase of my transformation was during the delivery of my baby. At this point, my body had bled, swollen, expanded, and nurtured an enormous child for me to expel. With the help of an epidural and two days of labor, I did just that—and then for the first time in almost a year, I was alone in my body. The absence of the second skeleton inside of me was magical and devastating, much like I imagine the come down is the morning after a werewolf's first full moon. To have such power only to have it evaporate in one gush of fluids, one last howl of pain, was the hollowest I've ever felt. The emotional and physical exertion of pregnancy, labor, and delivery resulted in absolute joy upon seeing my beautiful son's face—and a lingering trauma about the changes I experienced.

So, while I may still love horror, I can't watch it the same way I once did...because I lived it. And in my franchise? The survivors never look back.

CASEY GILLY is a comics writer, horror fan, and mother. The first two prepared her for the third.

Wow. Here we are, end of the universe and beyond. Where do I start?

Thank you, for sure. Thanks to you for reading this volume. I hope it resonated with you, comforted you, inspired you, entertained you, and – if I did my job right – scared you, at least a little.

Thanks to everyone at Top Cow – Elena, Vince, Henry, and of course Matt Hawkins and Marc Silvestri – and all of Image Central for taking chances on us and making this book happen. Thanks to the most cheerful artist alive, Andrea Mutti, for starting this with me; to colorist extraordinaire K. Michael Russell for bringing light to the Orpheus; to the patient Troy Peteri for lettering the hell out of it…and calling me out when there were too many damn words.

Thanks to my friends and family for everything, and thanks to my ever-patient and ever-brilliant girlfriend for being better than me at this whole writing garbage, but still being supportive as hell. Corny as it is, thanks to Neil Gaiman, and Shirley Jackson, and Ridley Scott/Dan O'Bannon, and Junji Ito, and, well, the list goes on and on. I stand on the shoulders of horror and sci-fi giants and I am inspired by their work daily.

But also…thanks to the bad times. Thanks to the miserable cross-country moves and the occupational hazards and the personal garbage and the random, senseless anxiety that creeps up on all of us, sometimes. Being a tortured artist is bullshit, sincerely, but this specific book wouldn't exist without all that doom and gloom.

INFINITE DARK was always supposed to be a book about survival. About staring down the bad stuff – be it fear, or guilt or depression, or cosmic monstrosity – and charging through it. And that's what this first volume – I hope – accomplished. These first four issues were what I pitched to Top Cow almost two years ago, and now that they're alive, and in your hands, I couldn't be happier.

But as Deva says at the end, while survival is most certainly a virtue, there's more to it, isn't there? There's something that comes next, after you beat your demons, and to be true to form, there's more to the story of the Orpheus and the people on it. The universe ended, but stories didn't – thank God.

So, if you've enjoyed what we did here, stick around awhile – there's a whole new story unfolding. Not just the aftermath of this one, but a horizon; what comes next isn't about surviving, but about setting forth. Though if you think this cheery afterword of mine means smooth sailing, rest assured – I'm far from done with terror on board the Orpheus. As you'll see in the next volume, the Entity was far from the last of their worries.

Check the pseudoreality field, grab your void-suit, and watch out for stray entropy bursts – it's full speed ahead, into the Infinite Dark.

Ryan Cady
January 2019

I wanted to close out this first volume with a very special DISPATCHES FROM THE VOID from my story editor, Alex Lu, who I owe so much and couldn't have written this volume without. Seriously, the dude's a genius…and a pretty nice guy. But first, I wanted to respond to some fanmail we received when we first started this segment —

I finally got my hands on your series and I find myself stunned. At first look, this series seems like a simple horror copy cat. "Oooooh a monster invading a space station." Didnt seem too intense or original. Picking it up, that is what I expected. However, as i read the first issue I found a connection, the feelings and cloudy emotions of Deva speak to how I feel most days. I dont know why or how, but the character connected to me. Which does not often happen to me with comics. I read lots of them. More than is healthy.

So I find myself adoring the work you have done. I am also sad it has not been pushed more heavily by the publishers. This is a gem. Even if it does turn into a run of the mill horror story. It's the emotion, or cloudy struggle to even feel emotion properly, that will have me here until the end of this wonderful series. Thank you. To the whole team. I am with you all to the heat death of your gorgeous series.
—Nelsen W.

Thank you, Nelsen! If it makes you feel better, I probably also read too many comics, when I have the time. I'm glad that the people on board the Orpheus resonate with you – the characters mean a lot to me, and that they could mean something to other people, too, just makes my day. Seriously appreciate your kind words on the series – and honestly, both Top Cow and Image have been wonderful to me as publishers. Let's hope more fans and retailers feel like you do, too, and pick up more copies as we move into volume two!

I just wanted to let you know how much I enjoyed Infinite Dark #1. I actually read it during a cancelled session (I'm a clinical psychologist) and it resonated with me more than I expected. Stories and story-making are therapeutic not just for escaping our problems and drudgery but for reminding us about our humanity. I think you've captured this with a finely executed premise that literally brings us to the brink of our existence. Can't get any worse than that so whatever's going on here in the real world maybe isn't so bad. We can get through it all, no matter what. I loved the artwork. Some great moments like the entry into the Dark Sector and Scheidt's exit into space. Beautifully eerie. While reading I was reminded of Lovecraft's bleak vision of ancient cosmic gods manipulating our reality. It was like a soft bass line throughout the story. Excellent.

Most frightening for me however was the idea of a super-AI doing my job while managing 26 other functions. Screw you Sm1th! No shrinks on the Orpheus? Not one? Not that I'm applying for the gig... Thanks to the whole team for making a little unexpected free time at work go by way too fast. I'm in for the ride and looking forward to what comes next.
—Juan Carlos M, PhD.

Anytime someone cites my influences, I'm truly flattered. And the idea of a psych professional reading our book and not hating it? Whew! Goosebumps. I'm glad we could entertain and add some chills. As you saw in Issue #2, there were some shrinks on board, mostly to manage and analyze SM1TH's data, but, uh, as you saw in this issue, well…Guess there's no job security in any fields at the end of the universe, eh? Yikes! Thanks for reading, and hope you stick around!

I've been struggling with depression, anxiety and cripplingly low self-esteem all my life and finally found the courage to reach out for help. I'm in therapy now, hoping to improve somewhat. I always find it kinda comforting to witness people doing what they love. Something I've been unable to do up to now, since I don't even know what I want exactly. I never looked at the horror genre like a balm for our sore psyche, but it makes sense, now that I think about it. Thanks for the perspective!

Infinite Dark #1 was a great start for the series, I enjoyed it very much and am thrilled to witness it continue. Know that you've won over an interested reader who might find some kind of solace in reading your story. This is the first time I've ever wrote a submission to a comic publisher. I guess your words reached me. Thank you for your hard work, keep it up as long as you're having fun doing it! I admire people like you. I really do.
—Greetings from Germany! Julian.

Julian, we're honored to be the first publisher you reach out to, and just as honored by your kind words. Very glad to hear that you're in therapy and seeking out the help you need – it's a long road, sometimes, but it's important to walk it and remember that you deserve that help. I hope things are only getting better for you, and that the conclusion to this first story arc only left you feeling a little more optimistic.

And now, for the last word on volume one, Alex.

DISPATCHES FROM THE VOID

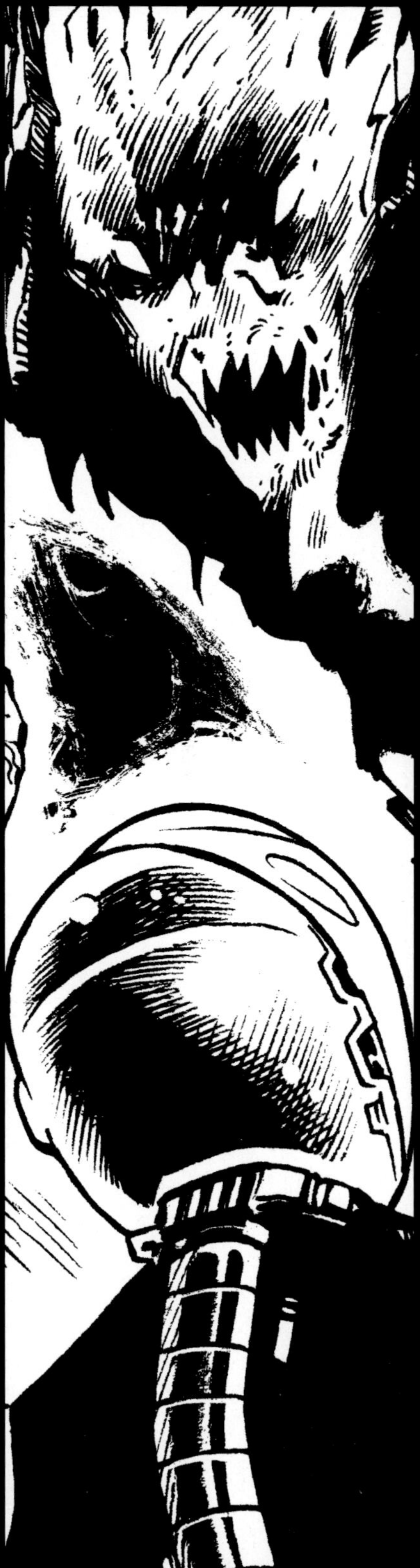

The very first time I encountered a Dave McKean painting, it was on the cover of a novel called *Coraline*. I was eight years old. I had no idea who Neil Gaiman was (or McKean, for that matter). All I knew was that I was scared. So I did what any red-blooded American would do.

I ran away, screaming. Ask my mom if you want proof.

All this to say that, historically, horror has not been my genre of choice. In part, I think that's because my mind is already so capable of scaring itself. At four years old, I thought that my parents were poisoning my meals. At five, I thought that murderers were inside my closet and underneath my bed, waiting for the cover of darkness to stab me through the heart. At six, I conflated the two nightmares and thought one of my parents would eventually step out of the closet with an axe and that would be that. Even now, I live my day to day life with so much mental stress and tension that an out of place noise in my apartment is enough to throw my entire night off.

Looking back, I think that I was afraid of horror because I was afraid to think about the dark parts of my own psyche. It was one thing to listen to My Chemical Romance and wear all-black outfits while looking up pictures of skeletons on the internet, but it was an entirely separate matter to think about why I thought the people who gave me life would want to kill me. As someone who has a complex relationship with their family and their identity, with all the privilege and struggles that those things bring, it was easier for me just keep moving forward, attempting to fashion a sense of self that blocked off the parts of my life that pained me, than it was to engage in a confrontation with those things. That's what horror is, after all—a confrontation with our darkest thoughts and the things we'd like to keep repressed.

Then, of course, 2016 happened.

Now, if you will, imagine Pandora opening her box. Imagine this endless array of horrors, plagues, and general darkness spreading out into the world from between her hands. What poured out of my mind at the end of that year was, to me, a hundred times worse.

What to do with all these shattered illusions of what America was? These repressed demons now flooding the world through a constant stream of tears? What do you do when the darkest parts of you are at your doorstep?

There's nowhere left to run, so you fight. You fight like hell.

That's what horror has always done—it has featured characters who have the bravery to stand up to their demons and do what I, for so long, could not. That's what the latest wave of horror stories—stuff like *Get Out* and INFIDEL—are doing to confront the bigotry and xenophobia that we, as minorities, as Americans, and as people of the world, can no longer pretend we've even begun to move past.

We stand and we scream. And this time, not because we're scared. But because we're ready to fight. We're ready to bleed. We're ready to survive.

ALEX LU is a freelance editor with credits at publishers including First Second, Papercutz, and Top Cow (he's credited in the book you're holding now). He likes good stories, good food, and good pictures of food. Find him on Twitter @waxenwings.

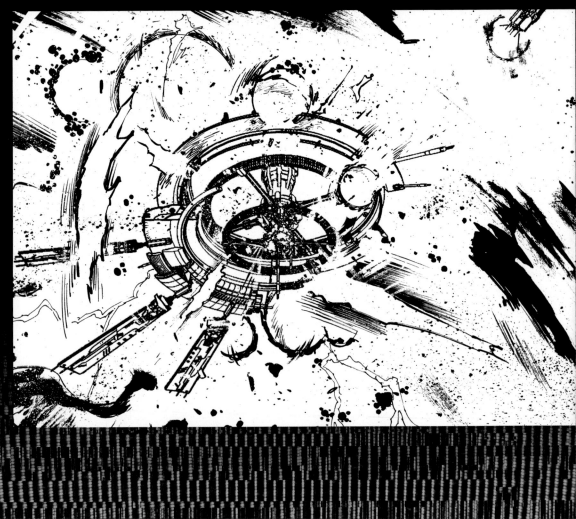

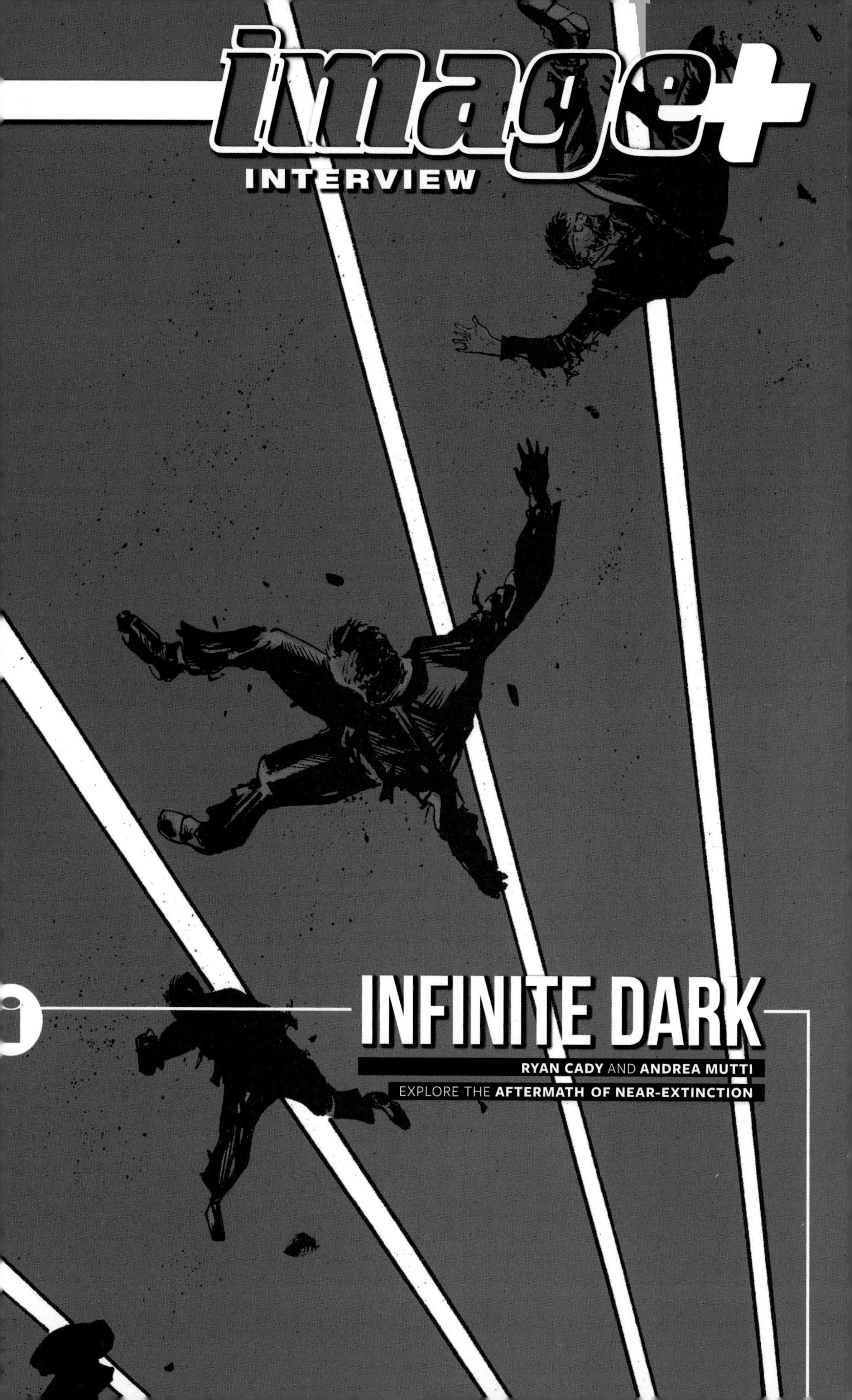

image+ INTERVIEW

INFINITE DARK

RYAN CADY AND **ANDREA MUTTI**

EXPLORE THE **AFTERMATH OF NEAR-EXTINCTION**

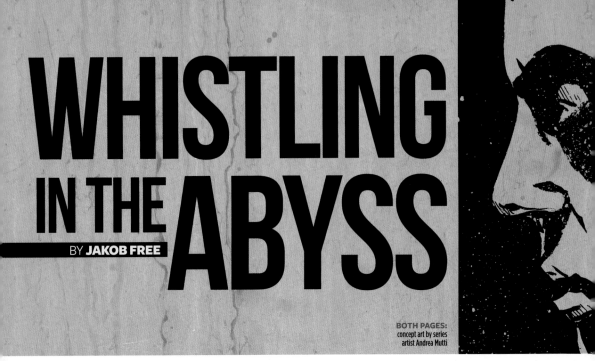

WHISTLING IN THE ABYSS

BY **JAKOB FREE**

BOTH PAGES: concept art by series artist Andrea Mutti

The heat death of the universe scares the shit out of Ryan Cady. And why shouldn't it? It's *scary* stuff. "I imagined a galaxy, a universe populated by our descendants," he says. "And then I started researching entropy. And oh boy. A no-win situation. The collapse of all existence? That's bleak as hell."

The theory of universal heat death entails a complicated process—and apologies to any physicists reading—whereby the cosmos approaches a period of energy's even distribution, aka the point of "total thermodynamic entropy." In this moment, all energetic reactions throughout the universe cease, and the universe stops dead in its tracks.

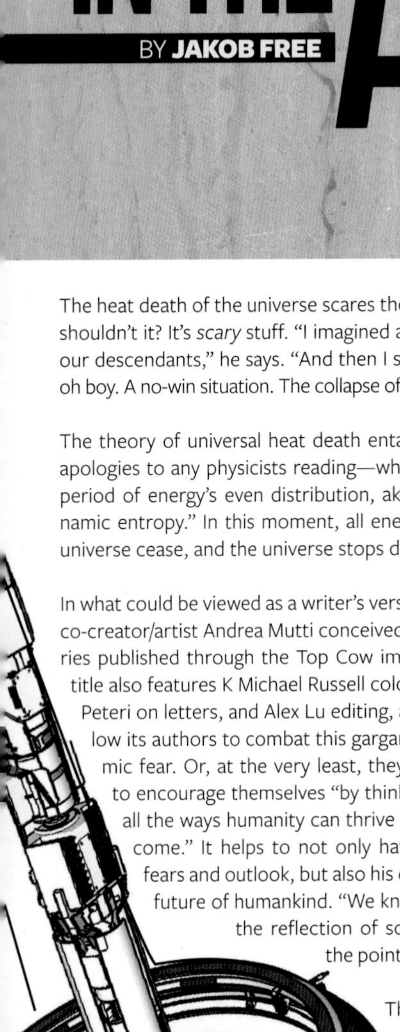

In what could be viewed as a writer's version of self-medication, Cady and co-creator/artist Andrea Mutti conceived *Infinite Dark*, a new ongoing series published through the Top Cow imprint. The title also features K Michael Russell coloring, Troy Peteri on letters, and Alex Lu editing, and will allow its authors to combat this gargantuan cosmic fear. Or, at the very least, they'll be able to encourage themselves "by thinking about all the ways humanity can thrive in the centuries and millennia to come." It helps to not only have a partner who shares Cady's fears and outlook, but also his desire to ask questions about the future of humankind. "We know that the stars we see are just the reflection of something dead," says Mutti. "So the point is where are we going and why?"

"WE KNOW THAT THE STARS WE SEE ARE JUST THE REFLECTION OF SOMETHING DEAD. SO THE POINT IS WHERE ARE WE GOING AND WHY?"

The "why" in the immediate sense is to "survive." But in the moments right after the heat death of the universe, survival would seem like an impossibility—especially given the way Cady and Mutti have accelerated the cosmic apocalypse.

"I've played it fast and loose with the science here," Cady says. "I wanted to use whatever I could to give the book as much looming hor ror as possible. I moved up the timeline quite a bit—w were wrong about entropy's pacing, and heat death be gins to accelerate and occurs 10,000 or so years fron now instead of billions of years from now."

To save themselves, an ingenious group of humans buil the Orpheus station, inspired by the tragic characte from Greek myth. The Orpheus is meant to weather th impending heat death and will serve as a life preserve for all of those that can make it to the station in time.

"Orpheus traversed the underworld—the outer dark ness—and made it back out alive," says Cady. "The gods granted hin a unique opportunity for a morta and that's what the builders of thi station thought they had done But much like how Orpheus' entir quest revolved around rescuing his wife, the Orpheus purpose was to carry tens of thousands of humans safe ly through oblivion. Orpheus looked back too soon, an his wife was sent back to the underworld—the statio was built too far away—and too slowly—from the colon ships that needed to reach it, and they exploded i entropy."

Instead of the 15,000 souls that the Orpheus was bui to rescue, the station becomes a tomb for the 2,000 o so humans who built it. As to whether or not those folk have any shot at restarting the human race: "Obviousl there'd be a bottleneck with a population that small, bu that's assuming a natural environment. The Orpheus wa controlled, planned, and prepared. Their medical tech i advanced enough that they can combat almost any dis ease, prepare ideal parenting combinations, etc. And they'r prepared for the long haul."

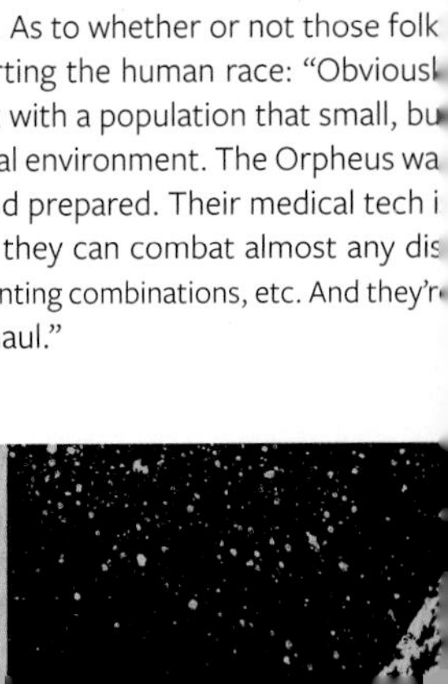

Image Plus Editor: Sean Edgar, Designed by: Sasha Head

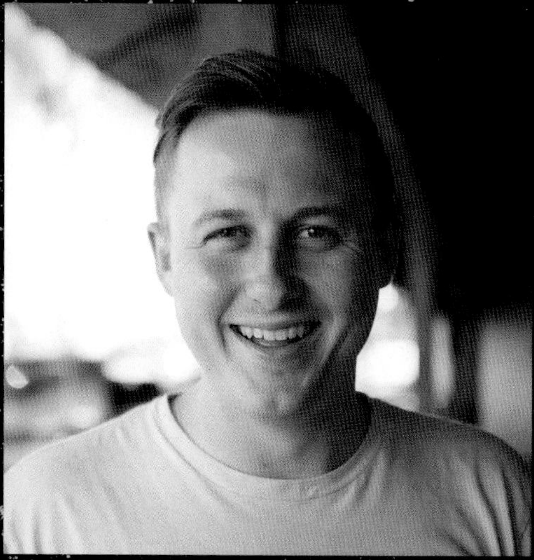

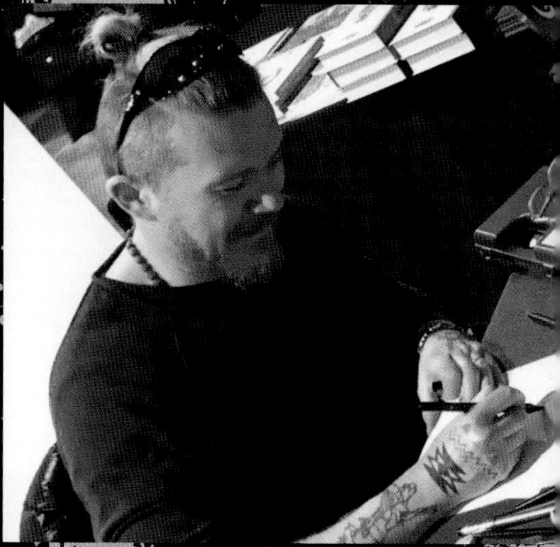

"DEVA [IS] KIND OF A POWDER KEG, AND FOLLOWING THE EVENTS OF THE FIRST ISSUE... THE FUSE IS LIT."

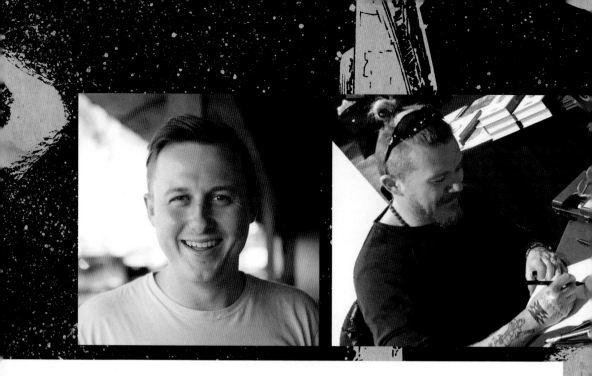

Even if humankind were able to hit the "restart" button, though, where would they go? Cady's thought of this as well: "The Orpheus even has limited terraforming equipment on board. Time doesn't really exist now that reality is collapsed, but presumably another Big Bang will happen (well, hopefully), and when that happens, the people on board were prepared to pick a planet, reforge it, and repopulate."

Until then, the Orpheus, and the minuscule society that lives aboard, are run by a Board of Directors. "They are absolutely not democratically elected. Basically, there were lots of plans in place for how human society would run on board the Orpheus... and then most of the population didn't make it. So, because it's the power structure they're comfortable with, something they could cling to, the staff on board the station just kept the same roles and officials they had while the station was being assembled and prepared." The Board includes Lynn Tenant, the director of project management, essentially a chief administrator; Ike Chalos, the director of human resources, a counselor and personnel manager; Alvin Scheidt, chief technolinguist, the station's number one programmer; and Deva Karrell, the security director, in charge of the security guards on site.

"And for the past two years, they've just sort of adapted those roles to fit the necessary leadership challenges that have arisen on the station... with arguable success," Cady says. "You can only run a society like a company or a project for so long."

As if the complete destruction of the universe wasn't enough, Alvin Scheidt has gone off the reservation, so to speak. He's left his post, violently abducted his neighbor, and set off for the Dark Sector—an area of the Orpheus that has been cordoned off and left to function with limited power. The Dark Sector *should not* have any people living in it, but Scheidt has seen something there that's changed his behavior. Finding out what that something is and why it's taken hold of Scheidt is up to Deva Karrell.

"Deva was a veteran cop before she took the security director job," Cady says. "She considers herself, first and foremost, a protector. So it doesn't really matter that there was no way she could've saved the rest of the universe—or even saved the colony ships that failed to reach the Orpheus—she still blames herself. Like many of us would, she runs through guilty fantasies and imagines ways she might've rescued those people. Coulda, shoulda, woulda. Deva [is] kind of a powder keg, and following the events of the first issue... the fuse is lit."

Fear of cosmic destruction may have been the impetus of Cady and Mutti's tale, but it's not the only fear that Cady must contend with. Despite working on licensed projects for years, *Infinite Dark* represents his first major foray into creator-owned comics.

"With for-hire work, there's always a target to aim for, a bullseye, and while you're throwing a lot of yourself out there, you've got these people to please and these structures already in place. With creator-owned, it feels purer, more free for sure... But that also means that we're only really answerable to ourselves." ●

"THE **COLLAPSE** OF ALL EXISTENCE? THAT'S **BLEAK AS HELL**."

ABOVE: series writer Ryan Cady and series artist Andrea Mutti

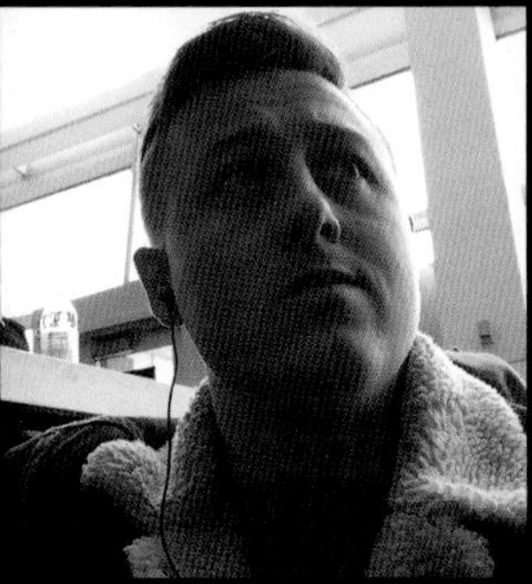

RYAN CADY is a writer of comics and horror fiction based in Southern California. A graduate of the DC Comics Talent Development Workshop, he has written for Marvel, Archie Comics, and others, on properties such as WARFRAME and The Punisher, and the book you're holding, his first creator-owned property with Image/Top Cow Productions. To this day, his early reviews of terrible fast food products for the OC Weekly remain his greatest creative triumph.

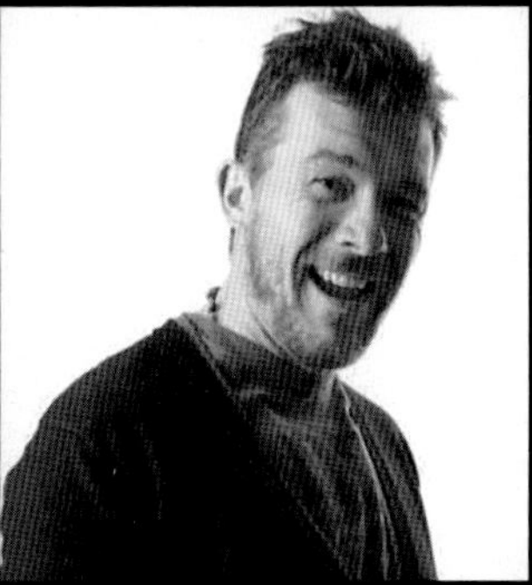

ANDREA MUTTI is an Italian artist who has worked in the comic book world for 25 years. He studied at the Comics School in Brescia and has worked with such US publishers as Marvel, DC, Dark Horse, Vertigo, IDW, BOOM! Studios, Dynamite, Stela, Adaptive and many more European publishers like Glenat, Casterman, Soleil, Dargaud and Titan. He lives in Italy and you can learn more about his career at his website **www.andrearedmutti.com**.

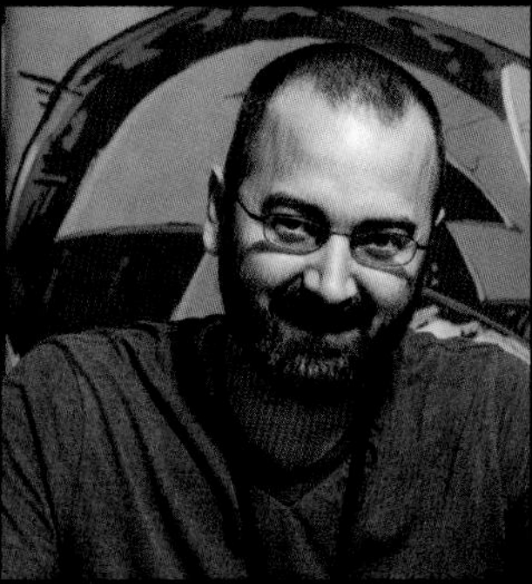

K. MICHAEL RUSSELL has been working as a comic book color artist since 2011. His credits include Image series GLITTERBOMB with WAYWARD & *Thunderbolts* writer Jim Zub, HACK/SLASH, *Judge Dredd* and the Eisner and Harvey-nominated *In the Dark: A Horror Anthology*. He launched an online comic book coloring course in 2014 at ColoringComics.com and maintains a YouTube channel dedicated to coloring tutorials. He lives on the coast in Long Beach, Mississippi, with his wife of sixteen years, Tina. They have two cats. One is a jerk. **@kmichaelrussell**

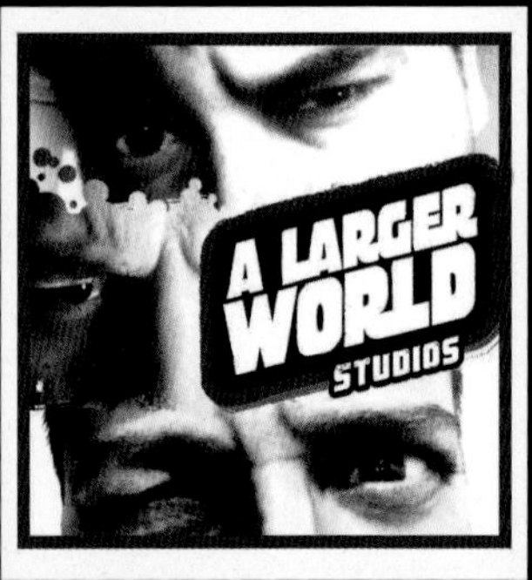
A LARGER WORLD
STUDIOS

TROY PETERI, Dave Lanphear and Joshua Cozine are collectively known as A Larger World Studios. They've lettered everything from *The Avengers*, *Iron Man*, *Wolverine*, *Amazing Spider-Man* and *X-Men* to more recent titles such as WITCHBLADE, CYBERFORCE, and *Batman/Wonder Woman: The Brave & The Bold*. They can be reached at studio@alargerworld.com for your lettering and design needs. (Hooray, commerce!)

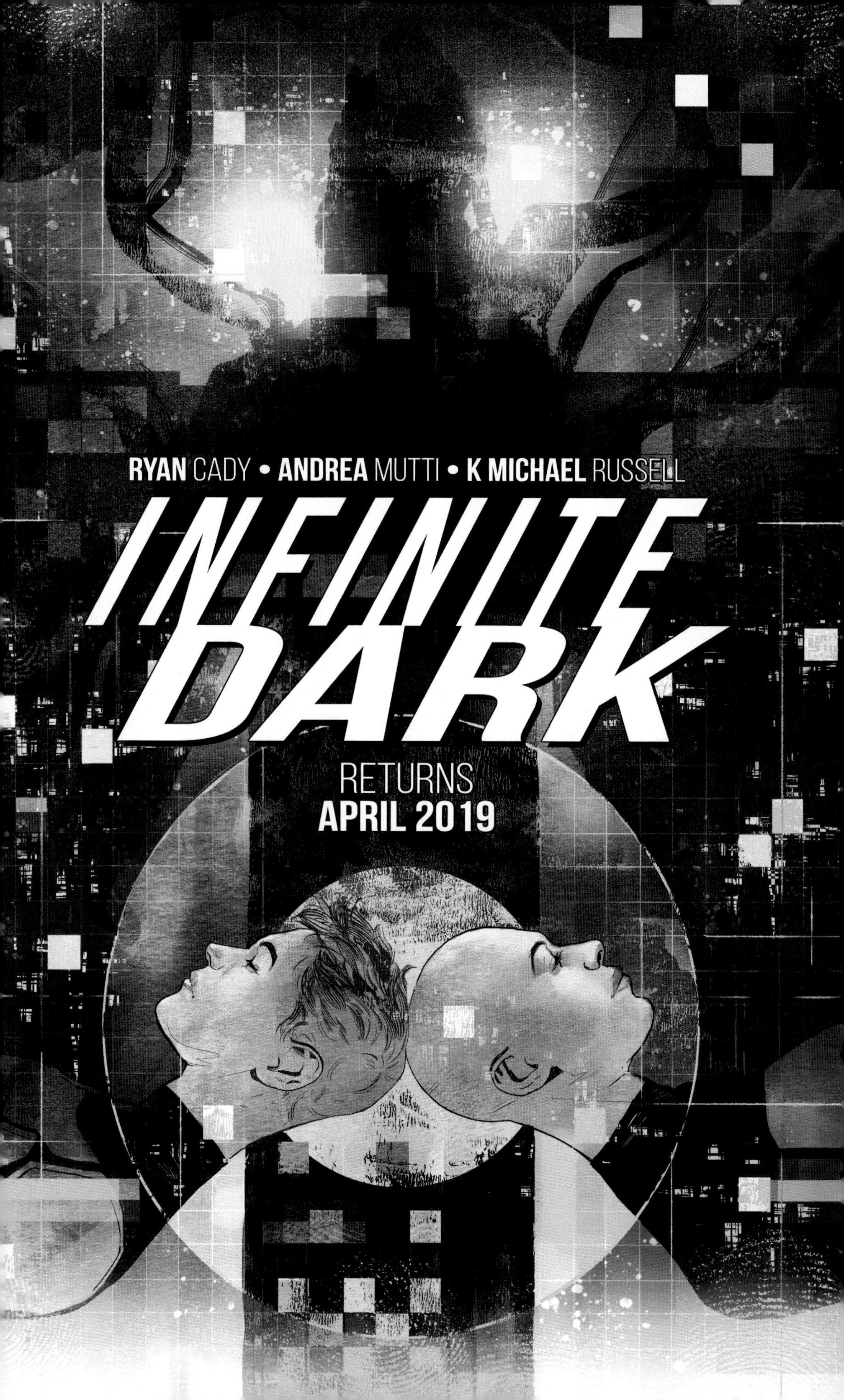
RYAN CADY • ANDREA MUTTI • K MICHAEL RUSSELL
INFINITE DARK
RETURNS
APRIL 2019

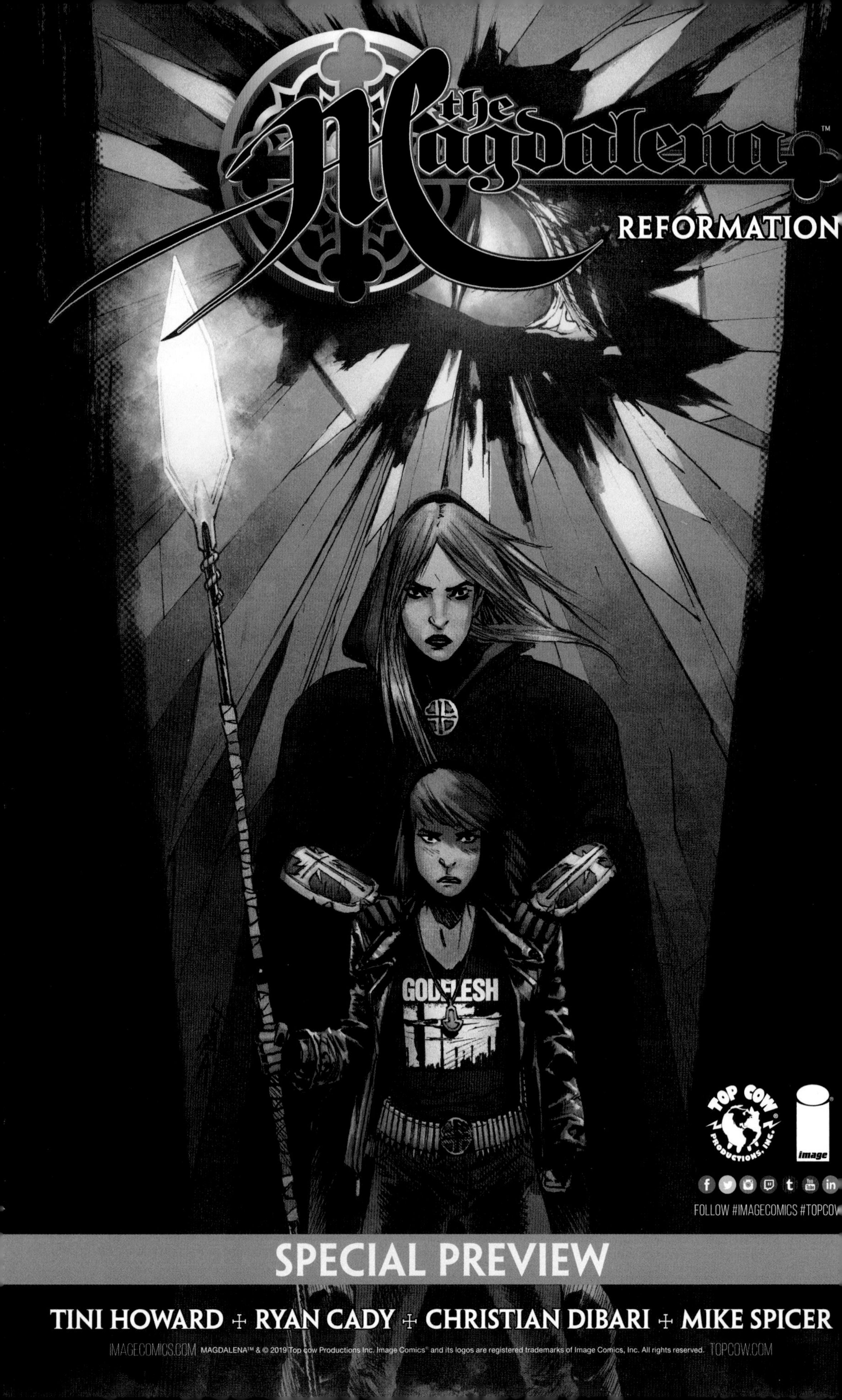
the Magdalena™
REFORMATION
GODFLESH
FOLLOW #IMAGECOMICS #TOPCOW
SPECIAL PREVIEW
TINI HOWARD + RYAN CADY + CHRISTIAN DIBARI + MIKE SPICER
IMAGECOMICS.COM MAGDALENA™ & © 2019 Top Cow Productions Inc. Image Comics® and its logos are registered trademarks of Image Comics, Inc. All rights reserved. TOPCOW.COM

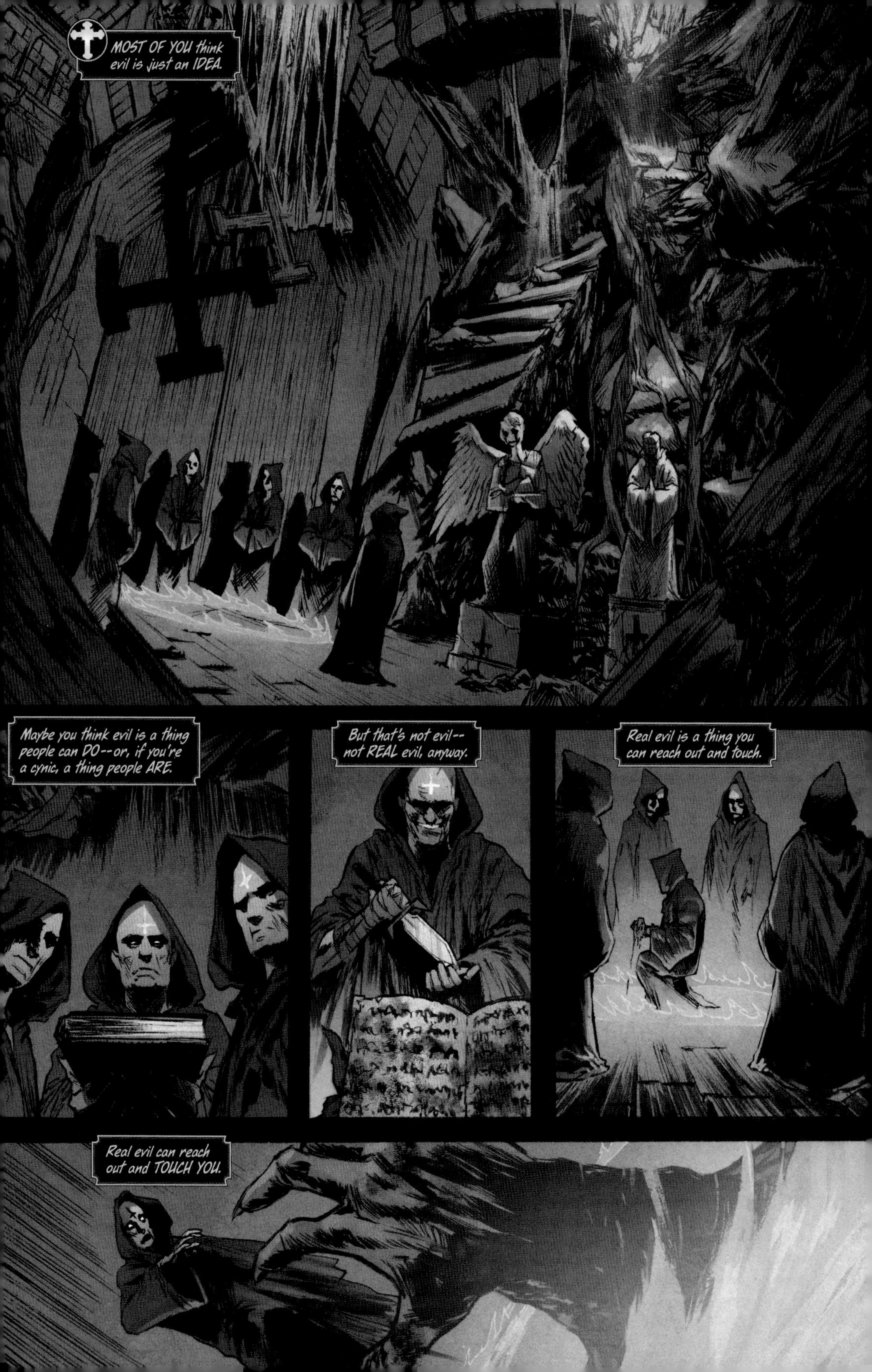
MOST OF YOU think evil is just an IDEA.
Maybe you think evil is a thing people can DO--or, if you're a cynic, a thing people ARE.
But that's not evil--not REAL evil, anyway.
Real evil is a thing you can reach out and touch.
Real evil can reach out and TOUCH YOU.

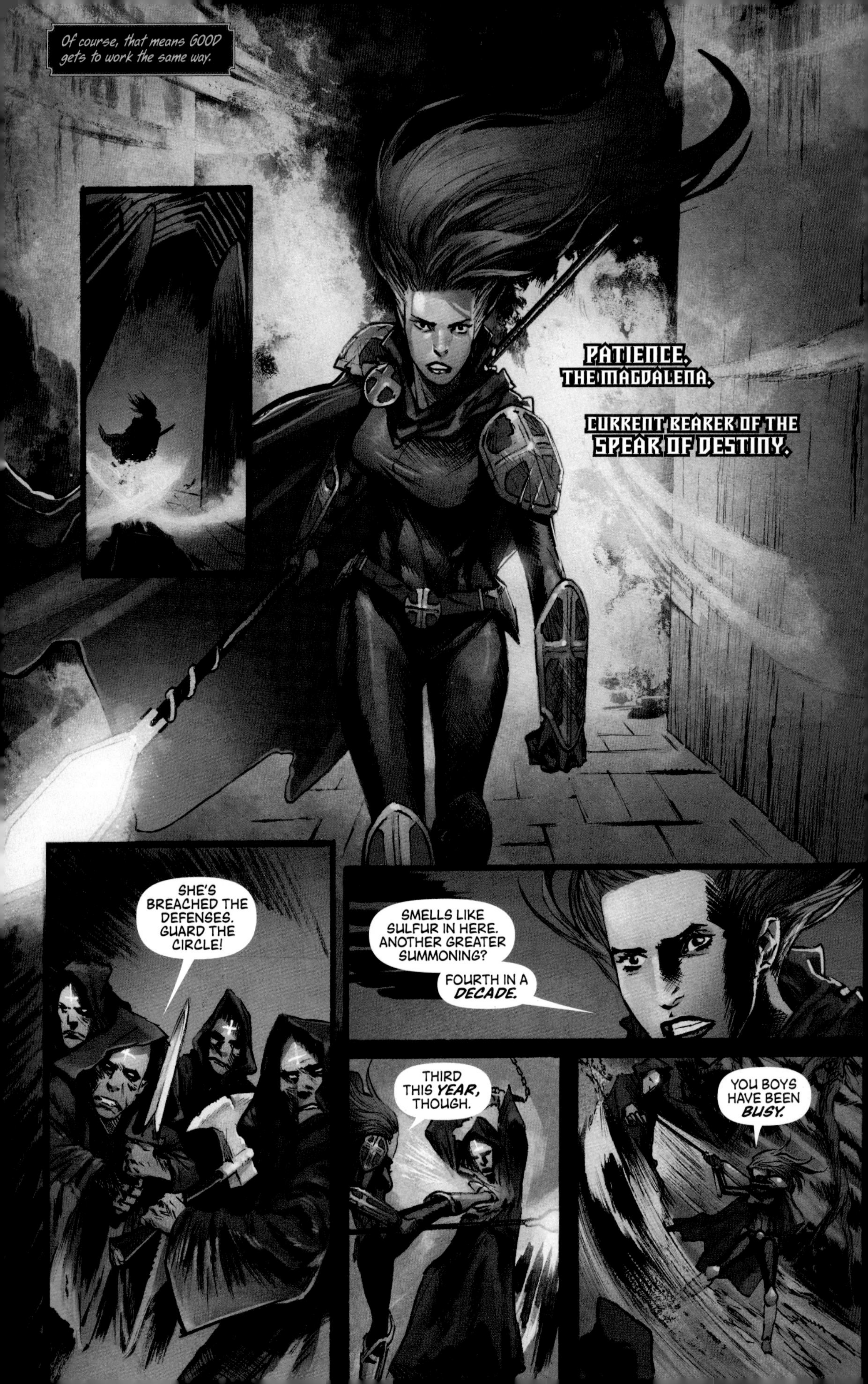

Of course, that means GOOD gets to work the same way.
PATIENCE. THE MAGDALENA.
CURRENT BEARER OF THE SPEAR OF DESTINY.
SHE'S BREACHED THE DEFENSES. GUARD THE CIRCLE!
SMELLS LIKE SULFUR IN HERE. ANOTHER GREATER SUMMONING?
FOURTH IN A DECADE.
THIRD THIS YEAR, THOUGH.
YOU BOYS HAVE BEEN BUSY.

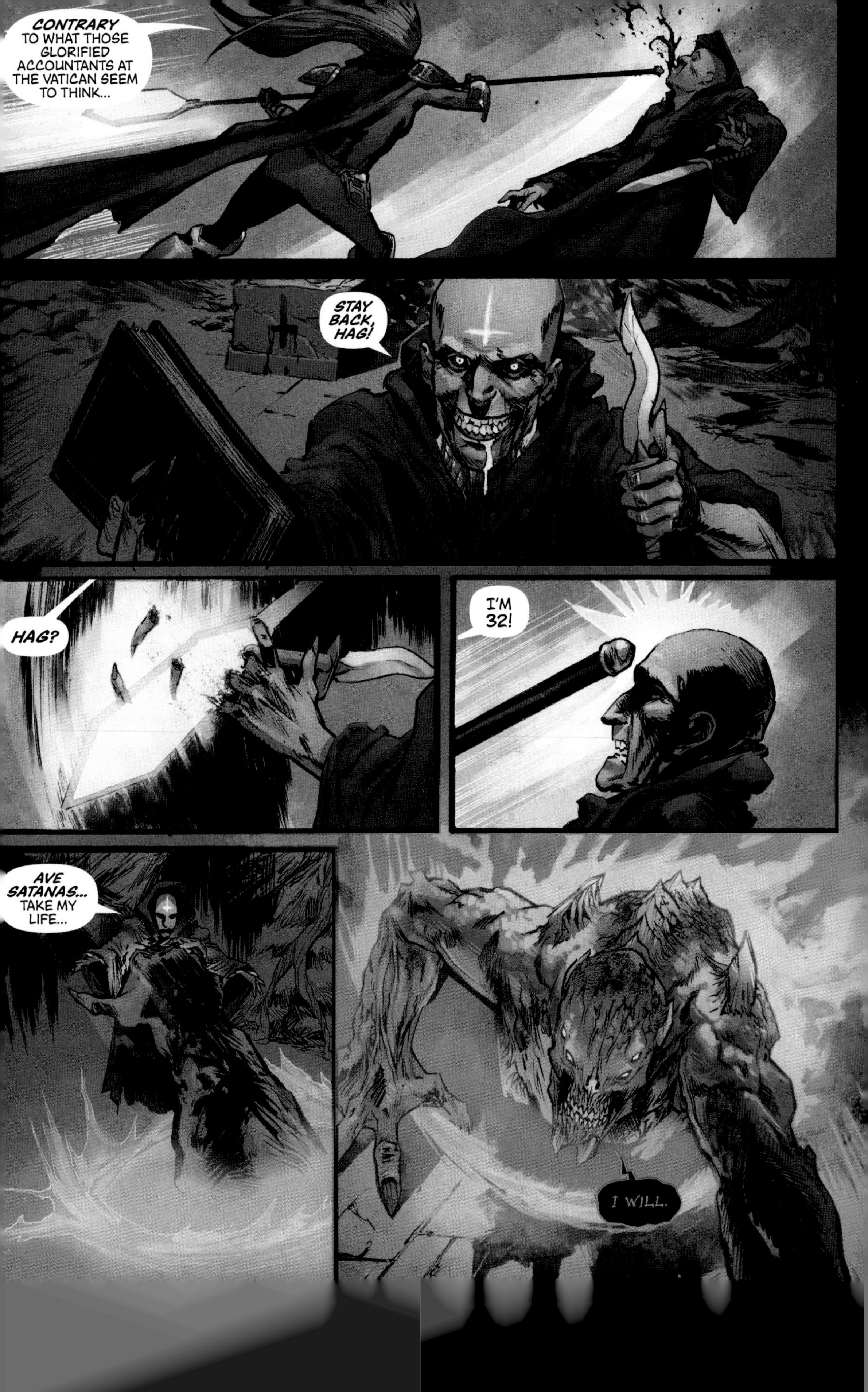
CONTRARY TO WHAT THOSE GLORIFIED ACCOUNTANTS AT THE VATICAN SEEM TO THINK...
STAY BACK, HAG!
HAG?
I'M 32!
AVE SATANAS... TAKE MY LIFE...
I WILL.

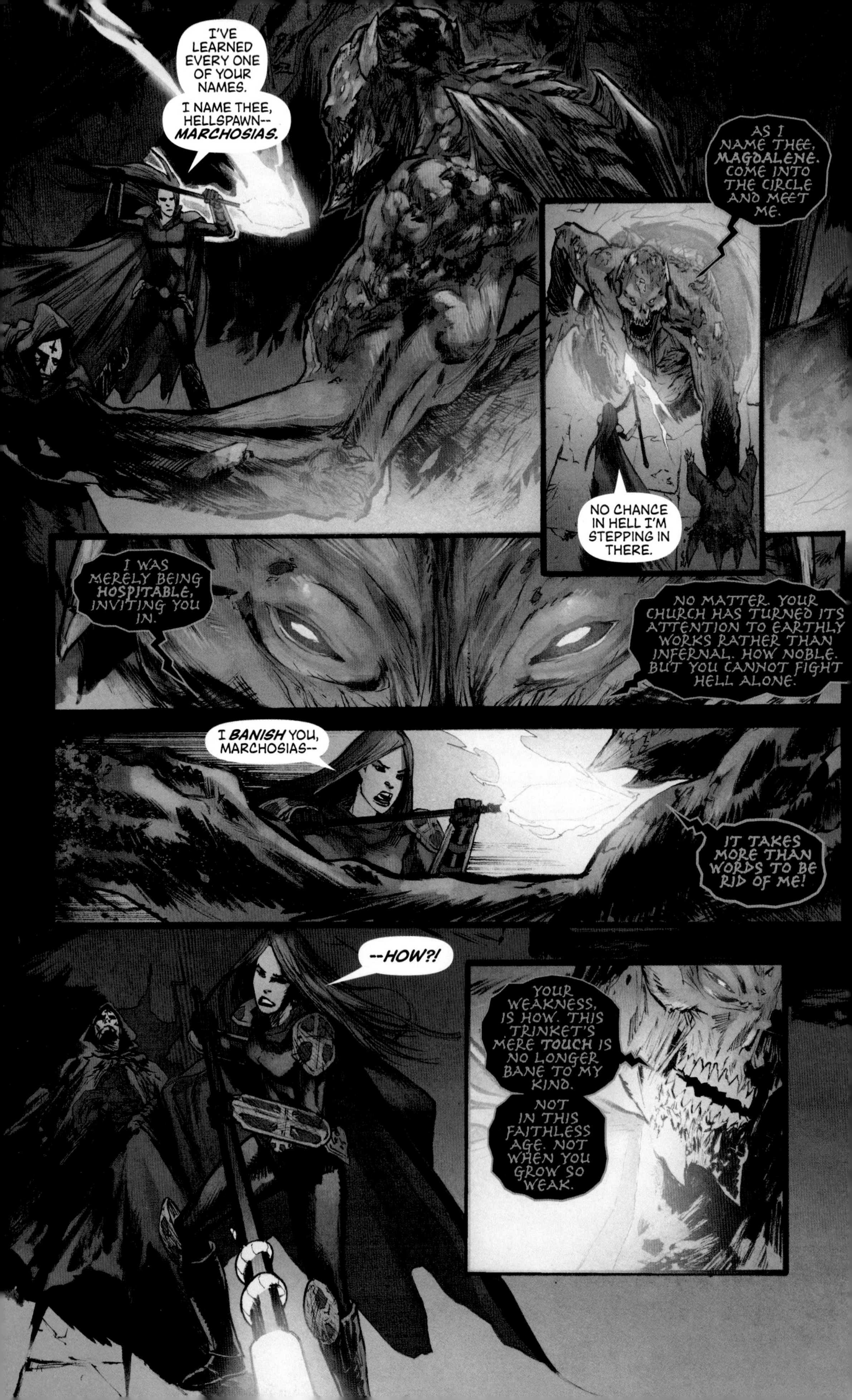
I'VE LEARNED EVERY ONE OF YOUR NAMES.
I NAME THEE, HELLSPAWN-- MARCHOSIAS.
AS I NAME THEE, MAGDALENE. COME INTO THE CIRCLE AND MEET ME.
NO CHANCE IN HELL I'M STEPPING IN THERE.
I WAS MERELY BEING HOSPITABLE, INVITING YOU IN.
NO MATTER. YOUR CHURCH HAS TURNED ITS ATTENTION TO EARTHLY WORKS RATHER THAN INFERNAL. HOW NOBLE. BUT YOU CANNOT FIGHT HELL ALONE.
I BANISH YOU, MARCHOSIAS--
IT TAKES MORE THAN WORDS TO BE RID OF ME!
--HOW?!
YOUR WEAKNESS, IS HOW. THIS TRINKET'S MERE TOUCH IS NO LONGER BANE TO MY KIND.
NOT IN THIS FAITHLESS AGE. NOT WHEN YOU GROW SO WEAK.

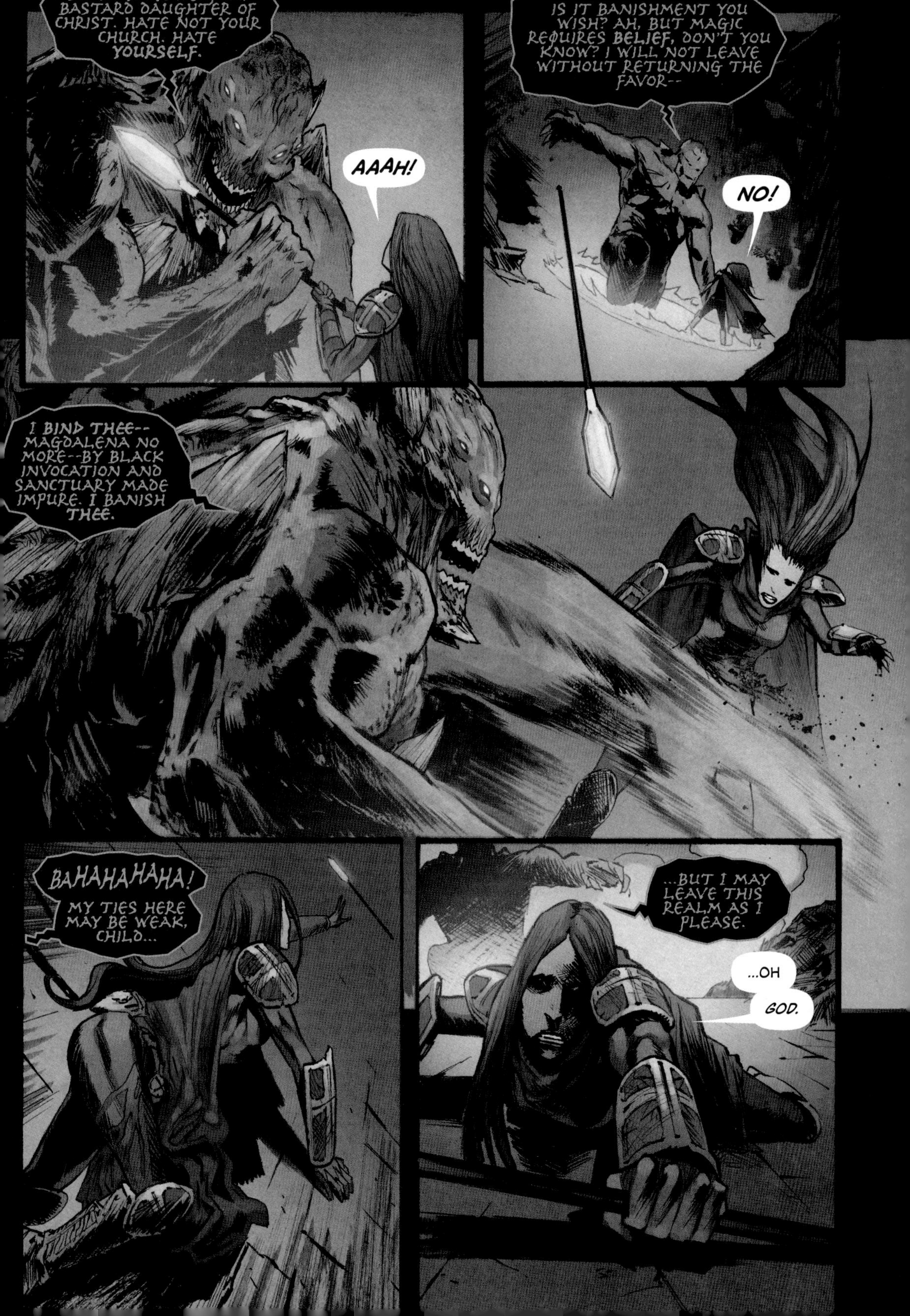
LET YOUR HOLY PAIN STAIN YOUR WEAPON, BASTARD DAUGHTER OF CHRIST. HATE NOT YOUR CHURCH. HATE YOURSELF.
AAAH!
IS IT BANISHMENT YOU WISH? AH, BUT MAGIC REQUIRES BELIEF, DON'T YOU KNOW? I WILL NOT LEAVE WITHOUT RETURNING THE FAVOR--
NO!
I BIND THEE--MAGDALENA NO MORE--BY BLACK INVOCATION AND SANCTUARY MADE IMPURE. I BANISH THEE.
BAHAHAHAHA! MY TIES HERE MAY BE WEAK, CHILD...
...BUT I MAY LEAVE THIS REALM AS I PLEASE.
...OH
GOD.

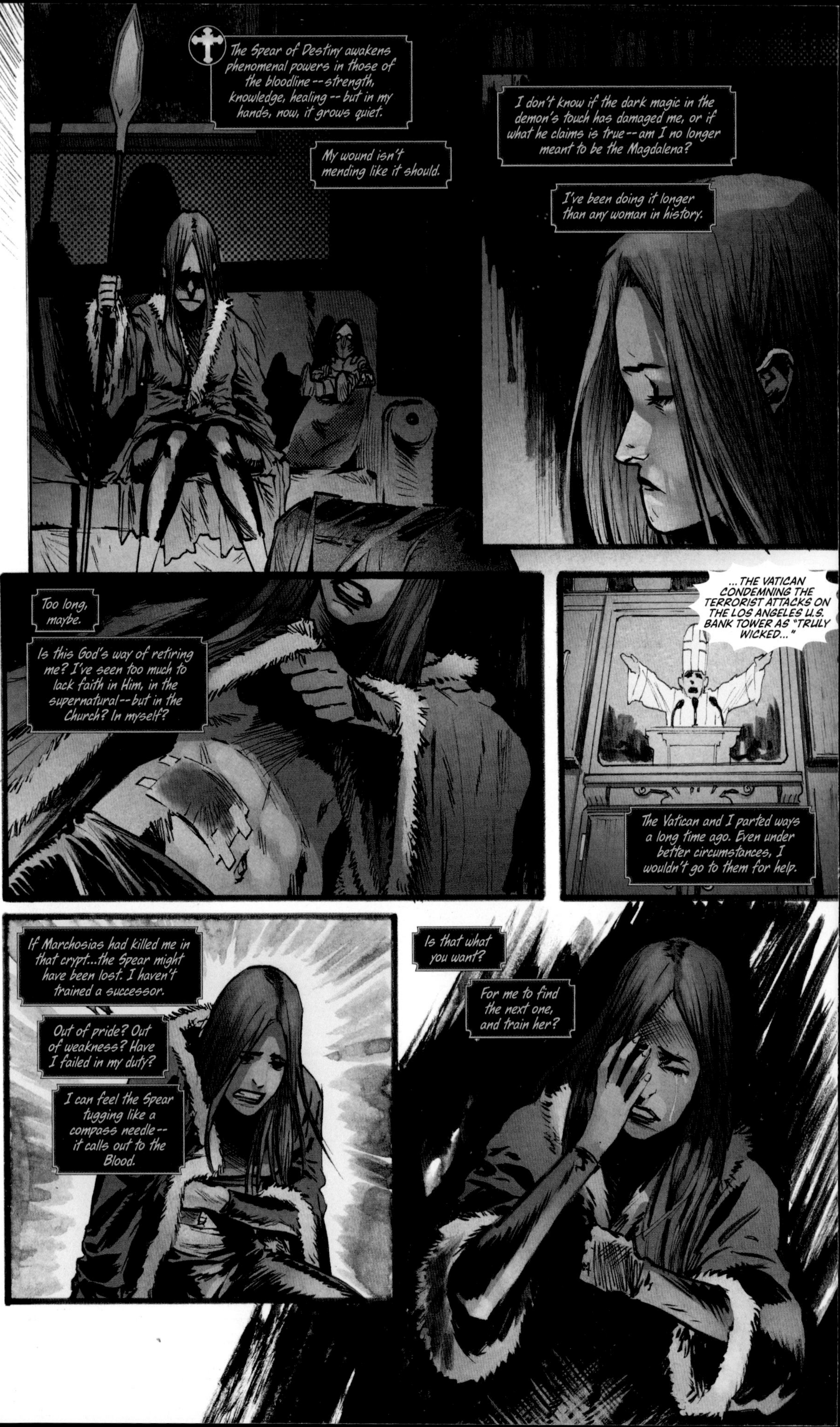

The Spear of Destiny awakens phenomenal powers in those of the bloodline--strength, knowledge, healing--but in my hands, now, it grows quiet.
My wound isn't mending like it should.
I don't know if the dark magic in the demon's touch has damaged me, or if what he claims is true--am I no longer meant to be the Magdalena?
I've been doing it longer than any woman in history.
Too long, maybe.
Is this God's way of retiring me? I've seen too much to lack faith in Him, in the supernatural--but in the Church? In myself?
...THE VATICAN CONDEMNING THE TERRORIST ATTACKS ON THE LOS ANGELES U.S. BANK TOWER AS "TRULY WICKED..."
The Vatican and I parted ways a long time ago. Even under better circumstances, I wouldn't go to them for help.
If Marchosias had killed me in that crypt...the Spear might have been lost. I haven't trained a successor.
Out of pride? Out of weakness? Have I failed in my duty?
I can feel the Spear tugging like a compass needle--it calls out to the Blood.
Is that what you want?
For me to find the next one, and train her?

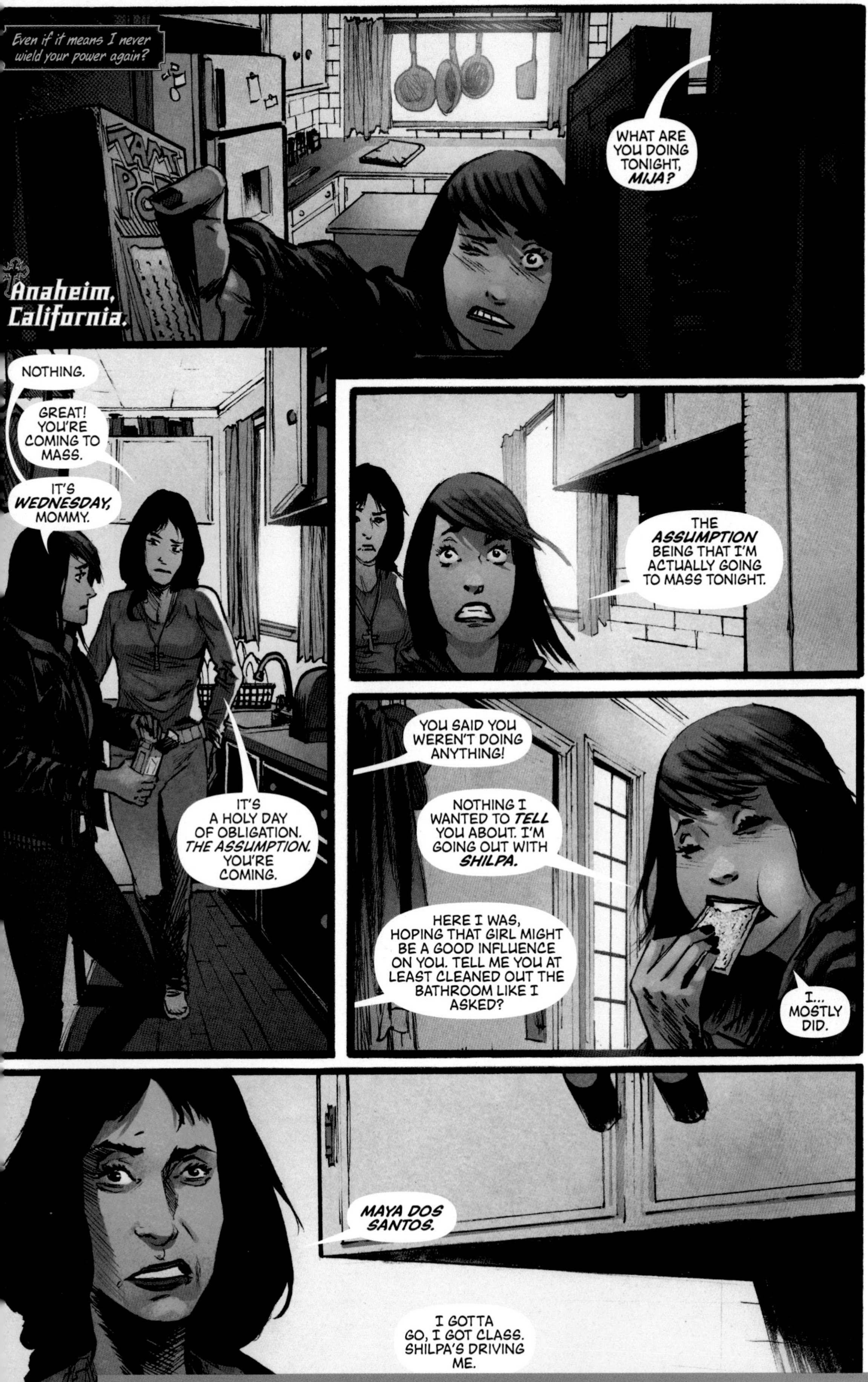
Even if it means I never wield your power again?
Anaheim, California.
WHAT ARE YOU DOING TONIGHT, MIJA?
NOTHING.
GREAT! YOU'RE COMING TO MASS.
IT'S WEDNESDAY, MOMMY.
IT'S A HOLY DAY OF OBLIGATION. THE ASSUMPTION. YOU'RE COMING.
THE ASSUMPTION BEING THAT I'M ACTUALLY GOING TO MASS TONIGHT.
YOU SAID YOU WEREN'T DOING ANYTHING!
NOTHING I WANTED TO TELL YOU ABOUT. I'M GOING OUT WITH SHILPA.
HERE I WAS, HOPING THAT GIRL MIGHT BE A GOOD INFLUENCE ON YOU. TELL ME YOU AT LEAST CLEANED OUT THE BATHROOM LIKE I ASKED?
I... MOSTLY DID.
MAYA DOS SANTOS.
I GOTTA GO, I GOT CLASS. SHILPA'S DRIVING ME.

CONTINUED IN MAGDALENA REFORMATION BOOK 1, AVAILABLE NOW

The Top Cow essentials checklist:

IXth Generation, Volume 1
(ISBN: 978-1-63215-323-4)

Aphrodite IX: Rebirth, Volume 1
(ISBN: 978-1-60706-828-0)

Blood Stain, Volume 1
(ISBN: 978-1-63215-544-3)

Bonehead, Volume 1
(ISBN: 978-1-5343-0664-6)

Cyber Force: Awakening, Volume 1
(ISBN: 978-1-5343-0980-7)

The Darkness: Origins, Volume 1
(ISBN: 978-1-60706-097-0)

Death Vigil, Volume 1
(ISBN: 978-1-63215-278-7)

Dissonance, Volume 1
(ISBN: 978-1-5343-0742-1)

Eclipse, Volume 1
(ISBN: 978-1-5343-0038-5)

Eden's Fall, Volume 1
(ISBN: 978-1-5343-0065-1)

Genius, Volume 1
(ISBN: 978-1-63215-223-7)

God Complex, Volume 1
(ISBN: 978-1-5343-0657-8)

Magdalena: Reformation
(ISBN: 978-1-5343-0238-9)

Port of Earth, Volume 1
(ISBN: 978-1-5343-0646-2)

Postal, Volume 1
(ISBN: 978-1-63215-342-5)

Romulus, Volume 1
(ISBN: 978-1-5343-0101-6)

Sugar, Volume 1
(ISBN: 978-1-5343-1641-7)

Sunstone, Volume 1
(ISBN: 978-1-63215-212-1)

Swing, Volume 1
(ISBN: 978-1-5343-0516-8)

Symmetry, Volume 1
(ISBN: 978-1-63215-699-0)

The Tithe, Volume 1
(ISBN: 978-1-63215-324-1)

Think Tank, Volume 1
(ISBN: 978-1-60706-660-6)

Warframe, Volume 1
(ISBN: 978-1-5343-0512-0)

Witchblade 2017, Volume 1
(ISBN: 978-1-5343-0685-1)

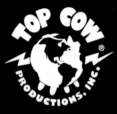

For more ISBN and ordering information on our latest collections go to:
www.topcow.com
Ask your retailer about our catalogue of collected editions,
digests, and hard covers or check the listings at:
Barnes and Noble, Amazon.com,
and other fine retailers.

To find your nearest comic shop go to:
www.comicshoplocator.com